PRAISE FOR THE MONTGOMERY JUSTICE NOVELS

"The Montgomery Justice series satisfies on all levels, with plots that dovetail into one another and characters that aren't always what they seem."

—*RT Book Reviews* on *Behind the Lies*

"Robin Perini is synonymous with stellar romantic suspense."

—*USA Today* Happy Ever After blog on *Behind the Lies*

"Perini refreshes romantic suspense."

—*Publishers Weekly* on *In Her Sights*

"This riveting book will keep readers on the edge of their seats and surprise them at the end. The tightly woven plot, quick pace, and complex characters make for a remarkable read."

—*RT Book Reviews* on *In Her Sights*

"Robin Perini will keep you perched on the edge of your seat. Danger, excitement, and romance . . . everything a reader craves!"

—*New York Times* bestselling author Brenda Novak on *In Her Sights*

"Robin Perini delivers the goods—*Game of Fear* is an intelligent, fast-paced romantic thriller that kept my heart racing and the pages flying."

—Karen Rose, *New York Times* bestselling author

"Robin Perini crafts the perfect blend of hot romance and chilling suspense that leaves you breathless!"

—Allison Brennan, *New York Times* bestselling author

"The world of computer hacking is taken to extreme levels in this exceptional action adventure. . . . The story moves quickly and captivates readers with every page."

—*RT Book Reviews* on *Game of Fear*

FORGOTTEN SECRETS

ALSO BY ROBIN PERINI

Carder Texas Connections

Finding Her Son
Cowboy in the Crossfire
Christmas Conspiracy
Undercover Texas
The Cradle Conspiracy
Secret Obsession
Christmas Justice

The Montgomery Justice Novels

In Her Sights (Luke's story)
Behind the Lies (Zach's story)
Game of Fear (Gabe's story)

FORGOTTEN SECRETS

ROBIN PERINI

The characters and events portrayed in this book are fictitious. Any similarity to real persons, living or dead, is coincidental and not intended by the author.

Text copyright © 2016 Robin Perini
All rights reserved.

No part of this book may be reproduced, or stored in a retrieval system, or transmitted in any form or by any means, electronic, mechanical, photocopying, recording, or otherwise, without express written permission of the publisher.

Published by Montlake Romance, Seattle

www.apub.com

ISBN-13: 9781611098891
ISBN-10: 1611098890

Cover design by Michael Rehder

Printed in the United States of America

For Mom.
Though her memories have faded, her presence reminds our family each day of her strength of will, power of faith, and all-encompassing devotion.
For Dad.
In sickness and in health have become more than a promise. They are truth. His patience is never ceasing, his loyalty boundless, his love absolute.
Together they are proof that love can be strong, real, and everlasting.
I'm honored and blessed to call you my parents.
I love you both. Always.

Courage is not having the strength to go on; it is going on when you don't have the strength.

—*Theodore Roosevelt*

CHAPTER ONE

No matter how far a man traveled, how fast he ran, or how hard he tried, it only took a moment for the past to ambush him like an enemy combatant lying in wait.

At this moment, Deputy Thayne Blackwood had no doubt he should've paid closer attention to his grandmother's words of wisdom. He tilted back his Stetson and gauged the distance between him and his target. What a cluster.

Normally, Clive's Dance Hall and Saloon would've been jumping during happy hour on a Friday, but the place had gone as silent as the Afghan desert right before everything blew to hell. And instead of canvassing a clandestine drinking hole with his SEAL teammates like he should be doing, Thayne was in a standoff with an SOB he'd known all his life. Still, whether he was in Singing River, Wyoming, or Afghanistan, a hunting knife, a short temper, and a jealous drunk made for a dangerous confrontation.

Ed Zalinksy pressed the serrated bowie more firmly against the throbbing pulse of his longtime on-and-off lover's neck. Carol's eyes widened, glazed with too much booze, her sallow skin and visible capillaries evidence of a decade or two of indulgence.

Thayne stared down the man and allowed a slight drawl to ease the tension in his voice even as his right hand inched toward his Glock. "You don't have to do this, Ed."

"I'm not leaving my house. She can't make me."

Slowly, Thayne raised his hands—soothing, conciliatory. "Let's take this outside. Just you and me, so Carol can get back to work."

Ed's knuckles whitened, his grip tightening around Carol's arm. Though nearly as tall as Ed, she whimpered.

Thayne sensed the panic mounting in the crowd hovering near the bandstand behind him. He didn't have to turn around to recognize what was happening. With each crunch of peanut shells, each rustle, he knew. A dangerous but well-intentioned few, their hands inching toward concealed weapons, hesitant but with just enough bravado to make a bad situation worse.

Thayne let loose a silent flurry of curses. Too many heroes could turn a tricky confrontation deadly in a split second.

What he wouldn't give for his SEAL teammates on his six. Having them at his back would've provided him a lot more options, but as Gram always said, *Wait for a wish, and you'll be waiting forever.* With half the sheriff's office—all two of them—gone fishing, Thayne's only reinforcement was fifteen minutes away. Rough estimate—the confrontation would be over in three.

"You don't understand." Ed's fingers twitched on the knife's hilt, his eyes desperate.

If he pierced Carol's throat, she'd bleed out from her carotid within a minute.

No time left. Thayne slipped the gun from its holster. Not his usual preference—he was partial to his SIG—but the Glock would do. He'd drop Ed with one shot if the man moved that blade a centimeter.

"Put the knife down, Ed."

"I gave her a place to stay when no one else in town would put up with her drunk, crazy talk. And how does she repay me? She throws my clothes on the front lawn and keeps my house, my TV, and my guns. My daddy left me those guns."

Ed tightened the arm wrapped around Carol's waist until she cried out.

"Please, Ed. I'm s-sorry," she stammered.

"You're a liar. Always have been. From the moment you got yourself knocked up to the moment your kid vanished while you were on a binge. You probably killed her and don't even remember."

A collective gasp escaped from the crowd.

What a bastard. Everyone in town—hell, in the whole state—knew about Carol's missing daughter, Gina. Fifteen years ago, she'd vanished without a trace. Carol had been one of the prime suspects, but Thayne's father, in his first year as sheriff, had ruled her out during the investigation.

A decade and a half later, Gina Wallace was still missing.

Ed jerked his head up and glared at the crowd. "What? Y'all've been thinking the same thing since it happened. I'm just brave enough to say it to her face."

Carol choked back a sob, tears streaking mascara down her face. "It's not true. Why are you doing this, Ed?"

"'Cause I love you, damn it. And you won't love me back." His hand dropped just a few inches.

Ed's mistake. Thayne's opportunity. He holstered his Glock and rushed Ed in a blur of speed. Before the man could so much as twitch, Thayne grabbed the wrist holding the knife and twisted it with a sharp yank. Ed bent over with a groan. The knife clattered to the floor.

Carol crumpled in uncontrollable sobs.

"It didn't have to be this way." Thayne snapped metal cuffs around Ed's wrists.

The room erupted in whoops and applause. Several women hurried to Carol. She clutched at a barstool and heaved herself to her feet, legs shaking. "I need a drink."

The bartender poured two fingers of Scotch and slid the glass to Carol. She downed it in one gulp, then crossed to Ed and slapped him across the face. "You bastard."

Ed heaved toward her, but Thayne's grip didn't give.

"Carol, go home. Sleep it off, huh?" Thayne tugged Ed out of her reach.

She crossed her arms and glared at Ed. "Not until I know he's headed for jail."

Carol's blood might be half alcohol, but she hadn't lost her fight. She had twenty years on Thayne, but he recognized the remnants of the woman his dad had told him about. Carol's homecoming court and state championship basketball days had long since passed. She'd had everything going for her until she'd fled the confines of Singing River for a summertime adventure on the rodeo circuit. A few months later, she'd come home with a lost scholarship and a baby on the way.

"The judge won't be back until Monday," Thayne said. "Ed'll be locked up until then."

She swayed. "Good."

"You gonna be OK?"

She lifted her chin and stared at Thayne through unfocused eyes. "I haven't been OK for a long time. Everyone knows that." She turned back to the bar and tapped the empty glass on the walnut surface. "I need another one."

Resigned to the fact that some people were their own worst enemy, Thayne straightened and stared down the rest of the dance hall. "Show's over. Make sure I don't have to come back tonight. Ed already ruined my Friday night rendezvous with paperwork."

A few chuckles at his words broke the tension, but Thayne hadn't been joking. With the sheriff's office being so shorthanded this weekend, and now having to process Ed, there'd be no privacy for his Friday Night Phone Fling.

He'd been waiting all week to talk to Riley again, to hear her voice. The woman was smart, sultry, and always surprising, but he hadn't liked her tension-laced tone during their last conversation. When he'd asked, she'd sidestepped his concern and abruptly ended the call.

The crack of a pool cue on the ball pierced through his memories. He glanced over his shoulder at the center table. The first time he'd seen FBI Special Agent Riley Lambert had been in this very room, perched half-on and half-off that pool table, sinking an impossible shot to win a bet. Except the wager hadn't been for cash, dinner, or even a drink. She'd been in full-on profiler mode, wanting an interview with any man in the bar who'd taken part in the search for Carol's missing daughter a decade and a half ago.

In that instant, Thayne had known Riley was different. How many women spent their vacation trying to solve a missing child's cold case? He'd asked her to dance, and she'd promptly shut him down, which made the passionate end to the evening all the more surprising. She'd left Singing River with no new information regarding Carol's missing daughter, and Thayne had returned to his SEAL team with seven days of memories that wouldn't stop replaying themselves in his mind.

During their entire location-challenged relationship, she'd never hung up on him—or refused to pick up. Until last week. He'd called twice more that night and once the next day, breaking their standing rule. She'd finally texted him that she was fine, just busy on a case. He believed her about the serial killer investigation, but she worried him. She wasn't herself. If it weren't for his father's precarious health and a promise to his sister, he'd have jumped on a flight to DC. As it was, his gut had churned for the last six days, and after a decade as a SEAL, he knew better than most to trust his instincts.

He'd just have to bend their rules again tonight and call as soon as he broke free of his duties. This time, he wouldn't let her avoid his questions. In fact, he might have to book that flight.

A few minutes later, "Friends in Low Places" blared through the jukebox speakers, and three couples hit the dance floor. The normal buzz of conversation and clink of glasses created a dull roar echoing off the paneled walls.

Thayne hauled Ed out the door, reading him his rights as they crossed the parking lot. "Damn stupid move, Ed. You violated probation."

"She loved me before that smooth-talking drifter got her pregnant." He stumbled. "Screwed up both our lives."

"Twenty-five years is a long time to stew on the past." Thayne secured Ed's arms to steady him, opened the back of his SUV, and pushed Ed's head down. "Maybe the judge will buy it."

After slamming the door shut, Thayne slid behind the wheel. Ed snorted from the rear. "What a joke. You in the front seat and me in back. I figured your daddy would've locked you up by now. Who would have thought? Thayne Blackwood, Deputy Sheriff. Or should I say, *glorified errand boy* until your daddy gets well."

"Don't push it, Ed, or I might forget I'm only a temp." Thayne rested his arm on the back of the seat, his gaze steel-serious. "You do know Uncle Sam has trained me to inflict a lot of damage without it showing—on the surface, anyway."

Ed paled.

Thayne faced front with a slight grin and started the engine.

By the time he pulled onto the highway leading the five miles into Singing River, the evening light had risen against the eastern summer sky along the Wind River mountain range. "You shouldn't have come back," Ed said, his voice sullen. "This place'll suck the life out of you."

Thayne couldn't argue. He'd worked his entire life to escape Singing River. Looking back, he'd initiated his quest at the age of eleven by pocketing a pack of baseball cards from the general store and receiving a tour of the town jail from his grandfather, the sheriff. By the time Thayne had hit fifteen, he'd graduated to joyriding down Main. His father's new sheriff's badge had still been shiny, but Thayne had done his best to tarnish it. His dad had locked him up for the hell of it.

In his wildest nightmares, he couldn't have imagined himself back in his hometown playing deputy to his father's sheriff. Just like his father and his grandfather. Yet here he was.

Upholding family tradition.

Temporarily.

He glanced in the rearview mirror. "Is that what happened to you, Ed?"

"Three choices in this town," he said. "Marry the head cheerleader like your daddy did. Get out of town—I thought you'd made it after ten years away from this place. Then, there're the ones like me. I screwed the class slut and, like an idiot, fell for her." He slumped in his seat. "A woman'll make or break you, kid. Most of the time, they twist your balls and enjoy it."

The ring of Thayne's phone saved him from responding. He glanced at the number and tapped his Bluetooth. "Hey, sis. What's up? You and Gram want company for dinner? 'Cause if I don't have to cook—"

"Thayne. It's happened again." Cheyenne's voice trembled, completely unlike his unflappable sister. "Someone's been inside the clinic." The phone went quiet. "Oh God, they're still here," she whispered.

Thayne's shoulders seized. "Get out of there, Cheyenne. Go to the sheriff's office—"

A door slammed open.

"No!" Cheyenne screamed. "Please. Don't hurt her—"

The phone went dead.

The world wouldn't stop spinning. Dr. Cheyenne Blackwood clutched at the carpet of her waiting room, her fingernails digging into the short fibers. She heaved herself to her hands and knees. Her head throbbed with every beat of her heart. She blinked, unable to focus. Why couldn't she see?

"Can't you do anything right?" The accusing voice sounded strangely far away, muffled.

Cheyenne's arms trembled and she collapsed to her side. Fighting against the waves of unconsciousness threatening to overtake her, she grunted and pressed her palms to the floor, forcing herself to rise.

"You won't escape." Two sets of hands pushed her back down to the floor. A large weight sat on her hips.

This couldn't be happening.

Hot breath puffed against her neck. "Don't fight. You can't win. No one ever wins."

Like hell she wouldn't fight. Cheyenne closed her eyes to keep the world from spinning and tensed her body. She could do this.

A weak whimper sounded from across the room. "P-please."

Gram.

Cheyenne bucked hard. She wouldn't go quietly. Her grandmother needed her. Her family needed her.

The weight on top of her shifted.

A damp cloth pressed against her nose, the sweet smell dulling her senses.

"Get the rest of the stuff. We're out of time."

"What about the old woman?"

"End her."

"Please, don't," Cheyenne begged against the cloth, her body strangely disconnected. She could feel herself going under again, leaving Gram at their mercy.

This shouldn't be. She wasn't finished. She had too much to do. Too many secrets left behind.

"Say good-bye." The order was soft, emotionless, final.

A tear escaped the corner of Cheyenne's eye and slid down her cheek. "Let Gram go. I'm begging . . ."

She couldn't understand the mumble that escaped her lips. Someone rolled her over. Her mind tried to force her body to action, but she couldn't fight, couldn't move. Couldn't help her grandmother. Or herself.

Her arms were yanked behind her, her wrists bound with a hard plastic zip tie.

Nothing she could do.

At least one person knew she was in trouble.

God, please get Thayne here fast. Save Gram.

With that last prayer, Cheyenne's world fell into a dark nightmare.

The mid-August evening sun beat down on Thayne's forehead through the windshield. He jerked the steering wheel, and the tires laid down tread around the corner. The sirens screamed out a warning when he sped through the stop-and-go light and a four-way stop.

Thayne couldn't care less that the few folks milling in front of several Main Street shops stood openmouthed, staring. All he could hear in his head was Cheyenne's scream.

A slow-moving Buick turned onto the road in front of him. Thayne yanked the SUV around the car without so much as tapping the brakes.

Ed fell to his side in the backseat. "You trying to kill us?" he shouted, speech slurred.

Thayne didn't bother to respond.

Almost there, Cheyenne. Promise.

He swerved back to the right lane of the two-way road. Singing River might be less than two miles from end to end, but Thayne could've sworn he'd already driven across the entire state of Wyoming.

He zipped past the empty sheriff's office. No more vacations for anyone. Ever. He slammed on the brakes in front of his sister's clinic and bolted from the SUV, Glock in his hand.

His backup was on the way—sirens wailed in the distance, growing louder by the second. He couldn't afford to wait. Two steps and he hit the door of Cheyenne's medical clinic.

The place looked like a herd of buffalo had stampeded through. His gaze lit on the bloodstain at the edge of the front desk, then whipped to the frail figure sagged against the wall of the waiting room, eyes closed, a bloody gash on her forehead.

"Gram!" He hurried over and knelt next to his grandmother. He pressed his fingers to her neck, searching for a pulse, any sign of life.

At first he felt nothing. His gut sank. He shifted his fingers along her paper-thin skin and held his breath. One second, another. Finally, he detected a faint throb beating in her throat.

The clinic door banged open. Thayne pivoted on his knees and raised his weapon.

Norma Baker skidded to a halt, her typically elegant silver hair in complete disarray. Her hands shot into the air.

"Get out of here, Norma," Thayne hissed. "Now."

Surprisingly enough, the retired sheriff's office dispatcher didn't argue with him like usual. She whirled and rushed out the way she'd come. He scooped his grandmother into his arms and followed Norma outside, settling his grandmother on the sidewalk.

Norma hovered over them, her starched and pressed tan pants reminiscent of her days working for his grandfather and then his father.

"Call for an ambulance. I've got to find Cheyenne." Thayne tossed her his phone.

"Be careful," Norma said, stroking his grandmother's face. "Even with her illness, she worries about you kids."

He ran into the clinic, activating his radio. "Pendergrass, where are you?"

The speaker crackled. "Just hit Main," the deputy responded.

"Assault and break-in at the clinic. Keep a lookout. You see anyone heading out of town, stop them."

Weapon at the ready, Thayne stepped across the threshold and held still and silent, even though his first instincts screamed to shout out for his sister. He'd learned better on the streets of Kandahar. Going in with guns blazing just got people dead.

He stepped over the stain on the floor. Too much blood.

"Cheyenne," he whispered, a chill piercing straight through his heart.

He eased up to her office and rounded the open door.

Clear.

And nothing out of place.

Closing and locking the door so anyone still hiding couldn't get in or out without making noise, he shouldered into the pharmaceutical supply room. Chaos. They'd ransacked the drug cabinet and emptied several shelves.

And no sign of Cheyenne.

Thayne spun around, his heart pounding inside his chest, fast and desperate. He'd faced fear before. He'd searched Kandahar neighborhoods, knowing insurgents could take him out each and every time he'd opened a door, but he'd never experienced such suffocating tightness clamping down on his chest.

His mind flew to the worst case. Cheyenne would've fought. Hard.

He burst across the hall into an exam room. Empty. He pivoted and without hesitation searched the last two rooms in the clinic. No sign of Cheyenne. His knees weakened, and Thayne held onto the wall for a moment. He bowed his head. He'd been willing to go to battle, to unleash fury against whoever had terrified his sister. He'd been primed to find and save her.

He hadn't been prepared to not find her—or for the sick dread building in his gut.

Jaw set so hard it throbbed, Thayne strode outside. No ambulance yet. He knelt beside Norma and his grandmother, gently taking her frail hand in his. "How's she doing?"

"She hasn't opened her eyes." Norma blinked several times. "Did you find Cheyenne?"

Thayne shook his head.

"Oh Lord. I saw blood. You don't think—"

"I don't know." Thayne studied Norma. "What made you burst into the clinic after hours? Were you meeting Gram and Cheyenne for dinner?"

Norma shook her head but avoided his glance. "I monitor the radio. I heard your call and rushed over."

"What were you thinking taking that kind of chance? If you'd interrupted them, you could've ended up—" He stopped himself.

"Maybe I could have stopped them."

A twitch pulsed in Thayne's left eye. Any other time, he would've ripped into Norma. She prided herself on her fifty years as part of the sheriff's office, but she'd gone too far. Again. "We'll talk about your eavesdropping on the official scanner later." He gave her the harshest glare he could to a woman who'd changed his diapers. "Or I might just let Pops and Dad do it for me."

Norma winced. "You've got no call to threaten me, young man." She dabbed Gram's forehead with an embroidered handkerchief. "Oh,

Helen." Norma looked over at Thayne. "She doesn't deserve this. None of you do. Isn't the Alzheimer's enough to deal with?"

Some things in life couldn't be fixed. Cheyenne's disappearance, though, he intended to do something about. Another sheriff's office vehicle screeched to a halt. Thayne stood and faced Deputy Quinn Pendergrass, his father's right hand for a dozen years. "Block the roads out of town and organize every person we've got. Dad can contact Lincoln, Fremont, and Teton counties and bring in the Wyoming Division of Criminal Investigation, if we need them."

"What happened here?" Quinn asked, scanning the scene. "Where's Doc Blackwood?"

Thayne hated saying the words, but he couldn't deny the truth. "My sister's missing."

CHAPTER TWO

The isolated cabin could have belonged to the Unabomber. Set back in a rarely traveled stretch of woods in Virginia's Blue Ridge Mountains, the location made for a perfect hideaway if you were a sexual sadist and didn't want anyone to hear your victims scream.

FBI Special Agent Riley Lambert double-checked her Kevlar vest and unholstered her standard-issue Glock. She gripped the butt of the gun and let out a long, slow breath. Five minutes and it would all be over. An unlucky first-grade teacher named Patricia Masters would be safe, and Vincent Wayne O'Neal would never hurt anyone again.

She had to believe that. She couldn't think about the two months she'd spent living on double-shot coffee and wasabi-flavored nuts trying to uncover the connection between a half-dozen missing persons cases.

It didn't matter that she wasn't the only member of a newly formed behavioral analysis unit specializing in the most heinous crimes received at the National Center for Analysis of Violent Crime. Or that no one on the multijurisdictional task force examining the case for the last year had come up with so much as one solid lead.

All that mattered was that two days ago Patricia Masters had been taken right outside an elementary school by the merciless psycho who'd been stalking the east coast for three years. Yesterday Riley found the connection—a common bus route, a few hotel bills, some grainy surveillance video, and one big mistake in the form of the deed to this cabin.

Today, the task force would save Patricia.

SWAT moved into position. Riley caught the team leader's hand motion. Sixty seconds.

She gripped her handgun tighter and glanced at her supervisor. "She's alive in there, Tom," Riley whispered.

He gave her that piercing you-can't-hide-the-truth-from-me look and drew his own weapon. "O'Neal usually spends a week playing with them. We've got a good chance."

Not wanting to face his impenetrable stare any longer, she focused on the cabin's door. Right here, right now was the culmination of a destiny that had started just one week after her tenth birthday.

The public would have called her a profiler. The FBI called her a special agent with the new, experimental Behavioral Analysis Unit 6.

Supervisory Special Agent Tom Hickok had pegged her to become part of the provisional team with the express purpose of embedding itself with local law enforcement task forces. Riley had jumped at the opportunity to take her psychological profiling skills on investigative assignments. The job hadn't gone quite as planned.

Three, two, one.

Riley sucked in a deep breath. SWAT stormed the front door. Guns drawn, Riley and her unit followed in their wake.

The raid took all of thirty seconds. The local authorities secured the scene with no need to search for their suspect.

There he stood. Vincent Wayne O'Neal. The mouse of a man waited in the corner, his calm, unafraid gaze triumphant. He didn't look like the stuff of nightmares. Riley had learned they hardly ever did.

He cradled a rifle in his arms. "You're too late," he whispered, staring directly at Riley. "I win."

He raised the barrel, aiming at her chest.

Riley dropped to the floor. Not fast enough. Red-hot heat sliced across her arm. She rolled to her back and squeezed off two quick rounds. A slew of bullets flew above her.

O'Neal slumped to the floor, dead.

Suicide by cop.

Riley's heart raced. Her head fell back to the floor with a thud. She lowered her weapon.

O'Neal's words, *You're too late*, chilled her very soul. He'd been too smug. She closed her eyes against the foreboding blackness creeping around her. Not again. This time had to be different. Patricia was here. Alive.

"Search the place," Tom shouted. "Find Patricia Masters."

The pounding of boots on wood thundered through the cabin.

Riley sat up. She had to help, but the moment she moved her arm she bit back a yelp. She glanced down at her shirt. Blood seeped through the blue cotton.

"Medic," her boss yelled, crouching beside her.

The red blotch swirled. Riley blinked in an attempt to focus. A paramedic knelt down, cutting her sleeve.

"It's nothing."

"Just shut up and let them do their job, Riley," Tom said. "We'll find her."

"Search behind the cabin," Riley hissed as the paramedic worked on her arm. "He wants them close." She didn't mention the spots swirling in front of her eyes.

A few minutes later, a slow thud of footsteps joined them.

Riley looked up. "You found her?"

"You were right in your profile, ma'am," the cop said. "There's a row of graves behind the cabin. Each marked by a rose bush."

"Patricia?" Riley swallowed deep. She couldn't bear the pity on the man's face.

"We were too late. I'm sorry. She's dead."

Riley froze. *No! Not again.*

She squeezed her eyes shut against the truth.

She hadn't been able to help Patricia.

Just like Riley hadn't been able to help her own sister.

The world tilted and swayed.

"Riley." Tom gripped her uninjured arm. "Stay with me."

Her wound burned. Blackness closed in on her. She was going to pass out.

What does it matter? Really?

She'd failed. Again.

◆ ◆ ◆

An unfamiliar clock's booming chimes roused Cheyenne through the fog in her head. Eight, maybe nine times?

She lifted her head from a hard pillow and squinted through the pitch-black room. A quick touch of the rough upholstery beneath her fingers told her she wasn't in her own bed or at the clinic. But where?

Her head pounded, and she gently palpated her temple. Memories sliced through her pain-filled mind. Someone had hit her. They'd hurt Gram. A sweet smell had overwhelmed her. She'd passed out.

Say good-bye. Cheyenne remembered the words, but being dead shouldn't hurt this much.

So, if she wasn't dead, she was alive.

For now.

A slow, metallic creak pierced the darkness. Footsteps crossed the floor toward her, coming closer and closer.

Her heart raced. Could her kidnapper hear the pounding against her chest? The whoosh of her pulse throbbed in her head. She closed her eyes and held her breath, biting back the groan of agony. Every survival instinct urged her not to move, not to reveal she'd regained consciousness.

A small click echoed from across the room. They'd turned on the light. She froze. The footfalls stopped. The room went silent but for a few jagged breaths above her prone body.

"Revive her," a deep male voice ordered. "The procedure must occur now."

"Yes, Father."

A door slammed, followed by a bolt locking them in. The sound sent agonizing ricochets through Cheyenne's skull. She didn't move. A sharp, stinging odor pierced her nose. She yanked her head away and gasped for air, unable to contain the cough.

Another sharp whiff and she snapped open her eyes. Her vision blurred from the tears. "Stop," she said, her voice cracking. "Please."

She pushed herself to a sitting position and swiped at her eyes, unable to focus. She heaved in a breath. The flow of air seized her throat. She clutched at her neck and erupted into a fit of coughing.

A hand thrust a cup of water in front of her face. "Drink." A boy of about sixteen hovered beside her. The teen tilted the glass to her lips.

Cheyenne drank and licked her parched mouth. For the first time, her eyes focused.

She gripped the loveseat's cushion. Her gaze fixated on one of the rustic log walls with two doors and no windows. The gray steel one was closed, its locks appearing impenetrable, the other opened to what appeared to be a small bathroom. She scanned the back of the large room and gasped. A woman lay on a twin bed, her face flushed and wet with perspiration.

The patient groaned, moved a little, and yelped, clutching at her belly. "Hurts," she whispered between pants. "Help."

Cheyenne shoved herself to her feet and shot the kid a glare. "What did you do to her?" She stumbled across the room to the bed, ignoring the throbbing in her skull, and placed the back of her hand against the woman's forehead. Burning with fever. She pressed her fingertips against the woman's wrist. Pulse 117. Not good.

"What happened?"

"Her stomach's been hurting for a couple of days," the boy said, chewing on his lip. "She collapsed right after lunch."

Cheyenne palpated the woman's abdomen. She whimpered a bit. When Cheyenne's hands moved to the right lower quadrant, an excruciating scream ripped through the room. Rebound tenderness.

"We have to get her to a hospital." Cheyenne stood. "It looks like an appendicitis. She could need an operation."

"We know," the boy said. He walked over to a table tucked in a corner and lifted a blue surgical drape.

Cheyenne's eyes widened at the array of medical supplies. She shook her head at the horrifying realization. "I'm not a surgeon."

The teenager sidled up to the feverish woman's bedside and clutched her hand, his expression obviously worried. "You're the only chance she has."

Cheyenne placed her hands on the boy's shoulders and turned him to face her. "Look . . . what's your name?"

"Ian."

"Ian, she needs a hospital. She could die."

The boy flinched, his eyes clouded with fear. "That's why Father arranged for you to come here, Dr. Blackwood. To save her."

A lock clanked and the door creaked open, revealing a woman with her hair draped across one side of her face. "Ian, Father wants a complete report on the *visit* into Singing River this evening."

Memories of Ian entering the clinic, of someone coming at her from behind, of her grandmother's cries, catapulted through Cheyenne. "You were there." She swayed, clutching at his arm to steady herself. "My grandmother? Is she OK?"

He hesitated.

"Please, don't anger Father, Ian."

The woman's pleading words sent a shiver straight to Cheyenne's core. *Father* obviously terrified both of them.

The boy nearly bit through his lip. "Yes, Adelaide."

He disappeared out the doorway. Pounding footsteps faded before a second door slammed shut in the distance.

"My grandmother?" Cheyenne repeated, facing Adelaide. "Is she OK?"

"You should be worrying about yourself." Adelaide's gaze softened in sympathy. "I'll try to find out for you, but I can't promise anything."

She frowned, and a tingle of familiarity niggled in Cheyenne's mind. She looked back and forth between her patient and Adelaide. Similar hair color, with that unusual tint of auburn. Similar mouth shape, bone structure, and height, except for the scar that began at the corner of Adelaide's eye and traveled to her chin. Related maybe?

Cheyenne's focus lingered on her patient. "She needs a hospital."

"I'm sorry. There's nothing I can do." Adelaide backed toward the exit. "You have everything you should need to help her. Father made certain of it."

Cheyenne shadowed Adelaide. "What is this place?"

"Take some advice, Dr. Blackwood. Focus on saving my sister and don't ask questions. No one can help you—or any of us."

The words captured Cheyenne's attention. Maybe she wasn't the only prisoner here. Taking a chance, Cheyenne lowered her voice. "My dad is the Singing River sheriff. My brother is his deputy. If you help me, I can help all of you."

Adelaide's eyes widened, her gaze darting to the opening. She leaned toward Cheyenne. "I'll come back later, if I can." Adelaide straightened. "I suggest you do your best to save my sister, Doctor." Her voice was loud and strong, obviously making certain someone outside the door heard the words. "Because if she dies, there will be nothing anyone can do to save you."

◆ ◆ ◆

Night cloaked Singing River with suffocating darkness. Pushing 10:00 p.m. and they hadn't found a trace of Cheyenne. Thayne's SUV flew through town. He clutched the steering wheel, urging the vehicle faster. Five hours. She'd been missing for five hours. He whacked the leather with his fist. Why hadn't he let Pendergrass take the drunk and disorderly call at Clive's? If he'd been closer to town . . .

He'd only missed her by a few minutes.

"Where are you, sis?" he muttered when he reached the edge of town and the Singing River Methodist Church.

Sitting on several acres of land, the church had always been a beacon. Now its steeple stood tall, illuminated against the night sky. A group of strategically placed floodlights bathed the building with strong white beams.

Four pickups from the Riverton Ranch sped past Thayne, heading toward the woods. The perpetual family feud hadn't stopped the Rivertons from joining the search. Thank God.

Thayne screeched into the church's parking lot. Several dozen vehicles sat empty in the grassland north of the church. A hell of a lot different than a SEAL op. Thayne usually found himself part of an eight-man squad or four-man fire team. Double that had gathered on the edge of the parking lot around the command center table, waiting for assignments. You'd have thought it was midday on a Sunday after services rather than late Friday night.

More than a hundred had searched for Cheyenne already, including his brothers. Hudson and Jackson had been the first to take a quadrant. Last he'd spoken with them, they'd found nothing.

Their father leaned forward, pointing at a map on the table. Clive nodded and handed flashlights to Olaf, the cook from the diner, and Yvonne, whose Cuts, Curls and Color Salon was a Singing River institution. They each grabbed a map and moved to the coffee station.

Thayne strode up to his father. Sheriff Carson Blackwood's jaw throbbed with tension, his lips pursed. Myocarditis had landed him in the hospital less than two months ago. His clothes still hung on his body, but he'd regained some color in his cheeks. He wasn't fully recovered, though. It could take another four months.

"I don't suppose I could convince you to go home and rest for a while," Thayne said, grabbing his mug and filling it with coffee from the next table.

"Anything?" His father bit out the words.

"Nothing. It's like she disappeared into thin air." Thayne shook his head, gripping the coffee, trying to shove aside the tension vibrating through his body. "Any news here?"

His father's shoulders sagged, and he shook his head.

"About time you got here." Three seventy-five-year-old voices spoke as one.

Norma, Fannie, and Willow glared at Thayne, but he recognized the worry behind their eyes. The women were his grandmother's best friends. They'd been part of his life for as long as he could remember.

"I've been suggesting that your stubborn fool of a father take a break for the last hour," Norma Baker said, crossing her arms. "He looks like he's about to keel over."

"You old busybodies." His dad's gaze narrowed in exasperation, and he sent Thayne a looks-could-kill glare. "When Cheyenne is home safe in her own bed, that's when I'll rest. And not before."

Norma's gaze softened. "Your family needs you, Carson. Cheyenne needs you healthy. You won't do any good to anyone if you're laid up in the hospital again."

Thayne recognized his father's famous temper on the verge of erupting. "Dad, what did DCI say?"

"They're shorthanded. They can only spare one investigator."

"DCI?" Fannie asked.

"The Wyoming Division of Criminal Investigation," Thayne said, facing the three women, who leaned forward with rapt attention. "They have a field office in Pinedale."

"Oh, like CSI," Fannie said.

Norma shook her head with a sigh. "That TV stuff isn't real."

"But more are coming, right?" The stark look on his father's face gave Thayne a chill. "We need the help."

"Maybe. In the meantime, Pendergrass will be using everything he learned from that forensic training he took at the DCI crime lab. He'll do a sweep and send any prints and evidence to them. Best we can do, except to keep the search going." His father swiped his brow. "What guts me is everything I love about Singing River is the very thing that will slow us down. A remote small town in a large, remote state with a small population. Hell, the nearest FBI field office is in Denver. We've only got a few resident agencies across the state, barely manned."

"Will they come?"

"They're stretched thin, too. One missing woman doesn't exactly float to the top of their list."

"So we're on our own." Thayne knew the statistics. They had about seventy-two hours to find Cheyenne. If they didn't . . .

"It's like before," Willow whispered under her breath. "Like that poor Gina Wallace, Carol's girl."

God, Thayne hoped not.

Norma straightened her spine. "Nope. We're finding Cheyenne. This time we know quicker. She's out there. We have hundreds of people combing everywhere."

"That's right," Fannie said, shoving a couple of her melt-in-your-mouth cinnamon rolls into a bag. "Cheyenne is a tough girl. She'll make it out of this alive."

"Of course," Willow said, her brown eyes troubled. Thayne knew why. Willow's late husband had been a tracker on the Gina Wallace search. They'd never found a single trace. The girl had simply disappeared.

Just like Cheyenne.

Thayne shoved away the memories. Too many differences to compare. Gina had been a child; Cheyenne was a woman. Technology had been in the Dark Ages fifteen years ago. They'd started this search within a half hour of Cheyenne's disappearance.

They had a chance for a different ending. "Anything from the BOLO on the black SUV Fannie saw heading north of town?" Thayne asked his father.

"We've alerted the surrounding counties to be on the lookout. No news yet."

"How could Cheyenne just vanish in broad daylight? Someone had to have seen *something*."

"Which is why I contacted the media and put out a request for any possible sightings or information. Like you said, we need all the help we can get."

A mud-splattered pickup screeched into the church parking lot. Deputy Michael Ironcloud hit the ground in a run, still wearing his fishing gear, his Shoshone ancestry undeniable, his presence and skills a welcome relief. He raced up to Thayne and his father.

"I thought you were gone for a week," Thayne said.

"Brad twisted his knee. We had to come home early. I dropped him off at home." Ironcloud shoved his hand through his hair. "I just heard about Cheyenne and the BOLO. I wish we'd known sooner."

Thayne froze at the deputy's words. "Why do you say that?"

"Because we noticed a black SUV heading toward Fremont Lake not long after Cheyenne disappeared."

CHAPTER THREE

North of Singing River, Wyoming, in the middle of nowhere, only the moon and dozens of stars offered any disruption from the utter blackness surrounding the vehicle. The bright headlight beams illuminated the dirt road in front of Thayne's SUV.

His gaze swept to and fro, searching for anything out of place, out of the ordinary, a glimpse of the plum dress Cheyenne had been wearing when she disappeared. He glanced over at his father, his dad's face even more drawn than two and a half hours ago when they'd left one of the deputies managing command central.

"We're going to find her," Thayne said, needing to hear the words as much for himself as to comfort his father.

"Of course we are. Good idea to search these dirt roads off the main route between town and the lake." He snagged the radio.

"Dad, you contacted the office less than fifteen minutes ago."

"Damn it, you think I don't realize that?" He closed his eyes. "We both know what could be happening to her, what they could be doing to her. If . . . if she's still . . ."

Still alive.

His father couldn't say the words aloud.

Neither could Thayne. "They didn't kill Gram. Hopefully that means something."

"Maybe." The sheriff of Singing River let out a sharp curse and tossed his badge on the dash. "The case is different when it's personal. A hell of a lot different."

"Yeah." Thayne recognized the expression. Anger, frustration, and desperation lying in wait just beneath the surface, clawing to escape. "My mind's going places it shouldn't," he admitted.

"Did I tell you I'm glad you're home and not on an op?" His father stared out the side window. "Your mother hated not knowing where you were for weeks or months at a time, if you were alive or dead."

"*Mom* always worried." Thayne understood the message. He could play along with the distraction—and with their standard worry game. Even though his mom had passed away five years ago, his dad still invoked the old standby excuse.

"Makes this damn heart infection worth it." The tough, no-nonsense sheriff cleared his throat and blinked. "Where's my little girl?" His dad leaned forward in his seat. "Where is Cheyenne?"

"We'll find her. We have to."

The SUV rounded a curve, its headlights forming a bright tunnel revealing a line of Douglas firs on one side of the road and a creek lining the other. They topped a small hill, and Thayne stepped on the brakes. A gate and barbed-wire fence blocked the road.

"Let me take a look." Thayne left the vehicle and studied the padlock, tugging at the rusted metal before slipping back behind the wheel. "No one's opened that gate for months." He turned to his father. "Cheyenne's smart and resourceful. She'll get word to us. We just have to keep looking."

He made a U-turn off-road and headed the way they'd come.

"I wish she'd call. She must have her phone. Pendergrass didn't find it at her office."

"Try the locator app again, Dad. We could get lucky."

"Apps," his dad huffed, tapping the screen. "When Jackson fought that fire in Arizona, his phone hardly worked at all. Today your brother is searching the mountains that back up to our ranch, but he could be on Mars and I couldn't tell. The terrain around here makes for one big dead zone. Hudson's on the south end leading a team. No reception there, either." With a frustrated hand, his father tossed the phone next to the badge. "I don't know why you kids gave me this damn phone anyway. I was perfectly happy with my old flip phone. This monstrosity doesn't tell me squat. Except that you're sitting right next to me. Sure as hell doesn't tell me if you're in Afghanistan or Pakistan or wherever you were last."

Thayne frowned at his father's outburst. "There's always a chance."

"We need satellite phones out here. It hasn't been in the budget, but I'm thinking we've got to find the money somehow." Thayne's father snagged the device and stared unblinking at the screen. "You gonna opt out, son?"

OK, the question came from nowhere, but sometimes the only way to cope with panic was to discuss the mundane. He wasn't fooled. His father's whitened knuckles gripped the phone. Not any different than Thayne's clutching the steering wheel.

The SUV bounced on the rain-savaged road. "Haven't decided. What would I do if I left the SEALs?"

"I could make that deputy's badge permanent. You could settle down, get married. Have a life."

A scoffing laugh escaped Thayne. "Come on, Dad. Of all your kids, I was voted least likely to follow in your and Pops's footsteps."

"Not by me or your mother. Jackson's the adrenaline junky. Hudson's heart is in the land. Cheyenne's tied to the people. But you, Thayne, you have that sense of justice, that need to right a wrong. You just feed the need on the battlefield fighting for Uncle Sam. You could do it here. Where you belong."

The SUV slammed into a pothole. Thayne eased up on the gas pedal. "Singing River is the only place on Earth Hudson could ever be happy. Cheyenne left for school, but only so she could come back."

"And you?"

"Singing River is . . . claustrophobic. Everyone knows my name, knows our family, knows what's expected. Gram understands. I couldn't even blow off a little steam without you and Pops knowing about it. Or be alone with my girlfriend. It's a wonder I'm not still a virgin, as many times as you guys interrupted—"

"That was your mother's idea." His father drummed his fingers on the armrest. "Why not come home, settle down?"

OK, Thayne had to figure out how to derail this conversation. Their superficial attempt at normalcy had just veered into dangerous waters. "There's no one here who makes me want forever."

"Does this have anything to do with a certain FBI special agent you spend hours talking to on Friday evenings?"

Thayne whipped his head around to meet his father's gaze. How could he know about the relationship with Riley? No one knew. Even Thayne had trouble wrapping his brain around the confusing emotions.

A small beep sounded from the app. "Thayne, I've got a signal."

"Who?"

His father blinked. "Cheyenne's phone. It's a mile off the dirt road leading to the old mill."

Thayne flipped on the sirens, pushing the vehicle as much as he dared on the dirt road.

The sheriff grabbed his badge off the dash and snatched the radio. "We've got a cell phone signal," he said, relaying the location. "Send backup."

Five miles onto the highway following the creek, Thayne skidded onto a dirt road. Dust kicked up, reflecting off the headlights like a curtain of sand.

"We should be closing in. How much farther?" Thayne asked.

"Almost there." His father tugged a spotlight from the floorboard. "About a hundred feet southwest of us."

Thayne stopped the car. They mounted the light and flipped it on. Ground cover rustled in a grove of fir and aspens. Thayne jumped from the running board and raised his weapon.

The branches swayed at the base of the tree. A coyote stared at them from among the twigs, then bounded away.

With a flashlight in one hand, Glock in the other, Thayne took the lead. His father followed close behind, monitoring the phone.

Thayne's flashlight beam swept side to side. He knelt down, studying the leaves and pine needles. His shoulders tensed. "Someone's been here," he said under his breath.

"Cheyenne?"

"Combat boot," Thayne whispered. He stilled, body coiled, listening for any sound, any hint of the unfamiliar.

For a moment, he could have sworn they were being watched. He peered through the trees, listening, waiting.

No movement.

He'd stayed alive through four tours trusting his gut. With caution, he ducked under a large tree limb and motioned his father forward. "I've got a bad feeling someone's out there. I can't tell which way he went. You?"

The man who'd trained all his children to track and survive bent down, squinting at the area in the flashlight's range, then slowly shook his head. "Guy knew how to cover his tracks. I can barely tell he wiped them away. He was here, but he could've headed in any direction, including back to the road. Trouble is, I didn't see any tire tracks, either."

Weapons drawn, they searched through the grove before moving into an area of wheatgrass. A glint drew Thayne's attention. He squatted down.

A phone. His gut twisted.

"It's Cheyenne's. I'd know that bright-red case anywhere." His father leaned over Thayne's shoulder.

Thayne shoved on a protective glove and scooped it up. Within seconds, he'd placed it into an evidence bag and tapped the screen through the plastic. The phone lit up. "It's locked. Do you know her password?"

"Her birthday."

"Damn silly choice. Too easy to break," Thayne muttered, but he tapped in the numbers. "It worked. When we find her, I'm making her pick a new code." Thayne searched photos, texts, and even e-mail. "She hasn't used it since she called me."

"No message? Nothing? I can't believe that."

"Whoever took Cheyenne must've dumped it."

"And then carted her off to God knows where." Thayne's father studied the road heading toward the National Forest. "It's too easy. They're not headed into the woods. They've covered their tracks well so far. Why point us in the right direction?"

"I agree. So, back the way we came?"

The sheriff grabbed his shoulder mic. "This is Sheriff Blackwood. Expand the BOLO for the black SUV and Cheyenne to all the neighboring states. And get Pendergrass out here. We have a secondary crime scene."

While his father barked out orders, Thayne walked the area around the phone's location, searching for anything they might have missed, some clue to lead them to Cheyenne.

He circled tightly, focused on the ground cover, but nothing appeared out of place until . . . He froze at a radius of ten feet, unable to move or breathe.

God, please no.

On the edge of a group of shrubbery . . . freshly sifted dirt, and just beyond that, a small ditch covered with dead branches and leaves. With a sidelong glance at his father, he hurried to the site. A fox scampered away, streaking below the evergreen leaves.

Thayne knelt down.

Please don't be here, Cheyenne. Please.

He braced himself and shoved aside several branches.

Buried beneath the logs, an old, shredded tent and a few fence posts lay embedded in the earth.

Thayne's knees gave way. He fell back in the dirt. Hard. *Thank God.*

"What'd you find?" His father's clipped voice jerked Thayne out of the intense relief. "Is it her? Is she . . . ?"

Thayne stood up and quickly strode to his dad. "It's not her. It's remnants of the last flash flood."

His father closed his eyes. Thayne hated being grateful they hadn't found Cheyenne, but for a moment, he'd believed he'd uncovered her lifeless body. He never wanted to feel that way again. Not ever.

The radio sparked.

"Sheriff. It's your mother. She's awake, but it's not good."

The streets of DC never slept. Even well after midnight. Horns honked nearby, a car alarm pierced through the dark, and Riley squirmed in the seat next to her boss. He'd been too quiet since they'd left the crime scene. His silence didn't bode well.

Tom pulled up in front of Riley's apartment building and shifted into park, the rumbling purr of his government vehicle nothing but a reminder that he'd been lying in wait since they'd left the hospital.

"You look like hell," he said, his voice soft but clipped, his gaze hard and knowing. "And not because of that bullet graze. When's the last time you slept more than a few hours?"

Her mind ticked back through the last week or two, buried in this case, getting to know, to appreciate, to really like Patricia. At the same time living in the heart of a monster, peeling back the dark layers of hell.

What could she say? She had no idea.

"That's what I thought." A long sigh escaped him. "What did I tell you after the last case, Riley?"

She ignored the question. What was the point in rehashing an order she could never follow? She couldn't do her job if she didn't make the case personal. It was her gift: getting into the mind-set of the victim . . . and the killer. It was how she worked. It was how she'd found O'Neal. She couldn't change now.

Riley met his gaze, her own unblinking, and he shook his head.

"We can't save everyone." Tom frowned at her, a furrow between his brows. "You know that." He steepled his fingers under his chin. "You still can't let her go, can you?"

"I joined the FBI to save lives. To save people like Patricia." Unrealistic expectations? Probably. That didn't change the sour taste rising in her mouth at tonight's failure. She should have anticipated O'Neal's behavior. That was her job, damn it.

"I'm not talking about Patricia Masters. I'm talking about your sister. You see your sister in the face of every victim and it's destroying you. You can't keep going on like this, Riley."

Her lips grew taut. She couldn't deny the truth, but she didn't have to admit it.

"Do you know why I chose you for this unit? Even though you've only been with the FBI for three years?"

"My winning personality and ability to get along with others?" she said, her voice dry.

"You're the best profiler to go through the training at Quantico in twenty years."

Her mouth dropped open in shock.

"You get inside these guys' heads. I need someone like you for this position because it's an experiment. The staff based at Quantico does more data crunching than investigating. The field agents take on that role. This team combines the two skill sets. It forces us to face the worst of the worst when we embed ourselves as part of local task forces."

"The unit's working," she said.

"Yeah. Our solve rate is higher than any of the other teams'. That's not the point. The very gift that makes you the best at your job is going to drive you out of it. You empathize, Riley. You live every horror with the victim, but you also immerse yourself inside the killer's head. You're not going to survive if you don't find a balance."

The words coming from the man who controlled her destiny with the FBI clawed at her throat, cutting off her ability to breathe. Desperate, she dug her nails into her palms to subdue the panic. "I can do this, Tom. I promise you."

He raised an eyebrow. He'd been a profiler for nearly thirty years. He didn't miss much.

"I want you to stay home. For a week."

"But—"

"You're injured. You're running on empty."

One glance at her bandaged arm reinforced the point. She'd let the serial killer get the drop on her. A few ibuprofens and the graze would heal. She'd be fine.

Unlike Patricia.

In some jobs, a failure meant a late report or a reprimand. For Riley, failure meant someone else died. Not something that could—or should—be forgiven. Or forgotten.

"Tom—"

He held up his hand. "Say anything else, and I'll make it *two* weeks. When you come back, I want you to report *exactly* how you plan to emotionally survive this job, because right now, I don't think you can."

Her boss walked around the car to help her out. "I'm not kidding, Riley. Seven days of serious contemplation. That's an order."

Without another word, he got into his car and drove away.

As the taillights disappeared around the corner, Riley's mind whirled in chaos. A week. She had a week to come up with an answer that would convince him that she could do the job she'd worked for most of her life.

She couldn't lose her position on the unit. She had too many promises to keep. The biggest one to her sister, Madison.

The streetlight above Riley flickered. A skitter of awareness tingled at the base of her neck. She clasped the butt of her Glock and hurried through the small gate leading to the old walk-up that had been converted into efficiency apartments a decade ago.

She climbed the concrete steps and unlocked the door. The old oak squeaked open, and she closed the outside behind her.

All was quiet in the foyer. She trudged up the stairs to her apartment. Her gaze darted from side to side with every step down the hall until she reached the last door on the right and inserted the key into the lock. It went in easily. Just like normal.

She pushed inside and quickly disarmed the alarm system, then reset it for home.

With the temporary cloak of safety in place, Riley walked directly into the bedroom, dropped her go bag, and sank onto the bed, her knees shaking. She buried her head in her hands, rubbing the grit from her eyes. Stark despair twisted her gut. She *was* running on empty, her energy sapped. It had nothing to do with her arm, and everything to do with Patricia's vacant, lifeless gaze. God, she'd wanted to save her.

Barely able to find the strength to move, she shucked her pants and shirt and slid beneath the covers. She'd wash her face tomorrow.

With a flick, she turned off the lamp beside the bed, but the room didn't go dark. A small night-light flickered from the outlet near her bathroom.

It never went completely dark in her room.

She hated the dark.

As a kid, she'd believed only bad things happened in the dark. She'd learned over the years the horrific could happen at any time.

But no one else had to know that. Too many demons, too many nightmares. Too many explanations she refused to provide.

No one needed to see the fears that welled up from deep within to suffocate her. They wouldn't understand. She folded her hands behind her head and stared up at the ceiling, the shadows twisting, taunting.

OK, not true. *One* person would understand. He always understood.

Instinct trumped logic. She reached for her cell phone. The screen glowed to life, blank and lonely. No new notifications. No new calls. No texts. No e-mails.

"Thayne," she whispered, tracing the screen with her finger, fighting the disappointment that clung to her like a wet wool blanket. She longed to hear his voice. She could feel herself falling into that dark place in her head. Thayne could rescue her from drowning in a sea of frustration and doubt with a few well-chosen words. Who would've thought that what started out as a single passionate week, followed by a few flirtatious phone calls, would have transformed into a lifeline.

His uncanny ability to sense her moods by just the sound of her voice terrified her. Of course, she could do the same with him.

She'd come to eagerly look forward to their weekly conversations. More than that, she counted on them. Thayne helped her keep her sanity. Most of the time.

Her finger hovered over the screen. One touch and his phone would ring. She would hear his voice.

He'd called three times last week, and she hadn't picked up. Was that why she hesitated calling now? Because he might recognize what she didn't want to acknowledge—that her job was eating her up inside.

She tucked the phone beneath her pillow and left her hand there. If he could, he'd call sometime tonight.

One punch on her pillow and Riley curled up on her uninjured side, searching the shapes cast through the room by the night-light. Though she tried, she couldn't fight the fatigue or the pain pills. She blinked. The grit behind her eyes hurt, but she didn't want to close them. She hated the moments before she fell asleep.

She hated the moments just before she awoke even more because the dreams wouldn't leave her alone and the nightmares never stopped.

Tonight would be no different.

A twisted shadow slid down the wall, devoured by the darkness. Riley's eyelids grew heavy, and she could fight no longer. Little by little, she sank into the oblivion of sleep.

Another shovelful of dirt sprinkled on top of Riley, covering her torso, pinning her arms beside her. The smell of fresh earth embedded itself in her senses.

She sucked in a deep breath. Dirt clung to her mouth. She looked up to the sky, blue and beautiful. It should be raining and cold. She couldn't die beneath a blue sky.

Suddenly, she was no longer in the grave; she was standing beside the hole, looking down.

She didn't want to look inside.

Her heart raced with an erratic pounding against her chest. She forced her eyes to peer into the grave.

Below her, Patricia Masters, terrorized, innocent, and dead, stared up at her, accusing. "Why didn't you save me?"

"I'm sorry. So very, very sorry." Riley's eyes stung with frustrated tears, unable to look away from the dead woman's face.

The vision morphed.

Patricia's blonde hair turned auburn. An adult's face transformed into that of a twelve-year-old girl.

Madison. Oh God, it was Madison. Her sister.

Riley screamed.

She jerked up in bed. Her heart wouldn't slow down. She choked in a shuddering breath.

With a groan, she sagged back into the soft down pillow cradling her head.

One swipe of her hand over her eyes and she knew she wasn't covered with dirt. She glanced over at the clock. Three forty-five in the morning. She'd slept all of an hour.

She closed her stinging eyes. She should sleep. Her body needed rest. So did her mind.

Breathe in, out. In and out. She lay there for several moments, but her mind burned with the memory. She could see it as clearly as if the kidnapping had happened yesterday.

Like Patricia and O'Neal's other victims, her sister's body was in a grave somewhere. Except Madison was still waiting to be found.

Riley couldn't give up. Not ever. No matter what it took, she would never stop searching until she found Madison. Never.

Fifteen Years Ago

"Madison and Riley Lambert. Get out of bed, girls. The bus will be here in fifteen minutes."

Madison blinked open her eyes, closing them again at the bright sun piercing through the window slats.

A snore sounded softly beside her just before two knobby knees ground into her back.

"Ow! Get off, Riley," Madison said, shoving her little sister off the bed. "Why can't you sleep in your own room?"

Riley hit the carpet with a thud and a groan. "What'd you do that for, Maddy?"

"I told you. It's Madison. Maddy is for little girls. Like you."

Madison walked over to the bedroom window and peered outside. She let out a small sigh. Thank goodness he was gone. She'd seen him on her way home from school every day for the last week.

Last night he'd stood below her window.

She hadn't told her mother. If she did, her mom would cancel the slumber party. Madison would tell her afterward. Until then, she'd just watch out for him.

She was in middle school now. Practically grown up.

Madison waltzed over to the closet and pulled out her new flare jeans and a halter top, then grabbed a scarf to use as a belt and some hoop earrings. She tossed them on the bed.

Riley reached out to touch the jewelry.

"Quit it. I told you to stop touching my things, Riley. You'll mess them up."

Her little sister looked down at the ink stains on her hands, but not before tears glistened in her eyes. Madison ignored the twinge of guilt. Maybe last year she and her sister had played Barbies together, but that was a long time ago.

Madison turned on the latest tune from her favorite boy band and danced into the Jack and Jill bathroom she shared with Riley. She opened the drawer.

"Riley! Get in here! Where's my lip gloss?"

Riley came to the door, biting her lip. "I dropped it on the floor. Flower got it."

"The dog ate my lip gloss?" Madison wailed. "Can't you do anything right?"

Madison slammed the door in Riley's face and locked it. She took out her brush and counted to one hundred as the bristles smoothed her long auburn hair.

Knocks pounded on the door. "Come on, Maddy. I have to get ready, too."

"No way. I'm getting ready all by myself from now on. And I'm locking my bedroom door so you can't sneak in at night."

"Maddy . . . ," Riley whined. "I get scared in the dark."

"Too bad. You're being stupid. Monsters aren't real. All you're doing is scaring yourself."

After all, a girl starting seventh grade knew ghost stories were told to scare you, and unlike her sister, Madison never got scared.

That night, however, Madison Lambert would learn some monsters are very, very real.

CHAPTER FOUR

Four years of medical school, three of residency, and an emergency medicine fellowship could never have prepared Cheyenne for this.

A dungeon—because that's the only way she could describe the windowless prison she found herself in—was no place to operate.

And yet here she stood, scalpel in hand. The other med students and residents had thought she'd gone crazy signing up for every surgery elective throughout her education, but she'd known coming back to Singing River to practice medicine, she'd be on her own. She'd imagined search and rescue, car accidents, someone on the wrong end of a bull's temper and no time to transport. Definitely not being kidnapped so she could perform an appendectomy in the middle of nowhere.

Right now she sent up a prayer of thanks for every moment she'd spent in those surgery rotations. She could do this.

But would her makeshift assistant survive without fainting?

She glanced over at him. Ian stood next to the instrument tray, his face pale but his posture determined.

They might actually pull this off.

She checked her patient. The sedative had taken effect. Cheyenne administered the local anesthetic. No way could she put the woman under with a general. Too risky. She had no one to monitor her vitals. Luckily, during her Emergency Medicine Under Austere Conditions fellowship, she'd learned how flexible medicine could be.

She made the first incision and set to work, letting instinct and training take over. Every so often she glanced at Ian, but he hadn't fainted yet.

"Retractor," she ordered.

His eyes grew wide and panicked. She pointed out the instrument, and he handed it to her.

She pushed aside the tissue and revealed the woman's appendix. Cheyenne froze.

Pink. Perfect. Healthy.

Oh God. What was she supposed to do now?

"Is something wrong, Doctor?" Ian whispered, tone laced with fear.

"Of course not," Cheyenne lied, her mind racing.

The door creaked open. Adelaide stepped in. "Father says you should be finished by now. He wants a report. Can I tell him Bethany's going to be fine?" Her trembling voice left no doubt Adelaide prayed Cheyenne could say just that.

So, Cheyenne finally knew her patient's name. "Bethany would have a better chance if you'd let me take her to a hospital."

"She can't leave." Adelaide took one step toward the makeshift operating table, her expression desperate. "Please, Doctor. Father must know. Will Bethany recover?"

"Yes, she'll be fine."

"Thank goodness." Adelaide turned to leave, then paused. "Father wishes to see her appendix," she said, tone apologetic.

Cheyenne's gut knotted. "I need to concentrate, Adelaide. Come back later, but please think about what I said before. My father can help us all."

Ian's eyes widened, but he said nothing. The woman bit her lip and nodded before locking them inside the room.

Cheyenne's gaze lingered on the steel door for a moment. Then she stared down at the healthy tissue, a plan forming in her mind. During most abdominal surgeries, the appendix was removed, since it served no function. She'd follow procedure and damage the organ so it appeared diseased. Giving in to her captors would buy her time. Time to convince Adelaide that she had a choice.

Saying a small prayer, she completed the procedure and dropped the organ into a metal dish.

"Bethany'll be all right now?" Ian asked.

Not hardly. Because whatever had caused Bethany's symptoms was still attacking her body. Cheyenne explored the open abdomen, searching for an obvious cause, but nothing appeared abnormal. She had no choice but to close the wound.

With the last of the staples in place, she stood back. "I've done all I can," she said to Ian. At least until she figured out what had made the poor woman so deathly ill.

"When will Bethany wake up?" he asked.

"I don't know." Normally a post-appendectomy patient would be awake within a few hours. Except Bethany hadn't needed the operation. And whatever was causing her symptoms hadn't been repaired. Cheyenne changed gloves and checked the IV antibiotic drip before lowering her mask. "I can't promise anything, Ian. She needs a hospital."

Ian swallowed. "Father won't be happy if she doesn't get better."

Cheyenne's knees shook, and she sank into the chair beside Bethany, studying her, searching for an identifying symptom. Ian hovered at her shoulder, watching, waiting.

Somehow, Cheyenne had to do the impossible: make healthy tissue appear diseased so Father would be fooled *and* diagnose her patient's symptoms.

If she didn't, she had no doubt that she wouldn't leave this room alive.

◆ ◆ ◆

The soft green numbers of the clock glowed another five minutes since the last time Riley had checked. There would be no more rest tonight. Resigned, she padded into the living room by rote, a path she'd followed thousands of times before. The kitchenette table hadn't been used for eating since she'd moved in three years ago. File boxes covered one side, filled with newspaper clippings, photos, interview transcripts, copies of forensic data.

A large map of the United States was pinned to the blank wall. Black pins peppered the view, representing stranger abductions of girls about the age of her sister. Red pins indicated victims who had been recovered—most of them hadn't made it. A few, like Elizabeth Smart, had survived longer than the seventy-two-hour life expectancy of missing children.

Stranger abductions might be a small percentage of those taken, but they were also the deadliest.

Riley knew all of this. She'd studied all the statistics. Her sister was dead, had probably died fifteen years ago. Riley owed it to her family to bring them closure. Somehow. Some way.

She'd made a little headway since joining the FBI. She'd searched the federal databases on her own time and had discovered a pattern. Madison wasn't alone. Too many girls of about twelve years old, red hair and freckles dotting across the nose, had vanished over the last decade and a half.

The map told the story. Many of them had been abducted within thirty miles of I-25.

Vanished without a trace.

Gone, but not forgotten. Not by their families. And not by Riley. Never by Riley.

One flick of a switch and her computer whirred to life. Tom might have kicked her out of the office for a week, but she could use the time. Trying to save Vincent O'Neal's last two victims had taken 110 percent of her concentration. She'd neglected Madison's case.

No more.

She logged in to the FBI's computer system. She'd review the HSK database for changes first.

What kind of world was it where a Highway Serial Killings Initiative database existed? The depravity of some human beings never ceased to shock her, even after studying the worst of the worst since she'd been able to sneak Ann Rule's book on Ted Bundy from the public library as a teenager against her parents' orders.

Digging into evil had become commonplace. Tom had no idea what she could handle. Riley narrowed the parameters, searching for new abductions of young females.

No records found.

Relief warred with frustration, because as horrible as the truth was, Riley was stuck. Unless the man who had taken Madison made a mistake or a new lead turned up, she didn't know if he'd ever be caught. It had been a while since someone who fit the victim's profile had disappeared. Could he have stopped?

She knew better. Sexually preferential offenders *never* stopped. They were drawn to a very specific type. A very specific age. They *couldn't* fight their urges for long.

She rubbed her eyes and stared at the screen. What was she missing? There had to be something. He was organized, methodical, careful.

The only commonality was the girls' similar appearance. And the fact that they came from middle-class or upper-class homes.

With one exception, of course. The first girl—taken from Singing River, Wyoming—Gina Wallace. Only a few months before Madison's kidnapping.

Gina's mother had grown up middle class but had fallen into a spiral of addiction. Riley almost hadn't flagged Gina's file. But the resemblance between the girl and Madison had been uncanny.

One year ago, on Riley's next vacation, she'd headed to Singing River. The trip hadn't broken open the case the way she'd hoped, but she'd met Thayne. And she'd fallen into his arms . . . mostly to forget.

From the bedroom, a faint buzz sounded. She stopped typing. Could it be him?

Thayne had never called this late before, but she really needed to talk with him.

Riley ran to her bedroom and grabbed her phone from under the pillow. She glanced at the screen and groaned. She tapped the phone. "Lambert," she said, her voice cautious.

"What are you doing, Riley?" Tom barked in her ear. "What were my orders?"

"To consider whether or not I should stay in the unit," she answered, trudging back to her computer.

"You logged in to the system. I set an alert to notify me immediately. What are you searching in the middle of the night? The case is over."

She didn't reply.

"Oh, hell, Riley." The anger left his voice. "You need a complete break. From this case and from your sister's case."

"I'm thinking about what you said," she said, her voice tight. "What more do you want from me?"

"I've changed my mind. Complete rest and relaxation, Riley. No logging in to FBI systems, no working on your sister's. That means *no investigations.*"

"I'm off duty. What I choose to do—"

"Don't push it, Riley. One write-up triggering an investigation and I'm certain they'll discover that you're using government equipment to research an unassigned, personal case. You'll not only get kicked out of the behavioral analysis unit but lose your job, too. And once you're fired from the FBI, there are no second chances."

Her body went cold. He couldn't. He wouldn't. "Tom . . ." What could she say?

"Your sister's been missing for fifteen years. It might be harsh, but one week won't make a difference. You need the break."

"My personal life is none of your business."

"It is when it impacts your ability to function. And my ability to trust you."

"You're wrong about me."

"Prove it. Get out of DC. Go see your family, take a vacation, knock toes with the Friday night phone buddy you try so desperately to hide from everyone. Anything that doesn't deal with murder and serial killers."

She stared at the phone. "How do you know about him?"

"You're not as discreet as you think. Eight o'clock most Friday nights your phone rings and you smile. I've seen that look before. In the mirror when I first met my wife. Besides, it's the only time you smile."

Mortified at her transparency, Riley nearly groaned into the phone. "Fine. One week." If believing she was going to see Thayne would get Tom off her back, she could live with the deceit. She *couldn't* lose her job. Not until she found Madison. Her sister trumped everything else in Riley's life. Including Thayne. She owed Madison that much.

"Don't go around me on this," Tom warned. "I can be your biggest supporter. I'll go to the mat for you. Cross me and I'll become your worst enemy if it's in the best interest of you and Unit 6."

He ended the call.

Riley tossed the phone onto the table.

Her computer beeped.

A message in bold yellow letters popped up on a red screen.

ACCESS DENIED.

Tom had done it. He'd really done it. He'd cut her off.

She leaned back in her chair and tucked her knees to her chest. Her mind whirled. The computer was silent. The mantel clock's second hand ticked, the click growing louder with each strike. The muffled sound of a siren echoed below. Ambulance this time.

Riley laid her head on her knees. Everything she'd worked so hard to achieve was slipping away. She couldn't stop looking for Madison. She'd promised herself. She'd promised her parents. Her mother.

That horrible darkness that had enveloped her the first year after Madison had vanished clutched at Riley's throat. She grabbed the phone back and stared at the lit screen.

Thayne. She needed to hear his voice. He'd butted heads with his SEAL team commander more than once over the rules of engagement. Politics trumped mission too often to count, and innocents died because of the choices of a few suits in a very safe room. Thayne might be the only person who would truly understand.

Her finger lingered above the screen until she squeezed her eyes shut and let the phone fall from her hand. Counting on him was dangerous. She could tough out this challenge alone. She had to, because she'd learned a long time ago. She really couldn't count on anyone but herself.

Hospitals possessed that odd smell of illness and strange lighting that put most anyone on edge. The double doors of the twelve-bed facility swung closed behind Thayne and his father. They didn't even pause at the main desk but veered to the right down one of the two hallways.

The Singing River sheriff pressed the phone to his ear. "You find anything, anything at all, I want to know." He shoved the cell into his pocket and scowled at Thayne. "The only prints on the phone are Cheyenne's. It's like she just vanished into nothing."

"Let me go, you old fool," a voice cried out. "I'm late. I have to get to class. The kids are waiting."

"Gram," Thayne said, meeting his father's startled gaze.

They hurried to room six and stood in the doorway. Gram might be small, but the fire in her eyes made Thayne smile with fondness, even as his heart broke. She sat on the side of the bed, trying to get up. His six-foot-one, burly grandfather stood beside her, eyes resigned—and pained all the way down deep to his soul.

"Helen, honey." Retired Sheriff Lincoln Blackwood leaned over her, pressing her gently back to the bed. Gram shifted, avoiding his touch. Pops lowered his arms. "You're retired, sweetheart. No class today."

Gram shook her head, staring at the hospital room floor. "You're lying to me. Why are you lying?"

The words saddened Thayne. She hadn't taught school for fifteen years. The first time he'd witnessed her living her past—right after he'd come home—he hadn't known what to say or how to act. He'd learned quickly that Alzheimer's leaves no prisoners, and he could do nothing but surrender to the moment.

"She woke up about two this morning and won't go back to sleep," Pops said.

Thayne crossed the room and smiled. "Gram, are you feeling better? That bandage on your head is quite the fashion statement."

Her hand touched the dressing on her scalp, and she winced. Her sharp eyes shifted to Thayne, and her eyes widened. "Lincoln? It's about time you got here. Get this old geezer out of here." She tilted her head toward Pops and lowered her voice. "He's trying to keep me here. I want to go home."

Those pleading words tugged at Thayne's soul. He hadn't realized he looked so much like his grandfather when he was young, not until Cheyenne had found a carousel of old slides. Thayne sat on the edge of the bed next to his grandmother and took one of her hands in his. Her pulse raced under his fingertips, and he cupped her face. "What's wrong?"

"I don't know him," she whispered, glancing at Pops. "I'm sorry I was mean. He looks nice enough, but . . . I don't know him." She clutched Thayne's hand with a grip that belied her eighty years. "I'm scared, Lincoln. Something's wrong with me."

Thayne blinked back the burning behind his eyes and forced a reassuring smile. "It's going to be OK. We're here to take care of you."

"Good. I like you, Lincoln. I might even marry you someday." She pressed his hand to her cheek, closed her eyes, and leaned against him.

He circled his arm around her. God, he hated this disease.

Not much helped when Gram lost herself like this. Her anxiety skyrocketed. Lately, she'd taken to biting her nails and gritting her teeth when the world became too confusing. But they'd discovered one thing that did calm her. Gram responded to music.

Thayne ducked his head and hummed the opening of a familiar tune under his breath, rocking her back and forth.

He'd heard the song's story a million times. Pops had surprised Gram for their twenty-fifth anniversary with a romantic picnic at the swimming hole on the edge of Blackwood Ranch. A warm summer night, a full moon, the water, and soft music in the background. "Could I Have This Dance" had played on their truck's radio. Gram had said nothing was more romantic than dancing in the middle of nowhere, underneath the stars, with the man you loved. When Thayne had learned to waltz, Gram had used the same song to teach him.

Thayne sang the first verse under his breath, his baritone soft and soothing. Her breathing slowed a bit and she opened her eyes. They had cleared for the moment.

"Helen?" his grandfather asked, voice tentative.

Gram lifted her hand to her head to touch the bandage gingerly and looked at Pops with concerned eyes. "Lincoln, honey? What happened to my head? Did we have an accident? Am I at the hospital?"

Pops sat on the other side of Gram and clasped her hand in his. "You were hurt, Helen. At the clinic. Do you remember what happened last night?"

Gram bristled. "Well, of course I remember. I was taking little Cheyenne to dinner with her boyfriend. She's going to marry him someday, you know." Gram smiled, but confusion slid over her expression. "She wanted ice cream for dessert, I think. That little girl is going to turn into an ice-cream cone someday."

"Honey," Pops said. "Cheyenne's grown up now. She's a doctor."

"A doctor?" Gram's forehead wrinkled in confusion. "No, no. That can't be."

Thayne patted his grandmother's hand and stood up. He walked over to his father. He recognized the sorrow in his dad's eyes. They were losing Gram a little every day. This time, though, panic laced his expression as well.

He grasped Thayne's arm. "She doesn't remember what happened to Cheyenne."

Gram was the only witness, and Cheyenne's life was at stake. Normally, they didn't push when Gram didn't remember. They just backed off. This time they couldn't.

Thayne crossed the room and knelt in front of her. "Gram."

She stared into his eyes, her own clear. "Thayne." She patted his cheek.

"Pops took you to Cheyenne's office last night. You were going to have dinner together while he played poker. Someone came in. They messed up the place. Do you remember?"

"I saw a triangle," Gram whispered, running her fingers over Thayne's military cut. "And red." She shook her head. "Get that nurse back in here so I can leave. I have to get ready for school, Lincoln. I can't be late."

Thayne rose, kissed his grandmother's cheek, and met his father's gaze.

His grandfather patted her hand.

"I'm not letting you touch me, old man. Keep your hands to yourself."

Thayne motioned to the nurse who hovered nearby. "Can you help them, Jan?"

"Of course."

Thayne and his father crossed the hall and stepped into a vacant room. "It could be in her mind somewhere," Thayne said. "Any idea what the triangle means? Or red?"

"No idea. We've never used a triangle brand on the ranch. It's used in military maps, but I don't know why she'd be aware of that. Maybe she's back teaching trig in her head?"

"Red could be the blood." Thayne stroked the stubble on his chin. "Maybe it'll come to her. She still recalls some short-term details."

"We can't count on her memory, and today's not a good day. The Alzheimer's has her living more and more in the past. And with her getting knocked out, who knows if she'll remember." His father rubbed his temple. "We have no leads."

Thayne studied his dad's haggard face. Since his illness, he appeared ten years older than his fifty-six years, but Thayne couldn't sugarcoat the truth. "I may not be a cop, but I don't buy DCI's knee-jerk theory of druggies on a spree. I think they're justifying not showing up, but it doesn't track. If all these guys wanted were drugs, they should have hurt or killed Cheyenne, not abducted her."

"You've got cop instincts." His father closed his shadowed eyes. "This reminds me a lot of the Gina Wallace case, son. And we never found her. I can't let that happen to Cheyenne. I won't."

Thayne knew what he had to do. He knew someone who could help. Maybe the only person who could. As much as he hated that he couldn't find his sister, he'd also learned early on in the SEALs to take advantage of each team member's strengths. He slipped his phone from his pocket. "I have an idea."

"Who are you calling?"

"Someone who sees leads in a crime scene no one else does." Thayne said. "Riley Lambert."

"Special Agent Lambert. Yes. She could help." His father stroked his jaw. "You may not like hearing this, but after I found out you were calling her every week, I contacted a buddy at the FBI. I wanted his take on her."

"You did what? I'm pushing thirty, not thirteen."

His father just shrugged without a modicum of apology. "A man needs to keep informed. Did you know she graduated high school at fifteen and earned a law degree by the time she turned twenty? She's on the fast track. He said she's scary driven, takes to a case like a rottweiler to a bone. And she won't give up. If you can get her to come, we could use her help."

Thayne's thumb paused over the screen. He hadn't known, and that didn't sit well, but it didn't matter. Because one thing he did know about Riley, she gave everything she had to her job, to her mission. They had the rottweiler mentality in common. Hold on with all your might and never let go.

The rest . . . He'd ignore the feeling of unease settling at the base of his neck. He tapped the very familiar number into his phone. After all those conversations, all those lonely nights, he'd dreamed of seeing Riley face-to-face most every day for the last year. He'd just never thought it would be like this.

◆ ◆ ◆

Riley couldn't remember falling asleep. She chanced opening one eye.

The morning light seeping through the slats of the window's shutters burned with the heat of a hot poker. She squeezed her eyes shut and shifted.

Her neck protested. She'd passed out on the couch.

With a groan, she moved her head. Something poked at her cheek. She lifted her right arm to brush away several small cardboard puzzle pieces stuck to her skin and winced. The bullet graze.

She stilled, letting the pain ease, before blinking several times so the room would come into focus. The coffee table was littered with a five-thousand-piece jigsaw puzzle three-quarters finished and a half-empty shot glass. The puzzle pictured a bowl full of colored marbles, each piece unrelated to any other.

A lot like Madison's case.

She eyed the three-quarters-full tequila bottle sitting on a small, empty spot of the oak table. She'd intended to make a bigger dent. She hadn't even lasted long enough to make a respectable stab at getting drunk.

Riley groaned and squinted at the wall clock. A little after eight. She had no idea what time she'd finally succumbed to sleep. The way her skull pounded, not long enough.

She let her head fall back against the sofa pillow and threw her good arm over her eyes, blocking out the light. Not only was it Saturday, but she had nowhere to be for a week. Well, she might not have access to the federal databases, but she had other sources of information.

She'd learned a thing or two at the FBI. This week would give her the time to revisit her sister's case from the beginning. Tom would never have to know.

A familiar buzz sounded, the vibration humming through the sofa cushions. OK, if she were paranoid, she'd wonder if Tom had read her mind.

No one else would call her this early . . . unless . . . She shoved her hand into the side of the couch, came upon what she hoped was stale popcorn, and after a few odd textures she didn't want to think about, gripped the cool rectangle that was her phone.

She snagged it on the third ring and scooped it up.

The moment her eyes focused on the screen her heart did that crazy flip-flop she tried to ignore. "Thayne? You've broken our Friday night rule, but I'm really glad you—"

"Riley."

His low voice sent a shiver, but not one of anticipation. She heard no seductive smile or teasing lilt behind Thayne's voice, only a solemn timbre. Like nothing she'd heard before.

That horrible sense of foreboding she'd felt more times than she wanted to admit shuddered down her neck and across her shoulders. "What's wrong?"

Thayne let out a long, slow breath.

Her breathing grew shallow. She could barely form the words. "Are you hurt?"

"I need your help. My sister's been kidnapped."

CHAPTER FIVE

Thayne searched the clear Wyoming sky south of the Singing River Municipal Airport for the Cessna Caravan carrying Riley. For the last ten hours, the entire town had turned up in an all-out effort to look for Cheyenne. Even the Rivertons had provided a plane. First to search, and a couple of hours ago to pick up Riley from Denver so she could arrive before dark.

Despite the hundreds of pairs of eyes here and in the surrounding counties, they were no better off now than they'd been this morning—except maybe checking off grids from the search area. They'd found no trace of Cheyenne since discovering her phone.

Thayne shielded his eyes, scanning the skies. A speck to the southeast appeared, growing larger by the second.

Riley.

After calling, he couldn't stop wondering if he'd jumped ahead of himself. Each and every hour, he kept expecting they would find his sister or that she'd find a way to get in touch. Right now he was glad he hadn't waited.

The buzz from the small plane's prop grew louder. Finally, the Cessna landed on the single runway with a few bounces and taxied toward the hangar.

In a few moments, he'd see her for the first time since they'd parted at the Jackson Hole airport a year ago, with a vague promise to keep in touch. The kind of promise used to make a permanent good-bye less awkward.

Except five days later—Friday night at ten eastern time—Thayne had been cooling his heels in a hangar waiting to jump on a cargo plane to Afghanistan, and he'd called her. Just to check in that she'd made it home, he'd tried to convince himself. She'd picked up and made him laugh, but more than that, she'd given him someone to miss.

Somehow that first Friday night chat had turned into a standing date—if he could call, he would and did.

But now, even after countless phone calls, he had to admit, his nerves reminded him of the last few seconds on a Blackhawk before a big op.

Was she everything he remembered, everything he believed her to be? Without any evidence, could she really do more than what they were doing already? She possessed the skills, but Thayne knew a thing or two about unrealistic expectations . . . he'd lived with them his entire childhood.

He didn't have to glance at his watch to know they were coming up on twenty-three hours since Cheyenne had disappeared.

Time was running out to find his sister alive.

The plane stopped, and he strode toward the aircraft. The pilot hit the ground to meet him.

"Thanks for doing this, Mac." Thayne shook the burly man's hand.

"Anything to help find Cheyenne," he said. "That girl's a gem." He frowned and pulled a duffel and computer bag from the cargo hold beneath the plane. "You haven't found her, I take it."

"Not yet."

"I'll top off the fuel and hit the skies again to join the search. Since we've got daylight until eight thirty or so this time of year, I can give it several more hours."

"The whole family appreciates it. Let Brett Riverton know."

"He's got his own problems, but family feuds don't mean much when one of our own is in trouble."

The door of the Cessna opened. Riley jumped to the ground, her gaze pinned to Thayne. His mouth went dry. A year apart had been too damn long.

His deployment and her cases had kept them apart. Now she stood a few feet away from him, and his feet didn't move. She unnerved him. Should he hug her like he wanted or let her make the first move? His mind whirled with an uncertainty he rarely experienced.

"Hope the ride was smooth enough, Special Agent Lambert," Mac said.

"We arrived fifteen minutes early." She shifted a satchel over her shoulder and smiled at the pilot. "The ride was perfect." She took in a deep breath and turned. "Hello, Thayne."

His name on her lips acted like a caress he couldn't ignore. Thayne moved to her side, so close all he had to do was lean in and she'd be in his arms. He swallowed. For the last year, when he'd needed someone to vent at, to talk to, she'd been at the other end of the phone, her voice surrounding him.

He lifted his hand to brush his finger down her cheek. He hadn't touched her in so long. Riley clasped his hand and squeezed, lifting her cinnamon gaze to his, full of sympathy.

"Riley," he said, his voice strangely deep, even to his own ears.

She wrapped her arms around his neck. "I'm so sorry about your sister," she whispered, her lips brushing his ear.

Thayne closed his eyes and embraced her, enveloping her warm body in his arms. He hadn't realized how much he'd needed her.

She tightened her hold, and he simply let himself feel for a moment, relinquishing the tight control he'd kept on his emotions. He didn't know how long they stood together. All he knew was that she'd come.

Mac cleared his throat. "I guess introductions aren't necessary."

Riley stiffened and pulled away from Thayne, leaving a chill and jerking him back into reality.

Thayne grabbed her bags from Mac. "We've met."

The pilot raised his eyebrow, eyes gleaming with speculation. "I'll leave you to it, then. I'll radio in if I find anything, Thayne."

"Thanks, Mac."

He disappeared into the airport office.

Thayne stared at Riley. His heart tightened in his chest. "I didn't think you'd be able to come. You're in the middle of a big investigation. I thought perhaps you could put in a good word—"

"The case is finished. We got the guy. He's dead. I was too late."

Damn. Shorthand for a huge cluster. He could relate. How often had achieving the mission come with too high a price? He wanted to hold her, comfort her, but he recognized the set of her jaw, clinging to control. He forced himself not to sweep her into his arms. Instead he settled for "I won't say congratulations."

"Thanks."

He wouldn't push. Yet. Soon, she'd need to talk. He nodded toward his SUV. "Let's go."

After opening the door for her, he slid onto the seat beside her. The fog of anticipation for her arrival had dissipated, and he studied her closely, taking in details he hadn't noticed during those first few seconds. She'd scraped her hair in a knot at the back of her head, outlining her hollowed cheeks. Over the last year, she'd lost weight she couldn't afford to lose. Her eyes were bloodshot, but that wasn't what startled him. The deep-seated circles under her eyes, the tightness of her lips, the tension stiffening her neck and back—she carried an edge to her that had nothing to do with determination or drive.

"You look like hell," he blurted out.

"I'll survive." Riley turned in her seat to face him, expression solemn. "I need you to listen. I've been thinking nonstop on the flight here. I've never investigated a case that's this personal. Except my sister." She sucked in a deep breath. "If I'm going to help, I have to take a step back from you and our relationship. I don't know of any other way to remain objective."

The words punched Thayne in the chest. "This isn't how I imagined our reunion would finally happen," he said, frowning at her.

She threaded her fingers through his and squeezed tight. "I'll do my best to help find your sister. I promise you that."

"I know you will." He cleared his throat. "I should brief you—"

She placed a finger against his lips. "Stop. I have my own methods. I don't want to know anything about the kidnapping. Not yet. I need to see the crime scene first."

"Won't it help to go in with the maximum intel possible?"

"Expectations color my perception. I want to see every element with fresh eyes, no preconceived notions."

So much time lost, though. His lips pursed.

"You look skeptical."

"Every minute is precious. Cheyenne's been in those bastards' hands for an entire day." He fought to keep his voice calm, when inside he wanted to punch out a wall.

She touched his shoulder, stroking him with the comforting warmth of her hand. Her caress soothed his burning anger, if only for a moment.

"You called me for a reason," she said softly. "I investigate differently. Let me do my job, my way."

"It's just—"

"Your sister. I understand."

What could he say? She *did* understand. Her personal investigation into her own sister's abduction was the reason they'd met a year ago.

Thayne started the engine and flipped on the sirens, speeding toward Singing River.

"Why didn't you tell me you were stateside?" Riley asked softly. "Because that deputy's uniform looks lived in for more than twenty-four hours."

Thayne winced, knowing he had no excuse. "Two months ago, Dad came down with myocarditis, an infection in his heart. He's recovering, but the doc in Casper ordered him to take a leave of absence from anything physically strenuous. I had a ton of leave built up that I had to use or lose, so I volunteered to wear a temporary badge and help take the pressure off the rest of the office."

"Two months," she said under her breath. "So that's why you've been able to call every week and didn't mention any missions. I assumed you were deep in classified ops."

"I'd planned to tell you, but you'd just picked up that serial killer case—"

"Don't put this on me." Riley tilted her head to look at him, challenge written on her face. "What's the real reason?"

He shoved a hand through his hair. All he could do was be honest. "I wanted to see you again, be with you, but I didn't want to screw up a good thing," he admitted. "As crazy as it sounds, long distance works for us. Hell, I haven't had a relationship last for an entire year. Ever."

"The worst part of listening to that load of BS is that I actually agree with you. So what does that say about us, Thayne?" She pulled out a blue notebook. "Don't answer that. How about we acknowledge we both need therapy and move on."

He couldn't stop the short laugh that escaped from him. "I'm glad you're here."

Her eyes softened and she looked as if she wanted to say something else, but then a cloak fell over her gaze. So familiar to him, so like the members of his SEAL team just prior to an op.

"Tell me about your sister."

Riley had slipped into special agent mode. Someday he'd have to grovel long and hard for deceiving her, but she was right. Cheyenne came first. "I thought you didn't want details."

"Not about the crime scene, but I do want to know about your sister. It's called victimology. If I understand her, it will help me profile who took her."

"Right." Thayne twisted his hands on the leather steering wheel, trying to rein in the ever-present fury. "Cheyenne's the only girl in the family, second oldest. Probably more stubborn than any of us, maybe even more driven, but with a soft heart. She'd bring home every injured animal she could find on the ranch and nurse them back to health. Drove Dad and Mom crazy. I always thought she'd become a vet, but she changed her mind while she was in college. Said she wanted to come home—which I never understood—to help people, so she applied for a loan that she wouldn't have to repay if she worked in a rural community. She laughed at that. Said they were paying her to do exactly what she wanted."

"Did anyone not want her to come home?"

"The whole town celebrated. We were down to two physicians in the county once Doc Mallard keeled over after seeing patients all day. He was seventy-five."

Thayne pulled into the parking space in front of his sister's office. "Cheyenne's been back eight months. She's the one who called me about Dad. Told me to get my butt home so he wouldn't do too much."

"And here you are."

He shrugged. "Family."

Before exiting the SUV, Riley grabbed her satchel. She strode to the sidewalk and then stopped, scanning the surroundings, her gaze laser-focused, taking in everything, particularly the flurry of activity kitty-corner to their location. "Sheriff's office within view. This took some guts—or desperation—to take the risk."

She pulled a camera from her bag and snapped photos from every angle. She pointed to a pristine white SUV, the only vehicle in front of the building. "Is that your sister's car?"

Thayne nodded. "We haven't moved it. Nothing was inside."

"No one noticed anything or anyone?"

"Friday night, just after five. Most of the shops on Main had already closed." He briefly mentioned the black SUV. "None of the BOLOs have popped."

Riley paused. "Did your sister have any enemies? Anyone she was afraid of?"

Thayne shook his head, realizing for the first time how little he actually knew about his sister's private life. Of course, why would he? He'd left Singing River behind with no pretense of coming back. Holidays and the occasional leave didn't make for an in-depth relationship. "Not that she mentioned to me. She's closest to Hudson. They're only a year apart."

"I'll want to talk to him later," she said.

"Sure." He paused in front of the door. Pendergrass had cordoned it off with yellow crime-scene tape. "Last week, she suspected someone had tried to get into the room where she keeps her drugs, but—"

"Stop." Riley held up her hand. "No details, remember." She opened her bag and snapped on protective gloves. "Who's been inside since it happened?"

"More than a few," Thayne admitted, opening the door. "I searched the place first, but my grandmother was hurt, and the paramedics worked on her. Since then, Deputy Pendergrass has processed the scene with help from a DCI investigator." At her questioning gaze, he added, "Wyoming Division of Criminal Investigation. Among other things, they run the state crime lab."

Riley froze with realization. "Your grandmother is a witness? Why didn't you tell me? What does she say?"

"She doesn't remember. Gram has Alzheimer's disease." He hated saying it out loud; somehow the words made it seem more real.

"Oh, Thayne. I'm so sorry." She reached for his hand. "Why didn't you tell me?"

"Gram doesn't want anyone outside the family to know," Thayne said, searching for the words to explain. "She doesn't want anyone to look at her differently. I guess that's why I don't say anything unless I have to."

Hurt flashed in her eyes for a brief second before she straightened her shoulders. "I don't know anyone with Alzheimer's. She can't recall *any* details of Cheyenne's abduction?"

"AD affects everyone differently, but we haven't been able to dig out much understandable information. That could change if she has a good day, but we can't count on it."

Riley let out a long sigh. "I'm so sorry. I met your grandmother when I was here. I couldn't tell."

"She hid the memory loss well, but she's worse now. She lives in the past half the time."

"I still want to talk to her," Riley said. "The smallest insight could help." She strode around the room. "Any hits on the fingerprints?"

"So far nothing, but I don't expect much. The place was full of patients."

"And the blood?"

"The smears on the wall are Gram's. On the floor . . ." Thayne clenched his jaw, reining in the compulsion to punch his fist through something—preferably the kidnapper's face. "We think that blood is Cheyenne's."

As far as crime scenes went, Riley had seen much worse. Oh, Cheyenne hadn't gone down easily, but the mess in the reception area of her clinic wasn't about destruction, it was about purpose.

Thayne knelt beside the bloodstains on the floor; his eyes were deadly focused, his stance lethal. If those kidnappers could have seen the man in front of her, they'd have left Cheyenne Blackwood exactly where she was.

"I don't want to start in here," she said. "Which room will tell me the most about Cheyenne and who she is?"

"The lobby is where they kidnapped her, where they hurt my grandmother," Thayne's voice bit out.

His frustration tugged at Riley's heart. He might be a deputy, but he was family to the victim. "I'll study the crime scene from every angle," she said, "but it's just as important that I study your sister. They chose her for a reason. I need to see her, feel her, before I can find her. It's how I work. You have to trust me, Thayne."

After a moment's hesitation, he gave her a sharp nod. "Cheyenne keeps this place professional. Except her personal office at the back of the building." He led her down a hall and through a walnut door.

Riley stopped just inside the entrance and let her gaze travel around the room. She breathed in deeply, lowering herself into the well that was Cheyenne Blackwood.

Neat, efficient, orderly. The doctor's priorities were clearly visible. The desk was a hand-me-down, probably used by the last physician and maybe even his predecessor, as was the rest of the furniture. Strangely enough, her medical degree hung in a small nondescript corner of the room, almost as an afterthought.

Thayne's sister cared about people, not things, not accomplishments. Not status.

Family photos littered the wall. Not portraits, but candid shots framed with care—and love.

"She's the mad photographer of the family. She's got enough blackmail material to own this town."

The affection in Thayne's voice was clear. So was the worry.

Riley crossed the thick carpet, her gaze searching inside the images of the relationships that had created Cheyenne Blackwood. One particular photo caught her attention. Thayne cut an impressive figure in his Navy dress whites, strong, disciplined, but with a glint of mischief in his eye and a slight smile tugging at his mouth. Riley's heart flipped once in her chest. She could imagine the hint of laughter beneath the timbre of his voice. She'd heard it enough.

Cheyenne had captured Thayne's personality in that one shot. She knew her brother well. Riley paused at a picture of Sheriff Carson Blackwood taken about a decade ago in his uniform, hugging a woman Riley assumed was Thayne's mother.

The room might not be purely professional, but Cheyenne didn't care.

She loved her family. She wasn't afraid to show how much.

A large floor-to-ceiling corkboard took up half the wall, littered with drawings from young patients. A few were colored blue with tears, but many more contained rainbow bright colors that jumped off the page.

With each minute, each small detail, the connection to Cheyenne became more and more real. Riley could just hear Tom now.

"You're getting too emotional again. Don't get involved."

Shut up, Tom.

She couldn't stop herself. She was already involved, notwithstanding her relationship with Thayne. Getting personal was how she accomplished her profiles; she had to build a tether between her mind, her emotions, and the victim.

No matter the price.

Riley slid a sidelong glance to Thayne. Cheyenne was very much loved. He would fight for his sister. With each second that passed, the line of his mouth tightened, but he stood silent, allowing Riley the time she needed. He didn't press. Most men of action like Thayne would be on her, asking questions, pushing hard. Somehow, he'd harnessed the discipline to wait. He really was something special.

"I can tell I'll like your sister," she said finally.

"I like her, too. And I want her back alive."

"I know, Thayne. Let me look at the . . ." Riley paused as an out-of-place photo called out to her. She tilted her head. The only image with no people. Just a few aspens and pines, a looming peak in the background, a pool of water. And a shadow. Odd.

"What is it?" Thayne asked.

"Where was this picture taken? Can you tell?"

"Oh yeah. The border between our ranch and the Riverton property. We used to play *Mountain Men of the West* and battle it out with the Riverton brothers. A feud with a family tradition."

"Singing River's own Hatfields and McCoys? That's a story you never told me."

He shrugged. "I haven't thought about it in years. Our families don't get along. Bad blood going way back and family loyalty make for a fierce rivalry."

"Cheyenne was in the middle of it? Was she the damsel in distress? The one who got kidnapped."

"Hell no. She's the one who drew up the attack plans."

Riley chuckled at the image of Cheyenne organizing Thayne and her other brothers, but his description didn't explain the photo. She'd have to let the disconnect simmer. "I'm done here."

After one last look around Cheyenne's private office, Riley walked down the hall. Would she see something, anything to help find Cheyenne?

Her heart wrapped in an oppressive darkness, a panic.

Please let us find her.

She opened one exam room. Untouched. Then a second, and finally the storage room containing supplies and medications.

Strange. In a high-risk robbery, she would have expected complete chaos, and yet, most items remained untouched, with only a few areas on the shelves empty.

She glanced down at the floor. "The kidnappers came after the supplies first," she mused, the reenactment playing like an out-of-focus movie in her head. "They used a garbage bag—"

"How can you know that?" Thayne interrupted.

"Because when they removed the bag from the box, several others tumbled out on the floor. The rest of this place is pristine. Your sister keeps her supplies orderly and well labeled. She would've folded the garbage bags and returned them to the box."

"Cheyenne's a neat freak for sure. Always has been." Thayne let out a low whistle. "You deduced all that from her office and this room?"

"That's my job," Riley said, moving about the small room, snapping more photos. Normally she'd have stopped to sketch as well, but the scene had already been compromised. She'd take the time later if she needed to. "Your forensic team is running the prints and trace evidence?"

"That would be our forensic expert of one. Deputy Pendergrass. And yeah, he sent off DNA samples and as much as he could find."

"Whoever broke in seems to have thrown in a mishmash of supplies." Riley moved to an empty pocket on the shelf, then to the next. "From first-aid to surgical. The medication storage area is different. They tore off the cabinet door and even the door to the refrigerated unit, but they didn't clean it out. I wonder . . ." She tilted her head, studying the shelf labels. "How often did she inventory?"

"Every Saturday after her half-day clinic, she updates the computer."

"What about her nurse or office assistant? I need to interview anyone who worked with her. They might be able to tell at a glance how much is missing."

Thayne shook his head. "She's been on her own since Doc Mallard's nurse retired to Casper last month to move in with her daughter. Medical professionals are hard to come by here."

"That'll make it tougher. She's dispensed a week's worth of meds." Riley peered at shelf after shelf, studying the orderly sections of missing drugs as well as the entire shelves left untouched. "They took pain pills for certain. Oxycodone, hydrocodone." She glanced over at Thayne. "They knew what they wanted. Which is the trend for break-ins at pharmacies. Thieves used to take everything. Now they tend to be more discriminating when they steal."

Riley bit her lip. Something felt off, but she couldn't quite wrap her mind around it yet.

"How does this help us find her?" Thayne asked.

"Whoever searched the supplies was sloppy—or nervous. More items tipped over, a bit more random. Whoever searched the drugs, they were organized, precise. At least two distinct personalities," Riley said. "They didn't try to keep quiet. Your sister heard them."

"She left the office long enough for them to come in unnoticed," Thayne said. "She walked across the street. Pops and Gram had gone into the general store to pick up her prescription. According to the schedule, Cheyenne's last appointment of the day canceled."

"I'll need that name," Riley said as she walked into the waiting room, recording the scene and view outside with photos from every angle. She opened the outside door. "No bell to alert the kidnappers. So, your grandmother and sister came back to the office, probably to close up."

"She called me. A few seconds later, she screamed."

Thayne's voice was devoid of any emotion, almost clinical. Riley wished she could stay so calm, but it wasn't part of her process. She needed to feel. Her heart raced, like she imagined Cheyenne's had. "Something alerted the intruders. Your sister's voice, your grandmother, something. Maybe they'd finished stealing what they wanted and were on their way out."

Riley squatted on one side of the room, scenario after scenario playing in her mind. They didn't fit. "Doesn't make sense," she murmured. "If they didn't want to be identified, why not kill your grandmother? It was either risky or stupid. Inexperienced." Riley studied the chaos. "It feels like a first-time crime scene. And yet they had a specific intent." She didn't mention that inexperienced perpetrators overreacted easily, and when that happened, victims tended to die. "It was planned. And confused. Someone pulling their strings maybe?"

"A drug dealer? Maybe Cheyenne interrupted them and they panicked."

"If they'd just been after the drugs, they wouldn't have hit the supplies. They would have left your sister here or killed her." Riley winced at the blunt words. For a moment she'd lost herself in the scenarios. She hadn't thought . . . She cast a quick glance over at Thayne, but except for the muscle in his jaw tensing, he showed no reaction. She had to remember he wasn't Tom. She couldn't simply talk through the issues. He was the brother of the victim as well as a local law enforcement officer. A LEO. She'd have to hold her tongue. "They wanted her, and they planned it for the end of the day. If your grandmother hadn't been here, if your sister hadn't been on the phone with you, who would have known? And when?"

Thayne rubbed the base of his neck. "When her Saturday clinic opened and she didn't show."

Riley surveyed the room. She chewed on the inside of her lip to stop the flow of impressions from escaping her lips. She didn't know how long the room remained silent until Thayne's hands settled on her shoulders, forcing her to face him and meet his gaze. His eyes flashed with frustration. "What are you doing, Riley? You've told me you talk it out when you go through a scene. Why so quiet now?"

Squirming under his questioning, she sighed. "Your family was attacked here. You don't need—"

"I need to hear everything," Thayne said through tight lips. "Wouldn't you want to?"

She couldn't argue with his words. She sucked in a deep breath. Her emotions were treading on paper-thin ice, but she'd want to know every detail, no matter what. "There are several types of blood patterns in the room." She stood with a clear view of the left half of the room. "Cheyenne placed herself between the thieves and your grandmother. She fought hard, probably harder than if she'd been alone, but they shoved her against the edge of the desk. Her head hit here, given the amount of blood pooled beneath the edge. She stumbled against the chair and fell to the floor, hence the smears and partial palm print. She probably lost consciousness."

Thayne's body stilled. His fists clenched with the effort to maintain control. "They took *her*," he said through gritted teeth. "Not Gram."

"Your grandmother was an interruption." Riley snapped off her gloves. "I need a report on the forensics, and I want to review Cheyenne's appointment book and medical files for the last month. Whoever put together this operation did some recon before today."

He nodded. "You'll have it."

Thayne paused, hesitating.

Riley recognized the uncertainty. There was one question he hadn't asked. Everyone did. She could make it easier, though the answer wouldn't help.

"Ask me," she said quietly, allowing herself to look into his eyes, his expression more cautious, more closed off than she'd ever seen him.

"Is Cheyenne alive?" Thayne asked. "Truth."

Riley tugged at the delicate half-heart bracelet on her wrist. She wanted so desperately to lie, to tell Thayne everything was going to be OK.

"I don't know."

CHAPTER SIX

Sunset fell over Singing River, and the road to Blackwood Ranch was deserted. Off in the distance, beams of flashlights began to flicker on in a wave, swinging back and forth, a reminder of what they might find. Thayne didn't want to let his mind imagine his sister's lifeless body, but he couldn't stop himself. He squeezed the steering wheel with knuckle-whitening intensity.

"You have a lot of volunteers looking for your sister," Riley said.

"One thing about a small town, folks might be hip-deep in one another's business, but when there's trouble, we take care of each other. We haven't let up the search for twenty-four hours. I doubt we could force anyone to go home."

"And you want to be out there, searching," Riley said.

She made the statement so matter-of-factly that Thayne didn't argue. He forced himself to relax his hands. "I'm an in-the-thick-of-the-action kind of guy. Not so good at watching and waiting."

"Or babysitting. I can find my way to your ranch on my own, Thayne."

"My brothers are out there. They're good trackers. You could need me when you speak with Gram. She's only been home from the hospital a few hours. Besides, I can provide background on most everyone and everything in town."

"You've been gone for a decade."

"Up until the last few months or so, Gram kept me in the loop with weekly e-mails and letters, depending on her mood."

The SUV rose over a small hill and Blackwood Ranch came into view. A broad iron arch with a BR brand at its center loomed above them, bathed in spotlights. The tires thumped across the cattle guard.

"This is where you grew up?"

Thayne hadn't remembered until then that she'd never visited the ranch. On her last visit, she and his father had met at the sheriff's office. "The place has been in the Blackwood family for generations. I lived here until I turned eighteen."

He drove down the long road. His father had parked his SUV in the driveway of the main house, but the building was dark.

"Dad must be at my grandparents'," he said, taking a right. "They live a few hundred yards in back. The main room is the original structure my great-grandparents built when they homesteaded around 1920."

Just close enough for his grandparents to enjoy the privacy. Thayne had loved racing down that path every day after school. His grandmother had made her famous apple cookies, and he'd scarfed down a half dozen with a tall glass of milk before his brothers and sister had made it to the front door.

Thayne parked, rounded the SUV, and opened the passenger door. "Yesterday wasn't a good day for Gram. You can't push her. If her memory's not there today, it's just not."

Riley placed her hand on his chest. His heart thudded against the warmth of her palm.

She looked up at him, sympathy lacing her brown eyes. "I'm so sorry."

"Me, too." A lump hit his throat. "Gram would hate this."

"What do you mean?"

"She lives for the family. If she realized she *could* help us find Cheyenne . . ." He gripped the inside door edge. "We need her to remember, but if she does, it will devastate her."

Riley stood, her body circled in the cage of his arms. Her hands drifted around his waist and she hugged him tightly. Thayne couldn't stop himself. He wrapped his arms around her and held her close, pressed against him, breathing in her scent, relishing the feel of her warmth.

This was what he'd been missing for the last twelve months. To hold Riley again.

He didn't want to let her go.

A wolf howled in the distance. Riley jerked at the sound, retreating from his embrace. "Was that—?"

"Welcome to Blackwood Ranch." Thayne touched her face with a light stroke of his thumb. She closed her eyes, leaning into his caress. So, she wasn't immune. "You feel it, too, don't you?"

She sighed. "I can't deny it, but Thayne—"

"Once we find my sister, I'm whisking you away from this town, and I'm doing everything I dreamed of doing for the last year. Count on it."

"You don't hold back, do you?"

"And you love that about me."

Her pupils dilated, but she blinked away the awareness. "I'm ready."

His brow arched.

"To go inside."

He led her toward the front porch. "Gram probably won't remember you. Don't take it personally. And if she asks you the same question over and over, just go along with it. Keep answering. Your responses might go into her long-term memory. Eventually."

"Some memories stick?"

"Yes. And on good days, she's able to recall more."

"If we keep asking, she could remember something anytime?"

He stilled and faced her, his eyes somber and warning.

"You know, Thayne, on the phone I could always tell when you were angry the moment you fell silent. You do quiet better than anyone I know. But face-to-face, I see that muscle in your lower jaw pulse." She touched his cheek, her gaze drawing his. "I get that you need to protect her. I won't badger her. I promise."

He wanted to protect Gram, but he knew she'd give him a tongue throttling if it cost Cheyenne. Talk about a no-win scenario. He threaded his fingers through Riley's.

"You love your grandmother a lot," she said.

"Gram's mine," he said simply. "Hudson and Cheyenne hung around with Pops on the ranch, especially after he retired. Jackson went off on his own into the woods. I connected with Gram."

"I wouldn't have guessed. Most boys don't exactly offer to spend time with their grandmother unless they're coerced."

"Gram isn't like anybody else. She was quite the adventurer before she married Pops. She learned to fly a plane after she read a book about Amelia Earhart, then left home when she turned eighteen to fly freight. Caused quite a scandal in Singing River back in the fifties."

"She sounds like an amazing woman."

"She is." Thayne pasted a smile on his face, dropped Riley's hand, and they walked through the door.

His grandmother stood across the room. She grinned broadly at him with recognition in her eyes. "Lincoln!" She sped over to Thayne. "You're home."

"Hi there." He didn't say anything about her calling him by his grandfather's name. He simply kissed her forehead and looked over her head at his father and grandfather.

"It's been a tough day," Pops said.

Cheyenne paced the perimeter of her four-hundred-square-foot prison, running her fingers along the wooden planks making up the walls. They didn't reveal one crack not filled with mortar. She passed the bathroom door. The small room didn't even have a window.

Bethany lay in a hospital bed at the rear of the room, diagonal from the daybed where Cheyenne had grabbed a few hours of sleep when her body just gave out.

She glanced at her watch. She'd been here more than twenty-four hours now, but if she hadn't had the timepiece, she'd never have known.

Only one way out, but the steel door through which Ian had left last night was solid, bolted from the outside. When he'd delivered supper, she'd seen two shadows behind him and a long hallway. She had no idea where she was, or even if they were in Wyoming. No idea if Thayne and her family were close to finding her. No idea if . . . She had to stop thinking about the man to whom she'd given her heart. He'd thrown it back at her. He probably didn't care if she was missing or not.

Her family wouldn't give up searching, though. Not ever. But they might need help. She had to find a way to contact them.

A pained groan sounded from her patient. Her escape plans would have to wait. She strode over to Bethany and pushed back the gown. The staples looked good.

She'd never been so scared in her entire life than when she'd cut into Bethany with a sixteen-year-old kid assisting. She had to admit he'd learned quickly.

Cheyenne scraped her hands through her hair. Even if Bethany survived the surgery, something else was killing her, and Cheyenne had no idea what. She'd ruled out the visible causes during surgery. In general the abdominal tissue appeared healthy.

With cautious fingertips, Cheyenne probed the area surrounding the incision. The woman moaned again. Her skin was hot and dry. Cheyenne studied her face and arms. Her cheeks were splotched with red; the rash extended down her shoulders to her forearms.

An allergic reaction.

Damn.

Cheyenne stopped the IV with the roller clamp so the penicillin would no longer flow into the vein and went to the refrigerator in the corner, flipping through the small bags. All penicillin, nothing else.

This wasn't good. Abdominal surgery without antibiotics, infection could set in fast. If the actual cause of her pain was a bacterial infection . . . either way, her patient could die.

She had to get both of them out of here. But how?

The now-familiar sound of a metal bolt sliding caused her to whirl around.

"Don't try it," Ian said, carrying in a tray of fruit and cheese.

He balanced the food before closing the door. The bolt slammed shut again from the outside.

He stared at the bed. "Why are her cheeks so red?"

"She's allergic to penicillin, and that's the only antibiotic you took from my office." Cheyenne crossed to him and looked him in the eye. He was just under six feet, and so was she. "Without another antibiotic, she's in danger of an infection. We need to get her to a hospital." She gripped his arm. "Please, Ian."

"No mistakes." He shook his head slowly. "Father's going to be very angry." His cheeks faded to milky pale. "He'll order punishment."

Cheyenne's neck muscles tightened at the fear on Ian's face. "It's not my fault you only have penicillin."

"*You* didn't fail. Father won't punish *you*." Ian gave Bethany a long look and bowed his head. "I have to tell him."

"Ian."

"Keep her alive, Doc. We need her." He scuffed his foot. "Especially the kids."

Ian was nothing but a kid himself, but the tone of his voice said more than his words. He loved her.

"I'll try to save Bethany, but I need your help."

"I know."

The kid's back stiffened, and he pulled in a deep breath before turning. He knocked twice, and the metal door opened then quickly creaked closed.

Cheyenne followed him and pressed her hand against the cold steel locking her in. "Be careful, Ian," she whispered. She didn't know much about this place she'd been taken, but it was obvious fear ruled over everyone.

"What happened?" a girl's trembling voice said from the hallway. "Bethany's not—"

"Hannah, I have to talk to Father and Adelaide," Ian said, a tremor in his voice. "Bethany needs more medicine."

"Oh no. We went there twice. We were supposed to have everything she needed." Hannah's voice choked. "Don't tell them. You know what happens if we make a mistake."

"Do you want Bethany to die?"

Soft sobs filtered through the door. Cheyenne closed her eyes against the helpless fury. They were terrified. And she could do nothing.

Somehow, she had to get out of here. Bring her father and the whole sheriff's department down on this place. But first, she had to survive the night.

She sat beside Bethany's bed, checking her vitals. Her temp was just under one hundred. She sipped on the hot tea and nibbled at the fruit and cheese. The warning reverberated in her head. *If she dies, you die.*

"Bethany." Cheyenne clutched her patient's hand and squeezed. "Bethany, listen to me. You have to fight to live. Don't give up. I'll find out what's wrong with you. I promise."

Cheyenne would have to pray Bethany was one resilient woman, because that was the only way they would get out of this alive.

CHAPTER SEVEN

Fifteen Years Ago

Twelve-year-old Madison stared at the bowl of sugar-coated cereal. "Mom, can't I have an English muffin? This stuff will make me fat."

Her mother turned and wiped her hands down her apron. She bit back a smile. "You're growing up." She placed a glass of orange juice in front of Madison. "OK. But you'll have to eat it in the car."

"Mom, where are my shoes?" Riley raced into the kitchen and skidded across the floor. "Whoa!"

Madison's eyes widened. The whole thing happened in slow motion. Riley toppled into Madison's arm. She lost her grip on the orange juice glass and it tumbled onto her, soaking her clothes.

Eeew. Wet and sticky.

"Riley! Look what you did!" Madison shot to her feet. "Mom, look at me!"

Her mother's lips pursed. "Riley, how many times have I told you not to run in the house? Why can't you be more like your sister?" Her gaze softened on Madison. "Go up and change."

Riley bowed her head and stuck out her lower lip. "I didn't mean to."

"Oh, get that pouty look off your face. You're acting like a baby," Madison said with a frown. "I thought when you turned ten, you'd finally grow up a little. But you're still a kid." She faced her mother. "I don't want Riley at my slumber party tomorrow night, Mom. She'll embarrass me in front of my friends."

"Madison, you can't! It's my first slumber party. I'll be good, I promise," Riley pleaded, her dark brown eyes wide.

One look and Madison could feel herself giving in. Then something wet dripped down her face. She patted her head. "I've got orange juice in my hair," she shouted. She glared at Riley. "No way. I can't trust you."

She stalked up the stairs, Riley's sobs dogging her every step. Madison hesitated. She felt bad. Kind of.

But the thought of her friends meeting Riley . . . That would never work. What if Riley got scared and wanted to sleep in Madison's sleeping bag or told them some embarrassing story?

She shuddered. No, this was better.

Madison hurried into the bathroom and tugged off her soaked shirt. Ugh. She was going to be late for school.

She turned the knob on the shower. One of Riley's Barbies was perched on the soap dish. Madison tossed it into the sink, next to a half-deflated birthday balloon Riley refused to get rid of.

Yep, Riley was still a baby. Madison would have to make sure all her sister's toys were out of the bathroom when her friends came over tomorrow night.

Madison stepped under the shower and quickly shampooed her hair. Five minutes later, she was styling her new bob. Maybe Mom would let them dip-dye the ends purple. As she waved the blow-dryer back and forth, a half-heart bracelet dangled from her wrist.

Riley's bracelet had the other half heart. It had been her birthday present to Madison last year.

Madison unhooked the chain and dropped it into the soap dish. Maybe next year, when Riley started middle school, they could be friends again.

With a final glance in the mirror, Madison scooped up her favorite lip gloss and hurried into her bedroom but slid to a stop before she could run out the door. Her curtains fluttered in the breeze.

Strange, she was certain she'd closed the window. Her mom didn't like wasting electricity, especially in the summer. Madison slammed them shut and looked into the side yard, half expecting the strange man to be back.

No one was there.

She let out a sigh of relief.

"Madison, hurry up. You're late for school," her mother called.

Madison sprinted down the stairs and followed her mother to the car. Riley sat in the backseat, pouting as usual. After her mother pulled the vehicle into the street, Madison looked out the window. Standing beneath the tree at the side of their house, a large figure dressed all in black stood, still and watchful.

"Mom, did you—?"

"What?" her mother snapped, frowning.

Madison bit her lip. Mom hated driving them to school before she'd fixed her hair and makeup, but she had to, since they'd missed the bus.

The morning sun glinted off the windshield. Madison squinted once, then twice. The man had vanished. Maybe she'd imagined him.

She dug into her backpack for her lip gloss, flipped open the passenger-side mirror so she could glide it on perfectly, and promptly forgot about him.

Later that night, Madison would learn a hard lesson. Some mistakes can't be taken back.

Some rooms exuded that lived-in feel that warmed you from the inside out. The Blackwood homestead's wooden floors, wall of family photos, and overstuffed furniture did just that. Riley didn't know if she'd ever been in another home that emanated such heartfelt emotions.

She couldn't take her gaze off Thayne holding his small grandmother in the center of the room. Helen Blackwood barely reached her grandson's chin, and she clung to him as if her life depended on keeping him close. Thayne cradled her with such tenderness, Riley's throat thickened with emotion.

How would it feel to be loved so much?

"Lincoln, I'm so glad you're home," Helen said to Thayne, her voice muffled as she buried it against his deputy's uniform. "I missed you."

Riley hurt for the pain on Thayne's face—for him, for his family—but she was at a loss as to how to comfort or help them. Except to find the missing piece to their family. The only thing she could offer Thayne was her expertise as a profiler.

Steeling herself against the empathy threatening to overtake her, she forced herself to look away and scan the room, past Thayne and his grandfather to the man she'd searched out a year ago for help with her own sister's disappearance.

A painful irony.

"Sheriff Blackwood." Riley walked over and stretched out her hand to shake his, careful not to jar her injured arm.

Gaunt was the only word she could think of to describe him. His illness and his daughter's disappearance had taken their toll.

"Thank you for coming, Riley." His tired but sharp eyes narrowed. "Do you have any leads?"

"Not yet. We were hoping your mother . . ."

"Lincoln?" Thayne's grandmother tugged at his shirt, her voice tentative and uncertain.

Lincoln Blackwood hurried to his wife's side. "Helen, honey?"

She looked at her husband with wild eyes. "Not you, old man."

She shoved at him, and his shoulders sagged, but he didn't press, simply backed away, giving his wife some space.

The room had gone completely silent. Riley had never been around someone with this disease. She didn't know what to do, what to say.

"What's happening to me?" Helen bowed her face in her hands. She squinted, staring around the room. With a furrowed brow, her breathing quickened, and she clasped her hand to her chest, panic in every jerky movement.

Thayne pulled her gently into his arms. "Gram. It's OK, Gram. I've got you."

"Lincoln. I don't understand what's going on. Everything is wrong." She gripped his shirt with trembling fists. "Please. Help me."

Thayne smiled down at his grandmother, his expression heartbreaking. "I know what always makes you feel better. Would you like to dance with me and make the world go away?"

She stilled and stared into his eyes before giving an uncertain nod.

Thayne met Riley's gaze over his grandmother's head. *Do you understand now?* his expression telegraphed.

The message slammed into Riley. The Blackwoods needed her to find a miracle, and she'd been counting on Helen Blackwood's statement to point the search in the right direction. Since Helen couldn't help, Riley had to start from scratch. She needed to review every photo she'd taken since she arrived, analyze every piece of evidence that had been gathered, and try to pull out that one sliver of information that several other sets of eyes had missed. The clue that would lead them to Cheyenne.

She'd have to ask for a vehicle and find a small space to hole up for several hours. No noise, no distractions, only quiet and the crime scene. Perhaps the sheriff had a spare—

"Dad, play our song, would you?" Thayne asked, then gently pulled his grandmother into his arms.

Riley's breath caught. This man could kill with his bare hands, and yet, right now he showed more tenderness than she'd ever witnessed.

Sheriff Blackwood flipped on the power of a stereo system. A smooth alto voice softly crooned words of need and love.

Thayne waltzed around the room with his grandmother in his arms, his box step slow and graceful. He bent his head low to his grandmother's ear. Straining, Riley could just make out his baritone voice humming and then singing a few verses.

Sheriff Blackwood crossed the room to stand beside her. "Music is one of the only things that calm her when she's confused. Especially tunes that connect to her past."

"Thayne looks a lot like his grandfather."

"Spitting image. She dotes on Thayne. One day he came home from school terrified of his first big dance at church. Mother spent a week teaching him after school so he wouldn't stumble over his feet. He was only twelve. 'Could I Have This Dance' is as much their song as my parents'."

Riley's gaze fell on Lincoln Blackwood, watching, protective, and so very alone. As if the sheriff had read her mind, he moved to stand with his father, placing a hand on the older man's shoulder.

No one spoke. Riley shifted toward the wall, feeling like an intruder. A numbing pressure grew inside her head, settling behind her eyes, threatening to erupt. She couldn't stop staring at Thayne dancing with his grandmother, such gentleness on his face, such love in his eyes. Such loyalty and devotion.

Her eyes burned with unshed tears, with overwhelming emotions she could barely keep contained. Another reason for her to get out of this house and go back to her job. She couldn't afford the complication of feeling any more than she already did.

As the song played, Helen Blackwood's tense body relaxed in Thayne's arms. Suddenly, she stopped dancing and closed her eyes. She squeezed them shut tight, then they snapped open.

Riley had never seen anything like the spark of recognition replacing the confused fog in Helen's eyes.

"Thayne," she said, smiling up at him. "You haven't forgotten how to waltz."

"You taught me the secret recipe, Gram," Thayne said, without so much as a blink. "One-two-three, one-two-three. Three-quarter time."

Lincoln eased toward her with a tentative hand outstretched. "Helen?"

She smiled at him and threaded her fingers through his. "What's the matter, honey? You look tired."

He kissed her cheek. "I'm fine. Just glad to see you."

Riley couldn't fathom what had just happened. As if a lightbulb had turned on in Helen's mind.

Her sharp gaze snapped to Riley. "I know you, young lady."

With a quick nod, Riley walked up to the older couple. "I'm with the FBI, ma'am. I'm conducting an investigation." Uncertain how to handle the interrogation, she turned to Lincoln. "May I speak with your wife, Mr. Blackwood? Somewhere quiet, maybe."

He gripped Helen's hand tightly and gazed at Riley, his blue eyes cutting through any nonsense. She saw a lot of Thayne in this man. He wouldn't hesitate to shut her down if he thought she would distress his wife.

"Oh, for pity's sake, I'm standing right here, young lady." Helen dropped her husband's hand and linked her arm through Riley's. "Let's go to my little sunroom."

Pops smiled for the first time since Riley had walked into their home. "The empress of Blackwood Ranch has spoken. But maybe Thayne could go with you, Helen."

"Only if he brings the apple cookies Fannie delivered. Not quite as good as mine, but not too shabby, either," she said, pulling Riley toward the door. "Lincoln built the sunroom for me, but I love it at night even more."

Twinkling stars appeared in a blanket of night above them. Riley couldn't stop staring at the expanse. Certainly not visible in the city. "Beautiful."

"And romantic." Helen strode over to a loveseat. "Sit down, dear. I want to show you something."

Riley settled on the soft cushion while Helen tugged a large sketchbook from a basket on the coffee table. She sat next to Riley and flipped through a few pages. The likenesses were uncanny. Her husband, her son, her grandsons and granddaughter. She pointed out every one.

"You're gifted, ma'am," Riley said. "I like your use of the 4B pencil for your shading. That's my favorite, too."

"You draw." Helen smiled.

"I dabble." Riley couldn't believe she'd revealed that detail. It wasn't something she shared. Not since she was a child. "What did you want to show me?"

Helen's eyes twinkled. "This."

She turned to a page revealing Riley and Thayne. The drawing had been sketched a year ago. The week they'd first met. They were sitting in the gazebo behind Fannie's Bed and Breakfast. Riley didn't have to be a profiler to recognize the adoration Helen had drawn on Riley's face. She looked like a woman in love.

Her cheeks heated. "Oh."

"Everything OK?" From the entrance, Thayne's words held a hint of worry.

Riley touched her red cheeks just before Helen quickly flipped to the next page. "We're fine, dear. Did you know Riley draws, too?"

"I didn't." Thayne sent Riley a pointed, pot-kettle look.

He was right. There were too many details of their lives they hadn't shared in their comfortable long-distance relationship.

Helen tsked at him. "Really, Thayne. You should know the most important things about a girl *before* you spend the night together. What is it with you kids today? I lectured Cheyenne and her too-serious boyfriend about the very same thing."

The Blackwood sunroom went silent, and Thayne whipped his gaze around to meet Riley's shocked expression. Even with Alzheimer's, Gram had a way of silencing a room.

"Gram, are you certain Cheyenne's dating someone?" he asked, sitting beside her.

"Of course. What do you take me for? That girl has jumped off a cliff without a bungee cord. I warned her, but do any of you kids listen to me?" She snorted. "Like I haven't experienced more life than you've even dreamed about." She looked up at Thayne. "So, where *is* Cheyenne?"

He didn't know what to say.

"She should be here tonight," Gram argued. "I need to have a heart-to-heart with her about that boy. It's important."

The only sounds to be heard were a few summer crickets chirping from beyond the glass-enclosed room.

When no one answered her, his grandmother's lip trembled and she bit down. Hard. Her brow furrowed, and he could almost see the effort to order the chaos in her mind. "Something's wrong," she said. "Don't lie to me. There should be no secrets between us. Not anymore." She clutched at Thayne's shirt. "Tell me."

"I'm sure she'll be home soon, Gram," he lied.

She sagged against the chair, and the sketchbook dropped from her hand. Her leg bounced in an anxious movement. "She's hurt, isn't she? I should know."

Gram whimpered and then began to rock, back and forth. "We were supposed to have dinner." Gram's hand shook, and she chewed on her thumbnail. "Or I thought we were. I hate when I can't think straight."

Thayne pulled her closer, and she laid her head against his chest. "It's OK, Gram. Everything's going to be fine," he lied, his heart heavy. He knelt down beside her and clutched her hand in his, calming the anxious movement with a light caress of her palm. "Pops dropped you off at the clinic last evening . . ."

"I remember." She nodded a couple of times. "That's right. Cheyenne was going to show me around her doctor's office. She's so proud. I'd already seen the place, but she wanted to show me again. I knew the truth, though. She wanted to talk to me about her young man. First time she's been serious, but . . ." Gram looked up at Thayne. "Secrets aren't good, you know."

Her leg bounced, and she fidgeted in her chair. "Something's not right."

Riley leaned forward. "Mrs. Blackwood, did you notice anything unusual when you went to Cheyenne's? Any detail could be important."

"There were . . ." Helen's brow furrowed. "Triangle."

The sentence didn't make sense, and Thayne recognized the problem. Gram had lost her words. Sometimes she made perfect sense, but sometimes an odd phrase would just pop out.

"You saw a triangle? On a car? A logo maybe? Or perhaps a tattoo?"

Riley hid it well, and not many would be able to tell, but Thayne could hear the frustration edging into her voice. He understood. God knows. But the whole family had learned that AD's effects couldn't be predicted or controlled.

"Gram said *were*." Thayne wished he could read his grandmother's mind. All he could do was guess. "That's plural. More than one?"

Her eyes widened and grew panicked. She tugged her hand out of his and chewed on her nail some more. Such intense effort, trying to concentrate.

"Damn," escaped Gram's lips.

Thayne's jaw nearly dropped open at Gram's use of a word he'd heard her utter only a handful of times in his almost thirty years.

She snatched up her sketchbook, flipped to the last page, and drew three stick figures. "Triangle."

She shoved the drawing at Riley.

"Three people were there?" she asked.

Gram nodded with a relieved expression. "There were . . . three. I'm drowning." She grabbed a glass from the coffee table and took two gulps of water. "Drowning. Water. Thirsty." She glanced at Thayne.

"Sometimes the right words don't quite come, do they, Gram? But eventually we figure it out."

Helen shook her head, pressing her hand to her head, tears in her eyes. "I'm s-s-sorry. I'm not good enough anymore."

Thayne kissed her forehead. "Nothing to be sorry for, Gram."

His grandmother nodded, but her eyes glistened. She glanced at Riley. "You're here to help, aren't you?"

"I'm going to try."

"I believe you," Gram said. "It's important to uncover the secrets. They destroy."

"Can you tell me what the men who hurt you looked like?" Riley asked.

Gram shook her head. "I don't remember."

"You mentioned red," Thayne coaxed. "Does that remind you of anything?"

She smiled at him. "Lincoln had red hair when we met." She flipped to the beginning of the sketchbook and ran her finger along an image of his grandfather when he couldn't have been more than seventeen. "You look so like him . . . except your hair is brown, of course. Like your mother's. A good catch."

She winked at Riley, leaned back in her chair, and crossed her legs. "Now, tell me, since the two of you are sleeping together, when are you getting married?"

After a decade in the Navy, Thayne hadn't imagined he could still blush, but as he stared at his slip of a grandmother, her eyes twinkling with a touch of the devil and smile widening, he couldn't help himself. "Gram!"

"Well, I'm not getting any younger. I need great-grandbabies to dote on before . . ." Her voice trailed off. "What was I saying?"

She sat up straight, and her gaze whipped around the room, desperate and confused, searching for something or maybe someone. Thayne wished he knew what was going on in her mind.

His grandfather strode into the room and cleared his throat. "Helen?"

She didn't say a word. She jumped up and ran into his embrace. He held her close, breathing in, closing his eyes and rubbing her back in comfort.

"I don't know what's happening. I'm scared." She let him hold her quietly.

Thayne sighed. At least Gram hadn't pushed Pops away. Each time she did, he could see the agony in his grandfather's eyes.

"I'll take it from here," he said.

Thayne drew Riley to her feet and toward the door of the sunroom. She paused and looked back, her lips tight with frustration.

"That's all we'll get for now," he said. "She's hovering between the present and the past."

Thayne stopped in the hallway leading back to the living room and his father.

"Somewhere in her mind she remembers, Thayne. She knows Cheyenne is in trouble." Riley clutched his arm. "Maybe if we talked to her some more—"

"Dad and Pops will do it, but we can't count on her information, Riley. The answers might be inside Gram unable to get out, or they might not be there at all. Then again, the situation could change tomorrow. She could have a great day, be completely lucid, and remember everything."

"What about this boyfriend of Cheyenne's? She seemed very certain."

"Her memories aren't reliable. Particularly recent ones." He thrust his hand through his hair and looked at her. "Gram is why I called you in the first place when we didn't find Cheyenne that first night. We need a miracle."

Riley closed her reddened eyes. He hadn't meant to put more pressure on her, but he needed her to understand. "Two months ago, you tracked down that pervert who snatched teenage girls off the street. There were no witnesses. No one thought the case could be solved."

"My team closed the case," she said, averting her gaze.

"Don't give me that. I was with you on the phone at least three or four times during the case. I know what you found, the pieces you put together. No one else could have, and we need you to do the same thing."

She rubbed her hands over her face, her mouth drawn with obvious stress. After a deep breath, she straightened her back. "We may need to consider another possibility. What if everything that happened in your sister's clinic was made to *look* like a robbery? What if Cheyenne *knew* her abductor? We're talking about an entirely different profile."

"Dad said most victims know their kidnapper," Thayne said, shifting closer to her. He didn't like the somber expression in her eyes. He'd grown accustomed to intensity and determination, but right now she seemed uncertain.

If only he could get inside that head of hers. He moved in so he could almost touch her. The narrow hallway offered her no escape.

"A stranger abduction is much less common," Riley said, her words certain, but a slight tremor underlying them.

She'd backed herself against the wall. Thayne didn't hesitate. He moved in and bowed his head down to her ear. "What do you need from me?"

"To talk to your brothers about Cheyenne's alleged boyfriend, especially Hudson, since you told me he's closest to her."

"No problem. Anything else?"

"Just keep searching." Riley raised her gaze to his. "I really admire you and your family, Thayne. Not all families pull together when times get tough."

The touch of wistfulness in her voice caught his attention. Family had been something neither of them had wanted to discuss during their long-distance affair. He had his reasons, of course, but he hadn't really considered hers.

Before he could ask what she meant, his cell phone rang. He tugged it out of his pocket and glanced at the screen. His younger brother. Jackson had been searching the mountains. "What's up?"

His brother didn't answer, and Thayne's heart seized.

"You alone?" Jackson asked finally, his voice tense.

Thayne peered down the hallway, then tugged Riley out a door to the back porch. "I'm with Riley Lambert, the FBI profiler I told you about. We're outside at Gram and Pops's. You're on speaker."

"My grid covered the old swimming hole at the southeast edge of the property. At first I didn't see it," Jackson said, his voice choked. "There's an unmarked grave, Thayne. And the digging looks fresh."

CHAPTER EIGHT

A waxing gibbous moon provided just enough light to recognize the mound of dirt in front of Riley. Several flashlights beamed over her shoulder, illuminating circles of the scene. She crouched beside the freshly displaced earth and shoved aside the familiar nightmarish dream playing through her mind.

There was no compost odor here, not like the rose garden where her team had uncovered her last victim—Patricia Masters had still been warm to the touch.

She hated this part of her job. The body had been buried, hidden either to prevent detection or as a sign of remorse. She'd know more when she viewed the remains.

Allowing her senses to grasp the minute details, she scanned the setting. An open hillside overlooking a large swimming hole. A thick tree limb holding an old tire hung over the pool. She could imagine the four Blackwood siblings cavorting during the summer in this place.

Behind a boulder, just inside the tree line, lay a low mound of dirt, six feet by three feet—unmistakably a grave.

She stood over it, feeling the intense stares boring into her back.

"Damn DC Feds always think they know better than we do in the flyover states," Underhill, the Wyoming DCI forensic investigator, muttered under his breath.

He didn't even try to disguise his annoyance with her presence at *his* crime scene. He tapped his foot, clearly irritated she'd horned in on his investigation. Well, she'd faced tougher obstacles than this guy. Pretty much every time the local LEOs requested her FBI unit's assistance, some prima donna cop got his feelings hurt.

Riley couldn't respect anybody who focused on their own ego more than the victim. She lived by a single tenet: The victim mattered more than anything. More than sleep, more than her own safety, and definitely more than pride.

Underhill knelt beside her with a smirk. "There's nothing left to see, *Agent* Lambert. We took photos. Now it's time to quit studying the mound and let us do our job and dig. It's a grave, and it's recent."

She stared him down with a cold gaze. "It's FBI *Special* Agent Lambert. And you're partly right, Underhill. It's a grave. That's all we know at the moment. Now step back and let me do my job."

Underhill glared at her but moved away.

Riley bit down hard on her lip. *Don't antagonize him.*

She had to be careful. If she provoked this guy, he might call her boss. Tom would order her on the first plane back to DC to face a very pissed-off supervisor and a disciplinary hearing. She couldn't let that happen.

Thayne's hand tensed on her shoulder. She wished he hadn't heard the investigator's comment. She wished she hadn't been forced to respond. She prayed Cheyenne Blackwood wasn't lying in this grave.

Riley slipped a sketch pad from her bag, angling the paper toward the moon.

"We need light," Thayne shouted.

Within minutes, one of the deputies had rigged a couple of spotlights. He ran the cord to the generator and flipped on the switch.

Night turned to day.

"Thanks," she said to Thayne when he returned to her side, her pencil flaring over the paper.

"We do have cameras," Underhill commented, his voice thick with sarcasm.

She ignored him, used to the skepticism. But she'd discovered over the years—particularly in an undisturbed crime scene—that the pencil and paper allowed her subconscious to take in the minute details that her mind didn't. Sometimes the smallest element provided her a lead. *If* the person buried here wasn't Cheyenne, a family was waiting for answers. Once Underhill processed the scene, the moment would be lost.

The sound of hushed conversations faded away, and she focused on each line and shape, then the shading. Finally, she closed the sketchbook and faced Underhill. "I'm finished. It's all yours."

"About time," he muttered and glanced expectantly over at Carson Blackwood.

"Dig it up," the sheriff said, his voice thick with emotion.

Riley frowned at the sheriff's sickly gray face. "Your father doesn't look too good," she whispered to Thayne.

"I tried convincing him to go home, but a blizzard wouldn't stop him from being here. A case of myocarditis definitely won't."

Thayne stood so near her, the heat from his body seeped through her clothes, even as the night turned the air cool. "Cheyenne's not in there, is she?"

Riley weighed the risk of telling him.

She must have paused too long. Thayne turned her to face him. "I want the truth, Riley. For my father."

"I hope not."

His hand tightened on her shoulder in a quick squeeze before he released her. Riley shut her eyes. *Please don't be here, Cheyenne.*

Underhill and Deputy Quinn Pendergrass troweled away the dirt slowly, methodically. Thayne's brother Jackson hovered over them as well. Their resemblance ventured into eerie when she saw them standing side by side. Same short-cropped brown hair, same ripped muscles, same determined gaze. And same haunted eyes. As a smoke jumper, he'd probably faced hell, just as Thayne had. But they shouldn't be watching. Not this closely. Not if they uncovered Cheyenne in this grave.

Riley faced them and straightened her spine. "You can't be here. Go to your father," she said, glancing over at the sheriff. "He needs you now. I promise, I'll let you know the truth as soon as I know."

Both men froze. Jackson glared at her, but Thayne gave her a short nod, trusting her with his sister in that moment.

Jackson cursed a storm before stalking over to his father. Thayne followed until the three Blackwood men stood together, stoic, tense, intently watching. The fourth, Hudson, was still out there searching.

With each shovelful of dirt, Carson's jaw tightened. Her heart ached for them. She knew exactly what they were going through. She'd traveled to countless—OK, not countless, exactly twenty-seven—grave sites since she'd turned eighteen, wondering if her sister would be uncovered from the earth.

Madison's body still hadn't been found.

A shiver skittered down her back, and she studied Thayne. As if sensing her stare, his gaze rose and met hers. His expression revealed nothing, not the stark effort of Carson's control or the raw despair of Jackson. Thayne betrayed no emotions. His SEAL training, perhaps? Or simply the need to shoulder the burden.

Her gaze fell to his right hand. Infinitesimal, rhythmic movements of his fingers, the only giveaway that Thayne wasn't calm and dispassionate.

She wanted to join him, to slip her hand into his, to let him know she was there for him, but she couldn't. Most profilers didn't work the scene like she did. But she'd discovered early on she needed to be present to immerse herself in the mind of not only the criminal but also the victim. So she stood alone, watching, waiting.

Minute by minute, a new mound of earth grew. Underhill slid the shovel into the dirt again. Riley detected a soft *clunk*.

The man froze, and the Blackwood men surged forward.

Riley quickly placed herself between them and the grave. "Don't," she said. "Let me."

"If it's Cheyenne—" Carson said.

She met his tortured gaze. "Sheriff, let me do my job. That's why you brought me here."

He gave her a tight nod. Riley shifted her attention to Thayne. He touched his father's shoulder. They backed off, Thayne still in absolute control.

Too controlled, actually. She understood the need.

Riley turned away, unable to face their stoic grief any longer. She and Underhill moved closer, with Deputy Pendergrass at their side.

She knelt down and pointed to a small sprig that had been stirred up. A hint of optimism for the Blackwoods ignited inside Riley. "Do you recognize that plant?"

"Of course. It's sagebrush. Probably broke off from that bush"—he nodded to his left—"when the perpetrator buried the body."

"The one with the small yellow flowers?"

Underhill nodded.

"Except the twig in the dirt isn't flowering at all."

Another time or place, she might have enjoyed Underhill's stunned-mullet look. Instead, she glanced behind her where Thayne stood with his father and brother. She lowered her voice. She didn't want to give them hope. Not until she was absolutely certain. Hope destroyed lives as often as despair. "I think an animal churned the dirt."

"Damn, you're good." Thayne's whispered words just behind her ear nearly sent her careening to the ground.

She rose and slapped the dirt from her pants. "Don't sneak up on me," she said, facing him with a scowl while her racing pulse slowed to normal.

"Those are wolf tracks," Thayne said, nodding to a set of prints.

"Just because a wolf sniffed around doesn't mean the victim isn't here," Underhill argued, though his tone lacked the same conviction as before.

"That's true," Riley admitted.

"Is it her?" the sheriff called out. "Thayne?"

A muscle in Thayne's jaw throbbed. His focus veered to the hole. "What should I tell Dad?"

"Let me finish here," she said, linking fingers with his for a brief squeeze. "Go to him. He needs you right now, and I need to be absolutely certain before I say anything."

Thayne hesitated.

"Please. If I make a mistake—" She paused. "I can't be wrong."

He gave her a quick nod and crossed back to his father.

Riley stiffened her shoulders against the penetrating and desperate stares searing her back. She knelt beside the hole, her artist's eyes noting every detail.

"When was your last rain, Deputy?"

"The night before Cheyenne vanished," he said.

She glanced at Pendergrass and Underhill, her brow arched. "I don't think a human being disturbed this site. The grave isn't wet enough. And from the sagebrush, I'd guess this is a six-month-old grave, dug sometime in winter. The hole was covered over before the abduction."

The DCI investigator couldn't argue. He gave her a grudging nod of respect. "You going to tell them?" he asked.

"Once I have absolutely no doubts. Do you mind?" She picked up a brush.

"You seem to know what you're doing."

She couldn't have hoped for more than that. Riley excavated methodically, pushing aside the dirt, layer by layer. Twigs, pine needles. The next scrape, she sensed resistance beneath the metal. She set the tool to her side and smoothed away the dirt with her gloved hands. Within seconds, the front portion of a skull revealed itself.

No flesh, only a bit of hair remaining.

Her heart thudded, and she bowed her head. Someone had buried a human being in the middle of nowhere. Thrown him or her away.

She looked over her shoulder at the Blackwood men. "It's not Cheyenne."

Carson's knees buckled. Thayne propped up his father. "You're sure?"

"These bones have been here long enough to decompose." She glanced at the DCI investigator. "How long for a body to skeletonize in this part of the country?"

Agent Underhill glanced at the soil. "The roots there were disturbed. This time of year, I'd guess three to six months."

Carson hugged his sons. They clung to one another, then Thayne picked up the phone. Obviously to call Hudson. Riley let out a small sigh. This grave might not belong to Cheyenne, but that didn't mean she wasn't buried somewhere else. Hopefully Thayne and his family could handle whatever happened next, though most couldn't.

Riley turned away and, with care, brushed aside the dirt until she could examine the entire skull. She was no forensic anthropologist, but she'd learned a few things—some from her training, most from the long hours of research and interviews she'd waded through searching for her sister.

The skull was larger than most women's. She turned it to one side. The ridge along the temporal line was definitely pronounced. Lastly, she looked into where the victim's eyes would have been and ran her finger along the lower section of the orbits. A relatively sharp ridge. Add that to the prominence of the arch above, and she was almost certain.

"It's a man," she said to Underhill. She turned the skull to the other side. A small, round hole right above where the ear would have been. Definitely not natural.

She rose to her feet. "Sheriff?"

Carson glanced up at her, his eyes swollen and red. "Riley?" He crossed to her and gripped her hand. "Thank you."

She'd done nothing but fail to find Cheyenne. She couldn't manage more than a grimacing smile. "Have any hikers gone missing in the last six months?"

"Not from Singing River, but I'll check the reports."

"Search for pairs of hikers first," she said.

"Why? Is there more than one body?"

"No, but this man didn't die of natural causes. He was murdered."

Cheyenne was dying. Her stomach cramped, and she whimpered, rolling into a tiny ball on the cot in her prison cell.

Her belly ached, acid burned in her throat. She shot to her feet and ran to the back of the room, flinging open the bathroom door.

She slammed it shut and fell to her knees in front of the toilet. By the time her stomach had emptied out, small flecks of blood streaked the clear fluid. She fell backward, heaving. Her pulse raced. She blinked and pressed her hand to her lower abdomen.

Biting her lip to avoid crying out, she let her head fall back against the wall, her breathing shallow, panting.

She'd never felt anything like this before. But she'd witnessed the symptoms.

In Bethany.

Her forehead beaded in sweat, Cheyenne struggled to focus. Causes of two people with identical symptoms.

"Come on, Cheyenne. Think."

Two possibilities. Infectious or environmental.

Her belly cramped again. She crawled to the toilet, and her body spasmed and retched, but nothing remained in her stomach. Dry heaves overwhelmed her until she collapsed onto the floor of the bathroom.

What was causing this? She fisted her hands, pressing short nails into her palms, trying to force herself to think.

Differential diagnosis. She'd done it hundreds, thousands of times.

Never hurting like this, though.

Start with Bethany. Cheyenne had eliminated all the obvious causes of the woman's pain. Ticking through the list of infectious agents she could recall, Cheyenne couldn't think of one with such a short incubation period.

So, if the problem wasn't disease or infection, that left one possibility. Something in the environment.

Except Ian and Adelaide weren't sick. No one else here had shown any symptoms.

Cheyenne pushed herself up from the floor, struggling to her feet. Legs shaking, she gripped the sink and splashed water on her face. She didn't know how long it took her to feel somewhat steady on her feet again. On weak legs, she walked over to Bethany's bed and sat down beside her.

"What is it, Bethany? What's making us sick? What's so toxic that in less than a day, I'd be showing symptoms?"

She scanned the room; she knew every inch of the space. She'd gone over the room herself with hospital-grade cleaning supplies before the surgery. She'd seen nothing to cause such an acute reaction.

Unable to avoid the one option left, Cheyenne clasped Bethany's hand. "I've ingested it, haven't I? So have you. Someone's poisoned us."

To her shock, Bethany squeezed Cheyenne's hand.

"Bethany? Bethany?"

The woman's eyes didn't open.

Cheyenne waited for several minutes, but Bethany didn't flinch again and didn't regain consciousness. Exhausted, Cheyenne stumbled to her bed and fell onto the blankets, her mind whirling with possibilities.

She couldn't think anymore. But she knew one thing. Whoever had planned the abduction *believed* Bethany's diagnosis was appendicitis. Why else steal the supplies and medication? Why force Cheyenne to operate?

The implications made her shiver.

Someone wanted Bethany dead. Someone who had access to this room or to the food and water brought into the room.

And given Cheyenne's symptoms, they wanted her dead as well.

◆ ◆ ◆

The rumble of engines broke the silence of the clearing. Odd sounds given the normal quiet of this isolated portion of the ranch. Thayne stepped through the tree line. He'd threatened to arrest a couple of reporters who'd found their way to the location. Damn locusts. They'd seen just enough to make for a juicy headline and endless speculation.

Cheyenne's abduction had gone national. This would mean their small town would have fifteen minutes of notorious fame.

The forensics team worked on the grid surrounding the grave under Jackson's watchful eye. Thayne joined his brother.

"Dad looks like he's going to keel over," he said under his breath, looking at his father at the opposite edge of the site.

"*You* want to try to convince him to go home, big brother?" Jackson whispered.

"Someone has to." Thayne rubbed his face.

When he caught sight of Carson swaying, he'd had enough. "Come on." He tilted his head toward Jackson, and they joined their father.

"You need to go home, Dad," Thayne said. "When we find Cheyenne, she'll chew us all out if you're back in the hospital. And I sure as hell don't want to face my sister when she's on a tirade."

A weak smile crossed his father's face. "She'd do it, too." He sighed. "I know when I'm outgunned." He flicked on his radio. "Status report?"

One by one, the search teams reported in. One by one, the bad news built. They'd found nothing. Not one sign of Cheyenne.

With each call, his father's shoulders sagged a bit more, and what little energy remained vanished.

Jackson cleared his throat. "Dad, I'm taking you home. The search teams won't stop. Thayne and Quinn Pendergrass will see to that. Besides, Gram and Pops need you."

Their father hesitated, but finally he nodded. "You'll call with any news. No matter what." He glared first at Thayne, then at Jackson, a warning in his tired but sharp eyes.

"Of course."

A rustle of trees and ground cover tore Thayne's attention from his father.

Riley stood just behind the tree line, her sketchbook in her hands.

His father followed Thayne's line of sight. "You and I both know Riley's our only hope." He clutched Thayne's arm. "If *we* were going to find Cheyenne easily, we already would have."

"I know." He faced his dad.

"Give her whatever she needs, Thayne. I'll call in every favor I have coming. Hell, I'll be indebted to whoever will help us for the rest of my life. As long as we find Cheyenne alive and well."

"Let's go, Dad."

Jackson led their father past Riley toward his truck. They disappeared through the woods as Thayne crossed to her.

"I'm glad you convinced your father to go home." She closed her sketchbook so quickly he couldn't make out what she'd drawn.

"Dad doesn't give in easily, and he doesn't know his own limitations these days. Cheyenne can get him to follow doctor's orders. She's the only one, though."

"Your family is bound to this land, aren't they?" Riley said. "I saw your initials carved on that tree, along with your brothers' and sister's. You have so much here, Thayne. Why did you leave home when you obviously love this town and your family?"

Thayne kneaded the muscles at the back of his neck. "My great-granddad homesteaded here. He became sheriff. Pops was sheriff. Dad was sheriff. I grew up facing the Blackwood legacy every single day. I couldn't breathe here. I had to find my own way."

"I get that," Riley said. "More than you know. After Madison, I faced my own set of expectations." She touched her bracelet. "Do you want to come back here permanently?"

"I never imagined moving home for good, but I got a call last week from my commander. I'm running out of time. I have to decide whether to continue with the SEALs and my Navy career or opt out. The team is one short. They need me."

"So does your family."

What could he say? Family trumped everything.

"Are you finished here?" he asked.

She nodded. The body had been removed and most everyone had moved off to continue the grid search for Cheyenne. Only Pendergrass and Underhill remained.

The rumble of an engine on its last legs shattered the darkness. Uneven headlights swept across the trees. The vehicle gave a loud hiccup, the backfire spewing exhaust. Oh boy. He recognized the POS truck. Carol Wallace jumped out of the vehicle and stumbled toward the open grave of the crime scene.

At the edge, she swayed and sank to her knees. "Is it her? Is it Gina?"

"Oh my God," Riley whispered. "Carol Wallace."

Before Thayne could move, Riley raced to the woman. Carol looked up at Riley and nearly toppled over.

"Y-you."

The slurred word told Thayne all he needed to know. By the time he reached Carol's side, the overwhelming smell of alcohol hit him.

Riley clasped Carol's arms. "Your daughter isn't here," Riley said. "Look at me, Carol. It's not Gina."

Her words didn't penetrate Carol's alcohol-soaked mind. The poor woman sank to the ground and just sobbed, tears flowing down her cheeks. Her fingers clutched at the dirt, digging into the ground.

Thayne grasped her shoulders and forced her to stand. "Carol, listen to me. It's not Gina. We haven't found your daughter."

Slowly, the cries diminished. She sniveled and looked at Riley. "But you're the FBI agent looking for her. If this isn't her, what are you doing here?"

"She's helping us find Cheyenne," Thayne said.

Carol's eyes widened. "Is she gone?"

Thayne could only stare at her in disbelief.

"Cheyenne was kidnapped Friday evening," Riley said. "I'm trying to find her."

"Like you found my Gina?" Carol blurted out the bitter words.

Riley flinched, and Thayne turned on Carol, his jaw throbbing. "Back off, Carol. Riley doesn't deserve that. She's the only Fed who's opened Gina's case in a decade."

Carol slapped her hand over her mouth. "Sorry. Ummm . . . Friday was rough," she said, unable to meet Riley's gaze. "I just want my baby."

In other words, Carol had been drinking since he'd arrested Ed. Thayne shook his head. "Pendergrass, I'm taking Carol home. Can you call someone in to drive her truck back to town when you leave?"

"Sure, Thayne. As soon as we're done here."

He looked at Riley. "You ready to leave?"

She stared down at the empty grave. "I need to regroup, so yes. I'm ready."

He escorted Carol to his SUV and helped her into the backseat. She wiped her eyes and leaned against the glass. Within seconds, she was snoring.

After opening the door for Riley, he slid in beside her, started the engine, and cracked open the front two windows to dissipate the sour odor.

Riley glanced over her shoulder at the passed-out woman. "When I saw her last year, she'd been dry for a few months."

"She keeps trying," Thayne said. "I'll drop her off at her place, then take you to Fannie's so you can check in to the B and B."

"I'm not staying," Riley said. "I need printouts of all the files and photos you've collected, my pictures printed, and a quiet place to work."

"We have most of that in the conference room at the sheriff's office."

"I don't want to see what you've done, Thayne. Not until I've run the two scenarios through my head and tried to come up with some kind of lead. I need quiet and alone time to focus."

Thayne pulled out his phone and gave the orders.

"Save the photos here." Thayne rattled off a web location. "I'll have the sheriff's office make copies and deliver everything to Fannie's. It could take a couple of hours, though."

Before Riley could respond, Thayne pulled up to Ed and Carol's house. He opened the car door. "Carol, where's your key?"

"Under the pot," she whispered. "In case my daughter comes home."

Thayne lifted her into his arms. Carol had to be five feet ten and weigh at least 160, but he carried her as if she were a ninety-pound weakling. Riley hurried in front of him and picked up the plant. The key lay there, to the side of a discreet key-shaped outline of dust, obviously recently used.

Thayne carried Carol into the cluttered house. A gun case stood in the corner, too many rifles to count shoved in it haphazardly. A stack of laundry, including men's boxers and several shirts that would have engulfed Carol, were strewn across the kitchen table beside a couple of bowls of half-eaten cereal and dirty coffee cups. Her husband maybe?

No one had cleaned the place in a long while, but one wall remained pristine, a shrine to her daughter. Thayne sighed. "Where's your bedroom?"

With a halfhearted flop of one hand, she pointed to a door. Riley grabbed the clothes strewn across the bed and sat them on a chair sitting in the corner while Thayne lay the woman down. "Sleep it off, Carol. Ed's locked up for a while."

He straightened, and Carol curled herself into a ball, shivering.

"I'm trying to hang on," she said through garbled words. "I don't know how much longer I can. I want my daughter back."

Riley covered Carol with a blanket that had fallen to the floor. She didn't know what kind of trouble Carol found herself in, but she could offer one bit of comfort. "I'm not stopping until I find out what happened to my sister," Riley said. "And your daughter. Carol, please, don't let the kidnapper win."

Carol's bloodshot eyes went dull. "He already has."

CHAPTER NINE

Riley took one last look at Carol before closing the door to the sounds of soft snores and even breathing.

"She's asleep," Riley said to Thayne.

Carol's words reverberated around and around in Riley's mind. *He's already won.*

How many times had she felt exactly the same thing? Facing the indescribable murders of too many victims. They called out to her. For justice. For answers. For closure. And with the questions she could never answer.

What took you so long? Why couldn't you save us?

Before Thayne could open the front door, she grabbed his arm. "Do you think Carol's right? Has the kidnapper won? Look what's left of her life."

"She has a right to feel hopeless. Her daughter's been missing fifteen years. Just like your sister," Thayne said, his voice quiet and pensive. "Except you've turned tragedy into helping a lot of people."

"Have I?" Riley shook her head, fatigue, both emotional and physical, pressing down on her, practically suffocating her.

They walked outside, and he locked up before returning the key to its location beneath the flowerpot. For Gina.

Riley took one step off the porch, and Thayne erupted in a curse. He grabbed Riley's hand and dragged her behind a tree before pulling out his Glock.

"What—?"

He placed a finger to his lips, and her eyes widened. She followed his gaze. A slight movement drew her attention. A figure crouched near Thayne's SUV.

She slipped her weapon from its holster. He signaled her to round the back end of the car while he slipped silently into the shadows toward the front of the vehicle.

If he hadn't seen the slight movement, they could have walked into a trap. Step by step, she crept behind a row of pines on the property line between Carol's house and her neighbor's. If the guy ran this way, she'd have him.

The man straightened and bent over the SUV's hood. Thayne shot up and raced across the yard. Before he could reach the guy, two shots fired from out of nowhere.

Thayne hit the ground at the same time as Riley. By the time she raised her head, the man had vanished. They crawled to take cover behind the SUV.

"You OK?" Thayne shouted. "Did you see which way he went?"

"I'm fine, and no."

He shot to his feet and yanked open the SUV's door. "Shots fired." Thayne barked out the address. He looked over his shoulder at her. "Did you recognize him?"

Riley shook her head, giving a vague description. Thayne added an estimated height to his verbal report and tossed down the radio receiver on the seat before joining her, Glock at the ready.

"The sniper could have taken out either one of us." Riley didn't mince words.

"Unless the shooter was incompetent."

"You don't believe that."

Thayne shook his head. "You can't hide from a sniper. I don't think he wants us dead."

"Then why shoot?" she asked.

"Maybe this gift is the answer." Thayne raised up and untucked an envelope from beneath the windshield wiper, holding it by one corner. He handed it to Riley. "It's got your name on it."

She snapped on a glove before taking the envelope from him, turning it over and over in her hands. Reaching into her satchel, she grabbed a plastic bag, and after carefully slicing one end of the paper, slipped it into the protective pouch.

"Can't be too careful these days," she said. "We still get regular anthrax alerts at Quantico."

She manipulated the plastic and pulled a sheet of paper from inside the envelope, unfolding it.

Stop looking or you'll be sorry.

◆ ◆ ◆

Getting shot at twice in two days made Riley wonder briefly about her choice of professions. Not that it had ever been a choice.

Deputy Pendergrass's taillights disappeared into the darkness, the letter and evidence going with him to be sent to the lab. Even after a thorough search of the area, they'd found no shell casings, no sign of where the shooter had hidden, and no witnesses, much less the person who'd left the threatening note. She twisted her lips in concentration.

"I can see the wheels turning in your mind," Thayne said.

"Two people. One organized, one sloppy, unorganized, and spontaneous." She slipped into the car, and Thayne joined her.

"Sounds like your description of the abduction. Pendergrass might find prints on the letter," he said.

"Maybe. But the attack doesn't make sense. A sniper could have taken us out if he'd wanted to. Why warn me off the case? We have no forensic evidence, and the search hasn't turned up anything in the last day," she said.

"A warning to back off."

"But why?" She tapped her finger to her lip. "We must be close to something. I need to rethink my profile and study the evidence to catch a break. Somewhere quiet, with no distractions."

"The sheriff's office is out," Thayne muttered. "The investigation team has taken over the conference room. That leaves one place in town where you can hide away without any distractions. For the most part."

He started the car and made a quick U-turn. It didn't take long before Riley recognized the route to Fannie's Bed and Breakfast. The same place she'd stayed a year ago—where she and Thayne had lost themselves in each other's arms. A lifetime ago.

He pulled up to the B&B, but before she could get out, he held her back. "We go into the building fast and quick, agreed?"

She nodded. Beneath the adrenaline burst of being shot at, a burning fatigue crept behind her eyes. No time to rest, though. She needed to rerun the crime scene through her mind, relentlessly searching for any small out-of-place element that would provide a lead. She needed the evidence because there was only one chance unless forensics hit pay dirt.

Profiling Cheyenne and the kidnapper.

Riley reached for her computer bag, but Thayne hooked the strap over his shoulder.

"I'll take it," Thayne said, his expression brokering no argument. "You look ready to collapse."

How could she argue?

He pulled his Glock out before exiting the vehicle and moving around the car to open her door. "Go!" he shouted. They rushed up to the porch of the B&B and raced inside, shutting and locking the door behind them.

Thayne checked the curtains and closed all of them.

The welcoming scent of vanilla created that just-baked feel, the antithesis of the tension still thrumming through Riley's veins. Her heart slowed a bit now that they were inside.

Fresh flowers adorned the elegant sitting room. A discreet check-in desk was tucked in the corner. Southern hospitality at its finest.

Fannie popped out from a door behind the mahogany counter, her hair expertly coiffed, dressed in a flowing chiffon gown and robe. A true southern belle, transplanted to Wyoming.

"I figured you'd get here eventually," she said with a frown, her gaze narrowed at them. "What's going on? Put away those weapons."

"Is Kade around?" Thayne asked.

Fannie frowned. "He's having . . . trouble."

"I'll figure something else out."

Fannie met Riley's questioning gaze. "My great-nephew just came back from the war. He's battling PTSD."

"I'm sorry, Fannie."

"Me, too. He's lost right now. So, why were you asking about him?"

"Someone took a shot at Riley. I'd hoped he might be able to help guard the place."

Fannie reached beneath the counter and pulled out a 12-gauge. "I can handle myself."

The sight of a woman in her seventies dressed in a negligee holding a shotgun should have been absurd. Fannie made the picture seem almost normal.

"I'm sure you can defend yourself, ma'am," Thayne said. "The shooter seems to have disappeared, but I think I'll stay around tonight anyway."

Riley hoped he was right. "You don't have to stay, Thayne. I can take care of myself. I'm a trained federal law enforcement officer, you know."

"Maybe so," Fannie chimed in. "But you need more rest. How are you supposed to find our Cheyenne if you're too exhausted to see straight?" She placed her hands on her hips. "You take better care of her, Thayne, you hear me?"

Thayne shrugged. "Yes, ma'am. I plan to."

Arguing would obviously get them nowhere. Riley reached out her hand for the key, but Fannie handed it to Thayne.

"Take her upstairs. Same room you stayed in before, dear. Breakfast is six to ten. Cheese grits, blueberry muffins, omelets, and southern sausage. And of course biscuits and gravy on Sunday. I'll set the alarm. Anyone coming in will have their ears blown out."

"Thank you, Mrs. Lonebear," Riley said.

"You just find our girl, Special Agent Lambert. You've got the room until she comes home. No charge."

"Thanks, Fannie," said Thayne.

The B&B's owner disappeared into her private quarters before Thayne and Riley trudged up the stairs. Thayne slipped the key into the lock and opened the door. "Where do you want this?" He lifted the computer case.

"On the table is fine." She sat on the bed, sinking into the comfortable mattress. Her body yearned to lie down. Her mind needed to work.

Thayne placed her suitcase on a luggage rack before closing all the curtains. He faced her, his expression solemn and concerned. He made the room seem small. He crossed over to the bed where she sat. All she had to do was reach out and touch him, let her guard down, and open herself up to the longing that had been building since she'd arrived. It would be so easy, but now wasn't the time.

"How can I help?" he asked, gently lifting her hand in his, the warmth of his touch so very nice. A loud ringtone intruded from her pocket. The moment was gone. Who could be calling her? Only Tom checked up on her. Had he discovered she'd flown to Wyoming? He'd know the significance. This call might very well be her termination notice.

Her gut churning, she slipped the phone from her pocket and reluctantly checked the screen. She blinked in shock, then tapped to answer and held the phone to her ear. "Mother?"

"Hello, Riley."

She braced herself. Her mother sounded tired, but then again, she'd sounded that way since the morning after Madison had disappeared.

"I suppose you know why we called."

The tone in her mother's voice conveyed clearly that Riley *should* know. She glanced at the date at the top of the phone.

Her twenty-sixth birthday.

For a moment, her breathing stopped. She'd forgotten, but her mother had actually remembered. For the first time in fifteen years. She'd even called.

The stunning revelation twisted her tongue. Riley couldn't believe it. She blinked several times. What could she say? *Thank you for treating me like a daughter. Thank you for not reminding me I've failed to find Madison.*

Maybe just a *thank you for calling* would do?

"The fifteenth anniversary of Madison's disappearance is next week," her mother said in that familiarly emotionless, clipped voice. "We're holding a very special memorial. It's important for you to be here. For us to show solidarity. We've arranged media coverage, and one of those crime shows is doing another reenactment of the case to try to generate some leads, since you haven't been able to keep your promise to bring Madison home."

Riley closed her eyes and held her stomach. She'd let her guard down for only a moment, which made the attack all the more painful.

The mattress shifted beside her. Thayne moved close enough for their legs to touch. He threaded his fingers through hers, and she met his sympathetic gaze. Had he heard her mother?

A pressure built behind her lids, tears threatening to come. Riley shot to her feet and hurried to the window, crossing her arms in front of her, staring at a curtain, imagining the night sky of Singing River, a bevy of stars twinkling, laughing at her hurt. For a split second, she'd thought her mother actually . . .

No, Riley. Don't go there. Why had she expected more? She should know better. And she had no right to want more.

Madison mattered more. Her sister was still missing.

With a tight grip, Riley cleared her throat so the disappointment wouldn't show in her voice. "I don't know if I can make it. I'm on a case."

She could almost see her mother's lips purse into that tight disapproving line, a perpetual expression whenever they spoke. "It's expected, Riley. You need to be here."

"For Madison." Her father's tentative voice uttered the words that sliced at Riley's soul.

"I'll try," she said finally. "That's all I can do. I have to go."

Before Thayne sees me cry.

She ended the call. A large presence warmed her from behind. Strong arms pulled her back against a muscular chest. Riley couldn't turn around; she couldn't face him. She had to protect herself. No one else would. She had to stay strong, stay tough on the inside and on the outside.

She squeezed her eyes shut. Thayne pressed her even closer against him, wrapping her tighter. She winced at the pressure on the bullet graze, but the physical pain hardly made a blip compared to the regrets twisting her heart. So she said nothing and simply let him hold her, still and silent.

She couldn't stop the tears from rolling down her cheeks.

The room had gone quiet, with only a faint owl's hoot and a whip-poor-will's song filtering through the window. Thayne encased Riley in his embrace. He hadn't been able to hear what her mother had said, but he'd seen Riley's gut-wrenching reaction.

She still trembled.

Riley needed someone on her side, and Thayne meant to convince her he stood in her corner. She deserved no less.

Special Agent Riley Lambert had impressed the hell out of him from the moment he'd entered the dance hall a year ago and seen her cleaning up at the pool table. He'd walked over to her, drawn to something he'd never felt before. She'd worn *tough* and *don't mess with me* like a warning sign, but Thayne had seen a hint of sadness behind her eyes that he'd wanted to chase away with a joke, a laugh, and a turn around the dance floor.

She'd refused the dance—she didn't dance, she'd said—but she'd laughed at his jokes, and when he'd driven her back to Fannie's place, she'd led him upstairs into a fantasy.

That first night had changed everything. Thayne had allowed himself to get lost in Riley. Not just her passion, though with one look or the lightest touch, his body had burned with want. He flat out liked her, and in the last year nothing had changed. Today had stamped an exclamation point onto his opinion. She had nerves of steel and courage that didn't end.

He'd come an inch away from falling head over heels in love with her a year ago. Not the woman-in-a-port kind of lust. Nope, this was the real thing. A Blackwood kind of love.

Today he was certain. Riley Lambert made him want the forever love.

He'd known it could exist. His parents had it; his grandparents had it. But they'd found each other by the time they'd turned eighteen. Thayne was nearly twenty-eight, and he'd started to doubt he'd ever find anything close.

Until Riley.

After a year of talking to her, of listening to her fears, sharing her excitement when she'd joined the task force; after sharing his frustrations with his missions, the politicians making his job impossible, his doubts whenever they lost another SEAL; he knew one thing. Riley could be his partner, could be his love, if he let her in. If she let him in.

Except they'd both kept their walls intact. Self-preservation. And he'd just discovered another one.

Her back pressed against him, she lifted her hand to her face. Probably to swipe away the tears. He wouldn't embarrass her by turning her in his arms, though everything inside of him wanted to. He just continued to hold her.

"Do you want to talk about it?" he whispered against her ear. "Maybe I can help."

"How exactly?" Her voice rose, and she whirled around, streaks of tears on her face. "Can you fix the fact that it's my birthday, and my parents didn't remember? Again. Or that the only time they pick up the phone is to remind me about my sister's kidnapping. Like I'd ever forget. Like I haven't obsessed about it for the last fifteen years. Like I haven't spent night and day trying to find her and bring her body home."

Riley slapped her hand against her mouth, her eyes wide with shock.

Thayne froze, stunned. He'd never seen her lose her composure before. Not once.

Her cheeks flushed, and she groaned, shaking her head. "Just shoot me now."

"Can't. I like you too much," Thayne said. He tilted up her chin. "So let me be the first to say, happy birthday, Riley."

He cupped her face with his hands, unable to look away. Her eyes glistened. If Thayne could have reached through the phone and strangled Riley's parents, he would have.

She blinked, attempting to hide the hurt. He wanted to heal her wounds. She deserved to be cherished. She deserved to be loved.

Ever so slowly, he lowered his lips to hers, gently, tenderly, barely touching them.

He folded her into his arms, determined to make her feel treasured.

In the past, he'd have simply scooped her into his arms and let the passion take over. Seduction would have been his normal MO. *Not* talking made relationships easier.

Except he and Riley *had* talked. A lot.

She needed to be touched, all right, but holding her tonight wasn't about passion. She needed more. He raised his head and met her gaze.

She shifted her weight, easing out of his arms, discomfort settling on her face. "Well, this is awkward. We were supposed to keep things professional."

"It's not awkward for me," he lied, unwilling to walk away from her. Not when she needed him, even if she didn't acknowledge the truth.

"Have you ever been awkward in your life, Thayne?"

He'd go with her less-than-clandestine attempt to change the subject. "When I was about twelve, my voice was changing; I was all arms and legs. Gram called me a human string bean." He shook his head wryly. "Anyway, there was this girl I really liked, and the school announced a formal dance. I really wanted to take her. Heck, it was a chance to hold a girl in my arms, but I had two left feet. Until Gram got ahold of me. That's how I learned to waltz." He quirked a smile and wrapped one arm around her waist, clasping the other hand against his chest, swaying side to side. "Everyone should learn."

"You know I don't dance." She fell silent.

"When's the last time you celebrated your birthday, Riley?" He willed her to raise her gaze to his.

Finally, she gave in, her expression cautious.

"Fifteen years ago. Before my sister was taken." She shrugged. "I didn't care the next year. Or even the year after that. I missed her too much. Then it didn't matter anymore. Too many things had changed. Birthdays were part of the past, when we were a real family. When Madison was there."

God, he hurt for the little girl whose childhood had been stolen. "I'm sorry for your loss."

Her fingers twitched, and she rubbed her temple. "Look, I'm tired, Thayne. And I need to work."

"Not yet."

Before she could speak, he opened the door and propped the latch so he wouldn't be locked out. Her body language had telegraphed much more than fatigue. Her words had drawn a picture of a family torn apart under the stress of Madison Lambert's abduction. For Riley, the wound had festered and never healed. He just hadn't realized how much.

He'd witnessed the mask Riley had so carefully constructed slip. He'd seen inside her tonight, seen beneath the smart, intuitive profiler, beneath the beautiful woman.

She should scare him. She needed more than he'd ever imagined giving. But with Riley, he knew he had to show her that he could be there for her like no one else ever had. That she wasn't alone.

He treaded down the stairs into the dining room. There they were: Fannie's famous muffins. He snagged one of her cinnamon swirl quick breads with cream cheese frosting, grabbed a knife and plate, and headed back up the stairs.

She'd closed the door on him.

The night wasn't over. He lifted his fist to knock. Soft, heartbroken sobs filtered from inside. For a fleeting moment, he hesitated, then very lightly tapped on the wood.

The cries immediately ceased.

For a moment, he could hear nothing from inside. Finally, tentative footsteps padded closer. The snick of a lock sounded, the knob turned, and Riley cracked open the door. "I need to work," she repeated.

He lifted the muffin. "Everyone needs cake on their birthday."

She looked at the treat, then up at him and took a shuddering breath.

"And no one should be alone," he finished. He pushed through the door, standing so close he could smell the sweet, fruity scent of her hair. "We can share. And you'll have to deal with the fact that I'm not leaving you alone tonight. Or ever. At least until we catch these guys."

She moved aside and let him in. "Why are you doing this, Thayne?"

"Because we just got shot at?"

"I mean the cinnamon roll."

He ignored her question as she closed the door. "Sorry I don't have a candle."

She'd taken off the suit jacket she'd worn all day, revealing a tailored white shirt. On the sleeve, a smear of red over what appeared to be a bandage drove his plan out of his mind. "What the hell happened to you? I thought you said the sniper didn't get you?"

She glanced down at her shirt. "He didn't. I should have changed the dressing sooner. It's not a big deal. I didn't duck fast enough Friday night. Just a graze. Hardly worth stitching up."

Thayne's heart pounded against his chest; his breathing tightened in his lungs. Deliberately, struggling to control his fury, he walked across the room and set the cake on the small table in the corner of the room. When he turned around and faced her, he couldn't stop the anger surging up his spine and scalding the base of his neck. "Exactly when were you planning to tell me you'd been shot?"

CHAPTER TEN

Riley had never seen Thayne truly pissed off. His eyes had narrowed, and his voice had gone cold and deadly soft.

"Don't go all hero on me, Thayne. I'm fine." She tilted her head at him. "Besides, I seem to recall a mission about six months ago where you didn't tell me for weeks that flying shrapnel had peppered your side."

"That's not the point. You were across the world and couldn't do anything. But I'm right here, and you didn't tell me the moment you landed!" The words snapped out rapid-fire. "Why?"

"Because right now I'm not important," she shouted. "Cheyenne is the only one who matters."

The fury thawed from Thayne's gaze, though not completely. The muscle in his jaw pulsed with barely contained frustration, but Riley refused to back down. She was right. They both knew it.

She appreciated his concern, but except for a few twinges, she'd almost forgotten about the injury.

"Riley—"

His ringing cell forced him to pause. "Blackwood." He paused, never once wavering his hard gaze from hers. "I'll be right down." Thayne pocketed the cell. "The files are here. I'll be right back."

His entire body stiff with irritation, he left the room. The moment he disappeared from view, Riley's knees gave way. She sank onto the bed as his footsteps thudded down the stairs, followed by the front door of Fannie's slamming closed.

She hadn't meant to yell, but she hated the idea of anyone seeing past the mask she wore. He'd looked beneath the surface and garnered a peek at the truth she hid so desperately.

FBI Special Agent Riley Lambert was a strong, confident, damn good profiler who could see the world through the eyes of the most depraved mind. That's who Thayne and his family needed right now.

The real Riley Lambert was a vulnerable woman whose twelve-year-old sister had vanished from their house never to be seen again . . . and whose family had never recovered from the tragedy.

Riley had never wanted Thayne to recognize her true flaws and vulnerabilities.

Why couldn't their relationship continue as it had been?

She scrubbed her eyes with the heels of her hands. The small birthday roll came into focus, mocking her from the table. Thayne might be a SEAL, but he also had a big heart. She really needed to make certain he didn't get any closer to owning hers.

He saw too much. He made her feel too much.

She rose from the floor and moved to the window. With cautious fingers, she pushed aside the curtains and peered through the small gap.

Below her, in front of the B&B, she saw him. Her body tensed in fear that a shot would ring into the night and he'd fall to the ground.

A car pulled away from the curb, and Thayne gripped two file boxes in his arms and ran toward the B&B like an IED had erupted behind him.

Riley sucked in a deep breath. She had a job to do. She couldn't let the threats or their personal relationship distract her from the task at hand.

She strode over to the sink and splashed water on her face before staring into the mirror at the circles beneath bloodshot eyes, at her pinched mouth. "Cheyenne. Where are you? Your family needs you."

Her heart thudded against her rib cage, knocking hard as if it were trying to escape, and her shallow breathing quickened.

The image of Sheriff Blackwood, Thayne, the entire family flashed through her mind.

Riley had to find Cheyenne. For the Blackwoods. For Thayne.

Her hands gripped the marble vanity in an attempt to quell the firestorm of panic rising within her. Normally her gut was her best indicator of the direction the investigation should veer. Not with Cheyenne. She doubted herself.

Every instinct told her Helen Blackwood had seen something important, but what good did that do? Riley had to go back to the beginning. Start over.

A half-dozen deep, shuddering breaths later, she lifted her chin. No more wallowing. No more overreaction. It didn't matter that grit scraped her eyes when she blinked. It didn't matter that regret swirled through her. She would give the search everything she had, every scrap of energy she could muster. Answers were all she had to offer.

The door pushed open, and Thayne walked in carrying the two stacked file boxes and a basket on top of them. In silence, he set the pile on the bed.

"Thank you," she said, hating the awkwardness that had settled between them.

"Where do we go from here to find Cheyenne?"

Riley could work with pretending nothing had happened between them. Focusing strictly on the investigation, that was something she could hold on to.

"I need caffeine and quiet," she said. "In that order."

"Fannie sent up extra coffee packets." He handed her the basket.

Riley filled the water in the coffeemaker just high enough for extra-strong liquid fuel, started brewing, and faced him.

"We have a conference room full of investigators sifting through the evidence at the sheriff's office," he added.

"Which is great. You can contact me when they identify any fingerprints or blood samples—"

"Preliminary results indicate the blood belongs to Cheyenne and Gram," Thayne said. "Cheyenne's military records have her DNA, and Gram has samples at the hospital, so they're sending them off for verification. As for fingerprints, they only found them in the exam rooms. These guys wore gloves."

Riley stilled. "No trace evidence at all?"

"They're working on it, but given this new information, they're doubtful." He paused. "I haven't told Dad yet, but we've got nothing except the black SUV, and still no results on the BOLO."

"I see." Organized and disorganized. The coffeepot began to bubble, and she took the top off a file box. "Thayne, please understand, I need to be alone for a while."

"I could help. Two sets of hands," he said, his voice quiet.

She could hear the need in his voice, but some things had to be done alone. "I'm sorry. I can't worry about what you might hear, how my thoughts will affect you. I need to explore scenarios in my head, and my words could hurt you. It's how I have to work. Alone."

"I see." He moved in close but didn't touch her, his gaze searching out hers. "I'm not going home. I'll be downstairs if you need me. You'll be safe. I promise."

"I have no doubt." Riley wanted to look away, but his intensity held her captive. "The kidnappers have made mistakes. We just have to find the oversight that will lead us to them."

They still had a chance to find Cheyenne alive. Despite the statistics.

Only 6 percent of predatory kidnapping victims escaped their captors without law enforcement intervention or their abductors releasing them.

That meant locating Cheyenne was on her and Thayne and the residents of Singing River. Unless Riley's first instincts were wrong, and Cheyenne had been taken by someone who knew her.

If that were true, she was either already dead, or her captor might let her go.

Two very different outcomes.

Riley had to figure out the truth soon . . . if they expected to bring Cheyenne home.

He nodded and strode to the door before turning back. "If you need me, I'll be here for you. Always, Riley. Don't forget that."

She blinked at the intensity in his gaze. "I won't."

"Please, find her." He shut the door, and the lock snicked closed.

We're counting on you.

She could almost hear the words.

A clock's chime sounded twelve times from downstairs.

First things first. She poured a large mug of coffee. A few sips would provide her with a second—or maybe third—wind.

Warmth seeped through to her hands, and Riley closed her eyes as the nectar of the gods slid down her throat, warming her insides. Two things about Singing River she would never forget: her week with Thayne and Fannie's special blend.

She wasn't sure what would happen with the first. The second, hopefully, would keep her going long enough to unravel the mystery of Cheyenne's disappearance.

She cleared the table and moved the birthday cinnamon roll to her bedside table. With one last look of regret for what the sweet bread represented—Thayne—she fastened her hair back with a clip and dug in to the boxes. Within minutes, her computer and supplies littered the round table. She removed a picture from the wall and tacked up Post-it notes with the very short timeline. From her briefcase, she pulled the case file that Thayne had provided and tacked up the photos of the primary crime scene and the layout of Cheyenne's office building on an improvised crime scene board.

Stepping back, Riley scanned the evidence, narrowing her gaze at the crime scene photos. Back and forth she strode, studying each image. She took a sip of coffee. The more she analyzed, the more she came to believe there was a purpose in what the thieves had stolen. But what? And why?

And more importantly, who?

Medical supplies. She crossed the room and bent over her computer, tapping the keys. A quick Internet search later, she found what she was looking for.

"Cheyenne Blackwood has the only doctor's office in town." Riley couldn't sit still. She paced, muttering to herself. "If they'd wanted drugs and supplies, they could've at least tried the county medical center, since it keeps more on inventory. The Marbleton clinic isn't that far away, only forty minutes or so.

"So they needed more than supplies. They needed a doctor. But why you, Cheyenne? Why here? Was it chance? Opportunity? Location?"

Riley closed her eyes, visualizing herself in the middle of the room. The getaway driver was waiting outside, on the lookout and ready to leave. "Cheyenne is strong, tall. They'd need at least two people to subdue her."

Her gaze pinned one of the crime scene photos. She squinted at the blood on the floor. Some drops, but not enough to kill.

A blow to the head or face. Enough to knock her out.

"Cheyenne didn't grab the door. No blood or prints near the knob." Riley paused working through the logistics. "She had to be unconscious when they took her."

And after five o'clock, no one had noticed because Main Street had closed down. That explained the choice of Singing River . . . a small town.

No witnesses except for Thayne's grandmother, and she couldn't help.

"Think, Riley."

Streets deserted. She fingered the map of Singing River and the surrounding area. A black SUV had been placed near a lake at the base of the Wind River Mountains, and Cheyenne's cell phone had been found northwest of town on the way to the mountains.

Riley placed red dots at the three locations.

She added a white dot at the Blackwood swimming hole; the body dumped there had been buried for six months or so. Probably unrelated.

She didn't like the distribution. The geographic profile was incomplete. She needed at least one more point, and even then she wasn't so sure. The kidnappers had planned well. They'd started out of town moving west and dropped the cell phone heading northeast.

One more pin. At Carol's house. Shots fired. Cheyenne's abductors had stayed near to watch the investigation. Part of the search crew, maybe?

Riley couldn't assume Thayne's sister was nearby, but she hoped she was.

Normally, this would've been the point in her process where she'd be working with a team or task force, bouncing ideas off each other. She'd have to do it alone this time.

More certain than ever the theft wasn't about money, she clicked a familiar link. Maybe there were other cases where medical supplies had vanished. She crossed her fingers when the login screen appeared and typed her credentials into the FBI's databases.

ACCESS DENIED.

Damn.

Tom hadn't been kidding about keeping her out all week.

She needed to run a few searches, and she preferred to do it herself. Sometimes local investigators ignored seemingly unrelated crimes. One thing her time as a profiler had taught her was to take a look at the beginning from a fresh perspective.

A text chimed on her phone. She glanced at the screen. From Tom.

Strike one!

Damn it. She had two choices. Call Tom and let him know she'd completely disobeyed orders or . . . ask Thayne for more help.

At the very least, she'd have to come clean to Thayne's father. He'd know that the Denver field office should be the one assisting in an abduction. There was nothing serial about this case, no real requirement for a profiler. She doubted Sheriff Blackwood would be surprised she'd come to Singing River outside normal procedure. He wouldn't know she'd taken a left turn at Albuquerque. But with his daughter missing, she doubted he'd question her much—if at all.

Riley plopped down on the bed and tucked her feet under her. The sparse crime scene board mocked her.

The forensic evidence hadn't given them anything to go on. So far.

She needed another viewpoint.

Reaching into her satchel, Riley pulled out a sketchbook and 4B pencil. She flipped halfway through the pad. What had she missed?

Drawing in her room would be second best—at the location before forensics arrived would always be best, but she'd learned to make it work.

She closed her eyes, picturing the clinic in her mind. She started in the front room.

Not looking at the photograph, Riley began to sketch. First Cheyenne's private office at the back of the clinic. Untouched. No prints. Photos on the walls. By the time she'd completed the sketch, her eyes were blurry. She lifted the drawing and compared it to the photo.

She'd drawn all the picture frames on Cheyenne's wall perfectly parallel to the floor. And yet, in the photo, one was slightly cockeyed. Riley studied it. All the other pictures were of patients, family, or locations Riley recognized. The ranch, the swimming hole.

Except one.

Settling back against the pillow, she traced the odd photo with her finger. She might be grasping at straws. Her vision blurred even more. She blinked, but it didn't clear.

Her mind had fogged. She let her eyes close. She'd rest them. For just a few minutes. Then she'd be able to think again.

◆ ◆ ◆

Thayne squinted against the morning light reflected off a silver dream catcher hanging at the entrance to Fannie's Bed and Breakfast. He waved at Hudson. His brother had guarded the B&B while Thayne had gone home to shower and change clothes. A light summer breeze caused the chimes to quiver. A melodious peal rode the wind but didn't welcome, only warned.

He hesitated before opening the door. In some ways, sunrise had come too quickly in Singing River. In others, not fast enough. He could tell his body ran on adrenaline now. His training made him capable of functioning with minimal sleep, but instinct wouldn't find Cheyenne. Thayne stroked his unshaven chin. He'd checked in on the way here. Last night had been a complete bust. No sign of his sister.

He and his father had discussed calling off the search. They'd disclosed the threat to the search teams, but almost everyone had lifted their chin, fire in their eyes. They'd appointed armed lookouts on each team. Like the investigation hadn't been challenging enough already.

Cheyenne's second night gone. At the sheriff's office, many wouldn't look him in the eye.

They believed she was dead. But they hadn't given up, either. Neither had he.

His head whispered the statistics. His heart shut down the mutterings.

Cheyenne was a fighter. She was smart.

Riley believed there was a chance, and he trusted her.

She'd pushed him away. He'd backed off for Cheyenne's sake, but when they found his sister, he and Riley were going to have a long talk. After he swept her away and kept her from thinking too much for a week, maybe two.

Thayne trudged up the wooden steps to Fannie's and opened the front door. Sunlight sliced through the open windows of the ground floor, wicked edges of brightness mocking him. Yeah, he'd have rather been nursing his third beer in a dark bar. Not because he wanted a drink, but because that would mean they'd found Cheyenne.

The cheerful décor grated. So did glancing at the door at the top of the stairs. He took them two at a time and rapped on Riley's door.

No answer.

He paused, leaning into the door. No sounds came from inside.

He lifted his fist to knock again.

"Don't you dare knock one more time, Thayne Blackwood." Fannie's southern drawl carried a threat he couldn't ignore.

This morning the curvaceous ex–beauty queen looked twenty years younger than her seventy-five years. Hair shellacked in place and a layer of makeup that had been expertly applied.

Not that he knew how she created the dewy mask. He just knew it couldn't be real.

Fannie frowned at him from the bottom of the stairs. "Get down here," she called in a stage whisper, her voice carrying to him. She wagged her finger at him. "I've got coffee on."

"Riley and I have an investigation to conduct," he said.

"She called up asking for another refill on her coffee fifteen minutes ago. She'll be down when she's ready. Leave her be." Fannie scanned him up and down with a critical eye. He squirmed when her gaze fell on his un-ironed work shirt and jeans. "You look like hell."

Knowing Fannie wouldn't leave him in peace, he tossed a resigned last look at Riley's door and made his way to the B&B's lobby. "Yeah, well, I didn't get a lot of sleep waiting for a sniper who never showed, and the searchers didn't find Cheyenne last night. Hell, they didn't find any sign of her. Six hours of stepping through search grids, arm's length apart, shining light on every inch of terrain."

"I know, hon." Fannie led him into the kitchen and lit the gas beneath a cast-iron skillet. "Sit down."

He pulled out the solid mahogany chair while she poured a cup of black coffee. Four cardboard boxes labeled CHURCH rested on the kitchen counter behind him. Stacked neatly, but the only items that didn't belong in the cozy room.

Fannie slid the mug over to him then turned back to the stove, layering strip after strip of bacon to cook.

The aroma hit him in the gut. "Gram used to cook for us kids on Saturday morning. Especially in the summer. Bacon, biscuits and gravy. All four of us scarfed them down then went out to the swimming hole."

"My recipe," Fannie said with a wistful smile over her shoulder. "Helen makes those biscuits better than I do. Said she added a secret ingredient to *improve* them. Never did tell me what it was. I'll have to ask her at church today."

Before she forgets forever.

The words went unspoken between them.

Thayne took a sip of coffee. Man, he'd have to take some of Fannie's blend back to the base with him when he returned to duty. "Gram saw who took Cheyenne."

Fannie shifted the bacon around in the pan. "Helen has more good days than bad. It might come to her."

"I wish I understood what goes on in her head." Thayne set down the cup. "If I did, maybe I could trigger the memory."

"I've seen you with her. You know how to reach her."

"Patience and time. Cheyenne doesn't have that luxury."

"Helen would do anything for her family if she could. You know that. Right now, it just isn't . . . possible."

"I know." Thayne pinched the bridge of his nose, trying to ward off the frustration building behind his eyes. "What has she said to you about her Alzheimer's? She doesn't talk about it. Neither does Pops. None of us do. Not really."

Fannie didn't speak for a moment. She adjusted the flame under the skillet and faced him. "We don't talk about it, either. What's to say? There's nothing we can do to stop it. All we can do is live with it as best we can. We've all made adjustments. I'm learning your gram's recipes. She wants them written down for you kids now that your mother's passed."

"I noticed her repeating a lot of questions when I came home for Christmas two years ago, but she was still the same Gram." Thayne stared into his coffee cup. "She's different now."

"She's changed over the last six months. Her meds aren't working as well. Helen, Norma, Willow, and I still have our book club meeting every Wednesday, but we discuss our all-time-favorite Agatha Christie novels, nothing new." She pressed down her apron. "Did you know that's how your grandmother first noticed the short-term memory loss more than five years ago? She kept having to reread sections that didn't stick with her."

"How long have you known?"

"She knew something wasn't right, but Norma knew first. Her mother and sister both had it young." Fannie sat across from him and patted his hand. "When Helen was finally diagnosed, we all had a good cry, but we'd known before then. It's an insidious disease, and we've adjusted for her, just like your family has. We spend more and more time living in the past where she's comfortable."

"Gram has good friends," Thayne said. "I never asked what she felt about what was happening. And now, I'm not sure if she understands."

"Thayne, the only thing Helen ever said to us was that she didn't want to be a burden to Lincoln and the family. She asked us to look after you all when she couldn't."

Thayne's throat thickened with emotion. "Sounds like Gram. If nothing can be done, she just pushes through."

"As we all do." Fannie's eyes gleamed with unshed tears. "Oh, enough of this. Helen would scold the both of us if she saw us getting all weepy for her." She rose and forked the bacon onto a paper towel–covered plate. "Keep asking her about that day, Thayne. Inside I know she wants to help find Cheyenne if she can. Even though she lives in the past sometimes, Helen still remembers a lot of what's going on now. Sometimes it just isn't at her fingertips when she wants it."

Fannie shoved a cinnamon roll at him and cocked her head, her eyes twinkling. "Go ahead. Made 'em fresh last night."

Thayne stared down at the roll. "You know, don't you?"

"That you pilfered one last night? That you took it up to Riley's room? Yes, young man, I know. I also heard you slam out of here not long afterward." She handed him a fork. "Eat."

Thayne stabbed the gooey roll, but he couldn't lift it to his lips. His mouth had turned to sawdust. He pushed the plate back at her. "She didn't need my help. No big deal. And I didn't slam."

Fannie snorted, in the delicate way only a southern lady can. "Poppycock. That girl gets under your skin, and I, for one, think it's a good thing. She's smart, she cares, and put the two of you in the same room and the air starts to tingle. I haven't witnessed those kind of sparks since your father chased after your mother."

"Oh no you don't, Fannie." Thayne shook his head. "I have enough trouble without becoming a project for the Gumshoe Grannies. You,

Willow, Gram, and Norma should keep to Agatha Christie and your book club."

"I didn't take you for a fool, Thayne Blackwood. Do you know how often the real thing comes along? Well, I'll tell you, once in a lifetime."

"Riley and I . . . It's complicated."

Fannie's eyes widened with utter shock. Thayne stilled, not even bothering to turn around.

"Very complicated," Riley said, her voice husky.

She stepped into the room and crossed the kitchen before pouring a cup of coffee and facing him with businesslike eyes, devoid of anger or frustration.

Or anything.

"But right now, we don't matter. The only thing that's important is finding Cheyenne."

CHAPTER ELEVEN

Bacon normally made Riley's mouth water, but she simply stood numb in the warm kitchen. She didn't even taste the coffee she sipped. Intellectually, she knew she was drinking Fannie's special blend, but the liquid sliding down her throat could have been hot water or hot chocolate.

Complicated.

The word definitely encompassed her feelings for Thayne. She wanted to let him see her heart, but something pulled her back. How could she give him what he had every right to expect—her whole heart and soul—when she knew with everything inside of herself that she needed every modicum of passion and commitment to find his sister? And her own.

Riley pasted on her professional FBI face. The expression might slip in the field on occasion—as Tom constantly reminded her—but she could keep it together. Until she found Cheyenne.

If she did.

Fannie cleared her throat and sent Thayne a you-really-put-your-mouth-in-it-this-time look.

"I guess we should be going," he said, his voice cautious.

"I'm ready." Riley set the barely touched coffee on the sink. She'd have to hope the five cups she'd downed upstairs would keep her going for a while.

"Are you headed to the church?" Fannie asked.

"Sheriff's office first. Then church." He glanced at Riley. "I thought we could check out any results on the BOLO and see if the court order came through for the medical records."

She gave him a quick nod of agreement. "I'd like to use your computer system for a few minutes."

Ignoring the quizzical quirk of his brow, she clutched the satchel of notes, sketches, and photos she'd brought along.

Fannie simply shook her head at the two of them, clicking her tongue. Finally, she pointed to the counter. "Thayne, would you take the left two boxes of goodies to the men at your office?"

"What about the others?" he asked.

"They're for the search-and-rescue headquarters in the fellowship hall at the church. I'm meeting Helen to serve food if she's up to it." Fannie took Thayne's hands in hers. "You and Riley will find your sister. I truly believe that."

He simply bent down and kissed her cheek before crossing the kitchen and lifting the two boxes. "The basket, too?" he asked.

She shook her head. "It goes on the back porch."

Thayne turned to her. "For Kade?"

"This morning, I found out he quit paying for his apartment and headed for the woods. He's having flashbacks."

Fannie's voice sounded so heartbroken, her expression so sad, Riley's heart hurt for the older woman.

"Has he gone for treatment?" Riley asked.

"Waiting list. Cheyenne did everything she could to get him in. She's been his saving grace," Fannie said. She gripped Thayne's arm. "If you see Kade, let him know he can stay with me whenever he wants. Please."

"And I'll inform the search team to keep an eye out for him," Thayne said. He grabbed his keys from his pocket. "You ready?"

"Just one thing." Riley faced Fannie. "The SUV you saw—did you notice anything strange about it?"

"Beside the tinted windows so dark you couldn't see inside?" Fannie asked, packaging up another bag of muffins and slipping them in a box. She tapped her foot. "Norma's always telling me to be more observant. That's why Miss Marple solves all those mysteries." Fannie placed her hands on her hips. "The car was clean as a whistle. I mean, waxy-shiny clean."

"Pristine," Riley commented. "Not surprising."

Fannie pulled strapping tape from a drawer and measured it the length of the box. She stopped just before she cut. "I do remember the license plate was mud-splattered. Blocked out the numbers and letters."

Riley's heartbeat sped up. "Did you see the color?"

Fannie closed her eyes tight. "Light blue or white, I guess. With dark letters." She grinned. "I remembered."

"Agatha would be proud," Riley said.

"Probably Wyoming. Maybe Nevada," Thayne said. "I can look up other possibilities when we get to the office."

Riley glanced over at Thayne. "If it's Wyoming plates, Cheyenne might not be far."

"Then go find her!" Fannie said.

Thayne paused at the door.

"Do you think anyone's watching us?" Riley asked.

"Maybe. Just keep alert."

"It's not like we can afford to hide out," Riley said.

They hurried to the SUV. Riley opened the back door for Thayne, and he slid the boxes of food inside.

"Any new information from last night?" she asked after he started down the road.

His eyes turned sober. "No sign of her. It's not fair, you know. All she's ever done is help people. The first thing I remember about my big sister was her hiding a stray cougar cub in the barn. The mother had been shot by a rancher after she'd killed a calf. The little thing should have died, but Cheyenne wouldn't let it. She nursed that cub back to health then cried for a week when the park service took it away."

Riley understood the disbelief. She'd felt it herself, but it was an easy trap to fall into, spending too much time thinking and imagining. "Were you up all night?"

"I'm used to it," he said. "How about you?"

She shrugged. "I'll sleep later." They pulled up to the sheriff's office, and Riley reached for the satchel beneath her. "I *do* need to use a computer in your office to do a little research."

"What about your laptop?"

She glanced away from him and gripped the door handle.

He grasped her arm to stop her from leaving. "What aren't you telling me?"

She was silent for a moment, gnawing on her lip. Better the truth now than when they were in the middle of a room of detectives. She twisted in her seat and lifted her chin. "I'm not sanctioned to be here. I'm on my own time."

"Vacation, you mean?"

"Not exactly." How was she supposed to tell him? She breathed in. "My boss suspended me. I can't get into the federal databases. They've locked me out." The words escaped fast and ran together.

With a stunned look, he fell back into his seat. "What happened? You're their ace. I saw the news scrolling across the television this morning when I went home to shower. The reporter may have given credit to the FBI for taking down the East Coast Serial Killer, but *I* know it was you."

"How can you be so certain?"

He lifted his hand as if to touch her, then dropped it. "Because you don't stop until you catch the bad guys. We talk every Friday. You run theories past me. And all of them were right."

She shook her head.

"Don't, Riley. I know you didn't locate the serial killer in time to save the first-grade teacher. It wasn't your fault."

She stilled. Why couldn't he shut up? She stared out the window, praying he would drop the conversation.

"Her death wasn't your fault. You know I'm right."

"But *I'm* the one who didn't see the connections fast enough." Her vision blurred, and the pain of being too late nearly doubled her over. "I couldn't save her, and God, I wanted to."

Her voice broke. Thayne let out a curse and tugged her across the seat into his arms. She pushed at him, but he pinned her against his chest and stroked her hair.

"You're the best there is, sweetheart. Sometimes we can't win. I don't like the truth, either. We're so alike, but we both have to accept reality."

"Now you sound like my boss."

Thayne leaned back and tilted her chin so he could see her eyes. "Why did he suspend you?"

She didn't like the speculation in his expression, like he was looking right through her. She gritted her teeth. "Why doesn't matter, except that it gave me time to help."

"You can tell me anything. I'll understand. We're friends."

True, but she'd come to realize she couldn't allow herself to love him. If she failed to find Cheyenne, she'd lose him anyway. Love came with conditions. She'd learned that truth the hard way in her own home.

So she said nothing and squirmed back into her seat.

Finally, he yanked open the car door. "After we find Cheyenne, you and I are going to have a long talk about what it means to be friends."

"Is our *friendship* real? Or just *complicated*?" Before he could respond to the barb, she grabbed her satchel and hurried into the sheriff's office.

For a Sunday, the place teemed with a blur of activity. The dispatcher fielded calls. A fax machine hummed; a printer churned. A uniform strode to a door labeled CONFERENCE ROOM with a map. He opened it. Three men sat, silently sifting through files. Behind them, a crime board took up an entire wall, the content similar to hers but with its own timeline and a different set of photos.

"Dad's office is over there," Thayne said with a resigned sigh.

A loud *clank* sounded at the back of the room. Just beyond an open door, a man stood in a jail cell running a metal camping cup back and forth along iron bars like a scene from an old western.

"Blackwood, get me the hell out of here, you SOB." A gray-haired man with a shadowed beard and bleary eyes shook the bars. "I ain't staying here one more day and night."

"Judge isn't in until Monday, Ed. That's tomorrow in case you lost a day." Thayne crossed his arms over his chest. "It's not my fault you decided to pull an idiot stunt on a Friday night."

"I didn't mean anything by it."

"You held Carol hostage with a knife. You threatened a deputy sheriff—me. Judge Gibson won't go easy on you. You'll do time for this one, Ed. No passes."

So, he was Carol Wallace's live-in.

Ed ran the cup across the bars again. "It ain't fair. You were a bigger screwup than me as a kid, Thayne Blackwood, and your daddy let you off."

"I may have done more than a few things I'm not proud of, Ed, but I never threatened a woman." Thayne stalked to the cell. "Give it a rest. Your blood's still about fifty-proof and at least you've got a bed here. Or are you gonna sleep on the streets? Carol kicked you out, remember."

"She'll take me back," Ed said, his voice confident. "No one else'll have her. Besides, I know what happened to her daughter, Gina. She's got no choice."

◆ ◆ ◆

A crick in Cheyenne's neck yanked her from sleep. She groaned at the ache in her belly, but at least she was a bit better. A soft snore rose from across the dark room. Bethany. Cheyenne's eyes snapped open.

Reality slapped her in the face. Not a hospital. Not by a long shot. Her prison.

Her body stiff from the nausea and vomiting, she sat up with a moan. She rubbed the sleep from her eyes and felt along the wall for the light switch.

With a flick, fluorescence illuminated the room. She had no idea if it was night or day. Not for sure. It could be eight at night or eight in the morning.

Cheyenne stumbled over to her patient.

Bethany had shoved the covers to the end of the bed. At least her face and cheeks were no longer splotchy red with the reaction to penicillin. But she was still flushed.

Cheyenne pressed the back of her hand to her patient's forehead. Damp. As were her gown and the sheets.

Bethany was burning up with fever. A result of the needless surgery.

Cheyenne had filtered through every possible cause of the illness. She dismissed the drug they'd used to knock her out. Its effects had dissipated. That meant the toxin had to be in this room, but since she'd disinfected the entire room, that left ingestion.

Cheyenne had only swallowed food and water.

Which might be why Bethany was regaining consciousness even though her fever had spiked. She hadn't eaten anything since Cheyenne had been locked with her in this room.

Light footsteps raced past the door, just outside the prison. Heavier footsteps followed, then a loud scream sliced at Cheyenne.

"Let me go! I want my mommy and daddy. Please!" a young boy cried out.

Cheyenne rose from the bed and stood against the metal door, her fists clenched, nails digging into her palms.

"They don't want you anymore, Micah." The woman's voice—Adelaide perhaps?—was calm and unemotional.

"I told you a thousand times, my name's not Micah."

"It is now."

"Leave him alone," she yelled, pounding against the cold steel.

A door slammed.

"No. Please, no," shouted Micah. "I don't want to go in there. I won't cry anymore. I promise."

Another door crashed with a clang, metal on metal. The boy's voice went completely silent.

"Oh God." She could feel the blood drain from her face.

She had no idea what they were doing to that boy, but her mind could only imagine the worst. She had to get out of here and bring help.

An iron key creaked. "Move away from the door," a familiar voice said.

Ian.

Cheyenne stepped back. The metal creaked open. Just beyond, she could see hands holding a gun.

Someone beyond that door was poisoning Bethany. And her. Who could she trust?

She'd counted down the numbers. Ian, Adelaide, Micah, Hannah, and the one they called *Father*. She had no idea if there could be others.

Ian entered the room, his face pale. "You shouldn't have yelled."

"That boy sounded so young. What's happening to him?"

"You don't understand. This is our home. The place we belong. Micah will learn."

The words were rote and unemotional.

Cheyenne touched Ian's arm. "Are you OK?"

His bloodshot eyes met her gaze, and he gave her a quick nod. "How's Bethany?"

"She has a high fever. I need antibiotics. Soon. Or she won't make it."

He walked slowly across to the bed, his movements stilted. He rested a hand on Bethany's cheek. "We can't survive without her," he said softly. "We need her."

Cheyenne placed her hand on his shoulder. He sucked in a sharp breath and shrugged away.

Oh no.

With a sick stomach, Cheyenne braced herself and tugged the neck of Ian's shirt to the side ever so gently. He didn't stop her.

A series of circular scars dotted his shoulder, most several years old. Red, angry skin peeked from just above his shoulder blade. The round burn mark had erupted in blisters. Very recent. Just below the newest injury, a series of long, thin scars crisscrossed his upper back. These marks were much older.

"Ian." Her eyes burning, Cheyenne couldn't bear to accept what this teenager had gone through—still was going through.

"It was worth it. For Bethany." He pulled away from Cheyenne's grip and faced her. "You'll have the antibiotics soon."

Steel glinted out of Ian's eyes. How could a sixteen-year-old kid show so much strength? Easily answered, of course. Ian had lost his childhood long ago.

"Can you get to Singing River? Go to my brother, Thayne. He's a deputy sheriff. He's a Navy SEAL. He can help."

Ian shook his head. "You don't understand. This is our home. The place we belong."

"I understand, Ian." Though in truth, she didn't. She had to get through to him. Bethany's chances were infinitesimal if she didn't receive antibiotics, and even then, Cheyenne could only give her a fifty-fifty shot. "You must know what's happening here is wrong. Hurting you is wrong. So is keeping Bethany locked up with me when she needs a hospital."

"We're a family. We have to stick together. If we don't—"

"Listen to me. Please. Please send my brother a message. Maybe we can save her. Together."

Ian stepped away from her and knocked on the door. "I can't do any more," he said, his voice barely a whisper. "I'm sorry."

Cheyenne's hopes fell. Ian might love Bethany, but was he afraid enough to poison their food or water? Cheyenne couldn't be sure. Until she knew who was responsible, she'd simply have to avoiding eating and drinking.

The door opened. Father stood just outside the door. Ian straightened his back. "We're a family. We stick together."

◆ ◆ ◆

The sheriff's office went silent, except for the humming of a printer. Thayne would've liked nothing more than to shut Ed up permanently. The drunk gripped the bars, a cocky grin Thayne would have gladly slapped off.

By his side, Riley stilled. She slowly faced Ed. Thayne could see the wheels turning in her mind, but something else glinted in her eyes. He only prayed it wasn't hope.

Ed rested his head between the steel bars of the jail. "I recognize you. FBI. The one searching for Carol's daughter. Well, I know what happened to her. I'll tell you if you get me out of here."

Thayne gripped Ed's shirt through the bars. "Quit flapping your gums. You have no idea." He paused. "Unless you had something to do with Gina going missing? Maybe you showed a little too much interest in Carol's daughter? Maybe things got out of hand?"

"That's sick," Ed spat. "I ain't no pervert, but I got information. 'Cause Carol talks in her sleep."

Riley clutched Thayne's arm, her nails digging hard into his flesh. He glanced over his shoulder at her face. Calm. Almost devoid of emotion, counter to her tight grip. She cloaked herself in that FBI profiler mask of hers—but her emotions ran deep.

"I'm always interested in information, Mr.—"

"Zalinksy. But you can call me Ed."

Thayne grunted at the pathetic attempt to charm her even as Riley smiled at the bastard. He released Ed. "Have it your way. But he's a perpetual liar."

Riley tilted her head as if studying Ed. "It may be because I'm an outsider." She shot Thayne a pointed look. "But I get the feeling you're in the know about pretty much everything that goes down in this town, Mr. Zalinksy."

"Oh yeah. Lived here all my life. I know all the secrets, including quite a few about the *good* deputy here. Some secrets hide in plain sight. Some are forgotten. But I got them all right up here." He tapped his head. "Lots of folks talk too much in the bar. And I can hold my liquor. I remember."

"I'm sure you do." She smiled at him.

Damn, Riley was playing Ed like a Stradivarius. She really was something.

Thayne leaned against the wall to observe the show. To Ed, Thayne would appear relaxed, but he could intervene in seconds if the guy tried to hurt Riley.

"What do you think happened to Carol's daughter?" Riley asked, taking out a thick red notebook from her satchel.

"It was that drifter who got her pregnant." Ed smirked at Thayne. "And that's all you're getting from me unless you let me out of this cage." He sauntered to the back of the cell, slumped onto his cot, and turned his back to them.

"You're looking at aggravated assault, Ed. You aren't going anywhere."

Ed glanced over his shoulder. "Carol needs me. She won't testify."

"I will," Thayne said.

"No one got hurt." He shrugged. "I was a little drunk. And I got an in with the mayor. I'll get probation if anything. Might as well let me out now."

"We've got a hell of a lot more important things to do today than dance to your tune, Ed. Forget it."

Thayne clasped Riley's uninjured arm and led her into the main office. He closed the door leading to the jail cells behind him. "He just wants out."

She nodded but didn't take her gaze off the door.

"Maybe," she said, her voice pensive. "Did your father talk to Ed when Carol's daughter went missing?"

"Of course. He was a suspect for a while, but Dad cleared him. Had a solid alibi from Deputy Pendergrass. The guy was in jail when she was taken, and he denied knowing anything."

"So part of his story could be true," Riley said.

"I wouldn't hold my breath."

Riley gripped Thayne's arm. "It's the first potential lead on my sister's disappearance I've had in more than a year, Thayne."

He couldn't look away from her tortured eyes. She'd visited Singing River for the first time because she had a crazy theory that her sister and Carol's daughter were linked. Thayne's father had been skeptical, but he'd agreed to meet because Gina's disappearance still gnawed at his gut. Otherwise he wouldn't have kept running the print they'd found at the scene through the Feds' Integrated AFIS database.

The conference room door opened, and Pendergrass motioned to them.

"Let him stew for another day," Thayne said. "He might talk. If he really knows anything."

"I agree. He's too cocky to trust right now," Riley said under her breath, walking with Thayne to the conference room. "What do you think he's got on the mayor, though?"

Thayne raised a brow, and his lip quirked. "I was wondering the same thing."

Deputy Pendergrass motioned them to have a seat.

"You have something?" Thayne pulled out a chair for Riley.

She shot him a surprised look, and he shrugged. Gram's etiquette lessons couldn't be unlearned, even by ten years in the Navy.

"An update on the blood evidence." Underhill took the lead from Pendergrass, shoving a couple of papers across the table to them. "Like we suspected, the blood type on the floor matches Cheyenne's, A-positive. Your grandmother's blood was found on and near the wall. She's O-positive. Another match. We expect DNA to confirm—"

"Not news," Thayne interrupted.

"Well, the last sample gave us quite a surprise, since the place had been wiped so clean we didn't expect to catch a break. We almost missed a small smear on the edge of the waiting room desk. It isn't your grandmother's or sister's, Deputy Blackwood."

"Could it belong to a patient?" Thayne asked.

"We checked the books. The blood was AB-negative. Very rare. No one with that type has come into the clinic for days."

Thayne leaned forward. "Do you have a big enough sample to test for DNA?"

Underhill nodded. "We're running it now. We'll let you know if the CODIS software gets a hit against the military database or the National DNA Index System."

The conference room door slammed open.

"Thayne!" The dispatcher raced inside. "Just got a call from the search party. They found something."

CHAPTER TWELVE

If Riley ever wanted to disappear, this isolated spot in the Wind River mountain range would be a good starting point.

She and Thayne hadn't received much detail prior to leaving the sheriff's office. Only that the search-and-rescue team had discovered evidence of Cheyenne near the National Forest. Since then they'd been out of communication. Cell reception in these mountains was spotty at best.

They'd not only left the paved road for a dirt one, they'd abandoned their vehicle at the base of this mountain. Of course Thayne trudged through the terrain like he was half mountain goat; Riley slapped away a pine branch, her legs and lungs burning in the high altitude.

The dirt trail narrowed, the pines creating a tunnel of evergreen, blocking out the morning sun. The air was nippy, even in August. Riley ducked beneath a tree, and by the time voices filtered through the trees, the so-called path beneath her feet had disappeared below the ground cover.

"I can hardly see the sun to get my bearings," she muttered.

Thayne glanced over his shoulder but didn't stop moving. "Which makes these woods especially dangerous. My brothers and I got lost over the next ridge when I was about thirteen," Thayne said. "Took Pops and Dad a day to find us, and we *wanted* to be found."

"Easy to get lost," Riley said quietly.

"Easy to disappear." Thayne broke through the forest into a clearing, and suddenly the loneliest stretch of wilderness in the world turned into a search-and-rescue convention.

A half-dozen volunteers stood at the perimeter. With the open sky above, the mountain range loomed to the east, and Riley caught a glimpse of Gannett Peak. She'd read it rose to thirteen thousand feet. One thing about Wyoming, everything in the vastness of the land appeared closer than it actually was.

"Ironcloud," Thayne shouted.

The deputy raised his hand in greeting but didn't move. He'd planted himself next to a couple of yellow flags.

"At least they're protecting the evidence," Riley said, hurrying across the grass.

She sighted a woman's purse at the same time Thayne stilled. Strewn beside the bag were a tube of lipstick, a small photo album, and a brush.

"Cheyenne's?" Riley sent Thayne a sidelong glance.

He nodded, clearing his throat before kneeling next to the items. Riley snapped a series of photos before tugging on a pair of gloves. She crouched beside the purse and reached out her hand.

"You're supposed to wait for DCI," Ironcloud said. "Underhill *ordered* us not to disturb the scene."

His tone communicated what his words didn't. Deputy Ironcloud had the same opinion of Underhill she had.

Judiciously, she picked up the purse. "I'll speak to him. I took photos, but we need to know what's inside and hopefully what's missing."

"We're running out of time, Michael," Thayne said to the deputy. "I couldn't care less about protocol at this point if Riley gives the OK."

Michael Ironcloud raised his hands. "Not going to argue. Underhill's a pompous windbag."

Riley unclasped the purse and opened it, fingering through the items as carefully as possible. "Her wallet is still here, ID, business cards, cash, credit cards. Car keys, spray perfume. Definitely not a robbery, and they obviously didn't care if we identified her things."

Because they don't plan on us ever finding her.

She didn't want to look at Thayne, but she chanced a brief glance. His lips had tightened, and his eyes held a haunted truth. He understood the implications, and she didn't have to say a word. She placed her hand on his arm. "They took her for a reason, Thayne. I still believe they wanted her specifically. And they wanted her alive."

He gave her a quick duck of his head, but she didn't know if he believed her. Not surprising, since with every hour that passed, Riley couldn't stop the pessimism from bubbling in her gut.

"Why would they bring her out this far?" Thayne asked. "There's nothing nearby but a few long-abandoned mining shafts."

"To disappear," Ironcloud said, stepping forward. "Truth is, we'd never have searched here if the sheriff hadn't ordered us to expand the grid another couple of miles in each direction."

"Good call." Riley replaced the purse exactly as she'd found it. "The bag hasn't been here long, not since yesterday. Otherwise the animals would have scavenged it."

"Thayne!" Jackson's shout carried from behind the tree line. He barreled through the branches, breathing hard and fast. "I found a footprint."

Thayne took off running, and Riley sprinted right behind him. A few hundred yards through the thick pines, Jackson skidded to a stop. He pointed at an indentation in the earth barely visible through the ground cover.

She had no idea how he'd even seen it. She stood back, knowing they'd surpassed her area of expertise.

Kneeling beside the track, Thayne studied the print. "Combat boots. Guy weighs at least two twenty." He motioned to Riley. "Do you have a photo of the track Dad and I found at the phone's dump site?"

She slipped an image from her satchel, and Thayne took it, placing the photo beside the boot print.

Even Riley could see the large gash in the tread. "A match," he said with a grim smile. "Gotcha."

Jackson strode about a dozen feet along the prints. "From his stride, he's at least six feet two."

"He didn't camouflage the tracks?" Thayne followed his brother's path. "There's only one set of prints." He didn't disguise his disappointment.

Riley could tell from the tone of his voice, the realization worried him. "If we go with our assumption there are three perps, what about the others who took Cheyenne? Did they split up? And where is she?"

"He's not carrying her," Thayne said. "Not enough depth to the tracks."

"Maybe there's a rendezvous point up there." Jackson stared into the distance. "The bastard could lead us to her."

"How do we find him in this thick vegetation?" Riley asked.

"If he's moving line of sight, he's headed toward the caves," Thayne said. "They'd be a good place to hide someone."

For the first time since Thayne had picked her up this morning from the B&B, a flash of hope sparked in his eyes. Her heart thudded a bit faster. Maybe . . . just maybe they'd caught a break. And a mistake.

"That's a gigantic *if*, bro." Jackson narrowed his gaze. "Why wouldn't the kidnapper switch course, lead us in the wrong direction? He's been ultracareful until now."

"Maybe he's in a hurry?" she said.

"Or he could be setting a trap." Thayne stared into the distance.

"How far are the caves you mentioned?" Riley took a swig of water from the canteen Thayne had thrust into her hands when they'd abandoned their car.

"At the base of the ridge," Thayne said, pointing toward a rocky hill. "Every year the local Boy Scout troops camp out here. They hike in to search for arrowheads and silver nuggets. Sometimes Wyoming jade will pop up."

"And you know this because the Blackwood brothers were all Eagle Scouts, I'll bet."

"Hudson and Jackson were. Me, not so much." Thayne picked his way over the rocks.

Jackson grinned. "What my brother is trying to say is that he kept Hudson and me from getting into too much trouble. He distracted our parents on a regular basis. Made us seem tame and well behaved."

Thayne ignored Jackson's obvious attempt to lighten the tense mood and looked at her over his shoulder, a frown furrowing his brow. "All the roads were built in the fifties and are long grown over. If he's up there, he's familiar with these mountains."

The implication of his words stopped Riley cold, but she had to be sure. "You don't get any mountain climbers or hikers?"

While Thayne zigzagged across the landscape, his brother faced her. "Not around here. Most visitors start at the base of Fremont Lake and climb in the National Forest. We're on private property now. The Riverton family owns most of the land as far as you can see."

A low whistle escaped her. "So we're in the middle of nowhere, and kids from Singing River have been coming here for years. Is there a more out-of-the-way place he could hide?"

One look at Thayne's profile, the hard set of his jaw, the fury spitting from his eyes, and a harsh foreboding returned to Riley.

Thayne met his brother's gaze. "The big cave?"

"Good idea," Jackson said. "It's barely visible, well hidden, and very few people know about it."

"How many people?"

"I could count them on one hand," Thayne bit out through clenched teeth.

"But you have someone in mind," Riley said, more certain now than ever.

He pinched the bridge of his nose. "Maybe. But it doesn't make sense. Kade wouldn't take Cheyenne. We grew up together."

"Fannie's nephew? The one Cheyenne's been helping?"

Thayne nodded. "And he knows the land."

"Your grandmother mentioned a boyfriend. Are Cheyenne and Kade dating?" This fit in with the second scenario Riley had considered. A relationship with Cheyenne explained a lot. Including the reason Helen was still alive and the perfect timing of the abduction.

Thayne met his brother's gaze. "If you'd have asked me yesterday, I would have said no, but now I don't know."

"If Kade took Cheyenne, will he let her go easily?"

"*If* he's kidnapped her and hurt Gram, then he's out of his head." Thayne looked over to her, and the lethal expression on his face made her shudder. "He's deadly."

A loud hoot sounded to the west. Riley jumped, and Thayne turned to the half-dozen searchers milling around behind them.

"Jackson and I will follow these tracks," he said, his voice raised. "Deputy Ironcloud will wait with you until we determine if it's safe."

A grumble hummed through the circle.

"I'm warning every one of you, I catch any civilians without a sheriff's escort and I'll toss you in jail and forget about you until we find my sister."

The men went silent, and Riley lowered her head so they wouldn't see her slight smile. Thayne knew his town.

He nodded to Ironcloud, and the deputy met up with them. "Don't tell my father about what we've found," Thayne said. "I don't want to get his hopes up." He unholstered his Glock. "And keep these guys from tramping all over the woods. We don't know what we're up against."

Ironcloud nodded and moved away to corral the onlookers.

Thayne turned to Riley. Before he could open his mouth, she shook her head and pulled her weapon. "Don't even think about it. I have the training, and you need backup."

Despite the flash of irritation in his eyes, he gave her a sharp nod. "Then keep us in sight at all times."

Thayne sidestepped the tracks and headed for the woods. After about ten feet, he stopped. "The guy's injured. His gait is uneven. He's putting more pressure on his right leg."

"Maybe that's why he needed a doctor," Riley offered.

"If he's up and walking now, though . . ." Jackson's voice grew thick.

No one finished the thought. If the kidnapper didn't have use for Cheyenne, he might have gotten rid of her already. They could be looking at recovering their sister's body at the end of the trail.

For a half hour, they pushed through the wildest terrain Riley had ever seen. No trails, no signs of civilization.

Thayne moved in complete silence. Even Jackson stepped on cracked branches here and there.

"Like a ghost," she muttered under her breath.

"Did you say something?" Thayne asked.

She flushed. "No."

Jackson sidled up to her with a conspiratorial wink. "Now you know how he snuck out every weekend during high school."

"I assumed he learned the skill during SEAL training."

"Nah, he was born sneaky. And invisible."

They trudged a few more minutes, passing a grove of aspen. The leaves quivered, creating a melodic tune within the forest. Riley's muscles shook, though she refused to ask them to take a break. If they could keep going, so could she.

Suddenly Thayne halted and held out an arm to block Jackson. He didn't speak but raised his hand and motioned for them to stop. He knelt down and ran his finger along the ground cover. Within seconds, he revealed a thin wire.

Booby trap, he mouthed.

They backed up the way they'd come. Thayne leaned in to Jackson. "Get to Ironcloud. Have him contact any other search parties in the area. Warn them to stay put." He turned to Riley. "You should go with him."

"You need backup."

She could almost hear the growl rumbling in his throat.

"I'll go as fast as I can," Jackson said. "Don't shoot me when I come back. And bro, don't get dead."

With a quick glance back, Jackson disappeared the way they'd come, moving fast.

"Walk precisely where I walk," Thayne hissed. "Man, I wish I had a green laser or even some Silly String."

She must have misheard him. "What?"

"Silly String is great for detection. It falls to the ground unless there's a trip wire."

Hopefully she'd never need to use that bit of information. She mirrored his footsteps. He carefully followed the thin metal to an old dynamite charge.

After a few moments studying the explosive, he pulled a utility knife from his vest pocket and snipped the wire.

"I'll send some guys out to handle it. The dynamite looks a half century old. If there's a crate of explosives up there, it could be unstable depending on how much the nitroglycerine sweated."

He stood with catlike intensity, but didn't move. Riley waited, unsure of what he saw or heard.

"I'd send you back if I could, but I can't chance it. Stay right with me, Riley. If I say run, you don't hesitate, just do it. You got me?"

Even if she'd wanted to salute Thayne at that moment, the deadly determination in his gaze would have stopped her.

Thayne picked his way through the woods, stopping regularly, silent, still, and waiting. Following exactly in his footsteps, pausing when he paused, Riley couldn't see or hear anything but a few birds and the skittering of what she assumed were animals.

Slowly, painfully, they moved forward toward the caves. With each step, each time she placed her foot on the ground where Thayne had hiked, her gut knotted.

When a natural fork appeared in the woods, he paused momentarily. The right appeared to be easier, more traveled terrain. Of course Thayne didn't hesitate. He headed left.

"You're sure?" she asked under her breath. "The other path looks to be more recently traveled."

"A single mine shaft is dug into the side of the mountain about five hundred yards from here. It's older than the rest. It didn't pan out. They moved up about a half mile and hit it big. If it were me, I'd go with the road less traveled. And this guy thinks like me."

Good enough for her. She gripped her weapon tighter, every sense on high alert.

Leaves shuffled to her right. She whirled around. A rabbit pounded across the path and streaked back into the forest. She let out a small sigh.

Over the next quarter mile, Thayne dismantled three more traps. If anyone else had come along, they could've been killed.

A few more feet and she could just make out a vertical rock face at least fifty feet above them. Thayne stopped, freezing, still as stone.

A blur of camouflage rushed into the cave.

A muffled explosion rumbled. An avalanche of rocks bombarded down. Thayne jumped back and threw Riley to the ground. He landed on top of her, letting out a grunt as rocks pummeled his back.

When it was over, a layer of dust covered them and Thayne's body covered hers. "You OK?" he whispered in her ear.

She coughed then nodded, blinking the dirt from her eyes. She looked over her shoulder. Her breath caught. "Thayne," she choked out.

A man dressed in woodland fatigues stood, his face streaked with camouflage paint, his black hair pulled back from his face in a queue. He carried an M4 carbine aimed at Thayne's back.

His eyes shifted from wide with fright to cold with purpose.

"Password!" their attacker shouted, digging the barrel of the gun into the back of Thayne's neck.

He lifted his hands. "Crimson," he said, his voice too calm.

Immediately the automatic weapon pulled away. Thayne rolled over but kept his body between Riley and their assailant.

The man's eyes were glazed, and Riley recognized the look. He was in a war zone, and they'd stumbled into the middle of his nightmare.

The man blinked. "Thayne? What are you doing here? You're supposed to be in Kandahar."

"New assignment," Thayne said. "Top secret, Kade."

"Who's she?" he hissed, nodding at Riley.

"CIA," Thayne lied without missing a beat. "Undercover."

"Damn spooks, always doing a deal that gets us killed," Kade muttered. He squatted down. "At least a half-dozen enemy swarming the woods. And they're not alone. I've seen more."

Thayne carefully stood. "Kade, what's your mission?"

"Get the team home," he said. "Strategic objectives have been compromised. They have hostages. It's a no-win."

A branch cracked to Riley's right. Kade whirled around, spraying the forest with gunfire.

Riley hit the dirt.

"What the hell?" Jackson's voice shouted in the distance.

"At ease, Kade," Thayne ordered. "We've got friendlies out there, too."

Kade's face went white. "Oh God." His weapon dropped to the ground. His entire body started shaking. "They're dead. They're all dead."

He whirled around and raced into the woods, favoring one leg and disappearing from sight.

Singing River had just become way too much like Kandahar. Thayne let out a slow whistle under his breath, the echo of gunfire still ringing in his ears. His gaze narrowed on the quivering leaves at the edge of the clearing behind Kade's disappearing figure just in case the man returned. He couldn't be trusted, not in that state.

Thayne could feel the tension thrumming through every nerve in his body, the fight-or-flight response he'd honed over years of training. He placed his hand on Riley's shoulder. "You OK?"

She shifted, facing him, her eyes wide, but she nodded. "Just had the wind knocked out of me."

"Sorry about that." He held out his hand and helped her to her feet.

"Better than being squished by a ton of boulders."

A stream of curses peppered the air from a few feet away. Thayne rushed to the edge of the clearing. "Jackson? You still breathing?" he shouted.

"Damn, that was close." His brother walked out from behind a large evergreen, dusting the twigs and pine needles from the front of his shirt and jeans. "You can keep your special ops work, bro. Give me a fire anytime."

Thayne grabbed his brother in a hard hug. Over Jackson's shoulder, Thayne winced at the damage the bullets had inflicted on the tree trunk. His brother could have been killed. He gripped him tighter.

"Let me go. I might think you care." Jackson quirked a grin at Thayne, but his eyes betrayed his relief.

Thayne could tell the attack had shaken his brother, and he wasn't the only one. "You scared the hell out of me. Don't do it again."

"Yeah, Dad'd skin you alive if anything happened to me." Jackson shrugged, the kind of shrug Thayne used when he'd come an inch from meeting his Maker.

Sometimes you had to say a prayer of thanks today wasn't your day to die.

"Dad gave you hell for getting me into trouble when we were kids," Jackson added. "If I were a different kind of brother, I might consider using this little fiasco against you. For the next ten, fifteen years, I'm thinking."

Thayne slapped Jackson's back. "I've got a blackmail moment or two, don't forget."

Now that Thayne knew his brother was safe, he glanced over his shoulder. Riley hadn't said a word. She had the strangest expression on her very pale face. He walked over to her. "You OK?"

"Of course. I've been in the line of fire before."

Something wasn't right with her, but he couldn't stay to figure her out.

"Don't remind me." He sent a pointed look at her right arm. "Somewhere inside Kade may know about Cheyenne. I have to go after him. I might have tugged him out of his flashback, but he could fall right back into it. Someone could get hurt." He turned to his brother. "Jackson, take Riley back to the base clearing. I'll be in touch." Thayne didn't need her as a distraction. God knows she was one.

Riley opened her mouth, and he placed a quick but firm kiss on her lips. Her eyes widened with shock. "Just in case." He leaned forward, his lips next to her ear. "For the record, I lied to Fannie. There's nothing complicated about what I feel for you. I just didn't want her to know exactly how much you've gotten under my skin."

He straightened, and not giving her time to respond, took off in a run following in Kade's direction. He trusted Jackson to keep her safe so he could focus on finding Kade, rescuing Cheyenne, and getting all of them out alive.

He still couldn't believe Kade would do this. Thayne had to keep reminding himself Kade's third tour had been the stuff of nightmares. Thayne's unit had cleaned up the aftermath of one mission gone horribly wrong. They'd discovered Kade near death, pinned below two dead teammates.

He'd been the only survivor of an ambush caused by bad intel.

Thayne didn't know what had happened in the firefight; the report had remained classified, need-to-know, but he could imagine.

Legs pumping, pushing him through the woods, Thayne followed the trail Kade left behind. An easy-to-follow path. That alone telegraphed to Thayne his friend wasn't himself. If Kade had wanted to hide in these woods, he could vanish and survive for years without being seen or heard from again.

The signs led Thayne around a bend. He stopped at a thick grove of aspens. A broken branch halfway down one of the trees grabbed his attention. He pushed it aside, revealing a crevice just large enough to squeeze through.

He'd thought he'd explored every inch of these woods, but he could see how he'd missed the narrow opening.

Kade's boots had left an impression in the ground cover. Thayne was close, but sneaking up on the panicked ranger wouldn't work. Thayne could end up shot. Whatever mental state Kade was in, he was a dead-on marksman.

Slowly, deliberately, Thayne eased through the tight crevice. Rocks scraped against his back. He tilted his head to maximize his view. No sign of a camp, any collaborators, or Cheyenne, though. Where was she?

A single shot exploded from a weapon, slamming against the rock a few feet above Thayne's head.

"Stay away!" Kade's voice choked. "I have to find her. I don't want to kill anymore, but I have to save her."

Thayne'd already be dead if Kade had really wanted to hit his target.

"It's Thayne." His entire body tense and ready to drop to the ground, he moved into the open. "What's going on, bud?"

His friend lowered the barrel slightly, but his wild eyes made Thayne pause. What did Kade see? Was he in that last firefight from hell?

"They're all around us. How'd you get through?" Kade aimed directly at Thayne's head. "You're one of them! You betrayed us."

Kade's body shook with fear, his finger trigger-light. Thayne had one chance.

"I was sent in to extract you," he lied—well, maybe not quite a lie, just a partial truth. "We need the intel to save the guys on the south ridge."

Kade blinked once, then again. "Intel."

"Where's your base?"

"This way."

Standing, he led Thayne across the dried streambed to a small campsite. A doused fire, a sleeping bag, some food from Fannie's.

Out of the corner of his eye, he noted a haphazard pile of items. Lip balm, a plastic bag with Earl Gray tea, Cheyenne's favorite. And a sewing kit he recognized.

A chill settled at the base of his skull. "Where'd you commandeer the supplies, Kade?"

"Found 'em," he said, his gaze blank.

Thayne straightened to attention. "Time and location, soldier."

"Twenty fifteen. About thirty clicks due west of here. On the side of the road."

"Was there a cell phone?" Thayne dreaded the answer he knew would come.

"Affirmative. Too risky to confiscate. They could use it to track me."

"Kade, it's very important. Can you identify the vehicle?"

"2014 Escalade. Nevada plates. Whiskey Hotel X-Ray 0501. Someone tossed a purse from the backseat."

"Did you recognize anyone?"

"Tinted windows," Kade said. "I couldn't see who was driving. A man threw out the purse and phone. Then a woman tossed something before they drove off."

Damn. Thayne closed his eyes, both disappointed and relieved that his childhood friend wasn't responsible for Cheyenne's disappearance. He was a witness.

Based on the timeline, a couple of hours after she'd been abducted, Cheyenne's kidnappers had dumped her purse and phone.

Too long ago. Careful to keep Kade in his sights, Thayne put on a pair of gloves and scooped up the items. He opened the compact. Just a mirror. "Is this everything?" he asked.

Kade shook his head. He slipped his hand into his vest pocket. Thayne tensed, tightening the grip on his Glock, until Kade pulled out a necklace. The thin gold chain was broken. A carved amulet hung down, the largest piece of Wyoming jade Thayne had ever seen. "*She* threw it."

Cheyenne? Slowly, Thayne approached Kade, still cautious. "Cheyenne's missing, Kade. My sister, Cheyenne. I think you might have seen whoever abducted her."

Kade frowned, his brow furrowed in confusion. His hands started shaking; his face dripped with sweat.

Thayne took another step toward Kade. Then another. "We're heading back to town, Kade. Hand over your weapon."

Suddenly a golden eagle swooped low, its squawk erupting above them. Twenty feet away, the sharp talons struck a rabbit and carried off its prey.

Kade whirled around, weapon aimed. He fired. Before Thayne could disarm him, Kade knelt down and took aim right at Thayne.

"You're one of them!"

CHAPTER THIRTEEN

A burst of shots pierced the air north of the clearing. Riley froze, as did the other men waiting, their low mutterings gone silent.

Thayne.

She stalked to the line of trees at the edge of the grass and peered into the forest as if she could see anything through the thick grove. Above, an eagle cawed, flying overhead.

Jackson crossed to her and clasped her arm. "You're not going out there."

She winced when he squeezed her right arm and pulled away. "You heard the gunfire. What if Thayne needs help?"

"Kade might have an elite set of skills, but Thayne is better. I trust my brother."

Riley recognized the worry in Jackson's eyes, though. "I saw Thayne's face. He wants to talk Kade down. It won't be an even playing field." She unholstered her weapon. "We've waited long enough. I'm going in."

Jackson didn't hesitate. He rooted himself between her and the forest. "If Thayne finds out I let you out of my sight, I'll never hear the end of it. Hell, even if he's dead, he'll probably haunt me."

Another dozen rounds blanketed the sky.

Riley planted her feet. "He needs backup. Are you going to let your brother stay out there alone, with no help?"

The muscle in Jackson's jaw throbbed, the reaction so similar to Thayne's it made Riley's heart hurt.

"Thayne wants you safe. Trust him. He knows what he's doing."

Scrubbing her face with her hands, she couldn't stand still, and Jackson shadowed her step by step, clearly not expecting her to stay put.

Her heart raced, her entire body tensed with worry. He had to come back. She couldn't imagine her days without being able to talk to him, without his smile, his touch. His presence.

Oh God. Did she love him, in spite of herself? Had her heart won over her head?

A half hour later, Riley once again peered through the gaps in the pines. Still no movement. She refused to wait any longer. She turned on Jackson. "I did it your way. I'm done waiting. Don't try to stop me."

"My brother knows better than that," Thayne's voice called out from behind.

Riley whirled around. Carrying several weapons, he strode into the clearing with Kade at his side.

Before Riley could throw herself into his arms, Deputy Ironcloud sprinted across the clearing. "On the ground. You're under arrest."

"Stand down, Deputy," Thayne said.

"You can't let him go. He could've killed you and your brother. And what about Cheyenne?"

"Kade didn't take her, but he got the license plate of who did." Thayne turned to his friend and held up his handcuffs. "I'm sorry. These are for everyone's safety."

Kade's eyes had cleared from when Riley had seen him last.

"What'd I do?" he asked, his voice barely above a whisper, his expression devastated.

"Almost killed Jackson and me," Thayne said, voice matter-of-fact.

"What the hell were you doing up here, Kade?" Jackson asked. "Why didn't you come to us for help?"

Kade's hands shook. "I can't take town. Too many noises. Too many old trucks backfiring. Sends me spiraling. I needed to be alone." He lifted his wrists. "God, I'm sorry."

Thayne snapped on the metal cuffs and placed his hand on Kade's shoulder. "Did you take any shots late last night by Fannie's B and B?"

Kade's brow wrinkled. "I've been on a mission since I found the supplies. I warned the enemy not to look for me, but they didn't listen."

"Did you have backup?" Thayne asked.

Kade nodded. "I delivered the note, but my contact kept the enemy from attacking."

Thayne closed his eyes. "We'll get you help."

"Kade threatened us?" Riley asked.

"Not us, the enemy. But the shooter's still out there. They used his illness." Thayne scowled. "Bastards."

She paused for a split second then walked over and punched him in the arm. "You left before I could say good-bye. Don't do it again." She reached up and brought his head down to hers, kissing him with all the fear and terror she'd lived through the past hour before shoving him away.

He didn't let her. "I told you I'd be back." He clasped her against his body with one arm.

A few catcalls sounded behind them, but Riley was past caring what anyone else thought. He could have died because of his hero complex to do the right thing and help a comrade in need.

He pressed her close, and warmth seeped into her side. How could she live without this? How had she lasted a year?

Thayne motioned to Jackson. "Call Hudson. Locate the nearest facility that treats PTSD. In the meantime, he can take Kade to

Fannie's." Thayne lowered his voice to a whisper. "Let Hudson know Kade's unpredictable. He'll need to be ready for anything."

"You got it."

Jackson steered Kade toward the edge of the clearing.

"Will Fannie be able to handle Kade?" Riley asked as, with apprehensive eyes, she watched Thayne's brother escort the soldier to the edge of the clearing.

"Her late husband battled PTSD, though they referred to it as shell shock back then. Fannie understands what Kade's up against."

Before they disappeared from the clearing, Kade planted his feet in the dirt, forcing Jackson to halt.

Riley tensed, but Jackson had a firm hold on Kade, and the soldier didn't try to escape. He simply turned to Thayne. "You need to know that after the purse and phone were tossed out of the SUV, they headed into the National Forest, not back to the highway." Kade cleared his throat. "I'm sorry, Thayne. If I'd realized Cheyenne was in that car, I would've done anything to save her. She's been there for me."

"I know." Thayne clasped Riley closer. "Not only did Kade give us a license plate, we have this." Thayne pulled an evidence bag from his pocket, containing a gold necklace with a carved stone amulet. "Jackson. Hold up."

His brother paused, and Thayne jogged over to him. "Do you recognize the necklace Kade found?"

His brother shook his head. "I've never seen it before. Sorry."

Thayne frowned at the jewelry. "Thanks anyway."

He returned to Riley with a sigh of disappointment.

"Whose is it?" she asked.

He shrugged. "I'd hoped Jackson knew. All Kade could tell me was a woman threw it from the SUV. I'd hoped it was my sister's, but I've never seen it before, either."

The piece looked expensive. Riley filed through what she knew of Cheyenne. She couldn't see the woman she'd studied buying herself expensive baubles.

"A gift, maybe?" she posed.

"Or she tore it off one of the kidnappers."

"Wouldn't they have stopped and searched for the necklace, Thayne? Especially if it could be used to identify one of them."

A shout on the other side of the clearing prevented Thayne from answering. Sheriff Blackwood stalked over to them, his face red with exertion—and anger. "We're having a serious conversation soon, Son, about keeping your little exploration from me. Until then, I want a sitrep. Now," he demanded.

His eyes flashed with a fury Riley recognized. Thayne had inherited that slow-burning temper from his father.

"Don't leave anything out. So help me," he ordered.

After walking his father through Kade's story and trying to calm down the sheriff—and not succeeding very well—Thayne handed him the necklace. "Do *you* recognize it?"

The sheriff let out a long whistle. "The stone alone's worth a small fortune because of its size and since all the naturally occurring Wyoming jade has been mined. Cheyenne would *never* have spent that kind of money on herself . . . not on jewelry. The clinic, maybe, but not a luxury."

Just as Riley had suspected. "Could someone have given it to her? Someone she's dating, maybe?"

"Cheyenne keeps her personal life . . . very quiet," he admitted. "I've never seen the necklace. You might ask . . ." He paused. "I almost suggested my mother. Cheyenne would've told her."

Except Helen Blackwood wasn't in any position to provide information. Frustration laced the sheriff's eyes, and Riley could understand. So many questions that only one woman could answer . . . except she wasn't able.

"What about Hudson? Thayne said he and Cheyenne are close."

"The last thing my daughter would do would be to mention her love life to *any* of the boys," Thayne's father said. "They'd either threaten the guy or tease her unmercifully."

Riley chewed on her lip. "Sheriff, there are two options: This necklace belongs either to one of the kidnappers or to Cheyenne. It's got an eighteen-karat-gold chain, a diamond clasp, and a unique carving. If it's one of a kind, we can trace the original owner." She paused. "Is there anyone else who might know if the necklace belongs to Cheyenne?"

Thayne and his father met each other's gaze.

"You've thought of someone?" she asked.

Thayne nodded. "Gram's book club, the Gumshoe Grannies. They know everything. We need to talk to Fannie."

◆ ◆ ◆

Coming down off the ridge could be much more treacherous than climbing up. Thayne had learned the dangers the hard way as a teenager when he'd raced his brothers to the base of the trail and come inches from catapulting over a two-hundred-foot drop. Only concern for Riley kept him from giving in to the urge to race down the hill at breakneck speed.

Cheyenne's life was at stake, and for the first time, they were looking at two solid leads.

By the time they made it back to the vehicle, the sun hung high in the sky. "It's Sunday. They'll be at the church," Thayne said as he slipped behind the wheel. "At least DCI came through with a dozen satellite phones so we can communicate up here."

He put out an APB on the license plate Kade had provided and waited for Riley to buckle up. She'd been a real trooper, but she was out of her element. He shoved the canteen at her. "Keep hydrating. It'll help with any altitude sickness, since you're based so close to sea level."

He squeezed her hand, then flipped on the siren and drove as fast as he dared through the mountains until he hit the outskirts of Singing River.

When they arrived at the church, the parking lot overflowed with vehicles. Thayne pulled up near the makeshift tents serving as search-and-rescue headquarters and a refreshment stand. Everyone stopped and stared, their faces rapt with a combination of fear and expectation.

He jumped out and slammed the door, the sound reverberating through the air. "Nothing yet," he announced to the crowd.

A bevy of groans waved through the volunteers. He could relate. He felt the same way. Bone tired and gut sick with disappointment.

At least Riley was by his side. She slipped her hand into his and squeezed, almost as if she'd read his mind. He needed her strength right now; he didn't want to admit the truth, but he'd let his hopes rise too high.

Now the adrenaline had worn off, and his body risked crashing.

Thayne walked over to the deputy manning the S&R headquarters. "Any news?"

The guy shook his head. "We ran the license plate. A white SUV was reported stolen from Marbleton two days ago."

"They switched the plates to the black SUV," Riley said.

"Another dead end." Thayne rounded on the deputy. "Coordinate with the Marbleton police. See if they have any leads that connect to Singing River or Cheyenne."

The deputy snagged his radio and reported in.

"Nothing's going to come of it," Thayne said under his breath, scanning the sea of volunteers.

"Probably not," Riley agreed.

At least she didn't lie to him. The disappointments kept hitting, and time kept ticking.

"We still have the necklace." She walked step for step with Thayne.

They crossed the asphalt to a table where Fannie and the other Gumshoe Grannies served coffee and food for exhausted townspeople pouring in from the surrounding woods for lunch. He could tell from the pitying looks they'd lost hope.

Well, he couldn't.

He waited while the last of the searchers had collected a good meal and trudged inside the church to eat. He wanted to speak to Gram's friends alone.

"Can I have a moment of your time, ladies?"

Fannie placed her hands on her hips and looked him up and down. "If you'll eat while we talk. You both look like you could keel over at any moment.

"Norma, get them a couple of chairs and some food," Fannie ordered. "Willow, lots of coffee."

Thayne simply shrugged at Riley with a clear message. Best to give in.

Within minutes Thayne bit into a roast beef sandwich and washed the food down with a long swallow of black coffee.

Fannie sat across from him, hands folded on the table. "What do you need, Thayne?"

He glanced over at Riley, and she retrieved the necklace. "We think either Cheyenne or one of the people who kidnapped her was wearing this. Do you recognize it?"

The three women met gazes, their eyes wide with wonder.

"I've never actually seen it," Fannie whispered. "I heard about the stone, though. I thought Old Man Riverton was telling a fish story all those years."

Thayne sat back in his chair, stunned. The Blackwoods and Rivertons had never gotten along that well, but he couldn't believe they'd be involved with a kidnapping.

Before Thayne could form words, Pops came up to the food table with Thayne's grandmother in tow.

Helen stared intently at the necklace. "Wyoming jade," she said softly, looking directly at Riley. "From the Rivertons. Where did you find it, dear?"

Lincoln smiled and hugged his wife. "You recognized the stone, Helen."

"Oh good grief, Lincoln, you're acting like I'm an idiot. Of course I know Wyoming jade when I see it. That's the stone Mr. Riverton found when he first dug in that hole in the ground. Beautiful." She smiled.

"Gram, do you know who the necklace belongs to?"

Thayne didn't mention Cheyenne; he didn't want to influence his grandmother in any way. Because of the gaps in her memory, Gram sometimes fit facts together that seemed logical. Thayne couldn't afford for that to happen now.

"The necklace is supposed to be a big secret." Gram took the evidence bag from Riley. "Cheyenne told me about the diamond clasp. She was right, truly beautiful. Of course, that's not why she treasures it so much."

Thayne met his grandfather's shocked gaze over Gram's head.

"The necklace belongs to Cheyenne?" Riley voiced the question Thayne couldn't form. "You're absolutely sure."

"Without a doubt." Gram lowered her voice and leaned in to Riley. "You know, dear, Cheyenne is enamored with that young Riverton boy. But we can't talk about it until Cheyenne gives the all clear. My granddaughter made me promise I wouldn't tell anyone until she knew her feelings were real."

Helen clucked her tongue at Thayne. "You should take this to your sister, dear boy. She'll be sick in the heart at losing her true love's gift."

"Sure thing, Gram." He stood and kissed his grandmother on the cheek. "Thank you," he whispered.

"Oh, get on with you, dear boy." Helen took Riley's hand in hers and tugged slightly so Riley stood up. "You two make a lovely pair."

"Yes ma'am." He grasped Riley's hand. "See you later. We need to return Cheyenne's necklace to her."

"Not yet, you're not leaving, young man." Helen beamed at them, slipping her hand into Lincoln's. "You've kept your feelings for your wife-to-be secret far too long. I'm tired of waiting to see if you've found the real thing. Like my Lincoln, here."

"Gram?" Thayne could barely speak.

"Kiss her, honey."

CHAPTER FOURTEEN

Riley couldn't have moved if she'd wanted to. Heat rushed up her cheeks, and she stared at Thayne's grandmother. What was she supposed to say?

Desperately she searched out Thayne. He appeared just as stunned. And . . . good grief, was her Navy SEAL blushing? She couldn't believe it, but yes, even his cheeks had reddened.

"Oh, for heaven's sake." Gram shoved Thayne toward Riley. "I know you two have kissed. At least once. I saw you at Fannie's."

Thayne stumbled into Riley, obviously not expecting the push. Riley reached out, and her hands went flat against his broad chest. Somehow he ended up toe-to-toe with her, looking down. The heat from his body seeped into hers, and her heart pounded. She moistened her lips, unable to escape his heated gaze.

She supposed she'd expected a small kiss, a platonic kiss, in front of everyone.

Instead Thayne cupped her cheek, wrapped his arm around her, and pressed her against him.

Her breath caught. She'd tried to keep their relationship professional, but her fear that he'd been shot had fractured the well-constructed walls around her heart. Thayne's grandmother had just shattered what little remained.

Riley kept expecting someone to make a joke, to say something, anything, to help them extricate themselves from this embarrassing situation, but no one said a word. Thayne didn't release her, and Riley simply gave in. She had no desire to pull away.

Beneath her touch, Thayne's muscles tensed. She gripped his shirt to steady herself.

His brown eyes captured hers, intoxicating her. His pupils dilated. Time slowed. Seconds seemed like minutes. Everyone but Thayne fell away from her view.

They could easily have been alone in her room instead of surrounded by God knew how many people. With his finger, he tilted her chin up and slowly, deliberately lowered his mouth to hers.

She could have pushed him away; he would've let her go, but Riley gave in to his touch, to the feelings that had been simmering inside for so very long. Her eyes fluttered closed. Her lips parted until his kiss captured her mouth. Very gently he begged entrance, his tongue dancing against her übersensitive lips.

She clung to him, leaning closer. Thayne Blackwood certainly could kiss. She'd forgotten how well, but her body remembered. Her heart skipped a beat. Her blood pounded in her head. Her knees trembled, and low in her belly, she tingled with memories of his touch. She belonged in his arms. She always had. No point in denying the truth.

A series of wolf calls and whistles finally pierced the haze. Thayne must have heard them, too, because ever so slowly, he lifted his head.

She didn't see the humorous twinkle in his eye she'd expected. No, this was something very different, almost cautious. He blinked, and she watched him paste a pleased grin on his face. And yet, the smile didn't reach his eyes.

"Satisfied?" he said to his grandmother, still holding Riley against his hardened body.

Helen beamed at them. "I knew you had it in you to fall in love, Thayne. A waltz lesson is a must-have now. So you can dance at your wedding."

Thayne leaned over and kissed his grandmother on the cheek. "You're right. I definitely need to polish up the waltz. But right now we have a job to do."

She smiled and patted his hand. "Come by before dinner. We'll practice." Gram looped her arm through Lincoln's. "How about we rehearse a bit, my love? And then explore our favorite rendezvous. Thayne and Riley have inspired me with a few ideas." She cut her husband a saucy wink.

Lincoln chuckled. "You're mighty frisky for a Sunday."

Riley couldn't remember seeing the Blackwood patriarch grin so broadly since she'd met him. He was obviously devoted to Helen. In sickness and in health.

Helen and Lincoln Blackwood truly loved each other. The real kind of love. The kind Riley had never believed existed.

He raised his wife's hand to his mouth and turned it over, pressing a kiss into her palm. "It's a date, my love. As soon as the rest of the first shift comes in and we feed those hungry folks lunch."

Helen frowned. "I hope they find that poor Wallace girl. Only twelve years old. It's a shame."

And just like that, Thayne's grandmother stepped back into the past, fifteen years earlier.

"That's why Riley's here, Gram. To help us find her," Thayne said, easily shifting into his grandmother's reality. He took her hand in his and folded his fingers through hers.

How many men would be so kind to someone so vulnerable? How could she not fall head-over-heels in love with a man like him?

The reality of her thoughts froze Riley. No, it couldn't be true. The Blackwoods had turned her belief system upside down.

Thayne bent down to Riley's ear. "Keep Gram busy while I talk to Fannie and tell her about Kade. Then we'll head to the Rivertons'."

Riley nodded and eased over to Thayne's grandmother.

"He's a good boy," Helen said.

"I know, ma'am." Riley took in Fannie's response to Thayne's news. He steadied the older woman with a hug.

"Thayne might be a strong warrior on the outside, but his heart is soft and caring. Don't hurt him, Riley. You could be the first woman I've met who actually can."

She had no idea what to say. As far as Riley was concerned, Thayne was the one who could tear out her heart. If she allowed herself to feel too much.

Thayne took a bag and thermos from Fannie. "Are you ready?" he asked.

One look at the twinkle in Helen's eyes, and Riley grabbed the thermos. "More than," she said, and hurried toward the vehicle, Thayne right behind her.

"What spooked you?" he asked as he slid in beside her.

She glanced over at him. "Umm . . ."

Thayne grinned as he put the car in gear and headed toward the highway. "Gram. She doesn't have much of a filter these days."

Heat rushed into Riley's cheeks. "I can't be mad at your grandmother." She gripped her seat belt. She was in Singing River to bring Cheyenne Blackwood home alive. With each passing hour, that looked less and less likely.

"I know what you mean. It's pretty much impossible," Thayne said, and gunned the accelerator down the freeway, lights flashing their urgency.

She hoped the Riverton lead led somewhere. Her so-called expertise had taken them nowhere. Riley prayed the necklace would bring Cheyenne home.

"How about breaking out those sandwiches? You need to eat, and I'm starved. We'll be on the Riverton land before long," Thayne said.

Relieved to have a distraction, Riley opened the bag and pulled out the remainder of their lunch. One bite into the sandwich, and the snap of spicy mustard layered on the turkey hit her tongue. She washed down the food with iced tea. "Do you believe your grandmother? About the necklace being Cheyenne's?"

"Would I surprise you if I said yes?"

"Can you trust her memories?"

Thayne didn't speak for a few minutes, then pinched the bridge of his nose. "One of the doctors described the disease in a way that helped me. Picture a spiral of memories that begins in the center when you're a child. A solid line circles outward with each year, laying down memories. Alzheimer's cuts gaps in the solid line. Some of the newest memories disappear, while some are still there. Then, bit by bit, the disease works itself backward, destroying memories in reverse. Gram will forget us, then the memory of Mom will fade, then Dad. Eventually Pops, and finally her siblings and parents. At the end, her brain will cause her to lose the ability to eat, drink, and swallow."

Riley gaped at him. "I had no idea. How terrifying."

"Yeah. It's our memories and experiences that make us who we are. Alzheimer's rips away what defines a person piece by piece. There's nothing good about the disease. Not one damn thing."

Thayne's voice grew thick. Riley had believed she understood a bit about what the Blackwood family was going through. She'd been so very wrong.

She hated to ask her next question, but she had no choice. "Then how can you believe your grandmother about Cheyenne's necklace?"

"If Gram repeats new information enough that it makes its way into long-term memory, it's there. For a while, anyway. I think that's what happened with Cheyenne's *boyfriend*." Thayne growled out the word. "Gram would've become obsessed with Cheyenne getting married. She's a true romantic."

"It makes sense," Riley said. "Whoever took Cheyenne knows the back roads and where the phone was dumped, and the Rivertons own the land."

The side of the road transformed from open spaces to a series of posts. "Speaking of which, we've now crossed the edge of Riverton Ranch."

"Their land must be thousands of acres."

"Try more than thirty thousand acres, almost fifty square miles."

Thayne's satphone interrupted them. "Blackwood.

"Hudson." Thayne listened for a moment. "Hold on." Thayne punched the speaker for the phone. "Repeat that for Riley."

"Cheyenne's been seeing someone for the past six months or so. She refused to tell me who. The only reason I knew was I stopped by her place on the way home from a buying trip. She wouldn't let me in. I heard jazz playing in the background, and she couldn't get rid of me fast enough. I got the picture. She shut me down when I asked her who the guy was. Figured she didn't want Dad or you running a background check."

"I never—"

"Don't try to deny it, Thayne. I might have threatened a horny football player a time or two, but once I left for school, you one-upped me. Everyone knows what happened to Cal Riverton when he put the moves on Cheyenne and blabbed about it. He didn't show his face in school for a week."

"It wasn't like that." Thayne grimaced. "I just gave him a shiner. He was too embarrassed to show his face at school knowing a guy three years younger got the best of him. I didn't hurt him that badly. Besides, he made Cheyenne cry."

"Yeah, Dad made you pay for it, though."

Thayne scowled. "Had to work a whole summer for the Rivertons, the first week at no pay."

"Hold it," Riley said. "Is Cal the guy you think Cheyenne's dating?"

"What the hell?" Hudson shouted.

"Cal left Wyoming, headed for California, and started some tech company," Thayne said. "He hasn't been back in years. I've got my money on Brett. He's a year older than Cal, runs the Riverton Ranch, and keeps trying to buy out Pops. It wouldn't surprise me if he's dating Cheyenne to get hold of the land."

Thayne didn't bother hiding his dislike of Brett Riverton.

"Just find her, Thayne. Call as soon as you know if Brett's behind this," Hudson said and ended the call.

The car reached a large stone and iron arch denoting the Riverton Ranch. Riley's gaze narrowed. "Those are high-tech cameras," she said.

"We also passed several motion detectors over the last mile," Thayne added, his tone dark. "Looks like Brett put them up recently."

"You noticed the stirred-up dirt at the base of the poles, too?"

Thayne nodded.

"Do most ranchers use cameras?"

"Quite a few. Rustlers, smuggling, but these are different."

The SUV rumbled over a cattle guard and turned in to a large ranch house surrounded by several buildings, including a barn, stable, and training facility.

"I thought you said the Rivertons were in to mining?"

"Money breeds money. Brett's passion is training quarter horses. He used to ride the rodeo when he was a teenager. Until his father disappeared. Rumor has it Riverton Senior got into debt to some mob guys gambling in Vegas and never came home."

Thayne pulled onto a long drive toward a large stone house.

Riley sat up straight in her seat. "Did you notice the men by the barn?"

"Armed guards. Even for Brett Riverton that's strange." Thayne stopped the car and checked his weapon. "Guess this won't be a simple interview."

He threw on his jacket to camouflage the holster and got out. Riley walked beside him, her back and shoulder muscles tensed. She could feel the hands watching. She glanced to her right, then her left, uneasy. Too many guns, and her arm still stung from a bullet wound.

"There are at least three watching," Thayne said.

He knocked on the door. A too-thin ranch hand answered the door, his eyes cautious. "What can I do for you, Deputy Blackwood?"

"We need to see Brett."

The man clicked his teeth. "Probably not a good idea. Come back later." He started to push the door closed.

Thayne widened his stance and stopped the movement with his arm. "Shep, I don't have the patience to spar with you right now. My sister is missing, and I'm interviewing Brett now . . . or I arrest him on suspicion of kidnapping."

The guy's skeleton-like face twisted, his visage bordering on horrific. Riley had seen the look before. The man probably had cancer.

"Let him in. I planned on visiting the sheriff after lunch anyway," a tired voice sounded from across the room.

"But Mr. Riverton, you're not well—"

"Don't argue, Shep."

"That's right, Shep. Let us in." Thayne shoved past the man.

Riley followed at his elbow, but once across the threshold, their steps faltered.

Surprise flickered through Thayne's eyes.

A man, face creased with pain, leaned on a cane and walked across the floor. He appeared decades older than Thayne had implied. Brett Riverton was obviously very ill. Maybe dying.

And Thayne clearly hadn't known.

"Damn, Brett. What the hell happened to you?"

CHAPTER FIFTEEN

The large oak door snicked quietly behind them, closing Thayne and Riley in the Rivertons' main house. Thayne surveyed the living area. He'd never been inside the place. Mahogany wood and plush furniture exuded money, but the room had been decorated for comfort and convenience, not for show. A couple of Remington paintings hung on the wall, and a large shadow box filled with stones, arrowheads, and other treasures held center stage in a massive wall unit.

Arms crossed, Shep stood silent between Thayne and his boss. Like Brett's right-hand man could stop Thayne. He'd heard Shep had lung cancer, and the rumors seemed to be true. Normally, he had a cigarette glued to his fingers. No nicotine stains. He'd quit at least a month or two ago.

"You look like hell, Brett."

"Thanks." He eased into a leather chair.

Thayne might not appreciate the guy and his seedy lawyers bugging Pops, but Brett was four years older than Thayne. He'd graduated a year ahead of Hudson. Brett had played on the football team. Defensive end. The guy had been fast, agile, and muscular.

Not anymore. Thayne could see Brett's collarbones recessed, his cheeks hollow, his skin gray.

Thayne shoved aside the sympathy for Brett's obvious medical condition. The moment Thayne had recognized the high-tech surveillance, the hairs on the back of his neck had shot to attention. Riley had cautioned him not to get his hopes up, that Gram might be drawing the wrong conclusions because of her AD. Good advice, but right now he had to wonder what Brett Riverton was hiding.

"I'm here about Cheyenne."

"You found her?" Something akin to pain flickered across Brett's features. Interesting. Guilt, maybe?

"Not yet."

Brett's brow furrowed into deep lines. "I'd hoped . . ." He let out a sharp curse. "I'm sorry I haven't been more help. As you can see, I'm stuck on the ranch for the time being. What can I do?"

"Answer my questions, Brett. You were headed to see my father today. What about?"

Brett's jaw tensed. He clearly didn't want to say anything. Thayne recognized the struggle on his face.

"When'd you upgrade the surveillance, Brett?" Thayne asked. "I recognize the models. The general public doesn't have access to them. What are you into?"

Brett's jaw tightened. "A few rustlers have thinned out the cattle too much to my liking."

"Really?" Thayne crossed his arms. "You can't lie worth a damn."

A fleeting smile tugged at Brett's lip. "I've been told I'm quite good at avoiding the truth."

"Did you lie to my sister?"

Brett's expression went blank. "That's none of your business."

"Everything about Cheyenne is my business until we find her." Thayne didn't like the slight thickening in his voice, but every hour that went by, the fear deep in his belly grew larger. "She's been missing for more than thirty-six hours." He glanced at Riley.

"After thirty-six hours, the chances of an abduction victim's survival drop to less than five percent." Riley strode across the room. "Special Agent Riley Lambert, FBI, Mr. Riverton. I'd be interested in your permits for some of this equipment. It was mounted on federal lands."

"I built the road," Brett growled.

"The government owns the land," she countered. "I could cite you."

"Leave him alone, Blackwood," Shep erupted from the door. "Either that or do your job so we don't have to."

Thayne tilted his head. "What's he talking about?"

Brett shook his head. His knuckles had whitened on the chair's arms. "Get my pain meds, Shep."

The hand scowled but rushed out of the room, slamming a door at the rear of the house.

"We've had some thefts since spring." Beads of sweat popped on Brett's forehead and upper lip. His grip tightened on the wheelchair's arms. "About six months ago, one of our hands took off after he stole some new equipment. I haven't been able to track him down to press charges."

Thayne studied the man who had been his older brother's rival in high school. Brett was tough to read. Normally Thayne could smell a lie. Brett had been right; he was a good liar, but he couldn't hide his physical condition or the fact that he was keeping a secret related to Cheyenne.

Determined to discover the truth, Thayne walked over to Brett and towered over him. "Where were you Friday night?"

Brett chuckled, the sound having little to do with humor. "Where do you think?" He swept his arm down his emaciated body.

"What about Shep?"

"In Cody. Getting chemo." Brett slouched in the chair. "Look, I had nothing to do with Cheyenne's disappearance. Believe me."

Thayne glanced at Riley. She nodded and handed him the necklace. From her expression, she agreed that Brett was hiding something. Thayne had run out of patience. He held the evidence in front of Brett's face. "Do you recognize this?"

If possible, Brett's face paled even more. "Where'd you get it?"

"I'm asking the questions." Thayne tilted the bag, the large stone gleaming even in the dim interior light of Brett's home. "What's it worth?"

He rolled backward slightly. "This is ridiculous. The price of the necklace is irrelevant."

"It's from your mine, isn't it?" Thayne asked.

"You know it is. It's got the color indicative of the vein of Wyoming jade my great-grandfather discovered."

"Actually, thanks for that information." Thayne scribbled something else into his notepad. "Expensive. Unique. I bet I could find the jeweler who you commissioned. You might as well tell me."

"You're crazy. I have no idea where your sister is or why she was taken. Hell, I donated Mac and the plane for the search. I encouraged my hands to help. I'd be there, too, if I could."

Riley stood beside Thayne. "It's quite common for perpetrators to insert themselves into the search or investigation."

Thayne could have cheered. He loved the way she'd piled on. Federal weight would help. Brett wouldn't be easy to rattle.

"That's BS." Brett's fists clenched, but his hands shook.

"You and Cheyenne were involved. We have a witness." No need to tell him it was Gram.

Brett remained silent.

"You're lovers." Thayne clipped the words. Normally, he'd have tried to ignore Cheyenne's private life. She was, after all, his sister. But he had no choice.

Thayne shoved the plastic bag holding the necklace into Brett's hand. "You gave Cheyenne a piece of jewelry worth a fortune. Either that or she stole it." Thayne didn't mention the other theory, but he could feel Brett crumbling. This was Cheyenne's necklace all right.

"You son of a bitch."

"If it gets my sister back, I've got no problem with that."

Riley leaned in. "Mr. Riverton, please. You're obviously trying to protect someone. Tell me about the necklace. It was found near Cheyenne's cell phone with some of her personal items. We think she was wearing it when she was taken."

Brett closed his eyes. "Damn her. I told her not to wear the necklace."

His right hand began to tremor; then a seizure moved through his body. Shep raced into the room. He glared at Thayne. "What the hell did you do?"

"Mr. Riverton?" Shep opened his mouth and shoved two pills down his throat. He looked around wildly.

Thayne shoved a glass of water into Shep's hand. He tipped it. "Drink up."

Brett swallowed. His eyes rolled back into his head. The muscles in his extremities jerked. He started to slide out of the chair. Thayne rushed to help. He and Shep stabilized him.

"I'm calling 9-1-1." Riley tugged her phone from her pocket.

"Don't," Shep said. "There's nothing anyone can do. Give the medicine a couple of minutes."

"He needs a doctor."

"They're doing all they can." Shep gulped. "Mr. Riverton's been poisoned and is being treated, but it's a slow process." Shep closed his eyes. "He needs to keep his illness as quiet as possible, or the board of directors will take over. It'll ruin him."

Thayne winced at Brett's trembling body. "We'll give it a few minutes. Then I call an ambulance."

Riley kept her phone out, thumb poised over the screen. Within two minutes, the tremors in Brett's hand lessened, and the sharp spasms transformed into flutters.

Thayne's satphone rang, and he glanced at the screen. "We'll be outside, Shep," Thayne said, "but we're not finished."

"Blackwood," he said into the receiver. "Hold on for a second."

He escorted Riley to the front porch. An armed cowboy strode toward them.

Thayne shifted his jacket back, showing his weapon. "Walk the other way." The man paused, but behind Thayne, Shep stood in the doorway and gave a quick nod.

Thayne led Riley to his vehicle. "We need privacy," he said and activated the speaker.

"We identified the body buried near the swimming hole," Deputy Pendergrass reported. "Special Agent Lambert was right. Midforties, time of death is sometime in the spring."

"Who is it?"

"We lucked out. The guy had dental records. He'd had a tooth abscess about a year ago. He worked for Brett Riverton."

◆ ◆ ◆

The murmur of hushed voices filtered through the locked door. Cheyenne reached out a hand to her patient's forehead. The fever had spiked again. With gentle fingertips, she took Bethany's pulse: 120.

Bethany groaned, glassy eyes staring out. "Can you hear me?" Cheyenne whispered softly. "You have to fight, Bethany. I'll do everything I can to save you, but you have to fight."

For a split second, her patient's gaze met hers. They were about the same age. Cheyenne could see a spine of steel in this woman. "Ian tells me they need you."

A lone tear slid down Bethany's cheek. "Help me," she whispered; then her eyes closed.

Cheyenne had had enough. She stomped to the metal door. Pulse racing, she lifted her fist, ready to pound against it, then stilled. Would she make matters worse for Ian and the others? She reached for the pendant she'd worn around her neck for the past six months.

They must have torn it off her sometime after they'd abducted her, and right now she wished she could clutch it in her hands, feel the smoothness of the stone, picture the man who had given it to her. Find strength in him.

He'd hurt her, more than she'd ever thought she could be hurt. Even then, there was so much she hadn't said. So much that could never be said. If she got out of this alive, she'd . . .

She sighed. What good would it do? Sometimes you couldn't go back. Only forward. She looked over her shoulder. If she didn't get those antibiotics, Bethany would die.

Even then, someone was out to kill both of them.

"Her words could be fabricated," a man's low voice said from the other side of the door. "You know we cannot trust anyone from the outside."

"Bethany could die, Father," a woman argued. "Is that what you want?"

There was a tad-too-long pause. "How dare you." A loud slap sounded. "She is my child."

"Then perhaps you don't trust Ian?" the woman asked, so softly Cheyenne could barely hear her.

"He's spent too much time with the doctor. Which gives me another idea. Perhaps we should keep the doctor with us? Permanently. She could train young Micah. He's shown a gift for science and math. He'd make an excellent physician."

Cheyenne's knees trembled. They were planning to keep her?

"A stranger?" Adelaide's voice rose. "Stay here?"

"Family *is* everything." The man sighed. "You're right. She'll betray us. They all do, and we can't take the chance. Once Bethany is well, we must dispose of the doctor."

"Father—"

"I've made my decision."

"Yes, Father."

"You're a good daughter, Adelaide."

A chime rang. "Time for music lessons," the man said. "Micah has a gift for the cello as well, did you know? His father very nearly broke his hand and ruined everything, but we got him away just in time."

"Only at your behest, Father." The woman's voice paused. "What about the antibiotics?"

"I'm concerned Ian can't handle the job alone. Go with him. You can report to me. And Adelaide, remind him of the punishment for disobedience." There was a pause. "I expect perfection, nothing less."

Cheyenne closed her eyes. Without help, how could she possibly escape? It was hopeless.

"Stop it, Cheyenne. There's always a way." If her grandmother had taught her anything, it was never to give up. *You can give in, you can give out, but never give up,* Gram would say.

"Not giving up, Gram. You'll see."

She entered the bathroom and splashed water on her face, feeling for the towel. They'd removed any sharp instruments from the room. She had no weapons . . . unless . . .

She looked at the wooden towel rack to the side of the sink. Maybe, just maybe. She grabbed the dowel and pulled with all her might. She'd become so weak. She'd hidden her food and poured out her beverages since she'd realized someone was poisoning her.

No use.

She propped herself against the wall and lifted her legs, jamming them against the wood. A loud crack echoed through the bathroom.

Her heart raced, and she kicked again. Finally, the splintered rod clattered to the floor. She knelt down and picked it up, turning it in her hand.

"I'm not giving up."

◆ ◆ ◆

Sweat trickled down the back of Riley's neck. The midday sun glared through the SUV's windows, but she didn't dare roll down the window. The car had created a wall of silence between them and Brett Riverton's guards.

"Cause of death?" Thayne asked.

"Your FBI agent was right on," Pendergrass said. "Sharp instrument inserted just behind the right ear. But the coroner also found evidence of trauma before he died. The guy was beaten. He may even have been unconscious before the death blow."

The deputy on the other end continued the report on the remains discovered by the swimming hole.

Thayne met Riley's gaze. She rested her hand between them on the seat, her small finger touching his, though just barely. He lifted his hand to her cheek and wiped away a stream of sweat. Damn Thayne for being so far beyond just an on-the-make Navy SEAL. Why did he have to be so much more? She wanted to lean into him, reassure him that everything would be fine, but she couldn't.

Neither one of them believed in coincidence. Another belief they shared.

A Riverton employee murdered. Brett Riverton poisoned and obviously involved with Cheyenne, who'd been kidnapped.

Yeah, all of that was a coincidence.

"Hurry it up, Pendergrass. We're baking in this car. What you're telling me is that Riverton's hand was murdered, and there's no evidence as to by whom."

"Sorry, Thayne. It's a dead end. Unless you get something from Mr. Riverton."

"Oh, I'll find out what he's really hiding," Thayne said. "How's my father?"

Riley kept one ear on the report of the sheriff's health, and at the same time peered through the window. One of the armed guards, a Winchester slung in the cradle of his elbow, caught her attention. Her gaze tracked his route. Armed guards paraded through the paddock but at a very specific pace and on a set path. Still, they repeatedly gravitated toward an outbuilding. She narrowed her gaze. Was she imagining it?

It didn't take long to recognize the pattern. Each man veered to a single building.

Finally, Thayne ended the call.

"I'm glad your father seems OK," she said.

Thayne frowned. "The stress and lack of sleep isn't helping his recovery. But Cheyenne is the only one who could get him to rest." He turned in his seat. "You noticed the building, too."

"Think we should take a look inside?"

"Brett's lying to us, and you read my mind. Now let's get out of this car before we roast."

Riley opened her door, and a cooling breeze hit her face. Instead of returning to the house, she and Thayne strode across the compound. Before getting halfway to the small building—a building large enough to hold someone prisoner—three armed cowboys stepped in their path, their weapons at the ready.

"I suggest you head back to the house, Deputy."

"Curtis, I'm searching for a kidnap victim—my sister, Cheyenne, to be exact," he said to one of his high school classmates. "I have evidence tying her to the Rivertons. I think Judge Gibson would throw your ass in jail in a heartbeat for impeding my investigation. Especially since you knocked up his daughter."

Curtis scowled. "Damn it, Thayne. The judge hates me already. And I need this job," he said, voice quiet so the other hands wouldn't hear him.

"You think your sob story trumps finding my sister?"

If this idiot thought he could take on Thayne . . . If any of them did . . .

"Open it, Curtis," Shep said from behind them.

Thayne cocked his head. Curtis unlocked the door.

Riley grasped Thayne's hand. "Let me go first," she said. "Please."

"I can't."

Sending up a small prayer Cheyenne was inside—and alive—Riley walked shoulder to shoulder with Thayne into the building.

A series of skylights illuminated the room. A horse snorted from the far side of the hay-strewn building. Thayne walked around a stall. One of Brett's prized mares was lying down, but she looked like she was dying. Her mane was ragged, her hair falling out. Beside him the Rivertons' vet stroked her belly.

"What's wrong with the mare, Doc?"

Dr. Tillman turned. "Copper poisoning. Brett transformed this machine shop into an animal hospital. We lost one of them today."

Riley turned. A dog lay in a kennel, ears flat, a rash peppering his skin, his paws covered in red mud. Beside him were three other kennels. One held a cat, the second what appeared to be a wolf. The third kennel was empty and newly cleaned.

"Will these others be OK?"

"Maybe. I'm giving them a chelating agent, and we're trying to find the source of the contamination." The doc cleared his throat. "I'm sorry about Cheyenne. I hope you find her soon."

Thayne nodded curtly. With one last look at the struggling animals, Riley followed him out the door.

Curtis ambled up behind them. "Don't let this get around, Thayne. Brett doesn't need any more trouble. He's a good boss."

"The EPA and CDC need to know," Riley said. "Mr. Riverton may not have a choice."

Curtis stopped in his tracks and shook his head before resuming his patrol. "Damn Feds."

"Don't take it personally," Thayne said to Riley. "It's a western thing. People get pretty upset that the federal government owns almost half the state of Wyoming."

On the way to the main house, Riley slowed her pace. Thayne matched it.

"Why would anyone poison Brett or those animals?" she said. "I'm not seeing an obvious connection between Riverton's difficulties and Cheyenne's disappearance."

"Just like my sister. She can't make anything easy."

Thayne tried to make a joke out of the situation, but it fell flat. Over the last few hours, Riley had hoped they were close to finding his sister. Unless their interrogation of Brett gave them a solid lead, they'd be where they started when Riley deplaned yesterday.

"Brett has to suspect who's got it in for him." Thayne glanced back at the makeshift animal clinic. "Why else have armed guards patrolling his place?"

They reached the porch, and Riley stopped. "How well do you know your judge, Thayne? Could you get a warrant to search this place and Brett's records?"

"Tough call. The judge is a fishing buddy of my dad's, but he's pretty high on individual rights. And, of course, Riverton's big money in this town. Still, for Cheyenne . . . it's worth a try."

"Brett cares about Cheyenne, and I don't think he wants a confrontation. He doesn't want what's going on here to leak. And he obviously needs medical help. You could push him."

Thayne gave her a grim grin. "I like how you think."

They walked into the house without knocking. Brett was bent low, speaking in hushed tones into a cell phone.

"Who are you talking to, Brett?"

He ended the call and slipped the phone in his pocket. "Just business."

"You've got some big trouble brewing here, Riverton. Riley has the CDC, the EPA, and the Bureau of Land Management on speed dial." Thayne crossed his arms. "I doubt you want the Feds on your land."

Brett rubbed his face with his hands. When he stared at Thayne, Riley could see the pain visible on his face.

Thayne rushed him and slapped the arms of the chair, the *thwack* echoing through the room. "Damn it. That body we dug up at our swimming hole was identified as one of your men. A man who stopped getting a paycheck six months ago."

"That can't be." Brett shook his head. "Six months. But that was before Cheyenne—"

Thayne grabbed Brett's shirt. "What's your game? What's your connection to my sister? Did you take her? Did she find out about something you're doing on your land? Or that your mines contaminated the water? Or is something else poisoning you and your animals?"

Shep slammed open the outside door and raced into the room. "Leave him alone. You don't understand."

Thayne whirled around. Riley had never seen his face deadlier.

"Back off, Shep." Thayne's grip tightened. "I'm not asking again, Riverton. Where is my sister?"

"I don't know," he choked out.

"Thayne." Riley placed her hand on his shoulder. "He's telling the truth. Look at him."

Brett's face couldn't have become grayer. He looked like he might pass out any second.

"He's an expert liar, Riley," Thayne spat, gripping Brett's collar. "If I weren't wearing this badge, I'd make you talk. I know exactly how to extract the truth. Hell, I still might."

The threat lingered in the air. Thayne sucked in a deep breath and thrust Brett back. "The way I see it, you're lying to me. You're putting Cheyenne's life at risk."

"I'd never do anything to hurt her." Brett met Thayne's gaze, his sunken eyes not backing down. "I . . . care about her."

"You're sure as hell not showing it."

Brett raised his hands and gripped Thayne's wrists. "You don't know what you're talking about. I'm trying to *protect* her, not hurt her."

Riley believed Brett. He couldn't hide the distress on his face.

For her, though, this new information changed her profile yet again. Except nothing fit together. She had too many unrelated facts that didn't form a cohesive picture.

"I want answers, Brett." Thayne didn't release his shirt, but gripped it tighter. "Did you hire someone to kidnap Cheyenne? Did they throw my grandmother against the wall?"

With what must have taken all his strength, Brett thrust Thayne off him. "Damn you, Blackwood, of course I didn't."

"Why should I believe you?" Thayne glared at Brett.

The man thrust his hand through limp, lifeless hair, then his mouth twisted into a frown. "Because Cheyenne is my wife."

CHAPTER SIXTEEN

The Riverton Ranch house's walls closed in on Thayne. His mind swirled, and he stumbled back at the shocking statement. "Impossible. Cheyenne would never—"

"What, marry a Riverton?" Brett let out a derisive laugh. "Imagine my surprise when she accepted my proposal—and then went through with it."

"After the way your brother Cal treated her, I would've believed hell would freeze over before she got near either one of you. Much less marry into the family."

Brett scowled at Thayne. "Thanks for bringing up *that* incident. Cal knows he screwed up. He apologized more than once. Cheyenne . . . well, let's say she tolerates him."

Thayne sank into the leather sofa across from Brett and stared at his left hand, where a gold band loosely rested against his knuckle. Riley sat beside Thayne, her leg up against his. He met her concerned gaze. Talk about throwing their entire investigation into turmoil.

"Cheyenne never walked a step off the straight and narrow. Perfect kid, perfect student, perfect daughter. She'd never just run off and get married. Especially to a Riverton. She'd do it the right way. Six-month engagement, church wedding, reception, the whole thing."

Brett's face had stiffened to stone. "And that's why you don't know."

"You're not making sense." Thayne's brain couldn't comprehend Cheyenne's out-of-character actions. How could he have misread his sister so badly?

"Being married to Cheyenne doesn't exonerate you," Riley said. "In fact, your relationship makes you our prime suspect."

"You can both go to hell," Brett said, shoving his hands through his hair. "You know what. Search the house, talk to Shep, do whatever you need to do to check me off your list. And when you're done wasting everyone's time, find her!"

Riley nudged Thayne's leg, and he met her gaze. She wanted to take over questioning. He wasn't getting anywhere, so he gave her a quick nod.

She leaned forward, resting her elbows on her knees. "Why keep your marriage a secret until we pushed you, Brett? It only increases suspicion."

For a moment, he didn't move, didn't respond. Thayne recognized the irritation flashing in Brett's eyes. Well, that was too damn bad.

"Answer the question," Thayne uttered through gritted teeth.

Riley shoved her knee into his thigh, harder this time. OK, fine. He'd shut up and see if she could do better. In Thayne's experience, threats worked well with the Rivertons.

She lifted her gaze to Brett's mutinous one. "Please. I want to understand. I get not announcing a relationship to the world, but why not tell everyone once you married?"

He rubbed the back of his neck, clearly uncomfortable with the question. Finally, he sighed. "From day one, neither Cheyenne nor I wanted to attract any attention. We reconnected when I drove one of my hands to her office after she first set up her practice. He needed stitches." He gave them a thoughtful smile. "By the time she finished sewing up the guy, I was hooked. She's wicked smart, has a great sense of humor, and it didn't impress her one whit that I have a ton of money sitting in the bank."

Thayne hated sympathizing with Brett, but he got it. He might not have the money, but his job attracted a set of groupies who wanted him for the prestige of being seen and sleeping with a SEAL, not because of who he was as a person. That's what Riley offered . . . she didn't care about his last name or his job. She liked the man who existed beneath his SEAL persona.

"I couldn't believe when she agreed to have dinner. We . . . clicked. Neither of us wanted to advertise our relationship, though," Brett continued. "You know how the town is."

Riley smiled at him, all sympathy. "I've experienced a taste of what you're talking about. Fannie, right?"

Oh, she was good. Brett had relaxed a bit more with each of Riley's questions, allowing Thayne to study his prime suspect, trying to read his every reaction, searching for his tells.

"Fannie and the Gumshoe Grannies are infamous. You'd think they had listening devices in every home in Singing River. Maybe they do." Brett narrowed his gaze at Thayne. "Your grandmother started that crazy group, didn't she?"

"Don't blame me," Thayne said. "I can't control them."

Shep brought Brett a bottle of water, and he took a sip. "The Rivertons and Blackwoods have been on opposite sides since settling here nearly a century ago. Families took sides. You know how it was when we were kids. Neither Cheyenne nor I wanted to reignite the feud. So we didn't tell anyone."

"Must have been tiring, though. It's hard to keep a relationship that private." Riley sent Thayne a meaningful stare.

Yeah, he got her point. Brett could very well be telling the truth.

"It's a long way from a secret affair to getting married," Thayne said.

"Your sister's quite the planner. We wanted to get away for a weekend, be in public without worrying who was watching. She lied about a Vegas medical convention; I lied about a cattle auction. We met in Vegas and indulged in a few too many drinks, and a few too much . . ." Brett cleared his throat. "I proposed. She accepted. What happens in Vegas doesn't always stay in Vegas."

"Why not come clean when you returned to Singing River?" Riley pressed.

"Cheyenne convinced me to have a real wedding instead. One your grandmother would enjoy . . . and remember for as long as possible. One that would have pictures Cheyenne could show your grandmother when the memories disappeared. Honestly, I think she didn't want to disappoint the family."

The Blackwood expectations struck again. Thayne rubbed his temple. But the idea of a real wedding. *That* sounded like his sister.

"I searched her house the day I arrived." Riley grabbed a blue notebook from her satchel and scribbled on the page. Then she brought out her sketchbook and flipped through it. "I didn't see any sign of you or a marriage. Or a wedding being planned."

"You wouldn't have," Brett said, his expression grim. "A month ago I began receiving some aggressive letters. They were anonymous, seemingly someone just venting. It happens. I have too much money, greedy landowner, miner, that kind of thing. I filed them away with other threats I've received over the years until one of the dogs took sick. Blue was a great bloodhound. Took a while for the vet to pinpoint the cause. Soon after, one of the hands came upon a wolf with similar symptoms. Then the mysterious illness began to affect me."

"Did Cheyenne know?"

"I hid my symptoms from her to keep her from worrying. She thought I had the stomach flu, but I knew what was happening. Since we couldn't figure out the cause at first, I had to do something before she got sick. My hired detectives came up with squat, so I had no choice. I sent her away."

Thayne crossed his arms. "Let's say I buy your story. There's no way Cheyenne would leave you, not if she suspected you were ill."

Brett looked down, away from Thayne's gaze.

"You know your sister well. She's stubborn, so I manufactured some lies. It took some doing, but I finally convinced her she was better off without me. At that point she was. I couldn't protect her. I couldn't even protect myself. She packed her bags and moved out. I told her to pretend I never existed to her and that I'd file for an annulment. She threw my ring in my face."

Brett's jaw throbbed, as if he could barely say the next words. "She promised she wouldn't wear the necklace, but she said she'd keep it to remind her how wrong she'd been about me."

Convincing. In fact, Thayne was beginning to believe Brett might not have had anything to do with Cheyenne's disappearance. He just had one more question.

"Why didn't you come to us when she went missing?" Thayne asked. "Keeping silent isn't the action of an innocent man."

"I sent Mac and as many hands as I could spare. Look, Thayne. I thought nobody knew about my relationship with Cheyenne. I didn't know she still wore the necklace until just now. If I had, I would've come to you, I swear."

"So why were you planning to visit Dad?"

Brett grabbed his cane and heaved himself up before shuffling to his walnut desk. He opened the drawer and pulled out an envelope. "Someone slipped this under my door earlier today. That's when I knew I had to come see you." He cleared his throat. "If . . . *when* you find Cheyenne, please don't tell her about this. She'd be mortified."

He passed the envelope to Thayne. With reluctance, Thayne grasped the packet but hesitated at the expression on Brett's face.

Riley snapped on a pair of gloves, took the evidence from Thayne, and folded open the clasp. She slid out a half-dozen or so pictures.

Her eyes widened. She glanced up at Brett, whose cheeks had reddened despite his illness.

"Well?" Thayne asked.

"Don't mention these to Cheyenne," Riley said and passed him the photos.

Thayne took one look, and the heat rose in his cheeks. He forced himself to avoid looking at his sister's face. The photos had been snapped to capture every angle of a very passionate encounter with Brett. He shoved them at Riley. "Someone followed you. Blackmail?"

"There was no note, but I have to assume there will be. They know who Cheyenne is to me. They're taunting me. Maybe they had something to do with Cheyenne's disappearance. I just know I haven't protected her as well as I thought." Even as weak as he was, Brett banged his hand on the desk.

"I recognize the location," Riley said, slipping them back inside the manila envelope. "Cheyenne has a photo on the wall of her office."

A small smile tugged Brett's lips. "Our spot. There's a waterfall on the south side of the property near the Wyoming jade mines. It's very isolated. No one ever goes up there."

"Where we used to play as kids?" Thayne asked.

Brett nodded and worked his way back to the leather sofa, sitting down with a groan.

Riley slid the photos into her satchel. "We'll have to take these in for evidence."

Brett hesitated, then reluctantly nodded. "She'll hate that."

"I'll try to keep them private." Thayne found he wanted to believe Brett. Not only did the man not have the strength to pull off the kidnapping, he truly seemed to care about Cheyenne.

It appeared whoever was trying to kill Brett could be responsible for Cheyenne's kidnapping. Or he was lying with Oscar-caliber skill.

"There's one more thing you should know," Brett said. "When the doc finally discovered the cause of my illness, we traced the copper toxicity to the stream feeding the waterfall."

Thayne stood up and pulled on his Stetson. "I guess our next stop is the waterfall."

◆ ◆ ◆

Fifteen Years Ago

The raucous laughter of after-school joy rocked the school bus. Madison wasn't interested in the class clown's latest impression of the Backstreet Boys. She couldn't stop looking at the new boy who'd transferred from San Diego. Bobby Frost.

One more time—for the final time, she told herself—she glanced over. He was staring at her. Her heart did a little flip inside her chest. Her face turned hot. Bobby's hair flopped down over one eye. He looked like he didn't care about anyone or anything. So cool.

The bus rumbled to a stop one street over from their house.

"Come on, Madison!" Her sister rocked back and forth, little-kid impatient.

Why couldn't their town be like every other where sixth graders attended middle school? Instead, Madison was still stuck in elementary school with the babies. Like her sister.

She tried not to pay attention to Bobby as she walked past him.

He winked at her. She tripped and went down on both knees.

The entire bus roared with laughter. Riley laughed the loudest.

Madison grabbed her backpack and raced to the exit. She jumped down the last step.

"Wait up, Madison," Riley cried, running after her.

Finally, her lungs burned, and she slowed down right in front of the house. She bent over and sucked in air.

"Why'd you run so fast?"

"None of your business," Madison snapped. "Let's go."

Riley bowed her head and scuffed her shoe on the dirt. That old twinge of guilt needled at Madison, but she didn't say anything. She opened the door.

Her mother stood in the kitchen, hands on her hips. Oh boy. Mom had that you're-in-trouble-now look.

"Riley Elizabeth Lambert. What did you do to your walls?"

Riley ran up to their mother. The poor thing had no clue.

"Did you like the picture, Mama? I drew my birthday party at the waterfall. I even put in the balloons and the cake."

Her mother swatted Riley on the backside and thrust soap and a bucket into her hands. "No dinner until you wash it off. Understood? And I want not a spot of color left, do you hear me?"

Riley looked down at the bucket. Tears rolled down her cheeks, but she didn't say a word. Head bowed, she trudged up the stairs.

"Do you want a chocolate chip cookie and a glass of milk, Madison?" Her mother's voice had suddenly calmed down, lost its edge. Mom just didn't understand Riley. At all.

"No thanks, Mom. I've got homework," she lied and followed her sister up the stairs. By the time Madison reached the hallway, Riley had closed her bedroom door.

Through the door, soft sobs echoed. Madison knocked, barely making any noise. She didn't want their mom to hear.

"Riley?" she said, her voice barely a whisper. "Come on, Riley, let me in."

The sobs stopped. Madison held her breath. The doorknob jostled. Riley opened the door, her eyes red, her face streaked. "What?"

Madison peeked into the room. A drawing of a blue and white waterfall, starting nearly at the ceiling, flowed down, ending with some brown rocks. It looked almost real. Birthday balloons floated nearby.

In the center was Riley—Madison could tell because of the shoulder-length hair and the bright purple ribbon tilted on Riley's head. Madison was there, too. Mom and Dad—grinning. OK, that might not have been exactly how it happened.

"You did this by yourself?" Madison asked.

"Yes." Riley crossed her arms, chin thrust out. "So what?"

"It's really good." With a grin, Madison walked over to the drawing of the birthday cake, candles lit.

"What's your birthday wish?"

Riley bit her lip, then looked away. She shrugged. "Doesn't matter."

Madison sat cross-legged on the floor. "Come on, Riley, tell me."

Her sister took a deep breath and looked at Madison with sparkling eyes. "I wanna draw pictures when I grow up." The words merged into one long one, Riley spoke so quickly. "I want to go to a museum and see my pictures on the wall." She stared at the bucket and sighed. "I don't want anyone to be able to wash them away."

Riley dipped the sponge into the bucket. She straightened, and a tear rolled down her cheek.

With a quick step, Madison stepped in front of Riley. The soaking sponge hit her right in the chest. Riley's eyes widened, and she winced. "I'm sorry, Madison. I didn't mean to."

Madison chuckled. "It's OK, Ri-Ri." She looked from the wall to Riley. "I have an idea."

She ran to her room and grabbed the camera her parents had given her for Christmas. "You might not be able to keep your drawing, but we can take a picture. And keep it forever."

Her sister grinned. "Really?"

Madison smiled. "Really."

She used up half the roll of film before she was satisfied. "When can I see it?" Riley asked.

"Not until we use up the rest of the film."

Riley frowned.

"Don't worry. I'll take a bunch of pictures at the pool today."

"OK." Riley's voice was small. "I'd better get started. It'll take forever."

"I'll help you," Madison said, running to the bathroom. She paused at the soap dish where she'd dropped the charm bracelet earlier that morning. She clasped it around her wrist and returned with a bath sponge.

The two girls stood in front of the giant picture. "It really is pretty, Riley."

Madison rubbed off the washable brown and black markers that had created the rock. She started singing "Puff the Magic Dragon," making up her own words.

> When things go bad, and life seems so unfair,
> Just hold on tight with all your might, and I'll always
> be there.

The song made Riley smile even as her masterpiece disappeared with each layer of soap and water.

Finally, the wall was blank.

"Do you think Mama will love me again if she sees the wall all clean?" Riley asked, her voice small.

"She loves you."

"When I'm good." Riley sat on the bed, but she didn't flop down like usual. "Can you teach me how to be good, Madison? So Mama will love me as much as she loves you?"

Madison blinked a couple of times and toyed with the bracelet on her wrist. How was she supposed to fix this? Because even Madison could see Riley pushed Mom's buttons without even trying.

"Come here, squirt."

Riley got off the bed and swiped her eyes. "What?"

"We're going to dance. It always makes me feel better." Madison held out her hands.

Riley took them, and Madison started to sing, her feet moving in the box step her mother had taught her.

When things go bad, and life seems so unfair,
Just hold on tight with all your might, and I'll always
be there.

She twirled Riley around. Riley fell back onto the bed giggling.

Madison chuckled. "We need lots of practice." She stared down at her little sister, whose eyes were still red from crying. "Tell you what? You can come swimming with me, and then we'll figure out a plan."

"To make Mama love me. Just a little?"

The words hurt Madison's heart, but she pasted a confident smile on her face, even though she had no idea exactly how to keep her promise.

"After we're through, Riley, Mom will love you the most."

Pine trees lined the road to the Riverton mine. The scent permeated everything. Riley took in a deep breath and shivered. Why did the most evil people plant themselves in the most beautiful, remote places?

The answer was obvious. Because no one could hear the screams.

She gripped the armrest with a death hold. Thayne covered her hand with his own, giving her a quizzical look. They were heading up a mountain road into another remote location.

She'd been there, done that, just two days ago.

"You OK?"

"I'm not fond of lonely dirt roads with two-hundred-foot cliffs on one side and no guardrail," she said, her voice dry.

"You should try the million-dollar highway in Colorado," Thayne said. "This is nothing."

"I'll take your word for it."

She glanced in the backseat. Shep sat, his back stiff, watching over Brett. He'd insisted on coming but now sagged against the door.

"How are you holding up?" Riley asked.

"Fine." He gritted his teeth, and his hands shook.

Brett obviously wasn't fine, but he clearly didn't want to talk about it. She faced front to give him some privacy from prying eyes. A glint on the side of the road grabbed her attention. Another camera, well hidden.

"More surveillance?" Thayne asked even before she could point it out.

"Cal's company has contracts with Homeland Security. I test the unclassified prototypes. It's a win-win. Just before your dad got sick, he arrested a group of rustlers that had been dogging all the ranchers in the area."

"I never would've thought your brother would become a Silicon Valley giant. I don't think he ever saw the high end of a C in high school."

"He's proud of that," Brett said. "He liked knowing he was smarter than people believed him to be."

Riley didn't like the suspicions prickling her mind, and she had to press Brett. "Do both you and your brother hold stake in the ranch?"

"He owns forty-nine percent; I have fifty-one. Whoever stayed to work the land received controlling interest."

"And you don't resent him earning money off your work?" Riley pushed.

"Dad wanted it that way. I think he hoped Cal would come back someday." Brett chuckled. "Besides, it's a fair swap. I own forty-nine percent of his company since I helped fund the start-up."

Thayne arched an eyebrow in Riley's direction, and at that moment Brett paused, narrowing his gaze at her.

"I should have seen this coming." His brow furrowed. "You want to know if Cal could have poisoned the water or kidnapped Cheyenne. First, he hasn't been back to Wyoming in years. He has no motive for the former, and he was the keynote speaker at a big tech conference in Hong Kong over the last week. He couldn't have done this."

"He could've hired someone."

"What's he got to gain?" Brett challenged.

"With Cheyenne in the picture, you could have children. If you died without an heir, he gets the ranch."

"Our money doesn't come from the ranch, Special Agent Lambert. Cal's company is worth billions. The ranch is small potatoes."

Billions. OK, so money wasn't a motive.

"I had to ask. Your relationship with Cheyenne puts a different spin on my profile."

"Do you always assume the worst in people?" Brett asked.

Riley winced at the truth in his words.

"Back off, Riverton. Riley's only focus is finding Cheyenne, so if she insults you, that's just too bad."

Thayne clasped Riley's hand, squeezing it in support.

"It's fine," she said. "I understand."

"Well, I don't have to like it," Thayne muttered.

Brett raised a brow. "Guess I'm not the only one with a clandestine relationship."

Thayne's knuckles whitened on the steering wheel. At least they were driving. She wouldn't have to keep Thayne from knocking out Brett with one punch.

Fortunately, the sign to the Riverton mine loomed at the right, framed by aspens. A series of cameras pointed down.

"How long has the surveillance been active?" Thayne asked.

"We started with two cameras at the mine's entrance." Brett's voice had turned gravelly with fatigue. "After I became sick, I added a few more."

"Do you have images of this road for the last few weeks?" Riley knew if she could get ahold of that tape, they might finally have a concrete lead to follow.

"Yes. Part of Cal's innovation was video compression technology. The cameras can record a year's worth of motion-detected movement. No need to erase data nightly or weekly."

Thayne let out a low whistle. "That technology could be a big help to law enforcement if it's not cost prohibitive."

"Cal's made it inexpensive and reliable. He freelanced out the development. Said he paid through the nose, but the manufacturing costs are low."

"You're proud of him," Riley said.

"Yeah, he thumbed his nose at his past and created a new future. I admire Cal for that . . ." Brett's voice trailed off.

Riley glanced into the backseat. Brett's eyes had closed. "Is he OK?"

"No. He shouldn't have come." Shep scowled. "Stubborn fool. He won't let me call his brother. All Brett's thinking about is Cheyenne, but he needs to take care of himself if he hopes to recover fully."

Shep took in a wheezing breath, and a painful-sounding hack erupted from his lungs. He yanked a handkerchief from his pocket.

The coughing fit emitted from deep within his chest. Speckles of blood stained the white linen. Finally, it stopped. He pocketed the evidence and blinked to clear his watering eyes. "There's a dirt road right beyond that big boulder at the top of the hill. Slow down. It's barely visible."

Thayne eased off the gas. A large rock at least six feet in diameter loomed a few hundred feet up the road.

"Is the lane always this deserted?"

Brett's eyes fluttered open. "The Wyoming jade vein was tapped out before my grandfather died. There's a bit of gold and quartz, but for the most part, we've opened it to tourists until the first snowfall. I closed it about two weeks ago because of the water contamination."

"Well before Cheyenne was taken," Thayne mused.

"Turn here," Shep interrupted.

Thayne yanked the SUV to the left. "Damn, that came out of nowhere."

"I warned you." Shep held on to the back of Riley's seat, his thin hands trembling with the effort.

The SUV rumbled onto a barely visible dirt road, grass nearly overgrowing the path. The vehicle rocked back and forth across the bumpy road.

"No wonder this place is deserted." Riley catapulted up, her seat belt the only thing keeping her from hitting her head on the roof. "You guys came here to play when you were kids?"

"Horses are a much more direct route," Thayne said.

"Two miles ahead," Brett whispered, his voice barely audible.

Riley's stomach roiled with each bounce. The road wound around hills following the flattest terrain, definitely not the most straightforward route.

Soon a large grove of pines appeared directly in front of them, in the middle of the road.

"Go around them," Brett said, his voice even weaker.

Riley hoped the road ended near the waterfall because she had no doubt he wouldn't be able to walk very far.

"It's like we're journeying into another world," Riley said. The trees thickened into pine walls on either side of them, hemming them in in a claustrophobic prison. "Like civilization doesn't exist."

Thayne focused on the road, the vehicle slowing down as they went deeper and deeper into the woods. "Any cameras up here, Brett?"

He shook his head. "This place is private. Our . . ." He cleared his throat. "*My* sanctuary."

The waterfall had been his and Cheyenne's place. Their special place.

With no cameras—whoever took the photos of him and Cheyenne had known that.

The road ended with a rock outcropping jutting up from the ground.

Thayne hit the brakes. "Now what?"

"We're here."

Brett opened the door, but Shep jumped out and rounded the SUV. "Stay put, Mr. Riverton."

Thayne shut off the engine. Riley opened the door and grabbed her satchel. The strong scent of lilacs overwhelmed her the moment she stepped out of the vehicle.

She stepped onto the ground, her feet sinking into red mud. Exactly like that found in the machine shop at Riverton Ranch.

"Thayne," she shouted, and pointed to the ground, flicking the mud from her shoes. "The poisoned horse was here." She bent down next to a stream and took a water sample to be analyzed.

"There's no need to collect samples. I've done extensive testing. Copper is the culprit," Brett said quietly.

"From your mines?"

Brett shook his head. "There lies the irony. None of these mines contains significant copper deposits. The metal shouldn't be in the ground or water in more than normal concentrations."

She walked behind Brett, keeping a close eye on his progress. He walked slowly over the rocks, stopping every ten feet or so to take a shuddering breath. The gurgling of flowing water followed them through the woods.

Thayne led them into the trees. Bright purplish flowers littered the ground. The honey-fruit scent nearly overwhelmed Riley. Another few steps and something else wrinkled her nose.

A scent she recognized all too well.

"Stop," she shouted and scrambled in front of Brett and Thayne.

Thayne had stopped, his expression flat.

"Death," he whispered. He palmed his Glock and pushed Riley behind him.

She grabbed her pistol. "Do either of you have a weapon?" she asked in a whisper to Brett and Shep.

Shep nodded and opened his vest. A Colt .45.

"Keep watch."

The thick thatch of trees kept visibility to less than a few feet in front of them. Thayne silently stepped over the ground cover. He paused. The putrid smell of decomposing flesh grew stronger, along with the rush of a waterfall.

One step beyond the trees, and a vision from a fantasy appeared. Water rushed down rocks, flowing into a mirrorlike pool surrounded by purple, pink, blue, and white flowers.

Just across the clearing, halfway into the woods, a body lay face-down, the woman's dress torn to shreds but still visible.

Plum. The same color Thayne had described Cheyenne wearing the day she'd been abducted.

Then Riley saw the victim's hair. Her heart stuttered, and she closed her eyes in pain.

Cinnamon-colored hair, halfway down the woman's back.

Just like Cheyenne's.

"God no." Thayne's voice shook. "Ch . . . Cheyenne!"

CHAPTER SEVENTEEN

The forest floor tilted. Thayne shook his head back and forth, over and over. This wasn't happening. That cold, unmoving body couldn't be Cheyenne. It just couldn't.

Brett shoved through the trees behind Thayne.

"No. Oh God, no!" Brett fell to his knees and would have sunk to the ground if Shep hadn't propped up his boss.

Unable to process what his eyes took in, Thayne simply stared, frozen.

In the middle of a firefight, adrenaline and instinct took over. Fight or flight. Gut decisions kept you alive.

This was different.

His sister was dead.

Riley touched his arm. "Let me go."

Her request shook him out of his shock. He gripped her hand tightly. "No. You can't. Whoever did this could be nearby." His mind had numbed, but his body knew what to do. He clutched his Glock like an old friend and surveyed the trees lining the clearing. He had to protect Riley . . . and . . . He gulped. The body.

The rustle of leaves shuffling snapped his attention to the left. His hand tightened around the weapon.

A squirrel skittered to a spot beneath a pine. The little animal paused, raised his head, sniffed the air, and darted off.

Thayne relaxed his grip slightly. He took a step toward his sister.

Riley placed her hand on his shoulder. "Let me take care of the victim, Thayne. She's why I'm here."

He struggled to process her words, but her tone was as gentle and coaxing as her hand stroking down his back.

He stilled and sucked in a long, deep breath, blinking to stop the burning tears at the back of his eyes. He couldn't look away from the bloody, crumpled body. Part of him didn't want to be certain, to deny the truth facing him, even though over the last twelve hours his certainty that they'd find Cheyenne had dwindled. His faith had taken quite a few hits, and hope seemed like a fool's journey leading to disappointment.

"I'm doing a perimeter search first," he said, clinging to procedure. Secure the scene. Always. He surveyed the area. Shep had propped his boss against a tree, but the tremors had returned. "With his condition, we can't afford a surprise."

Riley nodded and unholstered her weapon while Thayne took one last look over at Brett. The guy looked as if he might keel over right there. Any last doubt Thayne had that Brett knew what had happened to Cheyenne had vanished. Not that he'd really believed Brett was behind her disappearance. He trusted his instincts. They'd kept him alive for more than a decade.

His instincts hadn't helped Cheyenne, though. God, what was he going to tell his father? His grandparents? His brothers?

"Don't move until I come back," he said to Riley. "Keep watch."

With silent steps, Thayne methodically checked the perimeter. On a heading due west, he paused. The ground cover had been disturbed.

Someone had come this way and attempted to camouflage their tracks. Thayne squatted next to the area.

They knew the woods—and how to track. He slipped his pen from his pocket and shifted a layer of vines to the right. The edges of a footprint became visible. Perhaps a hiking boot. Not a large size. Maybe a ten? And a thin guy, maybe 150 or so.

Thayne noted the location but didn't disturb it any further. He completed the surveillance and returned to the clearing. "The area's clear," he reported.

Riley lowered her weapon, as did Shep.

"I may have a partial footprint. I think it belongs to whoever did this." He let his gaze return to the remains. He still couldn't bear to think of the crumpled form as Cheyenne.

"Are you ready?" she asked.

He gritted his teeth and nodded.

On the way across the clearing, Riley snapped on her gloves.

Thayne bowed his head. *God, please let us be wrong. Please.* He didn't pray all that often, less than he was brought up to, that's for sure, but sometimes prayer was all a man had to hold on to.

Riley held his gaze for a moment before giving him a last sympathetic glance. She stiffened her back and knelt beside the body. He could see the reality in her face. She hadn't wanted the search for Cheyenne to end this way, either, but had suspected it would all along. He could read it in Riley's eyes.

She rocked on her heels, then pulled out a measuring tape from her satchel. "Cheyenne's five nine, isn't she?"

"Yes."

"Weight about one thirty?"

He nodded.

Riley looked up at him. "This isn't Cheyenne," she said. "This girl is only five six and extremely thin. No muscle tone to her legs. She was almost wasting away."

"Not Cheyenne." *Not Cheyenne.* Thayne had to keep repeating the words to himself. They still had a chance to find his sister alive. Thayne blinked against the sudden burn in his eyes.

At the same time, Brett dropped his head in his hands. When he looked up, tears welled in his eyes. "Not her?" His head tilted back, and he looked up at the sky. "Not her." He seemed to be mouthing something and sagged back in utter relief.

"But it's her dress," Thayne said.

Riley tugged at the dress's collar. "Probably. But the size is all wrong for this girl. And this is a Dior. That doesn't fit with the closet I examined at her house. She didn't spend a lot of money on her wardrobe."

"She hated shopping." Thayne couldn't imagine Cheyenne having the patience to try on designer anything. Let alone spend the bucks to purchase it.

Brett cleared his throat. "That's Cheyenne's dress. I bought it for her in Las Vegas."

Thayne hunkered down beside Riley. "Why is this girl wearing Cheyenne's clothes? What does she have to do with her disappearance?"

"I have no idea," Riley said. "Her condition doesn't align at all with my theory that they kidnapped Cheyenne because she's a doctor and they needed medical care. The girl has sallow skin. There are marks on her wrists and ankles. She was restrained before she died . . ."

Riley didn't speak for a moment. "Bastard," she whispered under her breath and lifted the woman's hand.

Thayne had seen his share of missing limbs as a result of IEDs, but nothing quite like this. Her fingertips had been cut off, not from an explosive, but one by one.

With a gentle touch, Riley pushed aside the victim's hair and opened her mouth, wincing before sitting back on her heels. "Her killer pulled her teeth. She'll be very difficult to identify without fingerprints or dental records and with all the bruising on her face, unless her DNA is on file."

The poor girl's final moments must have been horrific.

"Who are you?" Riley asked quietly, staring unblinking at the body.

Riley's dedication to her job blew Thayne away. She confronted this kind of brutality all the time. He didn't know how she kept going case after case. Thayne had found a way to live with the violence of war by focusing on saving his teammates and those who were in danger from the enemy, but what Riley did every day meant she faced death at the hands of psychopaths. Yet here she was, treating this stranger, this victim, with the gentleness and caring of a dear friend, while her sharp eyes analyzed every detail with the detachment of a scientist.

She truly amazed him.

"Don't worry, I'll take you home. And I'll find who hurt . . . you . . ." Riley turned the woman's head ever so gently. "Thayne." She motioned him over and pointed to the back of the victim's ear. Blood had caked in her hair, and Riley probed a wound. "It's a small round hole. This woman was killed with the same type of weapon as the man we found yesterday at the swimming hole."

Thayne bent over to get a closer look. "Whoever killed Brett's employee killed her, too. Brett's connected to Cheyenne's disappearance, just not in the way we first thought."

Riley nodded. "He's now killed twice."

And would, no doubt, kill again.

Unless they found him first.

◆ ◆ ◆

Fifteen Years Ago

Screams echoed from all directions in and around the swimming pool. The sun reflected off the concrete and beat down hard. Madison had never seen the pool quite so crowded. Everyone was there.

"Maddy, look at me!"

She spun around, her gaze flying to the pool's edge. Riley laughed and jumped toward Madison, tucking her legs and letting the cannonball fly.

A wave of water splashed over her head. She grinned and waited for Riley's head to break the surface.

"That's your biggest yet, Ri-Ri."

Her sister shoved her hair out of her eyes and beamed with a smile so wide, Madison thought Riley's cheeks might split.

She hugged Madison. "Thanks for helping me with my room. And thanks for making Mom bring me," she said in an undertone.

Madison glanced over at their mother, covered head to toe with sunscreen, a huge floppy hat hiding her face from the light.

"Mom's having fun."

Riley sputtered with giggles. "She hates the pool. I'm not sure how long she'll put up with being out in the heat. Wanna play Marco Polo before she makes us go home?"

"Too many people." Madison's gaze swept the crowd. No one recognized her. That made it easier to relax.

"Ah, come on," Riley whined. "We played every time we came to the pool last summer."

"Oh, OK." Secretly, Madison loved the game. But like her mother said, when you grow up, sometimes you have to leave the little-girl games behind.

Not today, though.

Madison closed her eyes. "Marco."

"Polo," Riley shouted from a ways away.

Madison didn't delay turning toward the voice. If she waited too long, Riley would move . . . or the rest of the chatter would confuse the direction. Madison turned toward the voice. She bumped into someone. He let out a curse and swiped her legs under the water. Madison kicked at him. "Jerk," she said, then shouted, "Marco."

"Polo!"

With a quick dive toward the voice, Madison reached out blindly. She went under, then jumped up, sucking in a deep breath.

"You playing baby games now?"

Madison's eyes snapped open. The blonde hair was a giveaway, the disgusted look way too familiar. Madison straightened and pushed her hair out of her eyes. "Of course not."

"Polo!" Riley shouted. "Polo, Maddy!"

Madison ignored the call.

"I was thinking about coming to your slumber party," Ella, the most popular girl in junior high, said, her nose crinkling. "But I bet your baby sister will crash the party. Are you planning on playing Candy Land?"

"My sister isn't invited," Madison snapped. "But you wouldn't want to come. Truth or Dare might reveal too much about what you let Craig Gentry do to you in the closet at Olivia's birthday party."

"Don't try to sit at our table on Monday, Mad-deee."

"It's Madison," she said as the girl swam away, her blonde curls still dry and falling out of a topknot.

Madison turned around and faced a crestfallen Riley.

"I can't come? But you promised. After we finished the room, you said I could come." Riley's eyes gleamed.

It was probably the chlorine.

"Girls, we're leaving." Their mother stood, her eye makeup running down reddened cheeks.

Riley crossed her arms and glared at Madison. "You lied to me."

Madison rolled her eyes. "Look, we had some fun, but I'm grown up and you're still a kid, Riley. Maybe when you get into junior high, we can hang out together again."

Riley splashed Madison in her face and swam to the side of the pool. Her sister glared at her even as tears flowed down her cheeks.

"I don't need a sister like you, Madison. Why don't you disappear? I'd be happy again."

"I just might."

Neither sister would ever forget those words . . . or how true they would become.

◆ ◆ ◆

The beautiful clearing where Brett and Cheyenne had loved each other had become a crime scene. One more destroyed memory Riley couldn't stop from happening.

A loud zipper sounded across the clearing, closing the black body bag. The preliminary photos had been taken, and now the coroner's team was removing the body. Riley had gathered all the data she could, but she had more questions than answers.

Another victim. Nameless until they identified her.

Brett stood on the perimeter, swaying on his feet, his jaw drawn tight. Shep braced his boss with a thin shoulder. "Mr. Riverton. Please let me take you home. You need rest."

"All right." Brett gave Shep a tired nod but turned to Thayne. "How else can I help?"

"Give us access to your private investigators?" Thayne said without hesitation. "And we need any information you have on the man we found buried at the swimming hole."

Brett nodded. "Done."

Thayne stretched out his hand, and Brett shook it. "Go home. You look like hell."

"Call me the minute you find something." He swallowed. "Either way."

"Of course." Thayne looked down at Brett's left hand. "Cheyenne deserves your faith, Brett. She always did. Once we find her, don't screw it up again. Deputy Ironcloud will take you back to your place. Then put your PIs in touch with him."

"Do you think Brett will be OK?" Riley asked, watching him walk slowly away.

"Shep said he is improving." Thayne rubbed his temple. "But if we don't find Cheyenne, I'm not sure he'll want to get well."

Riley went quiet. What if something were to happen to Thayne? Would she want to go on? Could she?

"Where do we go from here, Riley?"

She'd been considering the question since the moment she realized the murdered woman was wearing Cheyenne's clothes.

"I think we start over. Your sister loves fiercely, doesn't she?"

Thayne crouched down to tie his shoe and looked at her strangely. "Of course. The whole family does. Sometimes to a fault."

"I can see that about you all." Riley paused for a moment, struggling to explain her theory. "Thayne, if Cheyenne discovered why Brett pushed her away, if she realized he was ill—"

"She'd do everything in her power to help him." Thayne rose to his feet.

"She might have stumbled onto something out here she wasn't meant to see."

Thayne grabbed her face in his hands and kissed her soundly on the lips. "You're brilliant. Have I ever told you that? I know the place to start. We're going west."

Thayne dragged Riley to the footprint he'd found. She squinted in amazement when he moved the ground cover away. "How did you ever see this? It looks the same as everything else around it."

"Not really. See the twig here, it's bent away from the others. Someone wandered through. But it's too high to be a bobcat or even a mountain lion or bear. Whoever made this was walking upright."

"Couldn't a bear do that?" she asked, searching with difficulty for the details that Thayne noticed so easily. A lot like what she did at a crime scene. Thayne was a wilderness profiler.

"Bears don't typically stand on their hind legs unless they're curious about something," he said. "I don't see any claw scratches marking the territory here, either. That's why I searched for a print."

"You think whoever killed that girl headed in this direction?"

"No other reason to hide the print."

"What's out this way?" she asked.

"Riverton land bumps up against the National Forest within a few miles. Nothing much between here and there but that ghost town and the vestiges of more old mines."

"Big enough for several people to hide . . . say, for a week?"

"Absolutely." Thayne nodded.

His satphone rang. "Blackwood."

"We've had another break-in. This time at the hospital."

◆ ◆ ◆

Late afternoon sun had dimmed the sky a bit when Thayne's vehicle screamed to the front of the hospital. He could barely stand not following up on that print, but he sure as hell wasn't about to leave Riley alone.

At least his brother had agreed to lead the team. Jackson was the best tracker in town. Next to Kade.

"This is a hospital?" Riley asked, taking a full view of the small building.

"A dozen beds. It's usually not too full."

Thayne checked his weapon and jumped out of the SUV, meeting Riley around the car. They strode between two sheriff's vehicles parked across from the entrance. A fire truck, lights flashing, waited in the parking lot.

A group of firefighters pushed through the sliding doors, mumbling, scowls on their faces.

"What's wrong?" Thayne asked, not wanting to know the answer.

"You'd better catch this son of a bitch, Thayne," one of the men groused. "Guy doesn't care who he hurts. Knocked old Nurse Crawly on the side of the head."

"She's OK, though?"

The guy shook his head. "Hit her just right. We lost her."

Thayne gritted his teeth. He was tired of being one step behind these killers.

"They're getting more desperate," Riley said.

"And we're no closer to identifying them—or finding Cheyenne."

Deputy Pendergrass met Thayne in the hallway. "Nurse Crawly . . ." The man's face was pale.

"I heard. Give me the full report."

Pendergrass didn't bother looking at his notes, but Thayne trusted his father's right-hand man as much as anyone on the SEAL team.

"They didn't come through the front in view of the cameras, so they must have entered through the side door."

"Those are locked, right?" Thayne said. He had no doubts because he'd assisted his father with the county emergency drill when he'd first arrived in town.

"They had keycard access. The hospital IT guy is looking at any anomalies in the record. They knew what they were doing, Thayne. It was well planned. They went directly to the hospital pharmacy. Nurse Crawly had the key. We think she got in the way."

"Just like your grandmother at Cheyenne's place," Riley commented to Thayne. "I'll bet the forensics will be just as clean."

"And this time they decided not to leave any witnesses." Gram had come so close to losing her life. He turned to Pendergrass. "Did Nurse Crawly say anything before she passed away?"

"She never regained consciousness."

"Damn it to hell." Thayne rubbed the back of his neck. "Any idea how many broke in?"

"No way to know."

"Maybe not for you and me," Thayne said, arching a brow at Riley.

"I'd like to see the crime scene before you go into any more details," she ordered.

"You got it." The deputy led them down the hall and through a set of double doors plastered with crime scene tape. They entered a room labeled PHARMACY. Inside, a body was covered with a sheet.

"Coroner's on his way," Pendergrass said.

Jan, his grandmother's favorite nurse, walked up to them, sniffling. "I just left her alone for a minute, Thayne." She couldn't take her gaze away from the sheet. "Maybe if I'd been with her—"

"Nothing would have stopped them, Jan," Thayne said, his words certain.

She nodded and took in a few shuddering breaths. Thayne put his arm around her while she sobbed against his chest.

Riley eased away from them, but Thayne took in every movement. She scanned the room inch by inch, snapped on her gloves, and knelt beside the body before lifting the sheet.

Thayne watched that odd focus appear in her eyes. "Clear the room," he said softly.

"Now?" Pendergrass asked. "Don't you want to interview Jan?"

"She needs a break," Thayne said, gently handing her off to Pendergrass. "And Special Agent Lambert needs quiet to do her job."

Everyone but Thayne left the room, and he backed into the corner, taking his own inventory of the crime scene. Would he see what she did?

The place wasn't ransacked, not like Cheyenne's office, so they'd known exactly where to go and what they were looking for. Thayne knew that much.

Riley pulled the sheet lower, revealing the mottled bruises on her arms. "Someone grabbed her wrists, squeezed tight. You can see the bruising."

"Cowards," Thayne muttered. Nurse Crawly had been no threat to them.

Riley rounded a chest-high glass counter in front of the pharmaceuticals, then went up one aisle and down the next before stopping. "They took whatever was on this shelf, but nothing else."

"Just like before," Thayne said. "They knew what they wanted. But why more drugs? They didn't even clean out Cheyenne's clinic."

"Maybe they needed more?" Riley mused for a moment before retrieving her blue notebook from her satchel and flipping back a few pages. "Thayne, can you call Jan back in?"

Within a few minutes, Jan, red-eyed from crying, stood in front of Riley.

"Can you tell me which drugs were stolen?" Riley asked.

"Oh, that's easy, ma'am. I already made a list. Three different kinds of antibiotics, but they left penicillin," Jan said. "And they took all the oxycodone we had."

"Thank you," Riley said. "You've been a big help."

"Please, Agent Lambert. Find out who did this. Nurse Crawly . . . Well, she was like a grandmother to a lot of us. She didn't deserve this."

"I'll do my best."

Jan and Pendergrass left the room again.

Thayne joined Riley in the aisle, staring at the empty shelf. "Why come here? Why murder someone else?"

"They needed medication." Riley rubbed her eyes. "None of this makes any sense. It's as if I'm dealing with two different profiles."

She scanned the room once again. A glint off the glass counter caught her eye. She walked over and bent her knees so she was at eye level. "Thayne," she said, the pitch of her voice rising.

He hunkered down next to her. "What? The glass looks like it's been cleaned recently. So?"

"Look again," Riley said. "Most of the glass is smudgy, with fingerprints from the entire day. Except right down the center. There are two clean swipes. The surface was cleaned deliberately."

"What are you getting at?"

"Look at the center of the cleaned area. Do you see it?"

Thayne's eyes focused. Then he saw what Riley had noticed from across the room. For a moment, he couldn't breathe. "It can't be . . ."

In the center of the glass, pristine, perfect, and purposeful, was a single thumbprint.

CHAPTER EIGHTEEN

Cheyenne moistened a cloth in the small sink and filled another basin. The room had begun to close in on her. She was becoming weaker by the hour, but at least the sharp pains in her belly hadn't returned, proof that her suspicions had been correct. They were being poisoned.

The trouble was, the unnecessary surgery Cheyenne had performed—not the poison—would be the cause of her patient's death if she didn't get the antibiotics. And soon.

"Shh," she said softly, sitting in the chair beside the bed. She wrung out the rag and ran the damp cloth over Bethany's face and neck, then down her arms, torso, and legs. The fever was spiking again.

Cheyenne couldn't be sure if the antibiotics would help at this point. A post-op infection was raging inside Bethany's body.

She mumbled in her sleep. Cheyenne couldn't make out the words. The cloth had warmed, so she redipped it, squeezing out the excess, and started the process again. There was nothing else she could do for her patient.

After another stroke of Bethany's forehead, her eyes opened, glazed with fever. "I'm not going to make it, am I?" she whispered, her voice weak and hoarse. A tear squeezed from the corner of her eye. "I promised them. I promised I wouldn't leave. That I would protect them." She gripped Cheyenne's arm. "Please. You have to help the children. No one else can. No one else . . ." She coughed. "No one else knows."

"What's going on here, Bethany? Who are the children? What is this place?"

Bethany squinted at her. "Father. He . . . he took his children. Twisted."

"I got that. He's definitely a fry or two short of a Happy Meal."

The corners of Bethany's mouth tilted up. She breathed in, and a fit of coughing took over. Cheyenne raised her to a sitting position to help her breathe. A spattering of blood darkened the tissues Cheyenne had used.

"Dangerous," Bethany whispered, and her eyes closed.

"Bethany?" Cheyenne checked her pulse. A slow, regular thud throbbed against her fingertips. "Keep fighting. For the children."

Metal rattled metal. A key turned. The door pushed open. Ian walked in carrying a small duffel.

His movements stiff, he handed her the bag. "Is this what you needed?" He refused to meet her gaze.

Cheyenne rose and retrieved the satchel. She opened it and peered inside.

"Yes." She nodded. "Thank you."

"Good." Unlike all the other times he'd visited, he turned away from Cheyenne and Bethany.

"Ian? What's wrong?"

He hesitated and opened his jacket. Blood splattered his shirt.

"Are you hurt?"

"Not me. I couldn't . . . couldn't stop it." He blinked, but the rapid movement didn't stop tears from leaking out. He swiped at them. "I can't let anyone see. We don't cry."

He hurried to the door. She couldn't imagine what the poor boy had been forced to do. Whatever hold *Father* had on everyone here was strong. Her only hope was convincing Ian and Adelaide to help her. Bethany had run out of time. Cheyenne had to take a chance.

"Don't leave," she said. "I need your help."

"I can't. They suspect . . ."

"I'll be quick." Cheyenne grabbed a pouch containing cephalosporin and motioned for him to come with her. While she hung the IV, she sent him a sidelong glance. "I heard Father talking to Adelaide. He thinks I influence you."

Ian nodded.

"Have I?"

"I forgot about my life before I came here," he said, biting his lip. "You reminded me."

"You don't have to stay," she said, taking a deep breath. He had a conscience. She had to trust someone. "Ian, Bethany didn't have appendicitis."

"What? But you cut her open. I saw her appendix."

"I thought she needed the surgery, but her organ was healthy."

He shook his head in denial. "She was sick. I saw her."

Cheyenne touched his shoulder. "Someone's been poisoning her. And me."

Ian's knees buckled.

"Sit down, put your head between your knees, and take deep breaths."

He sat on the foot of Bethany's bed and sucked in air. Soon he raised his head, tears gleaming in his eyes. "How?"

"Either food or water or both. I haven't eaten anything since then. I'm feeling better, but whoever's doing this will figure it out soon and finish the job. They want Bethany dead."

"No. Everyone here loves her. We need her." His desperate voice rose.

"Shh."

He slapped his hand over his mouth, and she grabbed his hands. "I need you to do something very difficult, Ian. Call my father and my brother. They can help us all. They could even find your parents."

Ian snorted. "My folks wouldn't care. They were never home. They probably never realized I disappeared." He looked up at her, and for the first time, the sixteen-year-old rock morphed into a frightened kid. "It's impossible. No one leaves here."

The door slammed open. A man with red hair, sprinkled with silver, walked into the room, cane in one hand, a frown on his face. His suit appeared to be Armani, perfectly pressed. His shoes gleamed with a recent shoe shine. She'd never seen someone who oozed with perfection to quite this degree.

He really gave her the creeps.

"Ian, I was afraid I'd find you here. Micah needs your guidance. He refuses to obey, and I do not wish to be forced to punish him. Or you, since he is your charge. Go to him. Now."

"Yes, Father." Ian gave a slight bow of his head.

Cheyenne stared at her cot. She had a makeshift knife under her pillow, but she couldn't get to it. Ian walked past them, touching Bethany's cheek once before leaving the room.

The man she knew only as Father faced her.

"Doctor Blackwood, how is my Bethany?"

"If you'd taken her to the hospital when she first became ill, she would be well by now," Cheyenne snapped.

"Your family taught you no manners, I see," he said with a strange calmness in his voice. "Good breeding always tells."

The dead cold of his eyes sent a shiver through Cheyenne. He took a step toward her patient. Every survival instinct inside of her urged her to keep away from him, but she forced herself to stand firm and meet his gaze, unwavering.

"You have your medicine. When will Bethany awaken?"

Until now she'd assumed Father had poisoned them, but if so, why ask about Bethany? Some elaborate ruse? The children loved Bethany, if Ian's words were any indication. And she loved them. Was he jealous?

The room's silence prickled at Cheyenne's nerves. He didn't blink, didn't look away. He simply stood, watching her, taunting her with his stare, waiting for her response.

She refused to submit to him.

The corner of his mouth lifted just a tad. "Well done," he said. "You have courage. Unfortunately, it's misplaced. I shall ask you again. When will my daughter awaken?"

Cheyenne wasn't going to win against this man. To get away, she'd have to bide her time. Adelaide was her only hope now. Ian didn't have the strength. Until she could speak with Adelaide again, she'd have to play along with Father. In this case, honesty might actually work.

"I don't know. She may not make it."

Father's brow furrowed. He crossed the room and laid his hand on Bethany's forehead. "You can fight this, Daughter. I know you can."

For the first time Cheyenne saw emotion flicker across his face. He cared for Bethany. Everyone seemed to.

A loud bell rang, and Father knocked on the steel door. It opened.

Adelaide stood in the doorway. She refused to meet Cheyenne's gaze but stared down at her feet in a submissive stance.

Father paused at the prison cell's door. "I suggest you see to it that Bethany recovers, Doctor. If I am forced to return for a second visit, you'll wish I hadn't."

The door closed and latched shut. Cheyenne sank to the chair, her knees shaking. He'd shown her his face, and she knew what that meant.

If she'd doubted her fate before, she was certain now. She'd never leave this place alive.

◆ ◆ ◆

The small pharmaceutical dispensary had become quite crowded. Riley stood in the corner while the forensic team pulled the fingerprint from the glass. Whoever had taken the risk to place that print could very well end up saving Cheyenne's life. If they could use the information to find her.

"The damn thing is pristine," Pendergrass muttered as he completed the task.

"Run it against all the databases you can," Riley ordered. "Put a rush on the job."

Thayne stroked his chin. "While you're at it, run another check on the surrounding towns for any more medical supply thefts with a similar crime scene signature."

"You got it." Pendergrass grabbed his gear and raced out of the room.

Riley's heart skipped a beat, a small flicker of hope rekindling.

"A break," Thayne said, his words laced with astonishment.

"More importantly, an insider who's willing to take risks," Riley said. "They might be unable to contact us directly, but they left us the only message they could."

"They couldn't just write us a note?" Thayne mused.

"You caught that detail." Riley had been hoping to keep the little bit of information from him. She should have known better. He had a good instinct for the criminal mind.

"Anyone who has to resort to this subtle of an attempt at communication is living in fear for their life."

Riley couldn't argue with his logic. She simply nodded in agreement. "Hopefully we get a fast match. IAFIS has one hundred million fingerprints on file, though. The search could take as long as twenty-four hours." She sank down the wall, studying the room from another angle. "Whoever left the print is taking a big risk. The clock just started ticking even louder."

Deputy Ironcloud shot through the door and raced over to Thayne. He whispered to him.

Thayne turned to Riley. "Dad wants us at the sheriff's office. He's already started the daily press conference."

"We should keep the fingerprint quiet, Thayne. For our insider's sake."

"They'll push hard."

"Your father should imply we don't have any solid leads," she said. "If the kidnappers believe we're onto them, it could put not only the insider's life, but also Cheyenne's, in danger."

Thayne nodded. As they pulled up to the sheriff's office, Riley couldn't count the number of news vans blocking the street. Cheyenne's disappearance had made all of the major national news networks.

Sheriff Blackwood already stood at a podium in front of the building with a dozen microphones propped in front of him, making an opening statement.

Thayne tugged on her jacket. "Dad needs us."

Riley pulled back, shaking her head. "I can't be seen. I'm not here *officially*. You know that."

Before Thayne could join his father on stage, the introductions had been completed, so Thayne hung back with her. The sheriff could hold his own, and he gave away very little, thank goodness. She should have known he'd be discreet.

"Sheriff Blackwood, there have been three murders uncovered in the last forty hours in Singing River. How do you feel about not having any leads on your daughter yet? Do you think your daughter is still alive?" a reporter shouted out.

Riley sucked in a breath. "What a jerk," she muttered.

The color in Carson's cheeks rose, and Thayne started forward. Carson caught his son's eye and held up a hand. "I have confidence in my deputies, in the Wyoming State Department of Criminal Investigations, and in the FBI personnel on site to do everything they can to find her."

"We've been told DCI and the Denver field office only sent minimal support," another reporter shouted. "Do you believe the government has provided enough assistance to find your daughter?"

Brutal questions. Riley didn't know how Carson could stand there and take it. One sidelong glance at Thayne and she could tell he was seconds from either decking a couple of the reporters or launching himself onto the stage.

"Your dad's doing fine," she said under her breath.

Thayne gave her a curt nod, but his jaw throbbed and those fingers on his right hand had begun their infinitesimal but revealing movements.

"We're lucky enough to have FBI Special Agent Riley Lambert reviewing all the evidence. Special Agent Lambert was instrumental recently in tracking down Vincent Wayne O'Neal, the East Coast Serial Killer."

The sheriff looked over the sea of reporters directly at Riley. They all whirled around.

Riley groaned. When Tom got word, she was sunk.

"Sheriff, we have information you received a threat if you continued the investigation. Why would you put her life at risk by holding this press conference?"

The question came from a single reporter standing to the side. The group gasped and spun back toward the sheriff, shouting more and more questions.

His spine straightened, and he held up his hand. "I'm not free to discuss all the specific details of an ongoing investigation. Once we find my daughter, I'll provide more information."

"Impressive," Riley whispered to Thayne. "He's unflappable."

"Not on the inside. See his right hand twitching? That's his tell when nerves are getting to him."

Riley leaned closer. "Similar to his son's."

Thayne stared at her in surprise and glanced down at his right hand, stilling the involuntary movements.

"What about the fingerprint your department recently discovered at the latest murder location, Sheriff? Is that your best lead?"

"Son of a bitch," Thayne bit out. "We've got a leak."

The sheriff cleared his throat. "No comment for now."

The flurry of questioning escalated.

"One at a time. I'll get to all your questions."

Thayne and Riley backed away from the crowd. "We've got a big problem," she said. "Whoever left us the print is in imminent danger."

"We can't get them to hold the information; it's live coverage."

Riley's phone sounded off. She glanced at the screen. Damn.

"I have to take this," she whispered to Thayne, holding her head high and pushing her way past the reporters and camera flashes into the sheriff's station.

She didn't stop until she'd entered Sheriff Blackwood's personal office and slumped in his chair.

Thayne followed her in and closed the door behind them. She looked at him and sighed. He might as well witness the carnage. She tapped her phone. "Lambert."

"What the hell are you doing in Singing River, Wyoming, Riley?"

"Hello, Tom."

"Am I correct in the assumption that you connected a kidnapping in Singing River to your sister's abduction? Did you or did you not receive specific orders *not* to investigate your sister's disappearance?"

"I'm not investigating Madison."

"You just *happen* to be visiting?"

"The sheriff's daughter is missing. The family asked for my help. How could I say no?"

"No is a pretty simple response," Tom bit out. "The Denver field office is already on the case. I checked. How did *you* get involved?"

She sighed. "I visited a year ago right before I accepted the profiler position. I was on vacation, and I got to know the sheriff and his family." He didn't say a word. She cleared her throat. "I was doing a little personal research."

Tom let out a sharp curse. "I've got the special agent in charge of the Denver field office ready to fly to DC and hang me up by my balls, Lambert. I warned you. You're suspended without pay, pending a full investigation into all your activities. Get back to DC, Riley. You are hanging on by a very thin thread. It might take intervention from the president himself to save your job, and I think he's a little too busy to bother with an FBI special agent on probation."

Tom ended the call before she could even try to defend herself. Not that she had a defense. She'd known the moment she'd agreed to come to Singing River that she'd face this choice. Maybe somewhere inside she'd wanted the showdown.

Thayne's brow rose. "Your boss has a loud voice. Is it true? I knew you weren't sanctioned to be here, but you actually defied a direct order?"

Riley avoided his all-too-knowing look.

"You sacrificed your career for us?"

"Don't make me out to be some kind of martyr, Thayne. I came because I wanted to help you find your sister. I couldn't bear to sit in my apartment alone for two weeks twiddling my thumbs. But I came mostly because the only time I've ever felt like I belonged anywhere was the week I spent with you last year."

She slipped her badge from her satchel and turned it over and over in her hand.

"You joined the FBI to find your sister," Thayne said. "Go back to DC. You got us a long way toward finding Cheyenne. We can handle it from here."

"You want me to leave?" Riley couldn't believe how much his words hurt.

"Well, hell." Thayne gripped her shoulders and raised her to her feet. She winced, and he released her right arm. "*You're* the reason we found that fingerprint, and when we know the identity of the person, I don't want just any field agent investigating. I want you here, more than anything." He looked into her eyes. "But Riley, what happens if you lose your job? What about your sister?"

Riley bowed her head, avoiding his gaze. "I want to find my sister, Thayne, but I know in my heart she's dead. Cheyenne could still be alive. If I have to make a choice, I'm going to make the choice I hope any agent would have made fifteen years ago when my sister was taken. I'm not leaving."

A sharp rap sounded on the door. A man in a pressed suit flipped open his badge. "I'm Agent Nolan from the Denver field office." He cleared his throat. "I've been instructed to confiscate your badge and gun, Special Agent Lambert, and to escort you off the premises."

Riley didn't hesitate. She pulled her weapon from the holster and shoved the gun and badge at him.

Thayne stepped between them. "I don't think so, Agent Nolan."

"Look, Deputy—"

"You're in my jurisdiction right now at the request of the Singing River sheriff's office. I'd walk away if I were you. We need her skills more than we need yours."

Riley grabbed Thayne's arm. "Don't cause trouble. You need the resources. I don't matter. Only Cheyenne does."

Nolan shook his head. "Man, sometimes the job sucks," he groused, placing Riley's badge and weapon in a bag. "I'll have to report this . . ." He looked at his watch. "It's after five. I'll have time to write the report tomorrow."

"Thanks, Nolan," Riley said, unable to believe anyone would take a risk for her, especially someone she'd never met.

"I don't know what you did, Lambert, but I've never seen so many upper brass so pissed off." He winked at her right before he walked out the door. "Congrats."

Riley dropped her head in her hands. "Now I'm really on my own."

"Hardly." Thayne tilted her chin, forcing her to meet his gaze. "Look around you. We have all the support we need. You've even got Underhill convinced behavioral analysis might actually work. You provide a hell of a lot more value than a few databases, Riley."

"You don't understand." She looked away. "What I do is a team effort. I can see now I should've brought in Tom at the beginning. He's more experienced than I am. Maybe he would have seen evidence or patterns I didn't see. I put your sister at risk by not telling you everything the moment I deplaned."

He pulled her close. "You and I both know your unit wasn't going to come out here to help. They would've contacted Denver if they even responded to us. At the beginning there was nothing to tie this scene to anything other than a one-off abduction. What could your team have done?"

"That's the problem. I don't know! Maybe found Cheyenne."

Thayne bit back a curse. "Fine, then we start from here and double our efforts. We have more information now than at any time since Cheyenne was taken."

His phone rang. He glanced at the screen and picked up. "Hudson, is everything all right?"

"Not really. Gram's missing."

◆ ◆ ◆

Dusk had hit. Two days ago at almost this exact time, Cheyenne had vanished. Now Gram was gone. Thayne flicked the fob, and the SUV unlocked.

Riley slid into the passenger side.

"You don't have to come," he said, slamming the door shut. "They could get a hit on the prints at any time."

"And they can reach us at a moment's notice. I'm going with you."

Thayne turned on the air conditioner to full blast. Hot air raced out. "It'll probably be cool once we get to the church," he said with a worried frown. "Where could she be?" he muttered.

"Alzheimer's patients wander," Riley said. "Even I know that much."

"Gram hasn't. At least not yet."

"But she's getting worse."

"Obviously," he snapped. "Alzheimer's is not something you get better from."

Riley didn't say a word. Thayne let out a curse and slammed his hand on the steering wheel. "Sorry."

"You don't have to apologize."

"Yeah. I do. It's just . . . she's vulnerable. I hate this damn disease."

Thayne pulled into the church parking lot and rolled down the window. The entire area surrounding the building was filled with parishioners cupping their hands, calling his grandmother's name, where over the last forty-eight hours they'd been calling Cheyenne's.

Feeling like his entire world was imploding, Thayne yanked the gearshift into park and jumped out of the vehicle. He caught sight of Pops near the tents. He hurried over to his grandfather, knowing Riley was by his side. "Anything?"

His grandfather's face was pale. He didn't look good. "Nothing. She's never done this before," he said. "Does Carson know?"

"Dad's still at the press conference. I left word with Michael Ironcloud. He'll let Dad know."

"Hopefully by the time we have to tell him what happened we'll have found her."

Thayne scanned the church grounds. "Where could she be?"

Riley bit her lip. "I don't know her that well, but would she go into the woods?"

Thayne shook his head. "I doubt it. It's not her normal routine. Did she say anything, Pops?"

"Not really. She was muttering something about a redheaded kid, though. Seemed really upset about him. Then she said she had to go to the ladies' room. It seemed like another memory that she couldn't escape from, so I let her go by herself." He bowed his head. "I should never have let her out of my sight."

Thayne squeezed his grandfather's arm. "We'll find her."

Riley leaned over to Thayne, her lips near his ear. "She mentioned red in her statement to you just after Cheyenne was taken."

Thayne looked at her, his eyes widening. "Two nights ago. About this time."

"Cheyenne's clinic." The words came from Riley and Thayne at the same time.

"We may know where she is, Pops."

"I'm coming," he said.

Thayne shook his head. "It's only a hunch. She could just as easily come back here. If we find her, you'll be the first to know."

"I hope you're right, Thayne."

He'd never seen his grandfather look quite so vulnerable. Within minutes, he'd peeled out of the parking lot and set the sirens and lights screaming.

"Do you think she remembered something and that's why she went back to the clinic?" Riley asked.

"Maybe. Or she could simply be looking for Cheyenne."

The few cars on the road pulled to the side, and within minutes Thayne stopped in front of the clinic.

They jumped out onto the pavement. The door was cracked open, the crime scene tape ripped aside. Thayne unholstered his weapon, his entire being praying that Helen was here . . . and safe. "Damn déjà vu," he muttered.

Riley stepped to the side and silently pressed open the door.

He walked into the clinic, and his heart eased just a bit. Gram's small body was curled up in one of the waiting room chairs. Her head was bent over a large pad of paper, a slew of colored pencils at her side. Lead flew across the page. Immediately he lowered his weapon and motioned to Riley.

"Gram?" Thayne whispered.

She didn't even glance up. "Just a minute, dear. It's important I draw what I saw. Cheyenne needs me."

Helen's voice was clear, logical, and in the present. Her little tongue stuck out. Thayne didn't dare speak for fear she'd lose this precious moment of clarity.

Thayne met Riley's gaze, her astonishment clear. He understood. Those moments were always a surprising gift.

Gram smiled up at Riley. "You draw, don't you, dear? I seem to recall you telling me you sketch using a 4B to shade." Gram bit her lip. "At least I think it was you. My memory plays tricks on me these days."

Thayne knelt in front of his grandmother. "You're doing fine, Gram."

Her eyes widened, and tears welled in her eyes. "No, I'm not. I forgot about Cheyenne and those bad people." She added a few final touches, then shoved the drawing pad into Riley's hand. "What do you think? Does this look like the boy who stole my Cheyenne from me?"

Riley grasped the page and stared at it. "Red. He has red hair."

Gram's memory of red hadn't been about his grandfather after all.

"This is the person who took Cheyenne? Are you certain?" Thayne asked as he studied the image of a young man about sixteen, eyes wide with fright.

"Of course. I was here, wasn't I? Then someone hit me." She pressed her hand against her forehead. Her eyes grew misty. "I couldn't stop them. My poor Cheyenne. She fought so hard. Tried to help me. And I let her go."

"Them? Do you remember the others? You said there were three." If she'd been able to draw them . . .

"Gram, had you ever seen the boy before?" He took the sketch pad from Riley and laid it on his grandmother's lap.

"I don't think so." With a sigh, she sagged back in her chair and stared up at the picture hanging behind the office desk. "I painted that. It's the swimming hole. I love going there with Lincoln." Her cheeks tinged with red. "He's such a forward man, trying to kiss me and hold me whenever we're alone." She leaned over to Riley. "I let him."

Gram chuckled and gave Riley a conspiratorial wink. "Grab hold of love now that you've found it, young lady. There's nothing more worth holding on to."

Thayne had to try to get her back on track. "Gram, who else was here besides this boy?"

"Who else was where?" She laid down the pencil and blinked in surprise at Thayne. "What are you doing home? I thought you were with your SEAL team?" She leaned forward and cupped his face with her hands. "I don't like when you're gone. You worry your father. I think you should come home for good. He misses you."

Gram stood, and the sketch pad fell from her lap. She walked over to the waiting room desk. "Cheyenne needs to do a better job of keeping her office clean. I'll drag in Willow, Norma, and Fannie to do a spring cleaning next Saturday."

Without another word, she strode out of the clinic.

"I guess she's finished," he said, rushing out the door after his grandmother and into the dim light of evening at the same time he snagged his phone and dialed Pops.

"Thayne? Is she—" Fear laced his grandfather's voice.

"We found her at the clinic. She's fine."

"Thank God. I'm on my way." He hung up.

Thayne strode up beside his grandmother and hooked his arm through hers. "Pops is on his way to pick you up."

She looked up at him. "That's not right. I have to meet Cheyenne for dinner."

"There's been a change of plans."

"Oh." She frowned. "Cheyenne's gone off with that Riverton boy again, hasn't she? Nothing good can ever come of that. He's not what he seems. He has secrets. He's dangerous."

Gram knew a lot more than anyone realized. Brett Riverton definitely hid a lot more than he shared.

"I think Pops is expecting you for a date and dancing this evening."

"He's planning more than that, boyo," Gram said, with a twinkle in her eye. She patted Thayne's face. "You could learn a thing or two about romance from Lincoln. I'll tell him to have a talk with you."

"Yes ma'am," Thayne said, biting back a smile. He let himself chance a glance at Riley, who shook her head in bemusement. He could relate.

"You're a good boy, Thayne. Don't let anyone tell you differently."

A pickup screeched up beside them. "Helen!" Pops hurried over to his wife. He wrapped her in his strong arms. "I thought I'd lost you."

"I'm not going anywhere, Lincoln. Not until you kick me out." She leaned her head against his chest and held him. She closed her eyes, resting there.

Pops placed his cheek against her hair, the brightness of tears causing his eyes to sparkle. *Thank you,* he mouthed.

Thayne simply nodded. Pops and Gram truly belonged together. They had that Blackwood kind of love. For better or for worse.

Pops led her to his truck and lifted her slight body inside. She shifted in her seat closer to Lincoln, leaning her head against his shoulder.

Without saying a word, Pops raised his hand, and the truck drove away.

"You didn't say anything about the drawing to him," Riley said.

"I didn't want to get his hopes up. Not until we know more."

"How do you and your family keep up with your grandmother, Thayne? My head's spinning with confusion."

Thayne recognized the feeling. When he'd first come home, he'd had trouble following Gram. "Her behavior changes every day, or even every minute sometimes," Thayne said. "The trick is not having any expectations. Be thankful for the flashes of the Gram I know and remember and help her be comfortable whatever her reality is."

"I admire you all."

"We love her. That never changes, but sometimes it's hard not to wish for her back. Like now. She'd be able to tell us everything." He turned back to the clinic. "We need that sketchbook to put out an APB on the kid."

They walked back into the clinic, and he grabbed Gram's sketchbook and sat down.

"Is that the only sketch?" Riley asked, taking a seat beside him. "I usually draw several versions."

Thayne flipped the page. "Oh, Gram." He tilted the drawing toward Riley. The boy stood in front of the clinic's desk, a terrified and sad expression on his face, his eyes staring at someone in the distance. A dark SUV was visible through the front window. Gram had even drawn exhaust from the tailpipe. In one hand, the kid carried a bottle and what appeared to be a rag. Cheyenne lay helpless on the floor, unconscious, with what appeared to be blood on her forehead. A girl stood over her, crying. A girl with long red hair down her back who was much too slim.

Stunned at the detail, Thayne took in every stroke. "This is real," he said in awe. "This is what happened Friday night. Gram knew all along, but she couldn't tell us."

Riley pointed to the girl. "She could be the one we found at the waterfall, Thayne. She looks so familiar to me. That must be why."

Thayne's phone rang. He picked it up and pressed the speakerphone.

"Blackwood," he barked out.

"We got a hit on the print," Pendergrass said.

"You're kidding. So fast?" Thayne could hardly believe the good fortune. Maybe their luck was changing.

"He was in the NCIC database."

"A felon?" Riley asked. "Is there a warrant?"

"Not even close. The print belongs to a kid named Brian Anderson. He went missing six years ago."

CHAPTER NINETEEN

The clinic faded into white nothingness, and Riley fell back into the chair, unable to comprehend what Deputy Pendergrass had just said.

She stared at Thayne's cell phone. "Let me get this straight. You're telling me the young man who broke in to the hospital pharmacy, possibly murdered Nurse Crawly, and left a fingerprint was a missing child?"

"Yes, ma'am. He was ten when he was kidnapped."

"Which makes him sixteen now," Thayne said. "Still a kid."

"A kid who's now our prime suspect," Pendergrass added.

Riley's heart hurt, because she'd spoken with too many kidnap victims over the years, including long-term captives. Their lives were never the same. "He's also a victim," Riley snapped. "Do you have a picture?" she asked, flipping the sketchbook to the close-up drawing Helen had completed.

"Sorry, ma'am. But I can do better than just a photo. The Center for Missing and Exploited Children has his original photo *and* an age-progressed image. Thayne, do you want me to put out an APB on the kid?"

Thayne looked over at her. "He's our insider."

"If we put out an APB, we've put a target on his back, and maybe Cheyenne's, too." Riley squeezed the bridge of her nose. "Don't do it. Not yet."

"You heard her, Pendergrass. Hold off on the APB, but send the photos to my phone and Riley's." Thayne rattled off her number. "And let the sheriff know as soon as he finishes the press conference."

"Don't tell him before it's over, Deputy," Riley added. "We can't risk the press getting a whisper of any leads. It could put the boy in danger."

"You got it, ma'am. I never liked the vultures anyway."

"Keep the information close," Thayne warned. "Someone tipped off the press about the fingerprint. Until we find the leak, I want a tight lid on every aspect of this investigation."

He ended the call. A few seconds later, a tone sounded on Riley's phone. An image appeared on her screen.

First an auburn-haired little boy of six. Very familiar. She compared it to the sketch. "It could be him." She tilted the phone so Thayne could see it, too.

When the next image flashed on the screen, he sucked in a breath. "Gram could have drawn that age-progressed picture. They're nearly identical. It's a match. Brian Anderson was here."

Riley gripped the sketch pad and stared hard, back and forth, between the images on her phone and the drawing.

"Riley?"

"He looks so familiar," she muttered. The image staring back at her sent chills skittering through her entire body. She shivered, and the hairs on her neck stood at attention.

"Because of Gram's drawing."

"Something else . . ." Riley gasped. "Oh my God."

"What is it?" Thayne asked.

"Give me a second." Riley handed him the sketch pad and ran to the SUV, grabbing her satchel. She clutched it to her chest, her heart pounding so hard she knew he could hear every beat.

She sat down next to him. "I'm probably imagining things," she said under her breath, pulling a thick manila expandable file from her bag, bulging with red folders.

Thayne's leg rested next to hers, the heat from his body warming her frozen soul. Was she right? She pulled out the first record.

Her hands shook. She riffled through page after page, her face growing paler with each item she touched until she reached the photo she'd been looking for.

"This can't be happening."

"Who is it? Another suspect?"

She shook her head, fighting the confusion washing through her mind. "This can't be right. It just can't be."

Thayne gripped her hand to stop her shuffling. "Talk to me."

She handed him a photo. "Look at this girl." She pulled out another folder and went directly to a picture. Something in her heart squeezed tight. "And this one."

One by one, she handed him more. "Look at them." Her voice trembled. "Nine photos. Nine redheaded girls."

"Who are they?" he asked.

"Wait. There's more." She swiped her phone. "This is the age-progression drawing of Brian Anderson. He's sixteen."

She placed a series of photos on the floor in front of them. "These are age-progressed photos of the girls. Aged sixteen. What do you see?"

Thayne's entire body went numb. "Similar face shapes, similar hair color. All with blue eyes. They look alike. Those girls and Brian Anderson."

"Exactly."

"Who are they?" he repeated.

"Let me show you two more." Riley's hand trembled. She removed the last two red folders. She hadn't been wrong. She couldn't believe it.

When she removed the photographs, Thayne gasped. "Is that Gina Wallace?"

"Yes. And here's her at sixteen."

Thayne sank back in his chair and stared at her, his expression as stunned as she felt. "Brian Anderson, our prime suspect in Cheyenne's kidnapping, looks like a male version of Gina. That's impossible."

Riley's eyes burned and her head spun. "And then, there's this."

She set down the last photo gently and swallowed deeply.

Thayne picked up the picture. Something different about this one. Bright blue eyes and smiling mouth. Wearing a half-heart bracelet on her arm.

Just like Riley's.

The truth slammed into him like the butt of a rifle to the solar plexus.

"Is this your sister?" he asked.

She swallowed deeply and nodded. "That's Madison." She ran a trembling hand across the photograph of her sister's familiar face. She could see her now, the night she had disappeared. The night of that terrible fight.

The day she'd told Madison she wished she didn't have a sister.

I'm sorry, Maddy.

She dropped her head in her hands, rubbing her eyes with a force that should have hurt. She could barely process the reality of the stack of photos in front of them.

"Riley?" Thayne's voice was gentle but urgent.

She blinked and looked at him. "Brian Anderson, the boy who kidnapped Cheyenne. He looks like Gina. And my sister."

Cheyenne couldn't leave Bethany's side. She'd failed to convince Ian and Adelaide to help. They were too frightened of Father. How could she blame them? For someone who appeared so urbane, he scared the hell out of her.

A cloak of foreboding had settled around her, pressing down, making it hard to breathe. Bethany's fever had finally begun to break. The angry red of the wound had diminished. She still wasn't out of danger, but her recovery looked more promising.

Cheyenne had to wonder how long Father would keep her alive once he noticed the improvement.

She wasn't about to sit and wait for fate to step in. Blackwoods never went down without a fight.

Footsteps raced past the outside door. "Come here, Micah!" a girl's voice shouted.

"No! I want my mommy!"

"Don't you get it? She doesn't love you. She made your daddy go away."

"That's not what she said." Micah sobbed.

"She lied. They all lie. Only Father tells the truth."

The sobs didn't lessen. Finally, the girl let out a curse. "I can't do it, Father. I failed you."

"Have patience, Delilah." Father's calm and oddly unemotional voice made Cheyenne shiver. "He'll understand soon enough. Take him. He can have Hannah's room."

"Yes, Father."

A set of footsteps disappeared, and then a loud door slammed shut.

"Oh God. That poor boy."

After a moment of quiet, sobs filtered into Cheyenne's room. What had happened? After seeing Ian's bruises, she couldn't imagine any sort of punishment in this place was easy.

"Don't cry, Dee," Micah said. "I'm sorry I got you in trouble, but they won't listen. My name isn't Micah."

"Oh, Micah." A few sniffles sounded. "Please. You can't fight anymore. It's dangerous. Something bad could happen to you."

"I won't give up. My mommy never gives up. Neither will I."

"You have to," Delilah said. "Come sit in my lap. I know what will make you feel better." She began to hum.

A tune that Cheyenne hadn't heard in years, not since she was a child. But with made-up words.

Delilah's voice was clear and pure. Another voice, a tenor, joined in, in perfect harmony to the tune of "Puff the Magic Dragon."

> When things go bad, and life seems so unfair,
> Just hold on tight with all your might, and I'll always
> be there.

Bethany stirred. "Always be there," she whispered in a singsong voice from across the prison room.

The tenor went silent.

Delilah's voice paused, then started singing again, trembling but louder.

"Sing, Micah," she said softly. "Please."

The little boy stumbled over the words, but he sang.

A violin played from somewhere in the distance as a key clattered in the lock. Ian stuck his head through the door. He blinked and stared at Bethany. Shadows bruised the pale skin below his eyes. With a furtive look, he closed the door behind him and brought in a tray of food.

"I stole it from the dinner table. None of us is sick," he said as he set it down on the small dresser. He joined Bethany and sat beside her before taking her hand in his.

"How is she?" he asked softly.

"Better."

Ian gnawed on his lip and raised his gaze to hers. "I was happy until Bethany got sick. Until you and Micah came."

A kindle of hope burned inside Cheyenne. "Can you help us?"

"We're watched. All the time. Hannah was stupid. She thought she could get away with it."

"Who is Hannah?"

"She was my friend. She was supposed to wash your clothes, but she stole them and tried to make herself beautiful. She was caught. And punished. She's not coming back."

Cheyenne was afraid to ask, but she had to be sure. "What do you mean?"

"She's dead. She's not the first to be punished."

"H-how many?"

"I don't know. I try not to remember the ones who just went away. It's easier that way." His eyes glimmered with sadness, his face vulnerable. He stared into Bethany's closed eyes. "She's so brave. She stands up for us." He lowered his voice. "I'm going for help. I'm taking Micah with me. He won't ever fit in. We shouldn't have taken him. He's too little."

Where excitement and hope should have rushed through her, Cheyenne could barely breathe in fear. She grabbed his arm. "You have so much courage. Take Micah to Singing River. Find Deputy Thayne Blackwood. He and my father will help you."

The door slammed open. Father stood, framed by the door, Adelaide a pale, weak shadow behind him.

"Ian, what are you doing here?" Father's voice was low and threatening. "You're supposed to be with Micah."

"I b-brought broth for Bethany," Ian said, his voice shaky. "She hasn't eaten in days."

Father frowned and shook his head sadly. "Adelaide, escort Ian to the punishment room," Father said. "We must reinforce our lessons."

Adelaide's face went white. "Please, Father, don't make me—"

"Silence." He glared at Adelaide.

Ian stood with a stiff back. He raised his chin and faced Father. "I'm ready."

Without a word, Father took him away.

Several minutes later, a cry of pain pierced through the air.

Then the world went silent.

CHAPTER TWENTY

The sheriff's department buzzed with activity. Thayne could almost feel the anticipation from the investigation team on the other side of his father's office door while he stared at the phone, willing it to ring. Riley paced the floor, every so often stopping at the shuttered window to peer through the blinds at the sun disappearing below the horizon. Only a small line of bright orange kept the night at bay.

She couldn't seem to settle anywhere. Thayne's father had decided to make coffee for the third time since they'd raced into the building with Gram's sketch pad, Riley's files, and an unproven theory.

His father opened the door. "Did he call?"

Thayne shook his head. "Not yet."

"You think there will be a match, though?"

Riley sat on the hard wooden chair across from his father's desk, her leg bouncing with nerves.

"I always believed the man who took Gina, Madison, and the others fit the profile of a sexual predator. Textbook. They have a type. They abduct, abuse, then murder their victims when they no longer satisfy the urges." She rubbed her temple. "Now I don't know what to think."

Thayne held up the phone with Brian's photo. "Brian Anderson has a similar look as the girls. He fits."

She shook her head. "No, he doesn't. Sexual predators don't cross genders with their victims. Not ever."

"I hate to suggest it, but maybe he's the exception." Either way, Thayne would love to get the bastard who'd abducted these children alone in a room . . . not for a minute, or even an hour, but long enough so the SOB felt just enough pain he'd regret what he'd done to those kids for the rest of a very short life.

"Maybe," Riley conceded. "But if Tom gets a hit, it means I've been wrong in my profile this entire time." She gripped Thayne's arm, her fingernails digging into his flesh. "I've been working under a false premise, searching for the wrong guy for years, and these kids paid for it."

His father, in full sheriff mode, took a seat in the leather chair behind his desk. "How does Cheyenne's disappearance fit in? Not to mention Brett Riverton?"

The look of distaste on his father's face at the Riverton name made Thayne grimace. When they found Cheyenne, she had some explaining to do.

"All we're certain of is that Brian Anderson is the key," Riley said. "He tried to reach out to us, and we have to be ready when he tries again. Whoever leaked the information about the fingerprint put Brian in real danger, and he may not even know it."

"So, if your theory is right, somehow we have to find the person who abducted Gina, your sister, and Brian, and then we'll find Cheyenne?" The sheriff took a long sip of coffee. "I could use a shot of whiskey in this. That guy has been avoiding law enforcement for fifteen years."

In other words, how the hell were they going to find him now? "But this time, we have an informant," Thayne said. "This is the first chink in the guy's armor."

"Which makes me wonder why," Riley said softly. "What's different now?"

The phone's ringing exploded like a hand grenade on his father's desk. Thayne punched the speakerphone.

"Deputy Blackwood," he said, his voice clipped.

"This is SSA Tom Hickok. You requested a search on boys kidnapped matching the general physical description and MO of Madison Lambert?"

"That's right. Did you find anything?"

"Is Special Agent Lambert with you, Deputy Blackwood?"

"I'm here, Tom," Riley answered, kneading her pants in a show of nerves.

"I don't know what made you ask this question, Riley, but I pulled six files. And damn. You're on to something."

Riley met Thayne's gaze and nodded. "We have a thumbprint at a robbery and murder scene belonging to a missing child, Brian Anderson. Is he on your—"

Tom let out a low whistle. "He's on my list."

"We also have a witness who placed Brian at the scene of my sister's abduction," Thayne added.

"Then why are we just now learning this? Riley, we could've run a sketch comparison and probably hit on the identity already. What have you been doing out there, Lambert?"

"Back off, Hickok," Thayne snapped. He'd had enough of this guy attacking Riley, even if he was her boss. "The witness is my grandmother. She has Alzheimer's."

There was silence over the phone.

"Could your grandmother have seen the image somewhere else? A milk carton maybe? Brian's photo was rotated about a month ago."

"We have the fingerprint, Tom," Riley countered. "Brian is AB positive, which matches what was found at the crime scene. And my boss taught me never to believe in coincidences."

And Riley Lambert for a touchdown.

"I'm not reinstating you," Tom said, "but you have the support of the unit. We're on the next plane out if you need us."

OK, so maybe her boss wasn't all bad.

"SSA Hickok, this is Sheriff Blackwood. We'd appreciate all the help we can get. And you can consider this an official request."

"We'll see you tomorrow, then," Tom said. "And Riley, good job."

Thayne ended the call. Riley stood up. "I guess we have work to do."

Clutching the thick evidence folder, she strode out of the office, but before Thayne could join her, his father delayed him.

"If we solve this, she may finally learn what happened to her sister, and Carol may finally have closure on Gina," his father said. "That's a lot for anyone to handle. Her emotions could get the better of her. Can she do it?"

"She's stronger than anyone I know," Thayne said. "She won't let us down. Besides, we all know failure isn't an option."

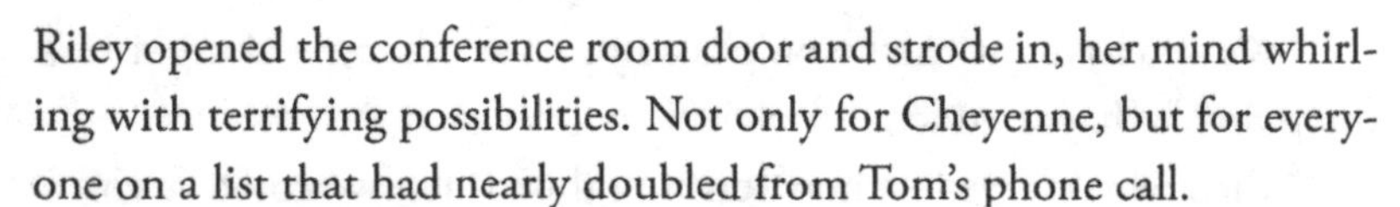

Riley opened the conference room door and strode in, her mind whirling with terrifying possibilities. Not only for Cheyenne, but for everyone on a list that had nearly doubled from Tom's phone call.

Deputy Pendergrass acknowledged her with a nod of his head. "We've added a panel to the investigation board as requested."

The door opened, and Thayne walked in with his father.

The room went silent. "We just received word from Special Agent Lambert's colleagues at the FBI that my daughter's disappearance is almost certainly connected to a series of abductions going back fifteen years. Including Gina Wallace's."

All the local deputies gasped. "Special Agent Lambert and Deputy Blackwood will take point. Riley?"

She opened the file and tacked up a ten-year-old boy's face along with the official age-progressed rendering. Carefully, Thayne pulled the sketch of Cheyenne's abduction and Brian from his grandmother's book. "Gram drew this," he said.

A low whistle escaped Pendergrass's lips. "Uncanny. If I hadn't seen it, I wouldn't have believed it. No offense, Sheriff."

"We all forget how much she remembers," Thayne said.

"Who's the girl?" Underhill asked.

"We think she may be the young woman found on the Rivertons' property, but we can't be sure. If you'll wait a few minutes, I think you'll understand why," Thayne said.

Over the next few minutes, Riley and Thayne posted the photos of the abduction victims on the wall-size board, one after the other. The string of images melded together. Side by side, they resembled one another in an uncanny way.

The room went silent.

"It's creepy how they all look alike," Pendergrass said.

"And why you can't identify the girl without DNA," Underhill said.

Riley nodded.

"Damn," Agent Nolan said. He passed Thayne another four photos. "These are the boys' photos that SSA Hickok e-mailed. His unit has gone to interview Brian Anderson's parents. They'll head here after they finish."

Riley faced the room of investigators. "One of Cheyenne Blackwood's abductors—Brian Anderson—was kidnapped six years ago when he was ten years old. This boy was alive two days ago, which gives us hope we'll find Cheyenne Blackwood, and maybe some of these other children alive as well."

"Assuming the same perp kidnapped all of them, why is Brian still alive?" Pendergrass asked.

"Most predators who are attracted to children want to control those who are smaller and weaker than themselves," Riley said. "Maybe he forced Brian to help lure the others, but now he's getting too old. Whatever the reason, Brian has reached out to us by leaving that fingerprint. He may know his time is running out."

Thayne grabbed Post-its, string, and markers. "OK, everybody, we're putting up a timeline."

An hour later, a fifteen-year time span emerged.

"Son of a bitch." Thayne's father walked over to the image of his first big case. Gina Wallace. He touched her photo. "She really was the first one?"

Riley set down her folder and faced the sheriff. "Agent Nolan searched back another decade from Gina's abduction. No girls or boys matched the MO. Gina Wallace was from Singing River. Cheyenne's abduction can't be a coincidence."

"Madison Lambert, Riley's sister, was second," Thayne said, "less than a month later."

"I need a map of the United States," Riley demanded. "To plot the abductions."

While Deputy Pendergrass gathered the supplies, Thayne motioned to Riley. "I'm calling for a status report on the signs near the Riverton waterfall. Interested?"

"Absolutely." They slipped out of the room and into the sheriff's private office. Thayne dialed his brother's satphone.

A crackling connection buzzed. "What's up, bro?" Jackson asked.

"I called to ask *you* the same question. Where did the trail lead?"

"It didn't. I found a few subtle signs, but all traces vanished within a mile. Whoever killed that girl knows these woods better than I do." Jackson's voice snapped with obvious frustration. "It's almost dark now, but I can expand the search in the morning."

Riley hadn't expected a trail of bread crumbs, but she couldn't deny being disappointed. A lot of criminal activity seemed to be centered at the Riverton waterfall.

Thayne met her gaze. "Do it," they said at the same time.

Jackson chuckled. "Hi, Riley. Glad to see you're in agreement with my brother. You may want to mark the date in the calendar."

Thayne spent a few minutes bringing Jackson up to date on the latest news. All in all, a frustrating conversation for everyone. "Before you go, how's Kade?" Thayne asked.

"Poor guy couldn't take being inside. Said something about searching for Cheyenne because he owed her. He gave Hudson the slip and disappeared from Fannie's B and B. I'm keeping an eye out for him, but no telling where he's headed."

"If he goes into flashback mode . . ." Thayne frowned. "The last thing we need during our search-and-rescue operations is an unpredictable army ranger in combat mode."

"Believe me, I'm well aware. He almost turned me into Swiss cheese. I hope a bed opens up at the VA soon."

"I'm sorry about your friend," Riley said after Thayne hung up.

"Me, too. I just hope he doesn't put himself in the middle of something worse. I have to wonder if we won't end up back in those mountains searching for my sister."

They left the office and crossed the main room of the sheriff's department.

"Let me out of here!" Ed shouted through the open door leading to the jail cells. "I see Gina's picture in there. I know you've found something!" He shook the bars, his eyes wild.

Riley paused, her gaze speculative. "Mr. Zalinsky." She tugged out her notebook. "You knew Gina."

"Yeah. So. I ain't changing my story. You ain't pinning that on me."

"I understand." Riley crossed to less than a foot from the bars. "I've been reading Gina's file. You dated Carol around the time of the abduction? Isn't that correct?"

He flushed. "I kept an eye on her . . . Carol was my girl, before that guy knocked her up."

"You were stalking her. You have been since you were both in high school. Isn't that right?"

Ed's face had turned the color of cooked beets. She'd hit a nerve.

"Stalking implies she didn't want it," Ed sneered. "She did then. She still does."

"She kicked you out. Stay away from her, Ed," Thayne bit out.

"Ask her, *Deputy.* She's coming over to bail me out. Should be here any minute."

Riley grabbed Thayne's arm. "Let me." She moved closer to Ed's cell. "What do you think happened to Carol's daughter?"

"I bet that drifter who got Carol pregnant took her."

Riley leaned in closer. "Carol told me last year she didn't know the father's identity."

"Oh, she knew all right. Just didn't want to say because he up and abandoned her. He met her in Casper, then dropped her off like the slut she is. But he came through town when she was about to pop the kid out. Came back a few years later, too. By then she was too drunk to remember. But I did. I saw him checking her out, checking his kid out. Drove a Cadillac, had real money. Talked to the brat, gave her a stuffed animal or something, then hightailed it out of here."

"That was years before she was taken."

"Maybe, but every so often, I'd see a brand-new Caddy drive by her place, hang out on the street."

"How often would you say he visited?" Riley asked.

"Every year or so, around the girl's birthday."

"Did you notice the Cadillac again after Gina disappeared?" she asked, betting she knew the answer.

"After the girl was taken," Ed said, leaning closer, his face framed by two iron bars, "no new Caddy. Not ever."

He let out a long laugh, and the odor of alcohol nearly made Riley gag. She stepped back with a cough, but she had more than enough for a follow-up conversation with Carol.

"Can I bring you a toothbrush?" she asked with a false smile.

Thayne leaned in, took one whiff, and glared at Ed. "Where'd you get the booze?"

Ed just shrugged.

Crossing his arms, Thayne planted himself against the bars for the clear purpose of intimidating Ed. The man gulped so loudly Riley could hear it from across the room.

"I'm not leaving you alone until you give me a name," Thayne promised.

"If I tell you, will you let me out?"

Thayne placed his hand on his utility belt, near his weapon. "If you *don't* tell me, there's no chance, and I'm searching your cell."

Ed scowled at his nemesis, and Riley had to admire Thayne's way with the guy. He really was good at his job.

"Some reporter traded me a full bottle for a few pieces of inside information."

"Do you know what you've done?" Thayne's voice went soft and cold and terrifying. He grabbed Ed by the collar. "If your addiction for the bottle costs my sister her life, you won't find a hole deep enough to crawl into. I promise you that."

He shoved Ed back into the cell.

Thayne didn't say a word until they were clear of the room. He slammed the door shut. "Damn him to hell. I should have sent him home the first day. He always gets off anyway."

Riley grabbed his hands, wincing at Thayne's tortured expression. "Don't do this to yourself. You didn't know."

"Maybe not, but we should have kept the damn door closed. We would have, except I know from personal experience how claustrophobic that room gets. I gave the OK to leave it open. I gave Ed the opportunity. Because of that drunk, Brian Anderson could be dead right now and our chance of finding my sister may have died with him."

The stars' light pricked the midnight fabric of the sky. Riley pressed her face against the glass, peering into the darkened house.

Carol hadn't shown up to work in two days. Riley rapped on the door again. She glanced over at Thayne. "Do you think she's OK?"

Thayne pounded on the door, his fist causing the wood to groan. "Carol, it's Thayne and Riley. We know you're in there. Please. We need your help," he shouted.

Agent Nolan was looking into the Cadillac. Riley knew one had been seen in the vicinity of at least two of the kidnappings she'd studied, but she hadn't checked into the boys' abductions. She still couldn't get over the fact that she'd missed the connection. She'd analyzed those missing kids' files since she'd been old enough to realize she could.

She'd committed the unpardonable sin of making an assumption. The very thing she fought so hard to prevent by avoiding any contamination of the investigation in progress.

The curtain fluttered.

"Carol," Riley said, hitting the door. "Please, it's important."

Slowly, the doorknob turned. Carol's pale face appeared. "What do you want?" she asked, her voice slurred, her eyes bloodshot.

"We need to ask you some questions about Gina's father." Riley slipped her foot in the door so Carol couldn't close them out.

"Gina's dead." Carol tried to press the door closed, but Riley wouldn't budge. "Everyone knows I killed my daughter."

"That's not true," Thayne said.

"Just as good as did. I left her alone all the time because I passed out. I let men look at her. I deserved to lose her."

She flung the door open and stumbled backward. An acrid odor washed over Riley. A nauseating combination of meth, alcohol, urine, and she didn't really want to know what else.

Thayne shoved open a window to let in some fresh air.

Carol plopped down on the sofa and picked up a tall glass filled with ice. She twisted open a bottle and poured to the top.

Riley sat down across from the woman who could have the key to everything. "We think you can help us find Cheyenne."

"I can't help anyone. Not even myself." She chuckled, her tone sour and defeated. "Was supposed to bail out Ed, but the money's gone."

It was easy to see where. A recently used meth pipe lay on the coffee table.

"Ed's the only one I can count on," Carol said. "And I screwed it all up with him. For good this time."

Riley leaned forward and clasped Carol's hands in hers. "Who was Gina's father?"

Carol blinked. She looked over at Thayne and shook her head. "Not talking about it around *him*. Men don't understand. Ed never did. You're judging me right now. I can see it." She stood up. "Damn you, Thayne Blackwood." She pounded on his chest. "The Blackwoods. The perfect family. I was like you." She fell into his arms, sobbing. "I was just like you."

Thayne picked her up and carried her to the sofa. She collapsed, a limp body wasting away.

Riley shot to her feet and rested her hand on his arm. "I've got this. I think she'll speak to me if you leave."

Thayne nodded. "I'll be right outside. I so much as hear a strange noise, I'm coming in." Thayne walked out the front door, closing it softly behind him.

Carol rubbed her hands against her eyes. "I was like him."

"I know," Riley said, patting Carol's hand. "No one understands, do they?"

Carol blinked at her, eyes wide and foggy. "Your sister got taken. I remember now."

Riley nodded and pulled out a photo. "Her name was Madison. She was kidnapped soon after Gina."

"You know they're dead," Carol whispered. "No one admits it, but they are. She'd be thirty now. Probably would've had a kid. Maybe two. I'd have been a grandma."

"They're gone," Riley said, the words hurting her heart. "But I still want to bring my sister home. For my mother. Don't you want Gina home with you?"

Tears rolled down Carol's cheeks. "Will it help?"

"I don't know." Riley sighed. "I'm not sure if knowing the truth will be worse or not, but I have to try." She rested her hands on her knees. "Can I tell you something, Carol? Sometimes I dream that Madison walks through my front door with a smile on her face. It's so real."

"Her ghost," Carol said. "I see Gina all the time in the dead of night. She blames me for her life."

"Then help me find them so we can do right by them. Who is Gina's father?"

"One-night stand. He showed up at a bar right outside the rodeo in Casper. I was trying to get in, but I was underage. They'd kicked me out a couple of times already." She frowned. "He was a college man from a real famous school in California. He spouted off words I'd never heard, but they sounded good." Carol closed her eyes, her lips upturned in a small smile. "He had soft hands, not like Ed or the cowboys around this place."

"He sounds nice."

"He was. At first." Carol's forehead wrinkled with thought. "We couldn't get into the club, so we went to his hotel room. He gave me some drinks. I don't remember much, except he made me feel special. I fell asleep in his arms."

Carol gulped down half the tall glass. "In the morning, he tugged on his pants and said good-bye. I asked him if I could go with him. He laughed at me. I wasn't smart enough or pretty enough. He walked out the door. Never saw him again."

Riley could just imagine a seventeen-year-old girl from a small town falling for a line. So easy for one choice to change a life. "Did you tell him you were pregnant?"

"I didn't even know his last name." Carol shrugged. "I thought I saw his car once. A Caddy. You know how much those things cost? But I was just dreaming." Carol's voice petered off. "Just dreaming."

She fell over onto the sofa, completely passed out.

Riley stood up. She walked over to a photo on the fireplace. A girl with auburn hair smiled back, though her eyes weren't exactly happy. Gina Wallace had lived a tough life from the beginning. What if Ed had been telling the truth? What if this drifter *had* come back? What if he'd taken Gina?

She was the first victim, and the first victim spoke the loudest.

A long shot? Yeah, but what else did they have?

She picked up her phone and dialed a familiar number.

"Hickok," Tom answered.

"It's Riley."

"What do you want, Lambert?"

"I need a favor. We have Gina Wallace's DNA on file, right?"

"Did you find a body?" he asked.

A good assumption, considering DNA, like fingerprints, could be used only as a comparison tool. It was valuable only if you had a match on file.

"Her father may be our perp. Can you run her DNA through the system, looking for a familial match?"

Tom let out a low whistle. "Do you know what you're saying? Are you crazy?"

"Maybe. But I'm also desperate. If I don't catch a break soon, Cheyenne Blackwood and Brian Anderson are as good as dead."

CHAPTER TWENTY-ONE

The glare of the streetlight created a halo. Thayne propped himself against the doorjamb. So far he'd heard a few tears, a bit of crying, and finally the soft murmur of female voices.

He drummed his fingers on his leg. A sense of urgency boiled within him. He had a feeling Riley and he were close to uncovering something big, but he could foresee nothing that pointed to saving Cheyenne, and he didn't have a clue how to find her.

Right now they'd placed all their hopes on a sixteen-year-old kid. What kind of delusional faith was that?

A rustle sounded off to the left. Thayne drew his weapon and crouched, peering into the trees at the side of Carol's home.

A loud meow pierced the night, and a cat streaked past him, hissing. Thayne didn't relax. Something had triggered the animal to flee.

A shadow moved to his left just as the front door to Carol's house opened.

"Stay inside," he hissed to Riley. "Don't leave until I come back."

The door slammed shut, and the dead bolt clicked into place.

Confident Riley could take care of herself barricaded indoors, Thayne rushed in silence to the trees. Somewhere hidden, perhaps in an alley or even down the road, a car's engine purred on the quiet street. Within seconds, the sound vanished.

No way he could track the getaway vehicle, so Thayne pulled a flashlight from his cargo pants and swept the ground. He sighted a pair of footprints impressed in the ground cover with a tread similar to the print he'd discovered not far from the Riverton waterfall and the unidentified girl's body.

Thayne dialed his phone. "Pendergrass, meet me at Carol's ASAP. Bring your forensics kit and someone who can watch over her house tonight."

"Will do."

With a tap, Thayne ended the call and gave the area one last look. Had he interrupted the sniper? A reporter? The kidnapper? The murderer?

Taking no chances, he walked the perimeter of the house until Pendergrass pulled up, lights flashing.

Finally, he knocked on Carol's door.

Riley flung it open. "What happened?"

"Someone was watching."

Thayne locked Carol inside and gave one of the additional DCI investigators the key. "Keep an eye on her."

The man nodded. Thayne kept his gun drawn, his body on full alert, until he escorted Riley to the SUV.

Her footsteps were dragging. She had to be exhausted. This roller-coaster ride searching for Cheyenne sucked energy more than a three-mile run in the middle of insurgent territory.

"Another dead end?" he asked.

"Maybe not," she said, filling him in. "The DNA's worth a shot. I should have thought of it before."

"You're too hard on yourself," Thayne said, pulling away from the curb. He had to stay alert and aware of anything out of sync.

Riley rubbed her neck, rolling her head from side to side.

"You need rest."

"I wanted to find Cheyenne today."

"So did I."

Riley leaned against the headrest and closed her eyes. "Take me back to the sheriff's office. I'll work the boards tonight. Revisit every one of those abductions. There has to be something."

Thayne put the car in gear. "I think you should sleep for a few hours. Your Unit 6 is working the Brian Anderson angle; DCI and the Denver FBI field officers are combing through the files. If we get a hit on the forensics, they'll contact us."

She shook her head. "Not going to happen. I should be there."

"We both know the golden hours are gone. Losing sleep won't save my sister." He let out a controlled breath. "If Cheyenne is alive, it's because whoever took her wants her alive." He turned the car toward Fannie's. "My family needs your intuition, your instincts, your ability to see what others can't. You need to rest."

She rubbed her eyes, wincing.

"You know I'm right."

She scowled at him. "I don't have to like it."

He stayed silent, waiting for her to acknowledge the truth. He was right this time, and she knew it.

"Fine. Just a few hours."

"Of course."

She tucked her leg underneath her and turned toward him. She opened her mouth to say something, but then closed it.

"You can tell me anything, Riley. We've been through a lifetime together the last two days."

"I don't know how the investigation will end, but I have to say this before everything goes crazy. And it will. Your family is strong," she said, her gaze boring into him. "Can I give you some advice?"

"Of course."

"No matter what happens, fight to keep your family together."

"Unlike yours?" he asked gently.

"It wasn't anyone's fault. Madison was the light of my mother's life. When she was taken, something broke inside Mom. I couldn't fix it. My dad didn't know how to, either. I'm surprised they're still together." She let out a pained chuckle. "Actually, a divorce probably would have required too much energy and passion."

He took her hand in his and threaded their fingers. "I'm sorry."

"I've investigated a lot of cases over the years. Officially, the last three years; unofficially, long before that. More often than not, an abduction tears the family apart. I'd hate to see that happen to you. Your family, they have something special."

"Well, I hated all that specialness when I was a teenager. It's the reason I left and the reason I stayed away."

"You're back now."

"I've come to reappreciate Singing River. And my family."

He pulled up at the B&B. Riley started to open the door. He stopped her. "Wait for me."

He exited and searched the area between the car and Fannie's for any unusual movements or signs.

Finally, when he was satisfied, he yanked open the passenger side and escorted her quickly across the lawn and into the lodging.

Fannie hadn't opened the curtains.

Riley faced him. "If you get a call—"

"I'll let you know. It'll be a quick trip, because I'm not leaving you alone tonight."

Cheyenne sat at her patient's bedside, nibbling on some of the food Ian had delivered, the small wooden stake she'd carved tucked in the waist of her scrubs. Bethany's breathing had improved, but she still hadn't awakened again. Instead of a feverish unconsciousness, though, she now slept easily.

A layman could tell the incision was no longer red with infection. The IV antibiotics had been administered, and Bethany would be awake soon. She'd be able to take oral antibiotics and eat and drink.

Cheyenne had become disposable, and Bethany would soon be again under the power of whoever had poisoned her.

A few hours ago Father had entered the room, forcing Cheyenne to show him Bethany's healing wound. He'd given her a small, satisfied nod and left without so much as another word.

If she got a chance to escape, she'd have to take it.

The door to her cell slammed open, the sound echoing throughout her prison.

Father strode into the middle of the room. "Doctor Blackwood, you spoke with Ian. What did you say to him?"

His overly calm tone gave Cheyenne chills. That and Adelaide's terrified expression as she followed him inside.

Cheyenne rose from her seat and faced the man who controlled her very life, but she said nothing.

His lips pursed. "I have no wish to punish you, but if you force me, I will not hesitate to protect my family. Answer me."

"Nothing of importance," she lied.

"You corrupted all my good work." Father's soft words belied the high color in his cheeks. "He was brilliant with electronics. Did you even consider what infecting his fragile mind with memories would force me to do?" Father paced back and forth, his hands behind his back. "Of course not. You live in a selfish world thinking only of yourself, never of the greater good."

As he spoke, Cheyenne almost collapsed with disappointment. Ian hadn't escaped. No one was coming to their rescue.

Her weapon dug into her side. She'd have only one chance to use it. She'd have to pick the perfect time.

She glanced over her shoulder at Bethany. She'd have to come back for her and pray her enemy didn't get to her first.

Father's brow furrowed. "I'd sincerely hoped this wouldn't come to pass. Adelaide, we have a punishment to administer. To all of them." He glared at Cheyenne. "Everything about to happen is your responsibility, Doctor. Ian was a good boy. Micah would have learned, and now . . ." He sighed. "Such a shame."

Father turned his back and started out the door. "Bring her, Adelaide."

Adelaide winced. *I'm sorry,* she mouthed and gripped Cheyenne's arm.

The empty hallway beckoned. One chance. She had to take it.

She shoved Adelaide out of the way and launched herself at the door, weapon drawn.

"Close it!" Father said.

The iron slammed shut from the outside. Cheyenne careened into the metal, jarring her body. She whirled around, backed against the door, weapon drawn.

She had nowhere to go.

"Silly, stupid child." Father rapped twice on the floor. Someone yanked the steel door open behind Cheyenne. She tumbled backward, and before she could move her arms, she was pinned to the floor, a familiar, sickly sweet odor permeating her nose and mouth.

Cheyenne tried to turn her head away from the sweet-smelling aroma. She held her breath and clenched her fists. If she could just . . .

She looked over at the woman whom she'd trusted. "Please. Adelaide. Help . . . escape." Her words slurred.

Father looked down at Cheyenne and simply smiled. A sickly satisfied expression that made Cheyenne's stomach roil.

"I'm sorry. I had no choice," Adelaide said, her face full of regret.

"You will join Ian and Micah for punishment," Father said.

Cheyenne blinked, tried to fight, but her mind lost focus.

"Ian," she whispered.

Darkness descended around her. The room went blurry.

A handcuff snapped onto her wrist. She tried to resist, but she couldn't move. She couldn't open her eyes.

"Bring her," Father said. "To the omega room."

Several voices gasped. "Father?"

"I have no choice. Guard her closely. We will fetch Ian and Micah."

Ian. I'm so very sorry.

Someone tied a cord around her waist. They dragged her along the floor. A small sniffle came from above her.

"Shut up," a female voice whispered. "Do you want to be punished, too?"

"N-no," the fearful girl stuttered.

"Then just do it. And never forget what Father always says. Family is everything."

◆ ◆ ◆

Fannie's B&B had never felt so small to Riley. Her heart skipped a beat at Thayne's promise not to leave until morning. The last time Thayne had told her he was staying the night, he'd stayed all week. The world had been a different place then.

"After you," he said, his face set in stone in a stubborn, don't-argue-with-me, it'll-never-work voice she'd come to know and hate during their Friday phone dates.

"I can still take care of myself," she said, because she felt obligated to stand up for herself, her job, and her training. "I may not have my badge, but you gave me a gun."

"We're being followed. Until we identify the source of the threat, you're stuck with me."

"You're being an overprotective alpha male, Thayne."

"That's my job."

Her lips curved upward. The truth was, she'd already decided to give in. She could use the company. With each step, her body grew heavier and heavier with exhaustion—emotional and physical.

Desperate worry for Cheyenne, a strange but surreal hope for finding answers about her sister and the other victims, and a gut-wrenching desire to make the bastard who had caused so much pain pay with his life had drained her energy dry.

"Come on, then." She headed up the stairs just as Fannie, Norma, and Willow peeked out from the kitchen.

Thayne paused, frowning at them. "You can't leave without an escort, ladies. The sniper is still on the loose. Understood?"

Eyes wide, they all nodded. Thayne put his phone to his ear. "Ladies, call when you want to leave. Deputy Ironcloud's stationed outside. He'll drive you home."

Whispering excitedly, they disappeared into Fannie's private quarters behind the registration desk.

"Do you think they'll stay put?" she asked, her voice weary.

"They may be mischievous, but they know how serious the situation is. They'll behave."

At the top of the stairs, Riley fumbled for the key in her satchel. He pushed her hands aside and took it from her, unlocking the room and taking her inside before shutting and locking the door behind him.

Except for the made bed, the room was exactly as she'd left it, crime wall and all. She stood in the center of the room, never feeling quite so awkward.

"Take a shower," he said softly.

Glad to escape, she headed to the bathroom, shucked her clothes, and stood beneath the water, letting the jets pulse into her back and neck. Steam rose, and by the time she was finished, she felt partly human again.

She slipped into a chemise and boxers and padded into the bedroom. Thayne had turned down the covers, and a cup of tea and a cinnamon roll sat beside the bed. She perched on the side of the bed and took a sip.

"Did you read my mind?" she asked.

"Nope, just got two of everything." He waited expectantly in the center of the room.

"Oh good grief, you don't have to ask. Hit the shower," she said.

"I didn't want to presume too much," he said with a wink.

Her mouth dropped open. If she'd had something to throw at him, she would have. The sound of the water acted like white noise. Her mind seemed to have shut down. She bit into the cinnamon roll, and by the time Thayne strode into the room in a pair of sweats, she'd consumed the last bite.

"Before you ask, no, I didn't bring a go bag. These are Kade's," he said, heading to the closet and grabbing an extra blanket.

Riley sat on the bed and tucked her knees to her chest. "Why does this feel so awkward?"

"Because a year ago, we burned hot and passionate for a week, without looking to the future. Now we know each other too well. And in some ways, not well enough." Thayne stood beside the bed. "And the future isn't so clear."

"You should be a profiler." Riley rubbed the base of her neck, groaning with the tightness.

"Let me," Thayne said. He climbed on the bed, his fingers toying with the hair at the nape of her neck before brushing it aside. "Try to relax."

She took a deep breath and closed her eyes.

He pressed against the tension that had settled at the base of her skull. His fingers unfurled magic on the knotted muscles. Riley groaned.

Immediately he removed his hands. "Did I hurt you?"

"Don't stop." She bowed her head forward.

He worked his way on either side of her vertebrae to a twisted pressure point, capturing the tangled nerves. They fired like sharp needles jabbing from the inside out. She gasped. He paused, but she didn't ask him to quit, and so he kept pressing.

Riley didn't know if she could stand the stabs any longer when suddenly they unfurled, relaxing in waves through her shoulders down to her ribs. A sigh escaped her.

"Lay down," he whispered.

She couldn't refuse. She sank into the mattress. Thayne rose and flipped off all the lights, except for the bathroom.

He'd remembered.

A few moments later, he climbed under the covers, pulling her back against his chest and the down comforter over them. For a moment, she stiffened.

"Don't worry," he whispered in her ear. "We both need sleep, but I love holding you, Riley. I always have."

Warmth cocooned Riley. For a few moments, sleep banished the horror of the world, and her body sank into oblivion, secure in Thayne's arms. She was home.

Fifteen Years Ago

"Time for bed, girls. I'll be upstairs in five."

Madison threw on her pajamas and made it to her bed just in time. Her mother opened the door. Madison feigned sleep. She planned to make a paper fortune-teller before she really went to bed.

Her eyes grew heavy. She was almost asleep when the bathroom door cracked open. Her sister tiptoed in.

"Maddy?" Riley whispered.

Madison didn't answer.

Instead of slipping into bed next to Madison, though, Riley tugged a pillow off the bed and lay down beside it.

Madison opened one eye. Riley had brought in her blanket. She was afraid of the dark, and Mom wouldn't let her have a night-light.

Madison reached over the bed and plugged in the little night-light she'd rescued from the trash when her mom had tried to throw it away.

"Thanks, Maddy. I'm still mad at you," Riley said with a yawn.

"Me, too."

Madison closed her eyes. Little sisters sure were a pain.

A lone owl hooted, its eerie cry drawing Madison out of a sound sleep. A soft breeze blew across her cheek. She shivered and drew her blanket tighter around her.

A cricket chirped, its song loud and close, as if the insect had found its way into the bedroom.

Strange. Normally the night noises weren't so loud.

A soft slide and faint click sounded from the window. Madison stilled, squeezing her eyes tight. Her heart pounded against her chest.

A whimper echoed from behind her bed.

Riley.

Madison's eyes snapped open.

A large figure bent over her bed. He placed his finger over his lips. Madison opened her mouth to scream. The man shook his head. "If you scream, she dies."

The man had Riley, one hand covering her mouth. Riley's eyes were wide with fear.

The scream died in Madison's throat. She nodded.

"Get out of bed. Put your shoes on."

Madison shook at her very core. The man's grip tightened on Riley's neck. He bent down and whispered something in Riley's ear.

Riley nodded.

Without a choice, Madison scurried across the room. She paused a few feet from the closed bedroom door.

"You're too smart to make that kind of mistake," the man hissed. "I've been watching you, Madison. IQ of one sixty. You try to fit in, but you don't. You look out the window, crying, most every night. You had your first drink tonight. And your first kiss. You are headed down a destructive path, but you have been chosen.

"Your destiny awaits. Now put on your shoes."

Madison could hardly tie her tennis shoes, her hands shook so much. Her half-heart sister bracelet tapped against her wrist as she finished tying the bow.

She looked over at Riley. Her sister was getting that angry look on her face. Madison wiped her eyes.

With her entire body trembling, she stood and faced the large man.

He smiled. She could see his white teeth. He wore a knit cap on his head. She couldn't see his hair.

"Go to the window," he said. He picked up Riley and sat her on the bed. He bent down to her ear. He whispered something, then pulled out a knife. He turned her hand over and ran the knife across her palm. She whimpered. He placed his hand over her mouth.

Madison wanted to jump onto his back, but she knew deep inside if she did, Riley would die.

"Lay down," the man said.

Riley started crying.

"Do it, Riley," Madison whispered. "Please. For me. I'll be fine."

She knew it was a lie.

The man smiled at her and stroked Madison's cheek. "You are a very intelligent girl. I knew I wasn't wrong about you." He tightened his grip on Riley's throat. "Close your eyes. Count to fifty. Don't open your eyes until then."

He leaned over the bed, his gaze meeting Madison's. He whispered in Riley's ear again.

She clenched her eyes tight.

He released his grip from around Riley's neck. She didn't move. Thank goodness.

The man opened the window. He held a sweet-smelling cloth to Madison's nose. "Breathe."

She took a deep breath. The world went fuzzy and tilted. Her knees gave way.

The man scooped her into his arms against his chest. His mouth touched her ear. "You belong to me. If you do exactly as I say, I won't come back for your sister." He nodded at Riley. "If you disobey, your punishment will be severe. And your sister will pay the price. Am I clear?"

Madison blinked up at him. She couldn't see his face any longer. Her head flopped over. She saw only her sister.

She hummed a few bars of "Puff the Magic Dragon."

Riley lay still as death.

The world faded to black.

Madison didn't want to wake up. She prayed she never would.

CHAPTER TWENTY-TWO

"Madison!" Riley shot straight up in bed, her heart thudding against the wall of her chest, each beat racing through her mind. "I'm sorry. I'm so sorry."

"Shh. It was just a dream." Thayne wrapped his arms around her and stroked her back in long, rhythmic circles.

At first Riley pushed at his chest, wanting to escape, but he refused to let her go; he just held her tighter.

The dim light from the propped-open bathroom door allowed her to see his face. And him to see hers. He cupped her cheeks and wiped away the tears with his thumbs.

"Madison's abduction wasn't your fault," he said softly.

"You don't know," Riley whispered. "I've gone over that night in my mind so many times. I should have screamed, but I stayed quiet, just like he ordered me to. I let my sister be taken by a madman, and I did nothing to stop it."

"You were ten years old. What would you tell a victim's sister in the same circumstances?"

Riley closed her eyes against the truth. "Damn you."

"Be kind to that ten-year-old child who lost her sister. She deserves it."

Riley blinked once, then again. She wouldn't cry. She couldn't make herself weak or vulnerable to anyone. She clenched her fists against his chest.

She tried to avert her gaze from the tenderness in his eyes, but he refused to let her. Silent and still, he stared at her, unyielding. They lay together, bodies a whisper away from each other. She breathed in, and his scent wafted over her. He smelled so good. Her heart slammed against her chest. Her hands unfurled against his bare skin.

His eyes darkened, and his nostrils flared.

Desire. This she understood.

She clasped the back of his head and pulled his lips to hers. The passion between them exploded. She could feel his hardening desire, but before they lost themselves, he wrenched back.

"I want more," he whispered. "More than we shared in this bed a year ago; more than all the phone calls; more than the most erotic dreams. I want it all, Riley. I know that now."

"I thought I was enough." She couldn't keep the hurt from her voice.

"You're enough, Riley, but I want everything, with nothing held back. We keep telling each other it's not the right time, not the right place, but will it ever be? I'm tired of waiting for the right moment. Brett Riverton taught me that lesson today. *Now* is the time. *This* is the place." He stared unblinking into her eyes. "I love you, Riley Lambert. With all of me."

She could never have imagined hearing the words Thayne spoke. Not for her.

He loved her? Her gaze shifted from his.

"Look at me," he growled. "Don't hide. Not anymore, because I'm not. I want a Blackwood kind of love. I want everything you are."

Thayne lifted her chin with his finger.

"When your parents called and I saw your face, I hurt for you. I wanted to wrap you in my arms and protect you from a past I could do nothing about. When you went into Cheyenne's office and saw the crime scene with new eyes, I was in awe of your ability. You have a gift that I don't fully comprehend, but more than that, I witnessed your heart, your compassion. You represent the victims who can't speak. You put all your energy, everything you have, into finding my sister.

"You're special, Riley. And if you give me half a chance, I think we could find the love my parents had, the love my grandparents have." He bent down, his lips hovering just above hers. "Accept my love, Riley. Let me show you how it could be between us. Not just with passion. With tenderness. In good times. And in bad. No matter what. Unconditional, never-ending. Forever."

A shuddering breath expelled from her lungs. He was offering her everything she'd been afraid to dream of, and she wanted to feel an emotion she'd never believed possible.

With a trembling hand, she touched his cheek. His eyes burned hot with need, making it hard to breathe. Her heart raced even faster. The emotions that had been threatening to overwhelm her erupted with terrifying strength, washing through her mind and soul, destroying the walls she'd erected to protect herself from the hurt and the pain, laying her open and vulnerable.

She should be terrified, but when Thayne held her, she felt safe and whole. He evoked something rare and precious she'd thought had been crushed a long time ago. Faith and trust.

Sinking into the pillow, Riley gazed up into his eyes. They crinkled at the corner with a smile.

Ever so slowly, he lowered his head, his lips barely brushing across hers. Her mouth tingled; her breath caught in her throat. She licked her lips.

A groan rumbled in his chest. "Do you accept my love?"

She closed her eyes and nodded.

"Can you give me your love in return? All your love, all your faith, all your heart?"

She froze in his arms.

Riley had no doubt that she wanted Thayne or that she needed him. He could very well be the best person she knew. How could she not love a man who danced the waltz with his grandmother just to calm her?

When was the last time someone had believed in her and her abilities as much as Thayne? She didn't believe in herself that much.

What he asked was impossible. Wasn't it? Love didn't just go on forever. People fell out of love all the time. Love had conditions. What were Thayne's?

He sighed, long and slow. "You don't have to answer yet," he said, stroking his fingertip down her arm, eliciting a shiver from her. "Someday I hope you will."

Riley looked up at him, tears clinging to her eyelashes. "I can't . . . I don't know how to be what you want."

"I just want you." He tucked her against his body. "I'm all in with you, Riley. I'm seizing the moment and jumping in with both feet. I can wait."

◆ ◆ ◆

The August dawn sprinkled in through the curtains. The bed was cool. Thayne reached out across the mattress.

Riley was gone.

He propped himself up, listening for the shower. He heard nothing.

He padded across the bedroom and gently opened the bathroom door. A slight hint of steam lingered on the mirror's edge, but she was nowhere to be seen.

He looked at the bedside table. A small scrap of paper was propped against a cup of coffee. He picked up the note.

Gone to sheriff's office.

His attention turned to the plate beside the cup. One half of a cinnamon roll.

Thayne bit into the gift with a small smile. They'd shared the gooey treat together most mornings during their first week together. She'd remembered.

It gave him hope. Riley was a woman who had sacrificed her life to protect others, who had sacrificed her dreams to heal her family. Who would stop at nothing to finish what she'd started. It was one of the reasons he'd fallen in love with her in the first place. Which was why she'd left. But she hadn't forgotten.

With a quick prayer they would find his sister alive and well today, Thayne dressed quickly. He studied himself in the mirror. The SEAL still existed beneath the deputy's uniform, but right now he was needed here.

He strode down the B&B steps.

Fannie poked her head through the kitchen door. "Could you watch for Kade? He didn't come home last night."

"Sure thing." Thayne nodded over his shoulder.

Within five minutes, he'd arrived at the sheriff's office and walked in the door. Ironcloud gave him a quick nod, still watching over Riley.

She was in the conference room, deep in conversation with Agent Nolan. He headed toward them when his phone buzzed. He looked at the screen in surprise. "Blackwood. What's up, Wolf?"

"I heard about your sister, Cowboy. Anything we can do?"

"I appreciate the thought, but that's not why you called, Commander."

Wolf sighed. "They want a decision on re-upping. We've got a long-term op to prepare for, and they want me to finalize my team."

"You want my decision now? When would I have to report?"

"Three days."

"Three days?" Thayne repeated the impossible date.

A voice behind him gasped. Thayne turned. Riley had walked out of the conference room. Her face had paled.

He stared into her eyes. "I can't make that decision with my sister missing. If they won't give me more time, I'll have to go for retirement."

"I don't want to lose you," Wolf said. "I'll see what I can do."

Thayne would've thought the decision to leave the Navy would be more difficult. "Don't bother. I have people who need me here, not clear across the world. And I need to be there for them. Put the request through."

Wolf said nothing for several seconds. "We'll miss you, Cowboy. I wish I had someone I'd make that decision for. Good luck."

"Don't get dead, Wolf." Thayne ended the call surprisingly serene about the momentous decision.

Riley blinked, her expression stunned. He could tell she wanted to ask questions. They'd have time for talk and more. Later.

"Did Nolan find something?" he prodded.

She shook her head slightly and then refocused. "He discovered only three Cadillacs were identified at the abduction scenes. All different models and colors. It's a dead end."

Hell of a way to start the day. "Any good news at all?" Thayne asked with a frown.

"Actually, yes." She bit her lip, and her brow furrowed.

"You don't look happy."

"Because I don't like what I'm thinking. We ran Gina Wallace's DNA searching for a potential match with her father. I thought he might be a lead, if not the kidnapper."

"You found him?" Thayne stood up and motioned his father into the room. His father rushed in and stood by his side.

She shook her head slowly. "The lab discovered something very interesting. Gina Wallace and Brian Anderson are related."

Thayne steepled his hands beneath his nose as the news settled over him. "How is that possible? I specifically remember reading that Carol had no living relatives in Gina's file. Gina is alone in the world except for her unknown father."

"None that we knew of," Riley corrected. "Until now." She let out a long, slow breath. "Gina and Brian are half siblings. They share the same father."

The sheriff's office went dead silent.

Riley rubbed the back of her neck. "Gina is easy enough to explain. Her mother had a one-night stand with someone who stalked her throughout the years—if we can believe Ed. And I do. Brian is another story altogether. From his file, we discovered he was conceived through in vitro fertilization with a *sperm* donor."

"Gina's one-night stand is Brian's IVF sperm donor?" Thayne met his father's stunned gaze as he restated Riley's pronouncement. "What the hell have we stumbled on?"

"They're family," his father said.

"Which explains their similar features." Thayne walked over to the window of the conference room and scanned from photo to photo to photo the series of images—of very similar images—hanging on the wall.

"And the others on the crime scene board?" his father asked.

Riley leaned back against the wall. She pinched the bridge of her nose. "We discovered that more than half the parents of the victims went through some type of fertility treatment. When I first read the file, it just wasn't something we believed to be significant in regard to the kidnappings. Now . . . well, Agent Nolan is calling the other parents."

"This doesn't explain Cheyenne's abduction," Thayne said. "Do you have a theory?"

Riley squirmed under Thayne's gaze. "She has a similar hair color," she rushed out.

His father straightened, and Thayne caught the twitch of his right hand and the bristling irritation just beneath the surface. "I don't know what you think you're implying, young lady."

"Look, Sheriff, maybe you'd prefer we discuss this alone . . . ," Riley suggested gently, her eyes knowing.

Thayne's father met Riley's gaze, then he glanced at Thayne. A slight tinge rose in his dad's cheeks, and he cleared his throat. What exactly had Riley discovered?

"Fine. Lynette and I had trouble conceiving early on. She underwent a small procedure before Hudson was born, but after that, the babies came one after the other."

How many more secrets that had been forgotten or withheld would they uncover during this investigation? "You never mentioned anything to us," Thayne said, surprise evident in his voice.

His father shrugged. "It's not something we discussed with you kids. It didn't matter. She had some fibroids in her uterus, and Doc removed them. It's one reason she had a hysterectomy so young."

Thayne remembered his mother going into the hospital while he was in elementary school.

Riley looked down at her feet. Thayne could tell she really didn't want to ask flat out.

His father straightened. "Let me be perfectly clear, Special Agent Lambert. Cheyenne is my biological daughter. Her hair color is not a coincidence; she comes by it honestly. From my father. End of story."

"OK." Riley obviously didn't want to argue in public.

But Thayne suspected she'd already requested Cheyenne's DNA be run, which would be on file since his sister had served in the military.

"I want to run comparisons on as many other kidnap victims as possible," she said. "All of them have some sort of DNA and fingerprints on file. They were just beginning to be collected as standard operating procedure when Gina and Madison went missing."

Riley twisted her fingers in her lap and sent Thayne a sidelong glance. "You realize what this could mean? Madison might be my *half* sister."

Thayne let out a slow whistle. "Do you think your parents used IVF to conceive?"

She kneaded her temple, and he could see the headache from the previous night returning. "I have absolutely no idea. I'll have to call my mother. Can I use your office, Sheriff?"

"Of course." Thayne's dad cleared his throat. "I'm going to make some coffee. You two want anything?" With the more-than-obvious reason to give Riley some privacy, his father tilted his head toward his office door.

"Please," Riley said with an appreciative smile. "Black, and as strong as you've got."

"Pendergrass makes coffee that tastes like bad, weak tea. I'll brew it so hair will grow on your chest." His father walked toward the coffeemaker, and those in the room dissipated. Several investigators returned to the conference room, but everyone kept glancing back at Riley.

"Do you want to be alone to make the call?" Thayne asked. What a hell of a thing to discuss with parents at all, much less with ones who obviously had difficulty communicating about almost everything.

"Please. Come with me," she said simply.

A bit stunned at the invitation, Thayne gave her a brief nod, thankful she seemed to want his support.

They strode into his father's office and closed the door behind them. Thayne hitched his hip on the desk as Riley picked up the receiver and dialed her parents' number. She placed the call on speakerphone.

"Hello?" a male voice answered.

"Hi, Dad."

"Riley. This is a surprise. How are you?"

She closed her eyes. "I'm fine."

"Good, good." An awkward silence grew longer. Whispers filtered through the phone. "Umm, Riley, are you coming to the memorial?" he asked, clearly uncomfortable.

More sharp whispers that Thayne couldn't quite decipher hissed from the speaker.

"The entire town expects you to attend."

Laying the guilt on a bit thick. Obviously Riley's mother was behind the questions. Riley's family dynamics were so . . . bizarre . . . compared to the Blackwoods'. His family had to have come as quite a shock. This conversation explained so many of her comments about his family that he hadn't quite understood.

Now he did. The Blackwoods must have seemed like another species.

Riley cleared her throat. "Probably. Umm . . . there's been some information related to Madison's case that's come to light. Can I speak with Mother?"

"Adrienne!" her father called out. "Get on the other line. Riley has news."

"Really, Alan, do you have to shout?" Mrs. Lambert's voice came through the phone. "So, Riley. You finally have some information for us?"

Thayne wanted to reach through the phone and strangle the woman. Riley met his gaze and shrugged as if to say, *Yep, this is where I came from.* She could've picked up the phone or asked him to leave, but she didn't. She was allowing him to see her family up close and personal. Warts and all.

Thayne reached his hand to her and squeezed, giving her a supportive smile that he hoped told her it didn't matter or change how he felt about her.

Holding his gaze with hers, Riley took in a deep breath and cleared her throat. "Mother, did you ever go to a fertility clinic?"

CHAPTER TWENTY-THREE

Riley's chest closed off as if she were in a vise. She squeezed Thayne's hand, thankful he'd stayed and her family hadn't scared him off.

"Yes, we did," her father said. "We conceived Madison shortly after your mother starting receiving hormone treatments. She was a wonderful surprise. As were you. Why are you asking?"

Oh God. She couldn't believe she had to push her parents. "Mother?" Riley asked. "Is that how you remember it?"

"This is private medical information and none of your concern." Her mother's sharp staccato voice was colder than usual.

"It's important, Mother. I need the truth, no matter what it is. We're running a DNA comparison on Madison's blood."

"You can't do that. I forbid it," her mother snapped.

Riley had never heard her mother quite so panicked.

"Adrienne?" her father said. "What's going on?"

"Just more of Riley's excuses. I'm hanging up now."

"Mother, if you help me, I might be able to find out what happened to Madison. Don't you want to know? Finally?"

No click. Her mother hadn't hung up.

"Adrienne. Tell her."

Riley couldn't remember ever hearing her father's voice quite so firm.

"Adrienne. Do it now."

"You want to know the truth, Alan. Fine. The treatments didn't work. They never worked. Your sperm was weak. I told the clinic to mix the sperm with an anonymous donor and not tell me the results."

The phone went silent. After several moments, Riley heard a soft click.

"Why did you have to do this, Riley?" her mother asked. "You're always stirring up trouble. Do you take joy in making my life miserable?"

"It's what I live for," Riley said. "You want answers. Mother, I'm doing what I can to find my sister. I believe her *biological* father kidnapped her. What clinic did you go to? I need the man's name."

"Denver Fertility Solutions, but they went out of business in the nineties," her mother retorted. "And don't you blame me for Madison's kidnapping. We know who's to blame. If only you had said something when he took her, you could have saved your sister."

Her mother slammed down the phone, leaving only a dial tone.

The words hit Riley in the gut, and she practically doubled over with pain. Thayne grabbed her shoulders and whirled her into his arms. "She's wrong. You must know that."

Riley nodded against his shoulder but allowed herself to sink into his warmth anyway. She had the answer she'd been afraid of.

The phone on the sheriff's desk rang.

Thayne glanced down at the caller ID. "It's a Colorado number," he said.

Riley punched the speakerphone.

"Riley." Her father's voice filtered into the room. Of course she had to wonder if the man who raised her was her biological father or not.

"Dad? I'm so sorry. I had to ask—"

"No, Riley. Don't you apologize to me. I'm the one who's sorry. Sorry for not being the father you deserved all these years. Sorry for not defending you and having your back when I should have. I let Madison's loss numb me to everything."

Her throat thickened. "Daddy, it's OK. I understand."

"No, Riley, it's not. Don't listen to your mother, sweetheart. None of this was your fault. You were a little girl. I know you'll do everything you can to find out what happened to your sister. You may not find the answer today or tomorrow or even in a year. You may never find her, and that's OK. You're enough, Riley. I'm proud of the woman you've become, and I'm ashamed I haven't told you that before now. I love you, sweetheart. I just haven't shown it. But that's going to change."

Riley choked back her tears and said raggedly, "I love you, too, Daddy."

He paused for a moment. "Riley, whether or not my DNA runs through your body, you're my daughter. Never forget that."

"I kn-know." She didn't want to know. Not ever.

"And, sweetheart, whatever you find out, call me. Maybe I can come visit and we can have a long talk. Face-to-face."

"I'd like that." Her hand shaking, Riley ended the call. Her knees gave way, and she fell into the chair.

Thayne knelt in front of her. "You all right?"

"He said he loved me." She raised her gaze to Thayne's.

"You're very lovable."

She could hardly see him through blurred vision. She swiped at her eyes. "I'll take this information to Agent Nolan. Maybe we can find a tie to this clinic."

Thayne clasped her hands and rose, pulling her to her feet. He cupped her cheek. "You're going to solve this, Riley. I can feel it."

She looked into his eyes, marveling at the faith in him. "I hope so. Except now I have to call every one of the families who have lost their children and maybe bring up a secret no one wanted revealed."

"If it means closure and discovering who took their child, isn't it worth it?" he asked.

"Is it? Maybe some secrets are just better off buried?"

"The truth set your father free," Thayne said. "Or at least woke him up." He wrapped his arms around her and squeezed. "Think of it this way. Without the secrets, would you have been able to connect these cases sooner?"

"Maybe."

The door slammed open and Sheriff Blackwood raced into the room. "Jackson called. Kade just walked out of the woods covered in blood."

Most Monday mornings, Singing River wasn't a hotbed of activity. Not so today. Riley leaned forward in her seat as Thayne drove to the hospital. She reached for Thayne's hand, and he linked his fingers with hers. She had no idea what Kade Lonebear had become involved with, but the last time she'd encountered him, he'd tried to kill pretty much anyone in his path.

Had he succeeded this time?

Thayne might trust his friend, but all Riley could see was the unpredictable nature of PTSD.

Thayne's vehicle squealed to the side of the hospital where an ambulance had pulled up to the emergency entrance. The paramedics opened the rear door, and Jackson hopped out, his shirt and pants splattered red.

Riley and Thayne jumped out of the vehicle and ran toward them.

"So much blood," she whispered. But whose?

Thayne tried to reach for her, but she scooted away. What if the blood were his sister's? God. Her throat closed off, panic strangling her. Not because she couldn't handle violence—she'd lived with violence most of her career—but if Cheyenne didn't make it, how could she face the Blackwood family again? She'd be a reminder of their loss, and she refused to do that to anyone.

Jackson waved at them.

Thayne reached him first. "What the hell?" He grabbed his brother's arms. "Are you hurt?"

Jackson shook his head. "Not me."

Riley couldn't believe Jackson wasn't hurt covered in that much blood, until she got a look at Kade sitting in the back of the ambulance, the paramedics hovering nearby and uncertain. She could see why.

He'd secured a small boy in one arm and a rifle in the other. He held the wide-eyed child tight, but the left half of Kade's shirt was soaked with red.

"Stay back," Thayne warned her, throwing his arm out to block her path. "If Kade's having a flashback . . ."

"Do you think he did this?" Riley asked under her breath. "Could he have?"

"I don't know."

A doctor and a couple of nurses sped out of the small hospital, then stopped, eyes wide. Thayne signaled them to hold.

Thayne eased closer to Kade. "Soldier? Status report," he said.

"I found a print near the Riverton waterfall. Faint, but I tracked it and came upon them. I couldn't help them both," Kade said, his low voice filled with sorrow. "So hurt, but the other one crawled away to die. He hid and wouldn't come with me. I couldn't stay any longer. Under fire."

Kade's head bobbed, and his eyes lost focus.

"Location?"

"Three clicks from the Riverton mine. Due east."

"That's deep in the woods," Thayne said to Riley. He hunkered down in front of Kade. "And who is this?"

The boy of about six clung to Kade, his eyes wide with fright. "Sam."

Riley's eyes took in the red-brown hair and features. She recognized him from Nolan's list of missing boys. Her breathing quickened. "Sam Carlisle?"

He nodded.

"Sam was taken from Fort Collins, Colorado. He's the last . . ." She didn't finish the sentence, but inside her heart stuttered with hope. They were so close. Sam was the first victim to escape. She smiled at the boy. She had no idea how he could have done it at six. "Your mom is looking for you."

The boy grinned and puffed out his chest with pride. "I knew she would. I told Kade my mom would never stop looking."

Thayne placed his hand on Sam's head, streaked with blood. "Are you hurt?"

He shook his head. "Kade is. They shot him when he rescued me."

"Who did?"

"Father." Sam's lip trembled. "Only he's not my dad. My dad's in heaven. That man wanted to call me Micah. That's not my name. I kept telling them it wasn't my name."

Sam's voice rose in panic.

"It's OK, Sam."

Kade coughed, and Sam slipped a bit in his arms as Kade's breathing grew more labored.

Thayne held out his arms. "Sam, come to me."

Sam clung to Kade, who winced. "No. He needs me."

"He needs a doctor now. You did good getting him here." Riley kept her voice gentle. "See, they're waiting to help him."

Riley tried to meet Kade's gaze, but the man had closed his eyes.

"Soldier?" Thayne barked. "What are your injuries?"

"Bullet lodged in my shoulder." Kade's voice had grown weak.

"You're safe at base. I'm taking your rifle," Thayne said. "You need medical attention." He eased Kade's rifle from his arm.

He didn't protest and sagged to the side, unconscious.

"Medic!" Thayne shouted.

The doctor rushed in, followed by the nurse. Riley scooped up Sam. The boy clawed at her. "Kaaade!"

Riley held Sam tight against her chest. "Sam. Sam. He'll be fine."

"He saved me after Ian got hurt." Sam bowed his head. "We gotta go back for Ian. Father will punish him if he finds him."

A terrified shiver went through the boy.

"Is punishment bad?" Riley asked.

Sam nodded. "One girl—Hannah—was taken to punishment, and she didn't come back." He leaned in and whispered in her ear, "Ian said she's gone forever. Like forever, forever."

Riley knelt in front of Sam. How much could a six-year-old tell them? She'd find out. "How far did you walk before Kade found you?"

"A long time. It was dark. Ian and I were running away. Then the lights chased us, and someone jumped out at Ian. They hurt him. He crawled away, but they went after him. Father came after me. Kade grabbed me and ran, but Father shot him."

Tears rolled down Sam's face. "Kade saved me," he repeated.

"Do you know from which direction you came?" Thayne asked the boy.

"Down," Sam said. "Ian said to go away from that big star up there. It looks like the handle of a cup."

"They walked south," Jackson offered, pulling out a map.

Hopefully he could pinpoint a search area.

"OK, Sam," Riley said. "Why don't we go inside and get you checked out?"

"I wanna see Kade."

"In a little while. I promise," Riley said.

"OK. I'm hungry. Where's my mom? She'll get me breakfast."

"We're going to call your mom right now." Riley hugged the boy close. "I'm glad you're OK, Sam."

"I didn't like it there. I liked Bethany, but she disappeared. Ian said we needed to leave because they wanted to be my family." He yawned, and his head fell to her shoulder. "I told them I already have a mom, but they wouldn't listen to me."

Thick pine trees surrounded Riley. Another time, she might have taken time to breathe in the fresh mountain air, enjoy the pockets of wildflowers, and simply enjoy the blue sky peeking through the green canopy above her.

Instead, she crouched beside Thayne in the cover of a huge evergreen.

"What I wouldn't give to have my SEAL team here," he said softly.

A series of sheriff's deputies and agents was scattered through the forest. Between Kade's description and the blood splatter on the ground, they'd identified the location where he'd been shot.

Riley prayed the other boy was safe and alive nearby. Sam had called him Ian. She wondered what his real name might be. Evidently this *Father* character renamed his children when he took them.

She hadn't wanted to leave the little boy, but he'd taken a shine to Jan and wouldn't leave Kade's bedside. Rules be damned.

Thayne eased forward. Riley followed. Every few feet, they stopped and listened. They'd gone at least a hundred yards when Riley picked up a weak cry. She raised her hand. Thayne placed his finger over his lips. He'd heard it, too.

"H-help me," a feeble voice whispered.

Riley closed her eyes, trying to focus on where the sound had originated.

"H-help."

Thayne lifted his hand, signaling Deputy Ironcloud to his right. *It could be a trap,* he mouthed. She nodded, palming the replacement Glock Thayne had given her.

They crawled through the underbrush. A deep hole appeared out of nowhere, and they froze. Riley peered into the hole. A boy lay there, unmoving, his leg bent at a strange angle, his body splattered with blood. She recognized him.

"Brian Anderson," Riley whispered. "Sam's Ian."

Thayne tapped his radio to reach search headquarters. "Dad, we need a rescue unit. Covert if possible. Brian Anderson is at the bottom of what looks like a collapsed mine shaft. He's at least thirty feet down. Broken leg. No telling what else." He gave his father their coordinates.

"We got movement," Ironcloud muttered in Riley's earpiece.

She stilled, quickly scanning the perimeter. A grove of aspens quaked, and a man peered through the leaves.

Riley shot to her feet, weapon drawn, but not before he pointed a gun directly at her chest.

Thayne called out behind her, shouting at her to stop. He didn't have to yell. She wasn't moving.

She blinked at the man, his red hair very familiar. So like Madison's. The side of Riley's head throbbed. Her mind flashed to that night, fifteen years ago.

His features morphed into a younger version, threatening her.

"I remember you!" she shouted, lost in her own nightmare come to life. "You took Madison."

His eyes widened, then he smiled, a twisted grin that made her shiver. "I came looking for my missing children and found another. You're mine, you know. I should have taken you, too, but I have a rule. One child at a time. Your sister was the more gifted. We had to have her."

"Where is she, you sick bastard!" Riley swallowed down the nausea threatening to rise in her throat. Her hands shook as she held the weapon on him.

His face froze into a dark mask. "That's no way for a child to talk to her father. I've seen you on the news. This is all your fault. You've ruined the perfect life I created. Well, it won't matter. I belong here, in these woods, but I can re-create our haven again. My children will help me. I'm not alone."

"Drop your weapon." She tensed, trying to get sight of any other threat.

He refocused his aim.

Before Riley could pull the trigger, a shot exploded from the distance. Riley dropped to the ground. Within seconds, Thayne was at her side.

"Riley! Are you hit?"

She shook her head. "I never pulled the trigger. Someone else shot him."

The man called Father crumpled to his knees, his eyes wide, stunned. Blood seeped down the front of his shirt.

"Not possible," he whispered. He fell to his side and closed his eyes. "It's all supposed to be mine."

Riley had no idea what he was talking about, but she didn't care. Knees shaking, she stood. Thayne knelt by her side.

"Show yourself!" he shouted into the woods.

A woman, her red hair wild, held a gun in trembling hands. Five children ranging from the ages of around eight to eighteen hid behind her.

All with various shades of red hair.

The woman dropped her weapon.

"Thank God. You found us. Finally."

And she sank to the ground.

Staring at the six figures huddled together at the edge of their base camp, not far from where they'd found Ian—or, rather, Brian Anderson—Thayne could easily see the resemblance among them. Even without the DNA tests, he would bet they were related to one another.

Riley sat across from the oldest of them all, Adelaide, trying to eke out information. She'd given them directions to what she called the compound. Jackson had gone to search for Cheyenne and anyone else who might have been left behind. They had files on almost twenty children. They'd found only eight.

Thayne couldn't peg her age. She could be anywhere from twenty-three to thirty-three, but she'd refused to give her real name. In fact, she'd refused to answer any questions. All she'd wanted to know was if the man they called Father was alive or dead.

Thayne hoped he died on the operating table. Save the world some trouble.

The five kids sat strangely quiet behind her, obviously in a state of shock. None of them had said a word, and Riley hadn't been able to coax anything from them. The trauma was obviously too great.

Thayne hunkered down beside Riley. "Did you get anything from them?" Anything about Cheyenne.

Riley shook her head.

His jaw clenched. He could keep it together. They were so close. *Please be alive, Cheyenne. God, please let her be OK.*

He forced a gentle smile on his face. "Transport is on the way, but it'll be a while before we can get them down the mountain. We're well off the beaten track."

The woman's gaze flew up to him. "Where are you taking us?"

Her voice trembled; her gaze darted to and fro. She'd clearly been abused. A scar had marred one side of her face. If she'd been taken from the age of twelve, she could have been held by their captor for up to twenty years.

"Back to Singing River," Thayne said, keeping his tone low and calm.

Riley gave Adelaide a reassuring smile. "The hospital first, to check everyone out."

"We have to stay together," she said, her voice firm. "My family needs me. Family is everything."

Thayne had witnessed this kind of detachment in battle-weary veterans. The poor woman couldn't seem to grasp that they never had to go back to the place they'd been held captive. They'd never again have to see the man they called Father, but it hadn't seemed to sink in that they were free.

"Adelaide? Is anyone else at your home?" Riley pressed. "Was there a doctor with you? Cheyenne Blackwood?"

Adelaide toyed with the dirt at her feet. Furtively, she looked around. "Is Father coming back?"

"He's never coming back," Thayne said. "You don't have to worry about him ever again."

She swallowed. "He'll be mad if I tell you."

Riley leaned in to her. "Please, Adelaide. We have to help her."

"The doctor was kind."

Was. Thayne's heart plummeted.

Riley reached her hand to Thayne's. "Where is the doctor?"

"Father . . ." Adelaide's eyes welled up. "Father took her to the omega room for punishment. No one comes home after he takes them there. No one." She shuddered and buried her head in her arms.

Thayne struggled to keep calm. This couldn't be happening. How could they be this close and be too late? "Can you show us where the omega room is?"

Adelaide snapped her head up, eyes wide with fright. She shook her head side to side and started to pant. "No . . . one . . ." She couldn't catch her breath.

Riley moved in closer, not touching Adelaide but speaking to her in a calm, almost hypnotic voice. Slowly, she calmed. "It's forbidden. Father said no one would understand the meaning but him, and no one can get in once he's closed the door. There are four keys. That's all I know."

Thayne gripped Riley's shoulder. She looked up at him, sympathy bathing her eyes. He refused to let himself consider the option. Not until he saw proof that Cheyenne wasn't safe and alive.

"Where is the omega room, Adelaide?" Thayne asked. "Where is Doctor Blackwood?"

"Look for her behind the house. In a clearing beneath the cliff," Adelaide said softly. "You'll find all the secrets there."

One of the girls began to rock to and fro. She began to hum a familiar song, something Thayne hadn't heard since childhood. "Puff the Magic Dragon."

A boy of about ten began to sing.

> When things go bad, and life seems so unfair,
> Just hold on tight with all your might, and I'll always
> be there.

Riley gasped. "Where did you learn that song?" She grabbed the boy's arms.

The kid's eyes went wide. The other children stopped singing.

Thayne tore Riley's hands from the boy and pulled her away. "What's wrong?"

"The song. That's Madison's special song, Thayne. She made it up the day she was taken."

Riley's entire body shook. Thayne pressed her close, knowing he could say nothing. She was facing her greatest fear. They both were. All he could do was hold her. And love her. “OK, OK, we suspected he took her, right? We’ll find her. We’ll find them both.”

A rustle of trees and pounding footsteps jerked Thayne’s attention away from the trembling woman in his arms. Jackson rushed over.

“We found the compound,” he said under his breath. “And you’re not going to believe it.”

CHAPTER TWENTY-FOUR

The thick cluster of evergreens in front of them just appeared to Riley to be another dense wooded area. They'd traveled an additional hour to the location, which put them a good three hours from Singing River. Had Cheyenne really been only hours away?

Riley stood with Thayne and Jackson studying the foliage that concealed the entrance to the compound. The team had uncovered the mysterious black SUV well camouflaged at the end of an off-road trail barely wide enough to accommodate the vehicle. Without Adelaide's help, they never would have found either.

"I would've walked right past and not even slowed down," Thayne said.

They pushed through a thick grove of evergreens, ducked under some large tree limbs, and weaved their way through a series of large boulders. After navigating a second stand of trees, they emerged into the secreted clearing. A large, two-story stone house came into view, the front flush with the rock face on both sides. Thayne let out a whistle.

Jackson pointed to a bevy of satellite dishes that had been placed strategically to one side of the building. The place may be in the middle of nowhere, but it was definitely high tech.

Riley studied the perimeter, and a glint of metal mounted on the corner caught her eye. She elbowed Thayne. "Is that camera similar to Riverton's prototype?"

"How did he possibly get access to technology that's not available to the public?" She'd known the man who'd gone undetected for fifteen years had been smart, but she'd pictured the Unabomber, not someone as plugged in and sophisticated as this guy appeared to be.

"We have no idea, but Jackson contacted Brett and Cal. They provided my brother the intel to get past some of the security."

Thayne's satphone sounded out of nowhere. "Blackwood." He listened for a few minutes. "You have to hear this."

He punched the speakerphone, and Tom's voice came through. "You sitting down, Riley?" he asked.

"Not really a place to do that here," she said.

"We ran the rest of the kidnap victims. Every one of the missing kids is related to one another."

"That's not a surprise," she commented. "One look at the children we found side by side, and it's obvious they're siblings."

"How about this one, then?" Tom said. "We ran your perp's prints, and they were on file because of a DUI. His name is David Aaron McIlroy. We completed a DNA comparison. He's their biological father. All twenty of the missing."

Riley froze. Inside, she'd known, but to hear the facts aloud . . . The man who had destroyed so many families, so many lives. The man who'd terrorized her that night fifteen years ago and taken her sister. He was Madison's father.

The cold truth ricocheted around her mind before encasing her heart, chilling her to the core. That maniac was her sister's biological father. And perhaps hers as well. She wouldn't go there now. Maybe later.

"The guy sure got around," Thayne commented with a frown.

"To sperm banks near the I-25 corridor," Tom said. "Except for Gina Wallace, all the children were conceived using various fertility clinics. Seems he thought his genetic code was pretty damn valuable."

Riley shook her head, the should-haves, could-haves slicing at her conscience. "We've had the victims' DNA for years. I never—"

"Don't finish that sentence, Riley," Tom said. "Hindsight is always twenty-twenty. Why would we run the comparison? The matches weren't close enough to be used for identification. They were never flagged until we suspected a pattern."

"So this crazy guy was gathering his children?" Thayne asked. "Like some twisted Pied Piper?"

He clasped Riley's hand, giving her a comforting squeeze.

Jackson shook his head in disgust before biting out a sharp curse. Riley was right there with him.

"He didn't take all of his biological children," Tom said. "After interviewing a few of the fertility clinics still in business, they were willing to tell us Mr. McIlroy was a favorite donor. Great bio, I guess. He has other offspring out there, but except for Gina, the abducted children all have unusually high IQs and are from less-than-ideal homes. We believe he chose his targets quite specifically."

"Madison doesn't fit his profile," Riley said. "Our family was normal . . . until that night."

"The unit will keep digging," Tom said quietly. "I'll be in touch."

He ended the call. Part of her wanted to lock McIlroy in a room and force the bastard to tell her the truth, give her the why. The other half hoped he just disappeared so all those children would know this particular bogeyman could never come back.

The wind whipped up, gusting cold from the north. Riley shivered against the onslaught. "Adelaide said to look behind the house at the base of the cliff." Riley couldn't push aside the deep foreboding and odd sense of déjà vu. She'd been in similar situations too many times in the last several months. None had ended well.

Maybe this time . . .

Deputies Pendergrass and Ironcloud, followed by Agents Underhill and Nolan, joined them in the clearing.

"We'll search the inside," Nolan offered.

Thayne, Jackson, and Riley rounded the house to the back. A well-sculpted lawn with a volleyball net, tetherball, and jungle gym peppered the green. Such an odd place. On either side, sheer cliffs stretched hundreds of feet up. At the back edge, the landscape morphed into a rocky berm. Large shrubs, boulders, and pines created a barrier, but a narrow crushed-rock pathway snaked toward the rocks blocking the rear of the property. Just as Adelaide had described.

They followed the trail until the foliage ended. Riley's knees nearly gave way.

Fifteen gravestones were lined in three rows. Her gaze snapped to a freshly dug grave.

"Thayne," Jackson choked out.

"No." Thayne halted, shaking his head. "Not until I see her."

Adelaide had warned them the secrets were here. Riley wove her fingers through Thayne's. Did that mean all of the abducted children but the eight they'd rescued were buried in this cemetery as well?

"We need a forensics team," she said quietly.

Thayne gave a quick nod and moved away, speaking softly into his satphone, the lines around his mouth drawn and tight with more than worry. As if he were preparing himself for the worst. She recognized the pain he and his family faced, and she wouldn't wish it on anyone.

Riley squatted down, barely able to breathe. The smell of freshly turned dirt made her stomach knot. One more dead body. What was the chance Cheyenne didn't occupy the new grave? She'd never expected to find Madison alive, but she'd begun to hope, to believe they'd save Cheyenne.

Bracing herself, she allowed her gaze to move from name to name across the headstones. With each stop, she grew more and more confused.

"I don't recognize any of the names," she said quietly to Thayne. "These must be their aliases." And for all she knew, Madison was one of them.

Thayne frowned and shook his head. "He stripped them of their original identities completely. We won't be able to identify them until we compare dental records or DNA."

Are you here, Madison? Can I finally bring you home?

Deputy Pendergrass and Underhill joined them, and Jackson pointed to the fresh grave. The job of digging up the latest body began, and Riley looked away, unable to watch what they uncovered.

"This wasn't supposed to happen." Thayne stared at her, shocked. "We were supposed to find her alive and well and mad as hell."

He'd once looked to her with hope. Now only devastation remained. She'd been in awe of his optimism, even when the odds had compounded against him, but faced with what stood before him, that hope was gone. Resignation and grief had etched themselves onto his very heart.

Riley leaned in to his side, wrapping her arms around his waist, not knowing what else to do. "I'm so sorry."

"I'm glad Mom's not here," Jackson choked out. "She wouldn't have survived this."

An overwhelming despair welled up inside Riley. Tears flowed down her cheeks. She swiped at them, but they just kept coming, so she gave in to the reality. The monster who had destroyed her family—and so many others—had destroyed the Blackwoods' as well.

A movement grabbed her attention. Deputy Pendergrass stood up from the newly uncovered grave. "Thayne?" he called.

Thayne took a deep, shuddering breath. "Is it her?" he asked through a clenched jaw.

Riley steadied herself to hear the news.

"The grave is empty."

She squeezed Thayne's waist. His body shuddered.

"Where the hell is she?" he barked out.

"We'll search every inch of this place until we find her," Jackson said. "She has to be here."

Pendergrass jogged over to Thayne. "Underhill found something very interesting you need to see."

The agent pulled back a bush revealing a sixteenth tombstone, tucked away from the others.

The name carved on it: CALVIN RIVERTON, SR.

Cal and Brett Riverton's father.

An eagle soared above, its call echoing among the tall cliffs surrounding them. Thayne shoved a hand through his hair.

"We'll figure out Riverton's connection later," he said. "*Where* is Cheyenne?"

"If we can find the omega room, we should try there first," Riley said. "It's the last place Adelaide mentioned."

"Right." Thayne raced over the path and across the yard to the back door of the house, shouting out for Nolan and Ironcloud as he got closer. He didn't have to turn back to know Jackson and Riley followed behind.

The two men met him at the rear entrance.

"The omega room. Did you find it?" Thayne panted.

"I believe so," Ironcloud said. "But there's no door."

"Show us. Hurry."

They entered the house and rushed into a large schoolroom, then through a playroom, a music room full of instruments that clearly had been played extensively, an electronics workshop that was littered with the Riverton camera prototypes and new designs, a chemistry lab, and even a state-of-the art computer center.

"The twisted bastard gave them the best of everything," Nolan said.

"Except they were stolen from their parents and never allowed to leave," Thayne said. "And of course, there's that whole cemetery thing."

Ironcloud led them down a set of stone steps into a large brick foyer with no furniture and no exit. The only décor was a framed picture, and embedded in the wall just above it, a large omega symbol.

"I'd say this is either the omega room or its entrance," Riley said, squinting up at the symbol. "It's inlayed. Wyoming jade, I think."

Sure enough, the symbol had been created with the stone. "I'm no expert," Thayne said, "but it looks like the shade of Cheyenne's necklace."

"From the Riverton mine. That's odd."

Thayne's gaze moved down to a large print centered below. He recognized the double helix. Two men's faces he didn't recognize graced the left side. NOBEL PRIZE 1962 titled the poster.

Riley walked over to the image. "Watson and Crick were credited with discovering the structure of DNA."

Thayne studied the picture, searching for anything off. "It's slightly tilted." He tried to shift the picture, but it wouldn't move. He ran his fingertips along the edge until he encountered a notch on the left. "Hinges."

Carefully, Thayne pulled on the right side of the frame and opened the print like a door. Behind it, flat against the brick, was a pullout alphanumeric keypad next to a metal door handle. "What is this? *Alice in Wonderland* or *Harry Potter*? We're supposed to solve a riddle?"

"Adelaide didn't know the code." Riley ran her hand over the four rectangular digital displays to the right of the keypad. "Seems simple enough. Except there are ten digits and twenty-six letters. That's . . . I don't know how many combinations. But a lot."

"Can we break in to it or blow it?" Thayne grabbed his phone and called down the hill. "We need someone who can—"

Nolan raced into the room. "We have a problem. We found a huge number of explosives set along the mountain. This place was rigged to blow."

"Could we use some of the explosives to blow this door?" Jackson asked.

The FBI agent shook his head. "There might be trip wires. It could set off the whole thing. We need to get everyone out of here. The place is probably booby-trapped."

"Cheyenne might still be here." Thayne crossed his arms. "Nolan, clear the area and call in the bomb squad, but I'm not leaving until we find my sister."

The man left in a hurry, shouting orders. Thayne stared down Riley and Jackson. "You two get out of here."

"Like that's happening any time soon. Have you got a clue what to enter into the keypad?" Jackson asked.

"We know there's an alphanumeric combination with four entries." Riley rubbed her hands on her pants. "Let's think this through."

She closed the door and stared at the poster.

"The print is about DNA. McIlroy was all about sharing his genetic material."

"What are you thinking?" Thayne could practically see the gears turning in her head.

"I've spent a lot of time recently in forensic classes that cover DNA. It's made up of four chemical bases. Adenine, cytosine, guanine, and thymine. Try A, C, G, T."

"I have no idea what you just said, but it's worth a shot." Thayne pressed four buttons. The letters displayed to the right.

A loud siren roared. Above the doorway, a red strobe light flashed. The key panel blinked, and a screen above the keypad lit up with the time of five minutes.

Four fifty-nine. Four fifty-eight.

Thayne let out a loud curse and looked over at Riley's shocked expression. "We started a countdown."

Nolan rushed back into the foyer. "Everything's gone live. If I'm right, in less than five minutes, this entire area will be buried under a man-made avalanche."

"Damn it. We don't even know if Cheyenne's inside." Thayne rubbed his face. "Get everybody clear and safe, Nolan. We'll follow you out."

He rounded on his brother and Riley. "You have to leave."

"We have a couple of minutes," Riley argued. "I think I'm right. But it was the wrong order."

"I don't have time to try them all!"

Riley paced back and forth. "Let me think."

Thayne met Jackson's gaze. They glanced over at the clock.

"Keep trying," Jackson said.

"T, G, C, A," Thayne punched. Nothing. "T, C, G, A."

He couldn't track all the permutations in this time crunch.

"Riley. You've got to get out of here. One hundred twenty seconds left."

"Try A, T, C, G," Riley said. "DNA is structured with the base pairs of A-T and C-G."

Taking a long breath, Thayne punched in the letters.

A loud hiss rushed out, followed by a click. The panel slid open. Thayne took Riley's face in his hands and kissed her. "You're brilliant."

They ran inside. A figure dressed in scrubs was laid out on a metal table, bound and unconscious.

"Cheyenne?" Thayne bent over his sister and pushed aside her long hair. Saying a silent prayer, he placed his cheek against her mouth. A small puff of air caressed him.

"She's alive." He glanced to Jackson. His brother swiped at his eyes but wore a huge smile.

Cheyenne's face was bruised and cut. She looked like hell. But she was alive.

"Sis?" Thayne said. "We're getting you out of here."

"Thayne!" Riley shouted. "The timer is still counting down. We didn't stop it. It's waiting for another code."

"Try the same one again."

After a few seconds, she appeared in the door. "I can't stop it."

Thayne scooped Cheyenne into his arms. "Go! I'm right behind you."

Jackson and Riley tore up the stairs. Legs pumping, Thayne followed them out the front of the house. Just as they reached the far edge of the clearing, a huge explosion sent fire spewing into the sky, the sonic blast shoving Thayne to his knees.

A rumble hiccupped beneath the earth.

His gaze snapped around him. He met Nolan's. The man nodded. Thank God. Everyone was out.

Thayne fell back, cradled his sister in his lap, and simply stared. Sheets of rock broke from the cliff faces, tumbling onto the building that had been Cheyenne's prison, a storm of boulders and dust that darkened the sky above them.

Riley sank to his side. Jackson stood frozen, his expression shocked.

Thayne didn't know how long they watched, everyone awestruck at the sight. When the thunderous hammering finally stopped, the house had vanished, and the crag between the cliffs had been filled.

McIlroy's compound had been wiped off the face of the earth.

The woman in his arms squirmed.

"Cheyenne?" Thayne smiled down at his older sister.

Her eyelids blinked. She stared up at him, then Jackson.

"I knew you'd find me." She coughed. "Did you rescue Bethany, too?"

Not a name he recognized. He glanced at Riley. She shook her head.

"Who's she?" Thayne asked.

"The woman they wanted me to help. They drugged me. I don't know what happened to her."

Afraid he knew exactly what the poor woman's fate had to be, he grimaced. "We found Adelaide and seven children."

Cheyenne licked her lips. "Can I have some water?"

Jackson rushed away to fetch some.

"On its way."

"I'm glad Adelaide escaped. She was so frightened of Father." Cheyenne shifted, then groaned, clutching Thayne's sleeve. "Find Bethany. She needs a hospital. I did my best, but I don't know. Infection . . . she needs antibiotics, and she was poisoned. The children need her. She protected them."

Thayne glanced over at Riley. Her face had gone pale white. Bethany probably hadn't made it. And any answers to be found were buried under so much rock he doubted they could ever dig it out.

"I'm sorry, Sis. I'm afraid she's gone."

CHAPTER TWENTY-FIVE

Hospital waiting rooms didn't change much from place to place. Singing River's version might be smaller than most, but it contained the prerequisite six-month-old magazines, uncomfortable chairs, and bad coffee.

It was also deserted. Except for Riley.

She'd found her way to a quiet corner of chaos to sit down and catch her breath. Just for a moment. Before she faced the aftermath of their discovery.

Parents, family members, law enforcement from all across the country, the national media. They were all headed to Wyoming for answers. Except there would be no explanations other than those Adelaide, Cheyenne, and the children could provide.

Outside the waiting room, the small medical staff and other volunteers buzzed back and forth. Riley leaned back, her head resting against the wall, and kneaded the stiff cotton of the scrubs the staff had loaned her to replace her mud- and blood-caked clothes.

In all the operations she'd witnessed, she'd never seen a logistical effort quite as convoluted as the one the Singing River sheriff's office had pulled off transporting what seemed like half the population from the avalanche site up and down that mountain. A large contingent still remained, securing and processing what remained of the crime scene.

Thayne and his family were with Cheyenne. His sister was safe. The Blackwood family was whole again, and Riley couldn't be happier for them.

So why did she long to curl up into a ball and disappear? She rubbed her eyes. She couldn't let anyone see her like this. She had to rein in her emotions before they spun into oblivion. She still had a lot of work to do.

"Come on, Riley. Get it together." She clenched her fists, and her nails bit into her palms. She breathed in through her nose, out through her mouth, willing herself to stay calm and focused.

Despite every effort, the world turned hazy. Her heart raced, and she fought against the panic rising from her gut to her throat. Someone could come in at any time. She couldn't let anyone see her falling apart.

Desperate, she rushed out of the room. Somewhere off to the side, she thought she heard her name. She couldn't stop.

Her footsteps echoed down the hospital's hallway, disinfectant burning her nostrils. Finally, through watery eyes, she veered to a supply closet. She ducked inside and closed the door behind her.

The small space offered a haven. No one could see her here.

Oh God.

She shook from head to toe, unable to process unreserved joy, crushing guilt, and the despair threatening to overwhelm her.

They'd saved Cheyenne, Adelaide, and the children. But Madison's grave—and who knows how many others—was probably irrecoverable.

Riley had failed to keep her promise to bring her sister home. After fifteen years, hope had existed. Now it was gone. She wrapped her arms around her body and trembled, cold down to her very soul. She knew of only one person who could warm her.

"Thayne," she whispered. All she could see in her mind's eye was his heartfelt offer of forever. Together.

And she hadn't been able to say the words in return.

She'd driven him away. Now that they'd found Cheyenne, he'd return to the SEALs, but their relationship could never be reset. She'd lost the best man she knew, the best friend she'd ever had. Through her own actions.

A tentative knock tapped on the door. "Special Agent Lambert. We need your help. We can't get the kids to talk to us."

Riley pressed the heels of her hands against her eyes, took in a few deep breaths, and opened the door.

Jan frowned at her, looking her up and down with a critical eye. "Are you all right?"

"Of course," Riley lied. "What's wrong?"

"They won't speak, and they won't leave Adelaide's side. We can't get close enough to evaluate them or even verify their identities. They won't tell us their real names, and they refused to let us take their fingerprints so we can contact their families. I don't know what to do."

"Take me to them."

Riley accompanied Jan to the surgical ward they'd jury-rigged into a makeshift waiting room. She looked through the glass. Everyone but Adelaide huddled on one side, together.

That was odd. The dynamics weren't what she'd expected after observing them on the mountain. Silently, Riley studied them. Something didn't feel right. They should all be taking comfort together. They'd faced hell together. So why was Adelaide, the eldest and obvious leader of the group, excluding herself, keeping her distance? Did the children blame her for Father's death? It wouldn't be the first time victims felt pity for their abductor, especially if he'd taken them from already troubled homes.

After Riley had observed them for about twenty minutes, Adelaide turned, revealing the side of her face without the long-healed scar that had distorted her features. The hair on the back of Riley's neck shivered with a horrifying realization. She grabbed Gina's file out of the satchel and held up the photo.

There it was. When Adelaide turned just right, revealing an untarnished profile, her identity couldn't be denied.

Adelaide was Gina Wallace. She had to be.

McIlroy's first victim.

Adelaide stood and walked slowly, calmly, across the room and stared down at the oldest girl. Her lips moved, though Riley couldn't tell what she said, but the girl who went by the name Delilah shrank back, absolute fear in her eyes.

Adelaide turned, a small smile tugging at the corners of her mouth, satisfaction in her eyes, before returning to the other side of the room.

"Separate them." Riley snapped the order to Jan. "Right now. Get the kids out of there."

"They won't go."

"I don't care what the kids or Adelaide wants. Take those children to another room."

"I can't force them—"

Thayne entered the room and moved to Riley's side. "What's going on?"

His close proximity caused regret to engulf her heart, but her feelings would have to wait. "I've been watching them for a while." She held up the picture of Gina. "Compare this to the side of her face without the scar. Adelaide is Gina."

Thayne blinked. "That's great, right?"

"I'm not so sure. Look at how the children act when she gets close."

He studied the interaction through the glass barrier for a few minutes. "They're terrified of her."

"She was McIlroy's first victim. He worked on her the longest. We need to separate them, Thayne."

To her surprise, he didn't hesitate or ask questions; he simply rushed to the hallway and motioned to Jackson, Pendergrass, and Ironcloud. He spoke to them under his breath. All three looked as if they'd had the wind knocked out of them. Riley could relate.

"Let's go," Thayne said. "And if Adelaide causes trouble, handcuff her."

He opened the door for her, and Riley strode up to the woman whose eyes she could now see were blank where her soul should have been. "I understand your name is Adelaide, that it's always been Adelaide?"

The woman nodded.

Riley smiled, choosing her words carefully and placing herself between the woman and children, blocking her view for as long as possible. "I searched our databases, and we can't seem to find an Adelaide who went missing. Were you known by another name before you went to live with Mr. McIlroy?"

Adelaide's mouth pursed in frustration.

"We have to know," Riley said.

Behind her, Thayne and the three men helped the kids to their feet and began ushering them out of the room.

"What are you doing?" Adelaide shoved at Riley and lunged toward the kids. They huddled behind the men.

Riley gripped Adelaide's arms tight. "They need their real families. Just like you do . . . Gina."

The woman's eyes widened. She shook her head side to side. "I'm Adelaide!" she shouted. "You can't take them. They belong to me. They stay with *me*."

"The doctor needs to examine them. They can't remain here." Riley nodded her assent.

At her signal, Jackson and the deputies removed them from the room.

Thayne lingered. He headed her way, but Riley shook her head slowly. She wanted Gina to talk.

The woman wrenched herself out of Riley's arms, and she let her go.

Twisting her fingers, muttering to herself, Gina paced back and forth. "This isn't right. You don't understand. They *need* me." Eyes flashing, cheeks flushed red with anger, Gina threw herself at the closed door and banged on the wood. She pounded and pounded until her hands bruised.

Riley grabbed her wrists. "Not so easy to control the world around you when you aren't dealing with just children, is it?"

Gina went strangely calm, oddly quiet. "You don't have a clue what you're saying. He promised to build me a real family. That's why I went with him. That's why I stayed. They are *my* family. He took them. *For. Me.* Family is everything." She met Riley's gaze with hate-filled eyes. "Give. Me. My. Family."

The threat didn't faze Riley, but Gina's soulless eyes made her shiver. They were empty and dead.

A knock sounded at the door. Thayne opened it. Someone whispered, and he walked over to the two women.

"You played the game well, Gina. You might have gotten away with it except for two things. Special Agent Lambert saw through your disguise, and Brian Anderson just woke up." Thayne snapped handcuffs on her. "You're under arrest for kidnapping, child abuse, wrongful imprisonment, and murder. To start."

Outside the hospital, summer's air had grown crisp, and the light in the sky had dimmed to a soft blue as the day came to an end and the blush of dusk settled over Singing River. Thayne couldn't remember a day in which he'd been shocked more.

He'd be eternally grateful they'd found his sister, even now being watched over by his father and brothers.

Seven families would be reunited. Too many others would receive a very different phone call. Perhaps one they'd expected somewhere deep inside, but one they'd dreaded for years.

Perhaps the knowledge would bring closure, but Thayne doubted it. They still hadn't determined how or why Brett Riverton's father had ended up at the McIlroy compound. Adelaide was the only one who might be able to provide answers, and she wasn't talking. Not now. And he couldn't see them uncovering the truth. Not when half a mountain had buried the secrets until they'd be forgotten.

He wrapped his arm around Riley's shoulders and pressed her against his side. She leaned into him, but her body remained stiff and awkward against him. What was she thinking? He'd find out. Eventually. If she'd open up to him. They had reached a crossroads. They both knew it.

Another round of screams slashed through the air. Deputy Pendergrass winced and closed Gina Wallace into the back of his car. Once she realized she couldn't cajole them into letting her go, she'd snapped, threatening anyone who came near her.

Especially her mother.

Carol hovered just outside the car. "Gina, honey. Please, let me help you. It'll be OK," she begged through her tears.

"Get away from me!" Gina shouted. "I need *my* family. Not you." She banged her head against the window. "Where's Father? He'll make you all go away. He loves me."

Thayne met Riley's gaze. Did Gina not remember she shot Father in the back?

Carol stared after the retreating vehicle, her body hunched with devastation. Face streaked with tears, she looked over at Thayne and Riley. "You were wrong, Special Agent Lambert. Even when he lost, he won."

"Carol—" Riley started to speak.

"Don't." The woman tugged a set of keys from her purse. "I need a drink."

She shuffled to the parking lot. Thayne slipped his phone from his pocket and warned Clive to confiscate her keys. Thayne pressed Riley closer. "Do you think Carol will ever recover?"

"How can she? The daughter she believed she'd lost fifteen years ago, the girl she'd turned into a martyr, wasn't abducted at all. If we can believe her rant, she went willingly with McIlroy from the start, probably to escape all the men Carol brought home. In the end, she committed more crimes than the man I've been tracking since I can remember."

"She fooled me completely," Thayne said. "I believed she was a victim. What happened to her?"

"She was broken." It was the simplest answer Riley could give him. "In her own twisted way, she wanted someone to love her and someone to love. Like we all do."

Thayne kissed Riley's hair and tightened his hold. "I'm so sorry we couldn't bring Madison home for you."

"Me, too."

Her voice thick with emotion, Riley averted her face from him, but Thayne wouldn't let her. He gently turned her in his arms, his heart hurting for the pain she'd tried so hard to keep hidden. She couldn't, though. She blinked back glistening tears.

A siren squealing jerked them apart. An ambulance barreled into the emergency entrance. The paramedics jumped out, flinging open the rear doors, and a woman covered with dust and blood was wheeled inside.

"What's going on?" Thayne asked the driver.

"Your brother Hudson found her up near that crazy man's compound," one of the EMTs said.

"Another survivor?" Thayne rushed after the gurney, getting a quick glimpse at the woman's face before the doctor glared at Thayne and whisked the curtain closed to protect his patient.

Thayne raised his hands in surrender and turned to Riley. "She's McIlroy's daughter, all right. She has the same features as the others."

"Do you think she could be Bethany?" Riley asked.

"I hope so. Cheyenne was devastated we couldn't save her."

"Thayne, if this woman *is* Bethany, maybe we can get some answers. Maybe she knew Madison."

◆ ◆ ◆

Riley stood outside the small hospital room. She'd wanted to be there the moment the doctor finished examining the unknown patient, but Brian Anderson had asked for her specifically.

How could she say no to the boy who'd risked so much to save Sam and everyone else in that compound? He was a true hero.

She pushed open the door. The room didn't have any amenities. Brian lay pale against the pillows. A social worker sat across the room, watching protectively.

Riley pulled a chair next to the bed. "Brian, you asked to see me?"

He rubbed at the sheets. "They told me you work for the FBI. That you stopped Adelaide from taking the others. I wanted to thank you."

"We're the ones who should be thanking you. Running away took a lot of courage. You saved so many."

"Not enough." He looked away. "Is Adelaide gone?"

"She's going to be locked up for a long time."

"That's good. She hurt a lot of people." His eyes glistened. "I wanted to tell you about a girl we named Hannah. Adelaide punished her. I think she's dead. She didn't like to eat, so she was very thin. She had long red hair. I didn't want anyone to forget about her. Adelaide didn't put her in the cemetery behind the house. I don't know where she is."

Riley flashed on the painfully slight body of the girl they'd discovered near the waterfall. "We found Hannah, I think. I'm sorry. She didn't make it."

Brian fisted the sheets. "I knew. I just kinda hoped I was wrong."

With a nod, Riley pulled out her notebook. "We've been trying to find all of you for a long time. Can I ask you a couple of questions?"

He nodded. "I don't know how many I can answer, though."

"What do you know about Father?"

"He insisted he was our dad." He snorted and rolled his eyes. "I didn't believe him."

She inhaled, working out a way to break the truth. "Brian, did your parents tell you anything unusual about you when you were small?"

"I was loud, and from an early age I talked a lot. Like weirdly talked a lot. Full sentences and big words kind of thing. I took apart the television when I was about four, I think. Why?"

"But they didn't say anything about your birth?"

"Like what? I guess it was normal. I don't exactly remember it." He narrowed his eyes at her. "What are you not telling me?"

"David McIlroy . . . Father . . . when he was younger, he donated his sperm to several clinics to help women get pregnant."

His expression grew guarded. "Sperm banks?"

She nodded, and he threw back his head onto the pillow and closed his eyes. "He *is* my biological father. Oh my God. He's my real dad. That . . . It explains a lot."

Riley wanted desperately to leave Brian to his thoughts, but she needed a clearer picture, especially since they might never be able to investigate the crime scene any further. "When you arrived, how many of you were there besides Father?"

"Four."

"Was someone named Bethany one of them?"

"Yeah."

"What do you know about her?"

He opened his eyes and stared up at the ceiling, unblinking. "She's the only reason any of us are normal . . . and alive. She tried to make life bearable. When Father or Adelaide got mad, she'd intervene. Father loved her more than any of us. He would tell Adelaide that, and she'd get really angry. I think he liked it when she got jealous. That felt wrong, but I never saw anything . . . if you know what I mean."

"I do." He squirmed and glanced away, so she changed the subject. "Bethany took care of you all? She protected you?"

"Yeah. Is she OK?"

"We don't know," Riley said. "There's a woman down the hall being interviewed."

"It has to be Bethany," Brian said, his voice rising to a panicked level. "We need her."

"I promise I'll let you know who we found as soon as I do. For now, can you help us with the other kids? I recognize some of them from their missing children's reports, but others I don't."

"You need their real names?"

"If you remember any."

He held out his hand for her notebook. "I know them all. First names mostly, but some I know their real last names."

Riley smiled. "I knew you would. You're clever."

"Thanks to *Father*, I guess." He shivered and peeked over at her, his face wreathed in disgust. "He's really my dad?"

"Biologically only," she reassured him. "You were taken from a family who really wanted you to be born."

He grew thoughtful, and she kept silent, giving him time to digest what she'd told him.

Finally, he raised his head. "They didn't show it. Father gave me a family who loves me." He stared at the notebook and pen she'd given him. "If I tell you who everyone really is, they won't be my family anymore."

She didn't know how to respond, but in the end, she didn't have to say anything. He turned his attention to the notebook and started to write down all the names he could remember.

Brian's memory was supernatural. He recalled dates, names, and places. It was better than anything they could have come up with on their own. Matching the kids to their families would take no time at all thanks to him.

After he wrote the last name, he nodded off. She didn't blame him. His life had completely unraveled. Information in hand, she crossed the hall and opened the door to the new patient's room, sliding inside toward the back.

Thayne stood beside the bed. He looked over his shoulder and quirked a brow at Riley, but she leaned back against the wall and shook her head. After Adelaide, she wanted to observe the woman, focus on any possibility of lies or deceit.

He nodded his understanding and refocused his attention on the patient.

The nurse stood over the woman. "Can you open your eyes, please? We need for you to wake up."

The woman struggled to follow directions but finally managed to crack open her eyelids. She licked her lips. "Where am I?"

"In the hospital. You had an operation. Do you remember? Doctor Blackwood told me about your ordeal. The incision is healing well. We'll be running some tests to see what caused your abdominal pain, but if Doctor Blackwood's recovery is any indication, you'll be well soon."

"She made it out alive?" the woman whispered. "The doctor?"

"She did, and she's fine," Thayne said as he moved to where the nurse had stood. "Hi." He flashed his badge and introduced himself. "I need to ask you some questions. Can we start with your name?"

"Bethany." She grimaced and closed her eyes. "As long as I don't have to open my eyes or sit up."

The wince could be from the light, but it could also be an involuntary reaction to seeing a law enforcement officer in her room eager to question her.

Although Brian had insisted Bethany was the real deal, Riley had her doubts. Bethany had lived with McIlroy for a long time. As far as Brian knew, she hadn't tried to escape. That made Riley suspicious.

Bethany pressed her hand against her head and winced. "The last thing I remember was an explosion and rocks raining down on me. I wasn't fast enough to get out. I thought I was dead."

Thayne asked the nurse to dim the light. "That better?"

Bethany nodded.

"You're a miracle around here," he said.

She groaned as if in pain. "The children? Are they safe?"

"We're fairly certain we got them all. They're staying here until we find their parents."

"And Adelaide?"

Riley noted a touch of fear in the question.

"She's in jail."

A ragged sigh escaped her. "You figured her out."

"Our FBI behavioral analyst noticed something wasn't quite right in the relationship between her and the children."

"Poor Adelaide."

That sentiment caught Riley's attention. Why would Bethany pity the woman who'd so obviously terrorized them?

"She wanted a family so badly . . . relished the role of mother hen, but she didn't know how to be a mother." She cracked her eyes open. "Be careful. There's something wrong with her."

"What do you mean?"

"I don't know. Adelaide kept begging for a real family, so Father tracked down his biological children from a series of sperm donations he made to put himself through school at Cal Tech. I believed her act for a long, long time, but then she slowly started to lose her grip on reality and our punishments became severe. And then deadly. Even Father disapproved, wondering if she'd become too unstable. Your FBI agent must be very good at her job to see past Adelaide's pretense."

"You're not the only one who was fooled. Most of us fell for Adelaide's act. Even Doctor Blackwood. She didn't realize until it was almost too late that someone was poisoning you both. Based on what our team found, it appears Adelaide had become adept at causing copper toxicity. Do you know anything about a local ranch owner she may have had a problem with? Their name is—"

"Riverton," Bethany finished. "She had her reasons, twisted though they were."

"Really? We saw the grave, but we don't understand the connection. Can you help us?"

"Father was a Riverton. The black sheep, I guess. He was cut out of the will. I don't know why. He resented the entire family and believed he deserved to own the ranch. That's why he settled in those mountains. I can't tell you how many times he tried to buy the ranch. They weren't selling, so he was biding his time until he could arrange to claim or buy the land. Adelaide believed they would never sell, so she took matters into her own hands. She hated Calvin Riverton Senior. I tried to talk her out of doing anything rash, but she insisted he had to disappear. She thought she'd fixed Father's problem, but then one of the sons—Brett, I think—came home from college to run the business, and the cycle started all over. She made friends with one of the ranch hands, but he got suspicious, so she killed him. That was six months ago. Then she forced Ian to hack into the Rivertons' cameras so she could find pictures that could be used against them. I told Father she'd gone too far, and he was starting to agree with me. Finally."

She closed her eyes and let out a huge sigh. The interview was taking a toll on her, but Thayne pressed on.

"You became her enemy," he said.

She nodded with a small grimace. "Adelaide wanted us to be sisters. And in the beginning, I was so scared, I tried. She was my lifeline . . . and then they took others. Something changed; something inside her went wrong. She insisted on the perfect family. If any of the new members didn't follow the rules or tried to escape, she just got rid of them."

A tear slid down Bethany's cheek. Her reactions weren't fake. She cared deeply for the children, just like Brian had said.

Thayne leaned forward. "We saw sixteen graves in the cemetery behind your house. Were they all children except Riverton?"

Bethany moved, trying to find a more comfortable position, but winced instead. "Father chose those with talent who he believed weren't living up to their full potential. Even at sixteen, Ian is a brilliant engineer. He designs security cameras for one of Riverton's companies. Delilah is a violin prodigy. Edith was a computer wiz. She was punished last summer."

Eyes wet with tears, Bethany looked away. "I've lost so many of them. You have no idea how many times I wanted to leave, especially when I got older, but I stayed because someone had to protect the children. Adelaide kept getting angrier, and Father lost his ability to control her. I saved as many lives as I could from her anger. Not enough, though. Never enough."

They were so alike. Riley would've felt exactly the same way. She *did* feel the same way. But nothing that happened was Bethany's fault.

The words rang in Riley's ears. She'd heard them before. For the first time she might have begun to believe them.

Bethany yawned, struggling to keep her eyes open. She was clearly getting tired, and the nurse mouthed they had five more minutes before she would kick them all out.

Thayne cleared his throat. "I have just a few more quick questions and then I'll leave you to get some rest. Do you know the real identities of the children, especially those who didn't make it? We'd like to bring closure to their families."

"Father knows."

"Father died of a gunshot wound about thirty minutes ago. Adelaide shot him."

Shock flickered over Bethany's face, and her eyelids dropped as if they were too heavy to keep open anymore. "Dead?" Her voice sounded incredulous. "He's dead?"

"Yes."

"I should be happy." Confusion colored her cheeks. "I am, but . . ."

"It'll take time to process." A smile full of compassion touched his face. "No one here expects you to be doing cartwheels." He looked down at his notes. "We're in the process of contacting the families. We can do the same for you. Do you remember your real name?"

Her eyes downcast, she gripped the sheets. "What does it matter? I'm not who I was supposed to be. How can I be? I was raised by a madman."

Riley's heart hurt for the woman. She'd been cut off from her family for so long, she wasn't the little girl they remembered. The thought of reconnecting must be terrifying.

"You are exactly who you've always been," Thayne said. "You're a survivor. A hero to those kids. I think your family would want to know that."

For the longest time Bethany remained silent. Would she tell them? Riley began to doubt, but then the woman swallowed hard and lifted her gaze.

"Madison," she whispered. "My name is Madison Lambert."

A loud gasp sounded from across the room. "Maddy?"

A nickname Bethany—no, Madison—hadn't heard spoken in forever. She forced her eyes to look beyond the glare of the light burning her eyes. In the shadows, a woman hesitantly moved toward her. Her face resembled the memory of a young girl Madison used to know.

"It's me." The woman took Madison's hand and held it to her chest, shock making her breath ragged.

"I-I don't understand . . ."

Thayne tugged the woman forward. "Madison, let me introduce you to the woman responsible for finding you. This is Riley Lambert. Your sister and the gifted FBI behavior analyst who saw through Adelaide's facade."

Tears streamed down the woman's cheeks. It was hard to believe the one person Madison had wanted to see was standing in front of her. It had to be a dream. "Riley? My little sister, Riley?"

She nodded, and the most beautiful smile Madison had ever seen greeted her.

With a shaking finger, Madison swept a tear off her sister's face. "Oh my God. You're so grown up. So pretty. Is it really you? What are you doing here?"

"I never stopped looking for you," Riley said through the tears and that amazing smile. "And when I got old enough, I promised myself I'd work at the best place to find you. Easy answer. The FBI."

"She didn't give them a choice," Thayne said. "From what I hear, she aced all her tests and dazzled them with her skills. They're lucky to have her."

Madison laughed. "You were always clever. But somehow I thought you'd end up an artist."

"In a way, I did."

Madison cupped her sister's cheek. "I thought about you every day."

Riley closed her fingers over her sister's. "So did I." Fresh tears started to fall. "I'm so sorry. I'm so sorry I let him take you."

"What? Why would you say that? It wasn't your fault. Look at me," Madison said and forced Riley's eyes to meet hers. "Not for one moment did I *ever* blame you for what he did. I'm glad he took me and not you. Do you hear me? You were the sweetest, most joyous part of my life, and I would have done anything to protect you. Even when I was a pain those last few months, I would have done anything for you. I *always* needed a sister like you. I hope you know that."

She pulled Riley to her and felt the sobs shake her body. "Don't cry," Madison said through her own tears. "I love you so much. Thank you for finding me." She tightened her arms around her sister. "Thank you."

She kissed Riley's temple and held her until the sobs subsided. When they separated, the room was empty of everyone but them. Thayne stood guard at the open door, his big body blocking anyone from disturbing them.

"Are Mom and Dad—"

"They're okay. They'll be so happy to see you."

Madison's gaze moved between her sister and the very protective, and now scowling, deputy. There was a story there.

"I get the feeling he's more than just a local cop you work with."

Riley blushed, and her gaze slid to him. "He's my best friend."

"And then some?"

"And then some."

The nurse stuck her head in, clearing her throat. "Time's up."

As if the words signaled her, Madison's body began to feel heavy, and she could barely keep her eyes open. "I'm so tired." Yet she couldn't seem to let go of her sister's hand.

"I'll be here as soon as you wake up. I promise."

She squeezed Riley's fingers and smiled. "We have all the time in the world, Riley. I'm not going anywhere. Not without you."

Madison raised their hands. A half-heart bracelet on Riley's wrist swung against her skin. She stared at it and grinned, reaching beneath her hospital gown. She pulled out a necklace. A small bracelet swung on the chain.

"I thought it was lost," Riley said. "You'd taken it off."

"I put it back on that night," Madison said. "You were with me the whole time. You helped me remember who I was, deep inside."

Madison fit the two hearts together. Tears ran down her sister's face.

Riley placed a gentle kiss on her cheek. "And I'm going to make it my life's mission to be that annoying little sister you remember."

Madison's lips twitched, and her heart felt like it would explode with happiness. "I look forward to it. We have a lot of catching up to do."

CHAPTER TWENTY-SIX

Darkness had fallen over Singing River, the stars twinkling rays of light in a sea of velvet, when Thayne pulled his vehicle in front of Fannie's B&B. He turned in his seat and faced Riley. She still appeared to be in shock.

"I should've stayed," she said before he could speak. "Maddy needs me."

"They weren't going to let us see her again until morning," he said. "I had Ironcloud call your parents, and they're on their way. There's nothing more to do for her. Or anyone. Not tonight." He rounded the SUV, opening the door for her. He reached out a hand. "Come on. After the last seventy-two hours, you need some rest, then you and your sister can spend all day getting to know each other again."

Riley nodded, her expression pensive, but took his hand anyway. "I can't believe she's alive. I never thought . . ."

Her voice broke, and Thayne wrapped his arm around her. What could he say?

"Somehow we found a miracle."

"Your sister saved Maddy's life," Riley said, gripping Thayne's hand. "When she discovered the poisoning, she gave Maddy time to gain strength so she could escape."

"Cheyenne was thrilled to know Madison got away. I think they'll end up being good friends after all of this."

Thayne led Riley across the porch and into the deserted lobby.

"Thank God Fannie's not around," he said under his breath.

"I heard that." Fannie popped from behind the reservation desk and rushed across the carpet. She grabbed Thayne in a fierce hug, then gave one to Riley. "I knew you'd do it." Her face broke out in a smile.

"Kade broke the case wide open," Riley said to Fannie.

The woman beamed, but her eyes dimmed a bit. "He's still in the hospital, but he'll be fine. That young boy Sam won't leave his side." She cleared her throat. "Get upstairs, you two. I left you a surprise." And, with a flourish, she disappeared through the door to her quarters.

Riley stared up at Thayne. "What do you think she did?"

"I'm afraid to guess, but there's one way to find out."

They walked up the stairs, and Riley slipped the key into the lock. She opened the door. On the table, a bottle of champagne sat nested in a bucket of ice, and two covered plates waited for them.

Riley looked around. "Where's the crime board?"

Thayne cleared his throat. "I asked Pendergrass to take it away." He pulled out a chair for her. "Shall we?"

Riley sat down, and they dug in to the hot gourmet meal Fannie had left. As Thayne chewed his last bite, his throat had closed off. He had so much to say to Riley, he didn't know where to start.

"Riley—"

"I quit my job tonight," she interrupted in a rush.

Whatever Thayne had been going to say swept out of his mind. "When? Why?"

"While you were saying good-bye to your family and Cheyenne, I called Tom. I'm good at my job, but I need some time. To find out what I want." She twisted the napkin in her hands. "To get to know my sister again. To get to know Riley Lambert again."

He rose and pulled her to her feet, clasping her hands in his. "Are you sure that's what you want? You've worked for your career a long time."

"So did you. Now that Cheyenne's home, you could rejoin your SEAL team before they ship out."

He could see the vulnerability in her eyes, and the fear.

Thayne lifted his hand to Riley's face and cupped her cheek. He looked deep into her eyes. "I quit for two reasons. One, because I couldn't leave while Cheyenne was missing." He dragged his thumb over her skin.

"And the second?" Her voice had turned husky.

"Because I'm tired of a long-distance Friday night phone fling. I want more, Riley. I want you. Every day, every night. I'll do whatever it takes. I'll finalize my separation paperwork; I'll move to DC with you. You name it, and I'm there. I'm in one hundred percent if you'll let me."

Her eyes widened. "You'd follow me?"

"To the ends of the earth. You'll never doubt I love you. I'd give my life for you, do anything to make you happy."

She gripped his hand hard. He could see the hope brightening in her eyes.

He needed to seal this deal.

Ever so slowly, he pulled her against him. With each breath, he could smell the sweet scent that was only Riley. They fit together, the top of her head reaching his cheek. But more than physically, they simply fit, heart and soul. She understood him the way no one else did. He admired her strength, her determination, everything about her.

Her hand sneaked up his chest. His heart thudded against her palm, speeding up a bit.

She took a shuddering breath. "If we do this, we can never go back to the way it used to be."

"We crossed that threshold the moment you disembarked from the plane. There's no going back. Only forward." Thayne closed his eyes, memorizing the warmth of her against his body. "I want forever, Riley. I want the love my parents had, the love my grandparents have. I want what they've had for the last fifty years. With you."

He pulled back enough so he could see her eyes. "Accept my love for you, Riley. No conditions. No caveats. Nothing but all the love I can give you. Now until I breathe my last breath."

His words shattered the final wall around her soul, the last bit of frozen tundra that had begun one night fifteen years ago when a madman had stolen everything Riley loved.

Now she had it back.

But she wasn't a child any longer. She was a woman.

"Let me show you how it could be between us." He bent down, his lips hovering just above hers.

A shuddering breath escaped her lungs. She couldn't resist. She didn't want to. She'd been searching to belong to someone her entire life. Someone who would never leave, who would always love her, who wouldn't give up on her, no matter what.

Thayne was that man.

So why did she hesitate?

"I see." Thayne lifted his head and pulled away from her.

Her entire body went cold. What was she doing? Her sister had shown true courage for years when her life had been stolen. Taking this leap of faith wasn't scary. This was Thayne. Her best friend. The man she trusted with her life. The man who had saved her heart and healed her soul. She clutched his arms, her grip so tight her hands hurt. "No.

You don't see. I love you, Thayne. I've loved you for a very long time. I was just afraid to admit it. Even to myself."

Thayne smiled, one that lit his eyes. He didn't speak, he simply picked her up in his arms and carried her to the bed. She held her breath while he nuzzled her cheek, tempting her with his nearness but not his lips or his touch. Her nerve endings tingled; her body thrummed with anticipation.

She clutched his shoulders.

"This is forever," he whispered. With very little pressure, he parted her lips, just a bit. "No going back."

She instinctively tasted his finger with a small swipe. The taste of salt, the touch of him made her tongue tingle. She clasped the back of his head and pulled his lips down to hers. "Not ever."

The passion between them erupted, and the walls of protection melted away. Thayne pressed her lips apart and explored her mouth.

She wanted to be closer to him. She worked the buttons of his shirt and shoved the offending garment aside so she could feel his skin.

With a groan, Thayne took over. He stripped out of his clothes, then set to work on hers. Finally, bare skin to bare skin, he wrapped her close, letting his hands caress her.

Shivering under his touch, Riley lowered her lips to his chest, exploring his body, nipping at the sensitive skin until she flicked her tongue along his nipple.

Thayne let out a long, low groan. She fell back against the bed and pulled him down to her.

He willingly followed, inserting his leg between hers. She closed her eyes. His hands and mouth touched her everywhere, exploring every inch. He knew exactly how to touch her, evoking a whimper. He slipped on a condom and raised above her, his eyes growing dark with desire.

"I love you, Riley. Always and forever." With one thrust, he sank inside of her.

His hands moved down her arms to her hands. He folded her fingers into his and stilled, staring at her.

"I love you, too."

He shifted his hips, and she gasped, wrapping her legs around him, holding him close. They were one, and she'd never felt more complete, more whole, more wanted, more loved.

He rocked against her. Her body thrummed with each movement, her belly tightening. She never wanted this to end. She closed her eyes, unable to stop the groan from escaping.

Her entire being focused on Thayne and his love. He cherished her.

Her body clenched, rising taut with him until she exploded in absolute joy, clinging to Thayne.

As awareness rushed back, he laid his head on her breast. She clasped him to her, out of breath, heart racing and sheer contentment settling over her like a cashmere blanket.

"That was—"

"Incredible," he said, out of breath himself.

They lay still for a moment, wrapped in each other's arms until Thayne shifted off her, spooning her against his body. He threaded his fingers through hers and kissed the nape of her neck.

"My father offered me a permanent deputy's position. How would you feel about staying in Wyoming? With me? As my wife?"

Riley turned over and faced him. His mouth was tense, nervous. She smiled. "Wherever, whenever you want, I'll be there," she said. "Always."

EPILOGUE

One Week Later

A string of Christmas lights twinkled outside of Clive's Dance Hall and Saloon. Riley stepped out of Deputy Pendergrass's vehicle. "Thanks, Quinn."

Her practiced gaze scanned the area. She recognized most of the vehicles from the Blackwoods' ranch close to the front. The rest of the parking lot was filled to overflowing.

She had her hand on the door when she paused.

Tonight was for celebrating. She couldn't believe she was this happy, had never imagined being content. A year ago, her life had been all about living one day at a time. No future, and a past that haunted her. Now endless possibilities awaited, not only for her and Thayne and their life together in Singing River, but for her sister. She looked forward to every day getting to know Madison all over again.

The door opened in her hand. Sheriff Carson Blackwood, a huge smile on his face, pulled her inside. "Riley." He clasped her in a big bear hug and gave her a quick kiss on the cheek. "Thank you for giving me my family back. And for making my son happier than I've ever seen him."

She kissed his cheek. "I'm the lucky one." Her eyes searched the room. They paused at a small table where her mother looked completely out of place and her father looked like he wished he were sitting anywhere but there. Madison sat between them, a small frown on her face, twisting her long hair in her fingers, still pale. A few days in the hospital had helped her lose that gaunt look. She would fully recover from the copper poisoning eventually. Thank God.

"How are they doing?" she asked, nodding at her family.

"They're trying," Carson said. "Your sister's an amazing woman."

The tall, jean-clad figure of Hudson Blackwood crossed in front of the Lamberts. He held out his hand to Madison. She looked up at him with a grateful expression. Her mother reached out a restraining hand but dropped it when Madison frowned at her mother.

Fifteen years apart and no one knew what to say or how to act.

Madison stood and met Riley's gaze. She gave her a wide smile then took Hudson's hand and let him lead her onto the dance floor. No doubt to avoid the parents.

Just like old times. The two sisters against the world.

"Thayne's in the far corner," Carson whispered in her ear. "With my mother."

Her heart flipped, and she strode across the floor toward him. Every moment away, she missed him. His touch, his laugh, his smile.

Thayne's eyes glinted with laughter as he spoke to Helen. Thayne passed her off to his grandfather before heading over to the band's leader, whispering something in his ear.

The man nodded, and a familiar tune began to play. "Could I Have This Dance." Not a song Riley had heard until Thayne had hummed it to his grandmother for the first time. Now, it was their song as well.

Lincoln held out his hand to his wife, and Gram stood up. They glided across the floor as if they'd been dancing together for more than fifty years. Which they had.

At that moment, the door opened. A smattering of applause started, then swelled to whoops and hollers. The band stopped playing.

Cheyenne made a beeline for Riley and gave her a big hug. "I called Brett," she said. "Thanks for the push." She grabbed Riley's hand and led her over to the corner where her grandparents stood, along with Thayne. "Now I'm going to return the favor."

Cheyenne smiled. "Gram."

The look on Helen Blackwood's face was joyous at first, then a small frown furrowed her brow. "I forgot our dinner date, didn't I?" She bit her lip.

Cheyenne blinked, then grinned. She hugged Gram. "Of course not." She kissed her forehead.

Thayne met his grandfather's eyes, and Riley recognized the small hint of sadness between them. He signaled the band, and "Could I Have This Dance" continued to play softly in the background.

Helen must have seen the look as well. She took a small breath and closed her eyes for just a moment. Then she opened them again, eyes clear and bright. *A good day,* Riley prayed.

"We can't let this music go to waste, can we?" Gram looked over at Riley. "Dance with Thayne, dear." She turned to her granddaughter. "Cheyenne, why don't you dance with that nice Deputy Ironcloud?"

"I'm waiting for someone, Gram," Cheyenne said as she craned her neck to look through the crowd.

Helen tsked her tongue and patted her granddaughter's arm. "He's not coming, my sweet girl. Those Rivertons never could stand a social. Solemn to the bone, so I suggest you dodge that bullet and dance with a man who's staring at you like a man should."

Lincoln stepped between the women. "Stop your harping, woman, and dance with me."

He swung Helen into his arms.

Thayne stood waiting, searching Riley's face.

"I don't dance," she reminded him, then glanced at Helen, who gave her a wink as Lincoln spun her away.

Thayne slid his hand around her waist and pulled her against him. "You don't have to. Just follow me," he said softly.

"But—"

"Cheyenne is back. Your sister is alive. Shouldn't a bit of the Riley you've been hiding away for so long get to enjoy life a little?"

Hudson guided Madison past them and across the floor, gently, slowly. The bright smile on Madison's face lifted a weight from Riley's heart. She'd be forever grateful to have her sister back. Changed, but still Madison where it mattered. It was time to be brave, to let the old Riley, the joy-filled Riley, live life again. "Lead away. I'll always follow."

A few minutes later, the door to the dance hall opened again and Shep's thin figure stood there quietly. Through a crack in the crowd, Riley could just make out Brett Riverton leaning against his cane, his serious expression at odds with the laughter in the dance hall. He locked gazes with Riley and tilted his hat. Then his focus shifted. Riley followed his eyes, to where Cheyenne danced with Deputy Ironcloud. The look on his face was so hungry and so resigned. He whispered something to Shep and painfully started to make his way to her.

"I'll be right back," she whispered to Thayne and met Brett halfway.

He tipped his Stetson to her. "Special Agent Lambert. I wanted to thank you for finding my father. It was a comfort to know that he didn't abandon us. The irony is, if McIlroy had come to our father and told us who he was, Dad would probably have welcomed him with open arms. He didn't have to try to take the Riverton land by force. He could have been part of a family."

"Join us?" Riley asked, placing her hand on his arm. "I know Cheyenne would be happy to see you."

"I don't want to intrude. She deserves more." Brett sent a long look over to Cheyenne, and she crossed to him.

"Brett," she whispered.

"I just came to bring you this," he said quietly, handing her the Wyoming jade necklace.

Cheyenne's eyes clouded. "But—"

"It's better this way. There's a lot you don't know about me." He nodded to Shep and walked painfully into the night.

Cheyenne stared after him, gripping the stone. "Excuse me." She hurried out the door, Deputy Ironcloud following in her wake.

Riley sighed. Brett loved Cheyenne, but he wouldn't admit it. He was trying to protect her, and he only hurt her.

Once, Riley had made the same mistake. No longer. She walked across the room, directly into Thayne's arms.

He pulled her body against his. She closed her eyes and breathed in and out, allowing her body to sway back and forth, embracing the happiness of the little girl who danced across the room with Madison so many years ago.

Ever so slowly, they moved together as one. He folded her hand into his and pulled it to his heart. She leaned into him, breathing in deeply. Her cheek rested against his shoulder as he guided her farther onto the dance floor in the direction of his grandparents.

"Look at them," Thayne whispered.

Lincoln embraced Helen, gently, protectively, as if he never wanted to let her go.

"I love you, Lincoln," Helen whispered. "Even when I forget to tell you, I love you."

Riley's throat thickened with emotion at her words.

"You'll always be my love, Helen Blackwood. And don't you worry. I'll remember enough for the both of us."

Riley blinked back her tears. A Blackwood kind of love. She understood now. Thayne cleared his throat and pressed her even closer.

"We have a love like theirs, Riley." His voice was husky. He stopped any pretense of dancing and simply stared into her eyes. "Together, forever."

She gave him a bright smile and held out her hand. "Then dance with me?"

"For the rest of my life."

AFTERWORD

Forgotten Secrets grew in part from witnessing my mother's battle with Alzheimer's disease. We have learned to cherish and embrace the small moments of joy even as we navigate through the tears. If we have learned one truth, it is to be thankful for what we still have and not to wish for what used to be.

My mother's journey has been a long one, and my family would not have survived without our faith, friends, and the support of the Alzheimer's Association (www.alz.org, Alzheimer's Association, P.O. Box 96011, Washington, DC 20090-6011). The local chapter of this organization has provided us with knowledge, support, and understanding, and I cannot express my gratitude enough to everyone who has touched our lives.

I am donating 10 percent of the royalties I receive from this novel to the Alzheimer's Association in honor of my mother, my father, and all those who support them as they travel this difficult road. The Alzheimer's Association's vision is a world without Alzheimer's, and I pray for that day.

To that end, I have created the #1MemoryChallenge, an awareness and fund-raising campaign. This effort encourages the sharing of special memories before they are lost as well as support of the Alzheimer's Association and its good work. You can find out more about my personal story and the #1MemoryChallenge at http://act.alz.org/goto/1MemoryChallenge or at www.facebook.com/1MemoryChallenge.

If you have a friend or loved one who is facing Alzheimer's disease or another dementia, it can feel like a lonely battle. Please consider contacting the Alzheimer's Association (or a similar organization) for assistance, and please support the association through your time or donations.

You are not alone.

ACKNOWLEDGMENTS

This story has been a labor of love, and those who know me well recognize the joy and the challenges in bringing this book to life. To you all, I thank you.

Jill Marsal, literary agent extraordinaire—your support and faith never cease to amaze me. I couldn't travel this road without you.

Charlotte Herscher, editor—your supreme patience, kindness, and insight made this book what it is today, and I will be forever grateful.

Tammy Baumann, Louise Bergin, and Sherri Buerkle—your talent, honesty, and astuteness humble me. I couldn't ask for better critique partners or more giving friends.

And to my generous beta readers: Janie Crouch, Ruth Kaufman, Jane Perrine, and Sharon Wray. You are awesome, gifted, and talented, and I value your unique perspectives and perception more than you will ever know. You know where to find me!

AUTHOR'S NOTE

Thank you for reading *Forgotten Secrets*. I hope you enjoyed it! If you're interested in my other novels, the Montgomery Justice series—*In Her Sights*, *Behind the Lies*, and *Game of Fear*—is available. (Keep reading for an excerpt from *Game of Fear* at the end of this book.)

If you'd like to know when my next book is available or have a chance at special information and giveaways, you can sign up for my newsletter at www.RobinPerini.com.

You can connect with me on my website at www.RobinPerini.com, on Goodreads at www.goodreads.com/RobinPerini, or on Facebook at www.facebook.com/RobinPeriniAuthor.

If you enjoyed reading this story, I would appreciate it if you would help others enjoy this book, too.

Lend it. Please share it with a friend.

Recommend it. Please help other readers find this book by recommending it to friends, readers' groups, and discussion boards.

Review it. Please tell other readers why you liked this book by reviewing it.

Authors are nothing without readers. I thank you all for taking this journey with me.

BOOK CLUB QUESTIONS

1. Riley Lambert is an FBI special agent attached to one of the FBI's behavioral analysis units. She chose this career because of her sister's abduction.

    a. How did Riley's past impact her choice of career?
    b. How did Riley's past impact her character?
    c. Did you find Riley a believable character?

2. What do you think the greatest strength and greatest weakness of the following characters are:

    a. Riley Lambert
    b. Thayne Blackwood
    c. Doctor Cheyenne Blackwood
    d. Helen Blackwood

3. Alzheimer's disease is one of the top ten causes of death in the United States. In *Forgotten Secrets*, the hero's grandmother lives with the disease.

    a. Do you know anyone who lives with this illness?
    b. What insights did you gain about the disease from how Gram was portrayed in the story?

4. A series of flashbacks takes the reader through the day of Madison Lambert's abduction.

    a. What insights did you discover about the heroine's relationship with her sister?
    b. Did you find these scenes distracting, illuminating, or both, and why?

5. Madison Lambert chose not to escape to protect the other children whom the villain had kidnapped. What did you think of her choice? What else could she have done? What would you have done?

6. Which scene in the book did you find:

    a. The most suspenseful?
    b. The most unexpected?
    c. The most emotional?
    d. The most memorable?

GAME OF FEAR

The whir of the circling Bell 212 helicopter rotors echoed through the cockpit. New Mexico's Wheeler Peak, barely visible in the dusk, loomed just east, its thirteen-thousand-foot summit laden with snow. Deborah Lansing leaned forward, the seat belt straps pulling at her shoulders.

Far, far to the west, the sun was just a sliver in the sky.

"It's almost dark, Deb. We have to land," Gene Russo, her local search and rescue contact, insisted.

"The moon is bright enough right now that I can still see a little, and we have the spotlight. Those kids have got to be here somewhere!"

Deb squinted against the setting sun; her eyes burned with fatigue. They'd been at it for hours, but she couldn't give up. Not yet.

"All the other choppers have landed, Deb. This is too dangerous. Besides, do you really think your spotlight's going to find a snow-covered bus on the side of the mountain with all these trees?"

"Five more minutes. That's all I'm asking."

A metallic glint pierced through a thick carpet of snow-packed spruce.

"There! I saw something." Deb's adrenaline raced as she shoved the steering bar to the right and down, using the foot pedals to maintain control.

"Holy crap, Lansing. What are you doing?" Gene shouted, holding on to his seat harness. "You trying to get us killed?"

He didn't understand. The bird knew exactly what Deb wanted, and she didn't leave people behind to die. Not after Afghanistan. She had enough ghosts on her conscience. She tilted the chopper forward and came around again, sidling near the road toward Taos Ski Valley, where the church bus had been headed before it had vanished.

She dipped the chopper, scouring the terrain with the spotlight. A metallic flash pierced her gaze once again. "Gene, did you see that? Just south?"

The gray-faced spotter shook his head. "No, I'm too busy trying not to puke all over your windows." He swallowed deeply and adjusted his microphone. "Could you fly this thing steadily for a while?"

She sent him a grimace. "Sorry. I really think I spotted something. I had to go closer. I didn't want to miss it. I need to swing by one more time. Really look this time, OK?"

Gene groaned. "Deb, I know you're used to Denver terrain, but you can't treat the Sangre de Cristo Mountains this way. These gullies and drafts can buffet a chopper, especially in some of the gorges. Your lift will disappear, and you'll fly into the mountain."

A peak rose toward them, and Deb pulled up on the collective control stick. The Bell followed her lead easily, but the sun was gone now. The near-total darkness made flying treacherous. The moon was the only thing making the deadly terrain remotely visible outside the spotlight's range.

"At least there aren't Stingers or RPGs shooting at us," she said.

Gene shot her a look. "You were in the military?"

"Flew rescue missions," Deb said. She shifted the steering bar. "I know I saw something down there, too. I've got that buzz. Come on, baby," she urged the chopper.

Below, a blanket of snow covered a valley peppered with spruce, fir, and pines. The frigid temperatures, blowing snowdrifts, and icy roads had made the ground search difficult.

If Deb couldn't find them tonight . . .

"Return to base, Search Ten." The order crackled over the radio. "It's too dark. We'll continue tomorrow."

"Negative," Deb said. "I have a possible."

"This is Search Command. Give us the location. We'll add it to the coordinates to check first thing in the morning."

"By morning, those kids might freeze to death," Deb said. "If it's them, the least I can do is drop supplies." She flipped off the microphone.

"Uh, Deb," Gene said. "They can pull your license for this."

She shifted in her seat. "I know. Keep an eye out. I'm going in as close as I can." She rounded another hill. "Come on, baby, come on," Deb begged the machine.

She skirted the tops of the trees directly next to the road, flying a lot closer than was sane. Suddenly, down the slope, a hint of dark blue appeared. She hovered, sweeping the area with the searchlight. The beam glinted off broken glass and chrome. Several figures stood on and near a big school bus, waving. Others lay on the ground, some suspiciously still.

"Damn it," Gene said in a stunned tone. "You were right." He radioed in the location and stared at her, his expression awestruck. "You're good."

"I was lucky," she said.

"No, that was dogged determination. You just wouldn't give up. You might be crazy, Deb Lansing, but you're a hell of a chopper pilot."

All-too-familiar guilt twisted inside her. "I have my moments."

She hovered over the downed bus, and Gene dropped blankets, first-aid supplies, and food. Below, figures scrambled to the drop zone.

Banishing the haunting image of the desperate soldier she'd been forced to leave behind from her mind, Deb turned to Gene. "I can land in that valley we passed earlier. It'll be tight, but if there are any kids seriously injured, we may be able to transport some of them to the helicopter with the sled."

"What the hell. You've already pulled off one miracle tonight." Gene grinned. "Go for it."

Deb eased down the control stick and, with careful precision, her feet adjusted the back rotor. Just as she was guiding the helicopter down, another glint of silver reflected in the spotlight, far enough away from the bus that it wasn't likely to be debris from that wreck.

"Do you see that reflection?" she asked. "Is it another vehicle?"

Gene peered through the windshield. "I don't know. I saw something, though. I'll call in the position for that, too. They can check it later."

The chopper touched down, and Deb jumped to the snow-packed ground, ignoring the cold around her. For now, she had people to save. As Deb and Gene yanked out the sled to transport the wounded, two men ran toward her, one with his forehead caked with dried blood.

"Please, we need help. Some of the kids are hurt badly. They need a hospital."

Deb scanned the inside of the chopper. How many could she fit and safely make it back? If she left equipment behind, she could carry someone extra. Her boss would be furious she'd taken the risk, but she'd worry about her job later.

ABOUT THE AUTHOR

Photo © 2013 Kyle Zimmerman

Internationally bestselling and award-winning author Robin Perini is devoted to giving her readers fast-paced, high-stakes adventures with a love story sure to melt their hearts. A RITA Award finalist, she sold fourteen titles to publishers in less than two years after winning the prestigious Romance Writers of America Golden Heart Award in 2011. An analyst for an advanced technology corporation, she is also a nationally acclaimed writing instructor and enjoys competitive small-bore rifle silhouette shooting. Robin makes her home in the American Southwest and loves to hear from readers. Visit her website at www.robinperini.com.